Mike & Vicky

Another one so that the
actuary & his wife can have
a book each!

Lots of love

Liz + Mike

The Actuary's Wife

K T BOWES

ISBN-13: 978-1519548269
ISBN-10: 1519548265

DISCLAIMER

ACKNOWLEDGEMENTS

Thank you to my faithful beta readers and editors, Demelza, Maureen and Charlotte. You're the ones who nip tangents in the bud and provide the honesty I need.

I'm also grateful to my Market Harborough friends who refresh my memory of the town so I can bring it alive in my work. Thank you to Kim, who really was a vicar at St Di's, Tracey, who has the town's blood in her veins and Nicki, who almost got herself arrested taking covert pictures of the church so my characters could break in.

DEDICATION

For Freda, gone but never forgotten.
She loved her John with an honest passion and his loss was a knife wound which never healed. Freda was wonderfully outrageous and delighted to give me multiple heart failures as a mother. She fed my toddlers cranberry juice in silver goblets at a glass coffee table nestled on a cream carpet. They adored her. We all adored her. Her absence leaves a hole in this world which only an elderly woman with a wide smile, crazy hats and half-mast pop socks can fill.

Freda was one of society's 'outsiders'. She worked it like a boss.

CHAPTER ONE

Emma Andreyev looked at the phone in her hand, rubbing her thumb across the screen and watching the words move up and down. Her heart beat in a familiar tattoo, induced by fear and sustained by experience.

'Don't let him leave.'

Emma swallowed and texted back, *'Who is this?'*

The reply was swift. *'You know, Emma!'*

She stamped her foot in frustration. Her past life on the housing estate in Lincoln brought contact with thugs and criminals. Fat Brian's face floated across her vision accompanied by Big Jason's toothless smile. Two years of living on the estate and they'd never texted her. They'd hammered on her front door and accosted her in the street, yes; but never texted.

'Go away!'

Emma stuffed the phone into her pocket and gnawed on her bottom lip. The mysterious texts began the day her husband returned from a business trip to London.

"It's just a simple job, *dorogaya.*" Rohan sounded confident as he ran his large hand across Emma's soft stomach, fascinated by her budding pregnancy. "It's a retrieval but no complications." His deep Russian voice rumbled against her skin as Rohan kissed his unborn child. "No danger. *Obeshchayu.* I promise."

"Yeah, I've heard your promises before," Emma breathed, stroking his wavy blonde hair and smoothing it back from his forehead.

"I never lie!" Rohan Andreyev looked indignant, the scar on his chin puckering as he studied Emma with practiced intensity.

"That's debatable." Emma squealed as he tickled the soft skin on her waist and pushed her shirt up, exposing the vulnerable flesh over her ribs.

A week ago the texts began, showing up on Emma's new private number. The phone vibrated in her pocket again and Emma bit back a scream of frustration. She unlocked the screen and stared at the glinting message. *'DON'T let him leave.'*

Her eyes caught a movement in her peripheral vision as dread snaked round her heart. Rohan Andreyev moved into full view, wiping the glossy black car with a strip of leather to remove the drips. Over six feet tall and muscular, Emma's husband shined the car, working against the worsening weather and the failing light. He walked around the Mercedes admiring his handiwork, listing to the right as his prosthetic leg coped with the camber of the gravel. He bent to scratch at a piece of flaking paint on the wing with his fingernail.

"Mummy did it!" The small boy bounced into view riding a skateboard. His cheeks were pink from the effort of balancing and he trailed one foot along the gravel. "She can't drive this car. She swears all the time driving it. You should get her another car, Daddy. One with rubber round it to stop her dinging things."

Emma cringed and shrank back from the huge bay window, not wanting to acknowledge her failure. The glass muffled their voices and she squeezed the bridge of her nose, trying to put the texts out of her mind. The first threatened her not to tell Rohan, but she toyed with the idea of dumping the whole problem on his broad shoulders.

"Should I, Nikolai?" Rohan smirked and caught his son by the scruff as the skateboard tipped. He let go of the child and rubbed the cloth over the dent, smirking to himself at his wife's discomfort as he caught sight of her lurking behind the shutters. "A rubber car? You think she would be better in one? Good idea, *da*." Rohan's blonde hair ruffled in the sharp Arctic breeze and his blue eyes glittered like diamonds with amusement. He pivoted and looked straight at the window, narrowing his eyes at the beautiful woman hiding behind the glass. "*Zagadka?*" he shouted, splaying his arms dramatically and despite herself, Emma laughed.

"I don't know," she mouthed, unable to answer the Russian word for *puzzle*. "I don't know why I can't drive it. It's just too big!"

Rohan stuck his bottom lip out and pretended to wipe his eyes with a shaking hand and Emma watched his neat bum as he bent to pour the dirty water onto the front lawn. The bubbles tumbled happily into the acre of grass and disappeared. Emma glanced at her phone again and sighed.

"Help me do tricks, Dad?" the child implored and Rohan nodded.

"Later, Nikolai. I can teach you the physics but not show you, *da?*" He tapped the complicated piece of machinery making up his lower right leg and Nicky nodded.

"Yeah, that's cool. In a while then."

Emma sat in the window seat of her sitting room which dated back to the Norman Conquest, listening to the sound of her husband clattering around in the cavernous reception hall. He banged the front door shut against the elements and hurried along the corridor. Emma snuggled into the cushions and desperately tried to master her emotions. "Hey, *dorogaya*," Rohan whispered, closing the sitting room door against the draught that followed him inside. "I've checked the car and it has fuel for a few days. You'll be fine until I come home again." He sat heavily on the seat next to Emma's feet and cupped them in hands which felt freezing through her woolly socks. He massaged her toes and she moaned and laid her head back against the shutter behind her. "I cleaned it so it's easier to see the next set of scratches from your driving." Rohan smiled and then leaned forward, lifting Emma's chin with his finger. "What's wrong, Em? I'm not cross."

"I don't want you to go." She gulped, an old memory surfacing and taking her breath away. Rohan looked unnerved but also suspicious.

"I thought you were fine. We talked about the job when I got back from London last week and I explained it. Why didn't you say something then?"

"I don't know...I..." Emma exhaled and ran her hand across her stomach.

"Is it the baby?" Rohan looked concerned and reached out to cover her fingers.

Emma shook her head. "No. Sorry. It feels like before when I was pregnant with Nicky. It brings back bad memories." She gritted her teeth, her jawline becoming a hard outline in her pink cheeks.

Rohan's mouth opened and hurt flashed in his eyes. "I didn't know you were pregnant," he said sullenly. "And I didn't just leave, Em. I came home to see you before a deployment to Afghanistan. Captains in the British army can't decide they don't fancy going anymore and not show up on parade."

"I know! Forget I mentioned it!" Emma thudded her head against the shutter in anger, causing a clank of protest from the ancient wood. Guilt ran riot in her brain and she struggled with herself. "Tell me about the job," she asked, forcing herself to sound interested. "When will you be home?"

Rohan wasn't fooled. His handsome face looked rugged in the failing light and his blue eyes sparkled with curiosity. He obliged his wife but studied her as though she were a new mathematical equation in his world of risk management. "A laptop containing sensitive information was stolen from a vehicle in a secure government compound. It belonged to a senior cabinet minister and the backups went to a server in Whitehall. Someone diverted and encrypted the backups and then stole the laptop, so the government have nothing. There's a ransom to release the backups which they won't pay, but they need that laptop."

"What's on it?" Emma asked.

Rohan raised an eyebrow and slanted his head. His lips drew back in a sexy smirk. "If I told you that, I'd have to kill you, *dorogaya*."

Emma sniffed in indignation. "Whatever, Ro! So, where does the actuary work come in?"

"I've analysed the risk of *not* retrieving the device and it's catastrophic. There's enough evidence on it to cause civil unrest. Without the backups or the device, the government will flounder. How can they refute or deny something they can't see? Whoever diverted the backups was skilled enough to know what they wanted, but the laptop contained other sensitive items which the hackers may not yet realise they have. I've given advice on limiting the damage and the spin doctors are ready to act, but the cabinet want the laptop and every copy made of that particular string of incriminating emails. My new tech has traced most of them but I don't tell the client that."

"Why?"

Rohan rolled his eyes. "It's my job to be the hero, rescue them from their incompetency and then accept my fee. I might even send in my tech to offer cyber security advice; after I cash the cheque, obviously. If I make it sound easy, they won't appreciate paying me the astronomical retrieval fee I've negotiated."

"You're unscrupulous," Emma sighed.

Rohan kissed her delicate foot. "No, Em. I'm a businessman and a good one. It's not my fault their English nepotism leads them to employ morons."

"How long will you be?" Emma's voice sounded flat and Rohan observed her with expert suspicion.

"Emma!"

She jumped and looked guilty. "Don't stop rubbing my feet." She put a trace of sulk into her voice, trying to distract him. Rohan's strong fingers massaged her toes and he ran his thumbs along her sensitive instep.

"What's going on, Em?"

"Nothing." She shrieked as Rohan grabbed her ankle and tickled her foot, watching as Emma writhed until she almost spilled onto the floor. "Stop!" she begged, alarmed at finding tears so near the surface. *Tickle torture*, Anton used to call it, convincing the child-Emma that the Russian police used it all the time. At the thought of Rohan's late brother, the tears threatened harder and her bottom lip wobbled.

Rohan shifted position so he could sit next to her on the window seat. He wrapped his arm around her shoulder and kissed the side of her head. Emma pressed her face into his shirt and breathed in his familiar scent, running her finger across his strong abdominal muscles. Not satisfied, she tugged his shirt from the smart black trousers and touched her fingers to his flesh. Rohan tensed at the ticklish sensation and Emma smirked at his immediate interest. He inhaled and lifted her face with his finger, smothering her lips with his urgent kisses. He gathered her to him and bruised her lips with his, flicking his tongue into her mouth, his breath coming in gasps of arousal. "When's Nicky going out?" he whispered and Emma nuzzled into his neck, administering a quick nip to the sensitive skin.

"Soon. He's watching Leicester City in the cup final. That's why he's hanging around outside; he can't wait. Will's bringing him home and he'll text when they get near so you can open the gates."

Rohan moaned with pleasure and tugged at Emma's sweatshirt, pulling the hem up so it became stuck under her armpits. She placed her hand against his chest. "Ro! Not yet!"

He snorted. "Em! It's a manor house surrounded by acres of grounds. Nobody will see." His fingers went to work on the button of her jeans, struggling with the smooth metal.

"Only your son! And the cop who's picking him up!"

Rohan groaned and rested his forehead against Emma's back as she slid past him, making a dash for it as he tried to grab her round the waist. "Nicky's shouting for you," Emma snorted as she pulled away. "You promised to help him."

The sound of the small voice echoed along the hallway, reverberating around the huge reception hall.

"Daaaaaad!"

Rohan let go of Emma and stood, his eyes twinkling with unfulfilled lust. "Later then, Mrs Andreyev. I look forward to the *udovol'stviye.*"

"I'm sorry, I don't speak Slavic." Emma bit her lip and tried to dodge out of the way of her randy husband. He brushed his lips across hers and nipped her full bottom lip. His fingers strayed to her shapely bum and he winked.

"It means *pleasure*," he whispered.

"Yes, but whose?" Her eyes widened with feigned coyness and she turned away from him.

"Whatever!" he chided. "I'll have to show you then." Rohan strode towards the door and into the hall, calling to his son in Russian to be patient. The dog barked from the front step, excited at the promise of Rohan's presence.

Emma threw another log onto the open fire and felt the smile fade from her face as the phone in her pocket vibrated again.

CHAPTER TWO

"You're gorgeous." Rohan punctuated his adoration with a kiss, sighing with satisfaction as he cradled Emma's slight body in his arms. "I regret the wasted years." He buried his face in her hair and sighed.

"They weren't wasted." Emma yawned and snuggled closer, running her hand across his downy blonde chest. The sumptuous old bed groaned beneath them. "We both learned who we were. I'm not sure our marriage would have survived if we stayed together back then, not with the pressure of your mother and everyone around us. I'm glad your grandmother gave me safe haven when I needed it. Lucya was the best person to look after me then. I miss her."

"From what you've said, she sounds a lot like my papa." Rohan ran his index finger down Emma's bare shoulder and pressed another kiss to her temple. "He was a good man. Some of the things Nikolai says reminds me of him. Sometimes it makes me sad and other times I'm glad he lives on in my son."

"*Bednyy rebenok.*" Emma turned on her side and wrapped her arms around Rohan's neck. *Poor baby.* She fitted her naked body into his and played with the soft curls at the back of his head. She grunted as he pulled her on top of him, feeling his strong abdominal muscles like rock under her chest. "Ok, ok," she conceded with a giggle. "You're nobody's poor baby. Just mine."

"*Tvoye*," Rohan whispered. *Yours.*

"We should get up soon; Nicky will be home. The game must be over by now." Emma craned her head to see the clock. She left her neck vulnerable to her husband and he took advantage. "No!" Emma squeaked. "We have to get up or we won't hear them arrive."

"I told Nikolai the gate code." Rohan breathed into her hair, his eyes misting over with lust in the soft lamplight. "They can get to the front door."

"That gives you two minutes extra!" Emma laughed. "Your technique's slipping!"

"Hey! There's nothing wrong with my methods, *dorogaya*. You have nothing to complain about. I sleep with you once after six years and give you *rebenok* with my first attempt. I'm a big Russian stud!" Rohan pulled Emma tightly into him and ran his fingers across her buttocks. She dipped her head and teased him with her lips, covering his mouth and when he moaned and tried to deepen the kiss, pulling away. "You're a very bad *printsessa*," Rohan rebuked her in a husky whisper, running his fingers through the back of her long hair. When she tried to pull away again after making him breathless, she found herself pinned.

"Cheat!" she giggled, turning her face sideways to escape Rohan's kisses. He ran his stubbly chin down her neck to her shoulder and she squealed, finding herself flipped so Rohan lay on top of her. "You don't fight fair," she whispered.

"I don't want to fight you at all." Rohan's lips were soft on Emma's and she succumbed to the intensity of his kiss and the sensation of his fingers roving across her skin. His soft Russian endearments were a continuous, whispered love song as he gave and received pleasure to his beautiful wife, treating her as a Russian princess. His honed, muscular body softened from a weapon capable of inflicting pain, to one which brought desire and excitement. Their lovemaking was intense and they collapsed in a tangle of arms and legs, breathless and satiated.

Then Emma heard the sound of her phone vibrating in the sweatshirt she dumped on the bedroom rug. Rohan felt her body stiffen underneath him. "Is that your *krovavyy* phone that keeps ringing?" he asked, a note of irritation in his voice.

Emma gulped. "Don't swear. It only did it once, just then."

"*Net*, it rang a few times. Want me to get it for you?" Rohan lifted his head from Emma's neck and peered over the side of the bed, raking the floor with his blue eyes.

"Leave it, it's too far away. It won't be Nicky; he knows to call you, not me."

Rohan rolled onto his side and stroked Emma's damp hair away from her face. His eyes were perceptive as he studied her and Emma felt her heart give a nervous skip. Rohan was a human lie detector and Emma focussed on relaxing under his scrutiny. "What's wrong, Em?"

She sighed and leaned towards part of the truth. "I'm worried about you leaving me here. It's a big house and we're miles from anywhere. What if something goes wrong?" Her brow knitted and she bit her lip, trying not to cry genuine tears.

Rohan tutted. "*Dorogaya*, you'll be fine." He ran his thumb under Emma's eye and kissed the end of her nose. "I feel like we shouldn't have moved out here. You felt safe in town, *da?*"

"No, I wanted to move out here. Your brother left us the house and wanted us to live in it. I just didn't know you'd be heading off again, leaving me alone and pregnant." Emma struggled to keep the pique from her voice.

Rohan sighed. "We never discussed it, Emma. You knew how I made a living and I'd have to work away sometimes."

Emma swallowed. "I hoped you'd stop. Or at least not take another risky job until the baby came."

"This isn't a risky job, Em," Rohan snuffed. "It's one of the easiest I've done. Fred's bringing the whole gang and we'll diffuse it quickly."

"But you don't need the money." Emma heard the whine in her voice and knew she ran on thin ice with her husband once she went along that track. "Anton left me a fortune and you said your stocks alone made more than a million pounds since Christmas. You could stay home if you wanted."

Rohan's lips quirked into a lopsided smile. "Emma Andreyev! I'm shocked. Is this your way of forcing me to say I don't want to stay home with you? You devious little *obez'yana!*"

"Well, don't you?" Determination lit her eyes with inner fire. "You don't have to work as the Actuary if you don't want to."

Rohan inhaled deeply and Emma felt her fringe move as he breathed out again. She tensed. He ran his finger between her eyebrows, smoothing out the worry lines before tracing the outline of her nose. "Emma Andreyev, I keep no secrets from you. I don't work as the Actuary, *printsessa.* I am the Actuary. It's who I am and what I do. I won't ask you not to be an archivist and work with dusty photos because it's what you love.

If the school didn't pay you a salary, you'd just go anyway and do it for free. It's rarely about the money."

Emma blinked back tears unsuccessfully and they escaped down the side of her face and plopped onto the pillow. "Ask me not to do it and I won't. I'll stop work and stay home," she whispered.

Rohan shook his head, his fringe falling into his eyes. "I won't ask you, Em."

Emma put her hand over her mouth and tried to suppress the huge sob which began in her chest. As usual, the mathematician had checkmated her. The misery welled up quickly, spilling from her mouth without restraint and Emma was powerless to hold it. Her chest heaved and her words were unintelligible, punctuated by hysterical jolts. Rohan pulled her face into his chest and held her, his biceps bulging against her tiny fingers as she sought to cling on and keep him pinned down. She sobbed and fought for breath, knowing it was futile. The Actuary was as much a part of Rohan Andreyev as the oxygen he breathed and she loved all of him. "I didn't know you felt like this," he whispered. "I'm so sorry, Em. I'm truly sorry."

Emma collected herself enough to allay Rohan's suspicions, sliding from the bed and washing away her salty tears in the ensuite shower. Will phoned from the front door and Rohan donned his jeans and shirt to greet his excited son. Nicky powered up the stairs to seek his mother, waving a new Leicester City scarf and towing Kaylee behind him. "I won't be long, Nicky," Emma called. "I'm just getting into my pyjamas."

"Ok, Mum," he called back graciously. "Kaylee just wanted you to see her hat before she goes home."

"I'm coming." Emma swiped at her puffy eyes with a towel and pulled on her pyjamas. She pushed her wet hair back from her face and straightened her shoulders, fixing a tight smile on her lips.

In the bedroom, Kaylee bounced on the balls of her feet and as Emma emerged, performed a beautiful pirouette. "Look Emma! Daddy bought me a hat and Nicky a scarf. It's got Leicester City on it and the fox. Does it suit me?"

"It does!" Emma complimented her. "Blue suits you, Kaylee. How lovely of your daddy." She turned to face her son and her breath caught in her chest. Nicky observed her with concern in his intense blue eyes. He didn't smile and pulled the long woolly scarf from his neck, allowing it to trail on the floor.

Emma swallowed and dabbed at her red nose with a piece of toilet roll. "Let's go and thank Will for taking you to the soccer, Nicky?"

The child shook his head. "No, Mummy. You stay here. I'll take Kaylee back to her daddy and then I'm comin' up here to talk to you."

Emma opened her mouth to reply and then closed it again. Kaylee skipped into the wide hallway and Nicky started to follow her. He paused in the doorway and held out the scarf. "For you, Mummy."

"No, baby. Will bought it for you." Emma produced a watery smile for her son but could see he wasn't convinced. He threw it on the chair between them and followed his little friend to the staircase and Emma listened to them clump down the wooden treads. "Oh no!" She sank onto the unmade bed and put her head in her hands. Nicky inherited Rohan's interrogative nature and Emma worried for her ability to deceive both of them with any degree of success.

The phone buzzed on the rug again and Emma's patience snapped. Stalking across to the roaring fire, she seized the poker in an angry fist and smashed the handle onto her balled up sweatshirt. There was the sound of glass shattering as the mobile phone bore the impact. The noise shocked Emma and she stepped back horrified, the poker still raised.

At the sound of Nicky's feet on the stairs, she laid the poker back on the hearth and threw another log on the fire. Dry wood crackled against the super-heated coal beneath and after a moment's hesitation, the orange flames licked around it. Her phone was Rohan's Christmas gift and Emma felt sick at her foolish ingratitude. Misery descended around her head and by the time Nicky reached the bedroom, she was in tears again. "I knew it!" the boy huffed, pressing his face into Emma's stomach. "I seed you done cryin' from your red eyes."

"I'm fine," Emma sniffed, wiping her eyes on her sleeve. "There's nothing to worry about, Nicky. I'm sorry. The last thing I wanted to do was spoil your night. Who won?"

"Leicester. Love you, Mummy."

"I know, baby. Love you too."

"You don't need to tell me what's wrong." Nicky's tiny hands caressed the bottom of Emma's back through her pyjama top.

"I don't?" she asked, feeling a wave of relief.

"Na, I already know. You're scared like when we lived on the estate and you did cryin' at night when you thinked I didn't know." He tipped his head back and rested his chin on her stomach. "But it's gonna be fine, Mum. I'll take care of you just like I always did when we was alone."

"Oh, baby." Tears poured from Emma's eyes and dripped onto Nicky's head. "I'm just so tired of it; I want to be safe, I really do."

"But Dad's got big muscles. He can fight the baddies."

"Yes, he can," Emma sniffed. "I'm just being silly. Sorry, baby."

Nicky snuggled in, linking his fingers behind her back. He squeaked as his mother's tears dropped onto his head but didn't move. Emma smoothed his soft blonde hair and gathered herself, controlling her breathing and sniffing away her tears. "Nick, I don't want Daddy to know I had a little cry, ok?"

Nicky looked up at her, his eyes filling with suspicion and Emma scrabbled to qualify her odd request. "He's going away tomorrow for a few days and I don't want him worrying. I need him to concentrate and come back soon. Yeah?"

Nicky nodded. "Is he leaving us?"

"No, no! I promise he isn't. It's just work. He'll be back."

Emma's son looked doubtful and she chastised herself inwardly. He was six years old and already far too wise for his years and just as he started settling and behaving like a normal little boy, she dumped a world of problems on his slender shoulders. "Everything's fine, Nicky. I love you sweetheart. I don't want you to worry."

"Ok, I won't," he lied.

The dull thud sounded through the old house as Rohan closed the front door. Emma ruffled Nicky's hair. "Come on you. It's way past your bedtime. Have a quick wash in my bathroom and hop into bed as fast as you can."

Nicky nodded and dragged his feet towards the ensuite, maintaining eye contact until he walked into the doorframe. Emma laughed. "Idiot! Hurry, Daddy's coming."

Nicky wrinkled his nose and closed the door behind him with a click. Emma heaved a sigh of relief and wiped her sleeve across her face, struggling to disguise her desolation for Rohan's benefit as she heard his uneven tread climbing the stairs. "It's freezing out there!" He strode into the room bringing cold air with him and Emma shivered. Rohan wrapped his arms around her and Emma's face sank into his chest. His fingers moved her long hair away from her neck and he kissed the delicate space under her ear. "Where were we?" he whispered.

"Will you read me a story, Mummy?" Nicky stood behind Rohan, his clothes in his hand and his nakedness pale in the lamplight.

Rohan's body stiffened, caught out in his amorous intent. "Nikolai, it's late, *syn*. Time for bed, *da?*"

"I need Mummy." Nicky set his lips in stubborn lines and held his father's gaze. "I want to hug her."

"*Da*, I know the feeling." Rohan smirked and looked to Emma for direction, respecting her six year struggle to raise their son alone. She smiled by way of apology and Rohan's eyes widened, noticing her distress then. He cocked his head and Emma bit her lip.

"I'll just put Nicky to bed." She excused herself, pressing her warm lips against Rohan's. His face felt cold, making her shudder. Moving quickly from the bedroom she caught Nicky's hand and led him across the hall and into his room. "Come on, champ. Into your pyjamas and hop into bed."

Nicky pulled on pyjamas, watching Emma from the corner of his eye as she checked the tepid heat issuing from the radiator. "I need to get these checked again. Surely they're meant to put out more heat than this. I wonder if it's because we've turned some off in the empty rooms. The man said they're gravity fed so maybe it's that."

"Mum?" Nicky pushed his feet under the sheets of the double bed. "When Daddy's not here, can you sleep wiv me? I'll keep you safe."

"My darling, if I get scared, this will be the first place I'll come. I promise." Emma tucked her son into the big bed, his face tiny against the pillows. She climbed onto the bed and cuddled him, stroking his soft face until his eyes drooped. It took only a few minutes.

Emma looked around the room, the powder blue decor reminding her of Anton. His death still held a rawness in her heart and she put a hand up to her chest, remembering the painful reading of his last will and testament. He left everything to her, his stepsister turned sister-in-law and she still didn't understand why. '*From Russia, with love*' - his last words to her as the embarrassed solicitor cemented the legal hand over. Emma sighed, remembering the colourful childhood they shared, living his theatrical fantasies to escape the miseries of his murderous Russian mother. 'You will be the *printsessa!*' Anton's childish Russian accent giggled down the ages as he pushed her into the apple tree which formed their castle. '*Rohan will be the tsar.*' Only, Rohan didn't like the games. He lived in a different kind of escape altogether. His serious world was founded on fact and mathematical equations, always evaluating risk and steering a straight course; until the day he gave in and kissed his stepsister.

Emma touched her lips at the memory of the kiss which changed both their lives. The sensible Russian

Orthodox boy who was always bound for the ranks of British Army Officers, stopped in the street aged fifteen and kissed the full lips of his twelve year old stepsister. She'd been fighting an older boy at school when the tall Russian waded in and pulled her out. The crowd parted for the silent, authoritative Rohan and Emma felt ashamed, especially as she wielded the upper hand sitting astride the mouthy fourteen year old, ready to smack him in the face. Rohan gripped her wrist until it hurt and Emma threw the tantrum of her life in the middle of a risky housing estate, stunning him with its ferocity. And he kissed her.

It was the first kiss for both of them and the heat and lack of control was spectacular. "Mama will hear of this," Rohan groaned, that fact dictating the pattern of their lives for the next four years. Emma grew up living for the stolen kisses and delicate touches of their forbidden love. She excelled at school, desperate to impress the studious Rohan and yearning for the electrical jolt of his proud smile.

Emma felt the pull of the Russian's powerful magnetism through the solid walls of the old house. She left the lamp on in Nicky's room and stole across the cold hallway into their bedroom. At the doorway she paused. Rohan's white blonde head faced his laptop screen and his face creased in concentration as numbers scrolled up like film credits, performing a complicated calculation. His muscles showed through his clothes and Emma sensed her fingers twitch in acknowledgement of their hardness under his smooth skin. He removed his reading glasses and ran his hands through his hair. As he stretched, Emma heard the creak of the ancient chair under his powerful body and he groaned in satisfaction as his long body straightened.

Emma glided across the wide room like a missile, pushing her way between Rohan and the mahogany desk and planting herself astride his legs. She pressed herself against his strong body and Rohan smiled as his hands found their way under Emma's pyjama top and caressed the soft skin of her back. His intense blue eyes softened at the sight of her and his face relaxed. "Remember the first time?" Emma whispered, brushing his lips with hers. "After Gretna Green, when we were married?"

"*Da*." Rohan nodded. "Of course I remember, *devotchka*. Good Russian boys wait until marriage so I made it worth the wait."

"I was sixteen and scared," Emma continued, speaking as she stripped her pyjama top over her head. Rohan's eyes flared and his pupils dilated. "And you looked so hot in your second lieutenant's uniform." Emma bent her head and kissed him again, feeling his body tense under her. She let her lips graze his. "And you looked even hotter without it."

Rohan's blue eyes narrowed, his lashes brushing his cheeks. His whole body felt poised and Emma revelled in it, arching her back and pressing her breasts into his chest. He was rigid, fingers locked in place around Emma's small waist, his thumbs barely touching the underside of her full breasts. "I want it to be like that," she breathed. "Like we don't know what we're doing."

Rohan opened his mouth and Emma placed her finger over his lips, preventing him saying anything logical or literal to endanger the moment. "*Da*." He kissed the slender finger instead, softly turning control back to her. She could see from the intensity of his gaze how much it pained him. Emma ran her lips up the ridged tendons in Rohan's neck, kissing and nibbling and feeling him shift underneath her. His strong fingers subconsciously kneaded the soft skin of Emma's back as he groaned, allowing her access to his soft earlobes and the underside of his jaw. Then he snapped.

The compulsive control freak and the army captain came together in one unhealthy moment and Rohan leapt to his feet, keeping hold of Emma as she gripped her legs hard around his hips. His eyes flashed with danger as he stumbled towards the four poster bed and spilled Emma onto it. She felt the bed groan under her, another of Anton's restoration gifts to her. The oak four poster bed had seen generations of the Ayers family who slept, laughed and loved under the cover of its dark canopy. Emma bit her lip as Rohan stripped his tee shirt over his head, his eyes dark with passion. The long shrapnel scars across his stomach looked like purple lines in the flickering light from the fire and she sighed as Rohan climbed onto the bed, willing her lips not to smirk with anticipation.

Asking Rohan Andreyev to pretend naivety was like asking the sun not to shine. He probably had a mathematical equation for the probable outcome and already dismissed the odds as a long shot.

CHAPTER THREE

"What time do you finish today?" Rohan asked as Emma buttoned her blouse.

"I'll be home by 12.30. Why?" her fingers shook as she nurtured the faint hope he wouldn't leave before then.

"I'll ring you. I should be checked in by then so I'll have time to spare before my flight boards. My taxi's due in half an hour."

"Oh." Emma bit her lip and willed the tears not to come. "You won't be able to ring me. My phone's broken. I didn't want to tell you."

"*Chto?*" Rohan stopped and stared at Emma, his long fingers half way through fixing his tie. She knew he watched her squirm. She shook her head.

"I know, I know, I'm sorry. I'll get it fixed."

"You want the documents? Receipt and guarantee. I'll get them for you. It's new."

"No, it's fine. It was my fault so they won't cover it. Just ring the house phone while you're away and we'll talk on that."

"Show me, Em."

"No. You need to leave, so get ready. The taxi won't be able to get in the gate so you need to be downstairs." Emma busied herself fighting her curly hair into a long ponytail, irritated by the wet patch on the back of her blouse from its damp weight.

"Hey, go steady." Rohan took the hair tie from her wrist and stood behind her, gently smoothing her hair back from her face. He teased it with his fingers until the curls ran in the same direction and Emma closed her eyes against the feelings his touch revived. "I need to be able to contact you."

Emma gritted her teeth and yanked her head away, wincing at the pain as Rohan kept hold of her ponytail. He fixed the hair tie and pinned her by the shoulders, forcing her back into his chest. "*Da?*"

"You need to contact me but it doesn't matter that I can't contact you! I've no idea where you'll be or if you're safe, but that's ok - as long as you can contact me." Emma wriggled free, cursing herself for her temper. "Just go, Rohan!"

"*Net!* I don't want to leave this way, not with us *bor'ba*, Emma. I don't want to drive away when we're fighting. Last time that happened you were gone when I returned."

"You're not driving; you're leaving in a taxi." Emma pouted, knowing she was being facetious. It pained her but she couldn't seem to stop. Yesterday's clothes lay on the rug by the bed, condemning her with the smashed phone inside the pocket. She thought of Rohan choosing it in the shop, gift wrapping it with his careful fingers and felt her betrayal of him like a knife in her chest. The breath came as a sob and she pressed her hand over her lips to suppress it.

"Emma, nothing will happen this time. No kidnappers, no double crossing computer guys and no danger. I'll be home soon and I won't take another job until the baby comes. I'll sit at my desk and crunch numbers for the bean counters but I'll do no retrievals. Ok?" Rohan lifted her chin with his finger and Emma blinked, feeling stray tears roll down her cheeks. She nodded and they plopped onto the wooden floor. "Oh,

Em!" Rohan crushed Emma into his chest, ignoring the lipstick smear across his clean shirt. "You need to explain how you're feeling, *dorogaya*. This is where we went wrong before."

"If I tell you how I feel, Ro, will you stay? I don't want you to go and I'd beg you if I thought you'd listen." Emma wiped her eyes with the back of her hand, cursing as black mascara streaked the skin.

Rohan shook his head in exasperation and let her go. He wrapped his hand around the corner post of the huge bed and rested his forehead against it. The rose coloured drapes hanging from the oak rail shivered at his touch. "Where's this coming from? It's too late now, Em. You know how this works. I've taken the advanced payment so I have to go; I don't have a choice." Rohan closed his eyes and gritted his teeth. He banged his forehead lightly against the heavy oak and shook his head in frustration.

"This is never gonna work." Emma's voice sounded flat. "I can't keep living this way. I want security. Nicky needs a father and so does this baby." She smoothed her hand across her stomach, hope dying in her eyes.

Rohan ran his fingers through his hair and looked aghast. "This is ridiculous, Em! You can't dump our marriage over a miscommunication!"

"It's the same bloody miscommunication every damn time though!" Emma shouted. "You left me pregnant with Nicky and now you're doing the same again."

"I didn't leave you!" Rohan's anger spilled over, his eyes flashing with fury. "Stop saying that! I was deployed and I didn't know you were pregnant! Don't let Nicky hear you say that? Are you trying to destroy my relationship with my son?"

Emma shook her head. "No."

Rohan flicked his thumbnail on his teeth and paced. "You asked me not to take the job after Christmas and I didn't, did I?"

"No."

"You knew I met a contact in London last week, yet you said nothing until now. Why?"

"Because I knew you wouldn't understand. It wasn't just the job after Christmas; I was asking you not to take any more jobs. Not ever." She shrugged and wiped her nose on her hand. "You did it anyway."

Rohan exhaled loudly and looked up at the ceiling. "*Der'mo!*" He banged the side of his fist against the bed post. "No more jobs ever? Like, retire?"

Emma nodded. "We both nearly died last time you took a retrieval job, Ro. Nicky almost ended up an orphan."

Rohan sighed and watched his wife as her fingers writhed against each other in an agony of suppressed emotion. "Emma, listen. I'm sorry, ok. I didn't understand."

They both jumped at the sound of small feet thundering up the stairs. "Dad!" Nicky's voice yelled. "Daddy! The taxi's comin'. I pressed the button and let him in." His blue eyes were wild as he ran into the room, stopping at the sight of his parents standing stiffly apart. He hovered, looking awkward with one foot covering the other. "I shouldn't have done it, should I?" The child looked anxious. "I didn't know what to do so I let it in."

"It's fine, Daddy needs to go." Emma turned a wooden smile on her son. "Thanks baby. Get your coat and shoes on and we'll head off to school. Please can you give Farrell some biscuits and then let him out?"

Nicky looked unsure. His eyes went from Rohan to Emma and the years of it being just him and his mother won through. He walked along the corridor and Emma heard him slide down the bannister, exactly like she asked him not to a million times. Emma swallowed.

"We'll talk about this when I get back." Rohan's face was blank but the vein in his neck ticked, revealing his stress. "I *will* be back, Emma, I promise." His blue eyes flashed.

Emma shrugged and Rohan took a step towards her. Her eyes strayed towards the broken phone, nestling in the folds of her clothes. Now she couldn't even show him the foundation of her terror; the text messages hidden in the broken glass and crushed plastic. Rohan's hand felt rough on her face as he caressed her cheek. "What's this really about, Em?"

She stared at the fireplace, the ashes cold and dead in the grate, as numb as she felt. "You wouldn't believe me if I told you," she replied, a sad smile lifting her lips.

His thumb stroked the soft place under her eye and Rohan leaned in and pressed his lips over hers. "*Vy kogda-nibud' mne doveryat?*" His voice was a whisper as he asked her if she ever trusted him. "How can I earn it?" he questioned, waiting for Emma's damning answer. She shrugged again, grinding her teeth until it hurt.

The doorbell sounded downstairs in the cavernous hall and Rohan's hand jerked on Emma's face. She put her left hand up to brush his fingers away and Rohan clasped it, lifting it to his lips. "You have no ring," he said quietly. "*Net obruchal'noye kol'tso.* I married you and gave you no ring. No wonder you don't trust me. I'll make it right, Emma, I promise. I'll be home soon. Wait for me, *da?*"

Despite herself she nodded, wanting to cling to his legs and stop her beautiful husband leaving.

'Don't let him leave.'

She failed. Fear washed over her as she listened to his heels click along the floorboards and down the stairs. "I didn't let him leave," she whispered. "I just couldn't stop him."

CHAPTER FOUR

"I need to go to my office, Nicky. Just kiss me and join your class." Emma waved her arm towards Kaylee's hopeful expression but Nicky clung to her leg and pressed his face into her coat. "Nicky if it's about this morning, everything's fine. Daddy's coming back."

"No, it's not." Nicky shook his head against Emma's stomach and she cringed at the pressure.

"What then? I need to start work, love. Mr Dalton will get cross."

Nicky lifted his head, his eyes sparkling like pale blue diamonds. "Mr D is never cross and I'm waitin' for someone."

"Who? Kaylee's waiting for you, so it's rude to ignore her. Come on, Nicky, your class is lined up to go inside. Quick!"

"Oh!" Nicky's face lit up like a sunbeam. "Here she is!"

Emma's mouth dropped open as the elderly lady hauled a suitcase up the huge step into the walled playground. She wore a pair of exceedingly wrinkled knee high tights and her white knees were bare as the wind tugged at her tweed skirt. Skater shoes adorned her tiny feet, the tongue sticking up to her shins and she walked with a swagger. Her purple knitted hat sported a pom pom almost as big as a second head and her pale mackintosh flapped around her thighs, the belt dragging along the dirty floor. "Here I am, here I am!" she sang, spotting Nicky and making a beeline for his shining face.

"Freda!" He abandoned Emma and wrapped his arms around the woman in her ninth decade, hugging her slight frame until she nearly toppled. "Look, Mum. What a surprise, it's Freda!"

Emma scoffed. "What a surprise my a...armpit!" She glared at her son. "What's the story young man?"

"Nicky kindly invited me to stay at Wingate Hall while Rohan's away; so I packed my bag and here I am." Freda patted the suitcase with too much force and it fell over with a slap onto the playground.

"Did he?" Emma turned her forced smile onto Nicky, who winced.

"I should join my class," he said with an angelic pout of pure innocence. "Mrs Clarke will sit on me if I'm late." He leaned in towards Freda and whispered confidentially. "They never found the last kid she sat on."

"Oh, he's probably still up there," Freda whispered.

Emma pointed her finger at the line of bouncing six-year-olds and Nicky joined them, pushing in to stand next to his best friends, Kaylee and New Mo.

"I love his little black friend," Freda said with far too much volume and indignant adult faces turned in their direction. Emma pursed her lips and hoped her new job at the school lasted past today. "Coo-ee, Mo!" Freda waved to Mohammed and he smiled and waved back.

"Freda," Emma began. "I think there's been a misunderstanding. I'm happy for you to come and stay with us, but I have to work until lunchtime. Why don't I leave your suitcase in the staffroom and pick you up from your apartment when I'm finished?"

"Oh no, that won't do at all!" Freda exclaimed,

grinning at Emma. Her top set of false teeth clacked onto the bottoms creating a ghoulish expression. She shoved them back up with a gnarled finger. "I'm here to help you, dear."

"Help?" Emma gulped and felt sick.

"Yes! Nicky said you're going through old photographs and records for the 150th anniversary." Freda waved her arm to take in the expansive school building with its apex roof and Georgian windows. "This was my school. I can probably name everyone in the photos from 1930 to 1935 and many more besides. Mother came here too and my stepfather, God rest his rotten redheaded soul, so I'll recognise people from the town." Freda crossed herself in a traditional Catholic movement and winked. Emma knew she was Anglican.

The archivist in Emma desperately wanted to lock Freda in the office and not let her out until she'd named every last photo, but the realist in her prevailed. "I'll have to check it's ok with the headmaster," Emma began, halted by Freda's shriek.

"They're going in, they're going in!" The old lady battled her suitcase into an upright position and wheeled it up the ramp, following Nicky's gyrating class of fidgets. She joined the back of the wobbly queue and farted so loud, it must have hurt. Thirty children let out snorts and giggles and Emma put her hand up to her forehead, feeling the beginnings of a headache.

Mr Dalton was happy for Freda's help, thrilled with the prospect of two archivists for the price of one. "Ooh yes," he said, sounding enthusiastic. "I'll just grab a police check form for you." He bustled down the corridor and promptly forgot.

"A police check?" Freda sounded horrified. "Does

he think I'll steal the photos?"

"No, not at all. Everyone who works with children needs to be police checked."

"But we won't be working with children, just photos."

"Yes, but we might see the children; and this office is right next to the Year 1 and 2 toilets, so we're bound to bump into a few."

"Ohhhh." Freda looked doubtful. "I don't think I want to help them to the toilet. I wouldn't know what to do."

"It's fine," Emma reassured her. "You won't have to."

A low hammering on the door made Freda jump in fright. "Are the police here to do their checks?" she squeaked. "I couldn't get my corset done up to the top, so I'm underdressed."

"It's just Sam. He fetches boxes for me. I can't lift them from the attic so he gets them. This is his office." Emma flung the heavy door open and admitted the puffing caretaker as he peered over two large boxes filled with photo frames.

"Just these?" he asked, laying them on the bench and bending double to catch his breath.

"Thank you." Emma patted him on the shoulder and he reddened in embarrassment.

"Hi, Sam," Freda said and simpered like a teenager. She fluttered her eyelashes and beamed at the young man. "How old are you?"

"I'm er...I'm..." He gulped at the sight of the old lady in the strange shoes. Then he pointed. "Do they have wheels that pop out the bottom so you can skate?"

"Oh, I'm not sure." Freda plopped into a chair and

tried to lift her foot. Her tweed skirt slithered upwards revealing skinny white knees and a pair of bloomers. Emma stared, wondering if she could display them at the anniversary celebration. They looked old enough.

Sam looked to Emma for help. "Sam's thirty two, Freda. He came to this school as a little boy and works here. He's married."

"That's nice." Freda peered at the sole of her shoe. "Will you help me skate on these shoes, young man?"

"No way!" Emma panicked. "You're ninety years old. Don't be crazy; you'll fall and break something!"

"Maybe not." Freda smiled and her teeth did the strange clacking thing again.

Emma stared hard at Sam and jerked her head towards the old lady. "Don't even go there. It won't be as funny as you might think."

"Oh, he could put me in the tube. Do you think you could do that, young man? Can you fit me in the tube?"

"Tube?" Sam looked sick, his ruddy skin pinking again.

Emma's eyes widened in horror. "Not YouTube?"

"Yes, that's it. I want to be on your tube, skating on my shoes. Let's get the little wheels out." Freda scrabbled around on Sam's desk and retrieved a large screwdriver.

"No!" Sam and Emma lurched for the screwdriver at the same moment but he got there first, moving sharp objects out of Freda's way with frantic, haphazard shoving actions.

The door burst open and Mr Dalton stood in the gap, his tie resting over his left shoulder where the wind blew it as he chased a Year 3s drawing. "What on earth..?" he started, appalled by the sight of his archivist and caretaker laying into a defenseless old lady.

Emma and Sam darted backwards to reveal the elderly school visitor brandishing a long screwdriver in her gnarled hand. "Bloody 'ell!" he squeaked, clapping his hand over his mouth and looking around him guiltily at the impromptu slip in decorum. He waved the police check form in Emma's direction. "I'm not 'appy about this, Mrs Andreyev!" His Welsh lilt lifted his voice a few octaves and Emma bit her lip and looked crossly at Freda.

"She's got wheels under her shoes," Sam offered, snatching the screwdriver from Freda's hand. "We don't think it's a good idea for her to use them."

"Noooo!" Mr Dalton's eyes bugged and his lips puckered into an angry pout. "Certainly not! Riding any wheeled device is not permitted in our school!"

Freda looked disappointed and Sam leaned in towards the headmaster, speaking in an undertone of confidentiality. "Someone's already superglued them in."

"Oh!" Freda hooked her leg over her thigh and peered at the sole of her shoe, looking disappointed. The bloomers went on show again and Mr Dalton looked scandalised.

"I'll keep her in here," Emma said, screwing her face up in apology. She reached for the flapping form and Mr Dalton let it go, a look of concern on his face.

"Ok, then," he said. He whipped around in his usual high speed fashion and disappeared. The heavy door clicked shut and Emma heard him talking to a child in the corridor. "Oooh, lovely hair tie, Emily Parry. Verrrrry impressive."

"That was close." Sam looked at Freda through narrowed brown eyes. "I've only had this job a term and I don't want to lose it."

Freda ignored him, picking at the sunken wheels with a lined fingernail. She shook her head and the bobble on her hat wobbled like a loose boulder as she smiled up at Emma. "Can we look at the photos now dear? I want to see if my stepfather was as ugly a child as he was an adult, God rest his rotten redheaded little soul." She crossed herself again and Sam pulled a face and stepped back. He lifted a folder with the label, 'Maintenance Book' emblazoned on the front and skirted Freda to reach a set of keys hanging from a hook. His face was pure misery as he stuffed the keys into his overalls pocket and left the room.

Emma sighed. "Freda, you need to behave if you're staying with me this morning. Sam's sharing his office because there's nowhere else. If I get offside with him, I'll have to leave."

"Sorry dear." Freda looked momentarily contrite. "Can we look now?"

Emma dragged a large, collapsing cardboard box towards her. The sides bent to reveal several photographs in frames, the glass covered in a patina of tiny black flies and mildew. "When was your stepfather here?" she asked.

"Around 1914, I think. He might be hard to spot in the sepia photos. Everyone's hair will look red or brown." Freda sounded wistful. "I'd recognise my mother perhaps."

"Did everyone go to school?" Emma asked. "I thought your mother was in service."

Freda nodded and reached for the first photograph, pulling it from the rickety box with shaking fingers. Her brow crinkled in a mix of emotions as she wiped a thick screed of dust from the glass. Emma opened her mouth to urge the old woman to watch her fingers and stopped. Freda hadn't got to ninety by being told what to do. "It was illegal to employ children until they were thirteen, but my grandmother worked as Mrs Ayers maid so Mother went along most weekends and after school to help. My grandfather worked on the land and the family lived in a cottage with the other house workers. Grandmother was determined Mother should become a lady's maid and taught her everything she needed to know to take over from her. Mother was a clever girl and had her heart set on becoming a teacher. She was selected as a pupil-teacher after the testing but her parents forced her into service. She never forgave them and when the lady's maid to the youngest Ayers girl died unexpectedly, Mrs Ayers employed Mother. Poor Mother wanted to see the school year out but they removed her a day after her fifteenth birthday. Desperately unhappy, she found sympathy with Lady Celia, who was Mother's age. Lady Celia didn't treat her like her maid but as an equal, which is possibly where it all went wrong. The fanciful girl believed Mother and Geoffrey Ayers were in love and facilitated their meetings in locations around the house. I was conceived in the laundry room."

Freda stopped and rubbed her hand over her face, smooshing grey filth from the photograph under her eyes and across her forehead. Emma bit her lip and waited as the elderly lady peered through the glass at the small, serious faces beneath her fingers. She opened her mouth to speak and then looked up at Emma. "Yes dear?"

Emma cleared her throat, figuring she could clean Freda up in the adjacent toilets before morning tea time. "How do you know the details? I didn't think that generation talked about sex and conception, especially not affairs."

Freda nodded. "No, they didn't. Mother had dementia in her later years. My husband John, paid for me to fly home periodically to look after her and take the strain off my siblings. She rambled so much, we knew pretty much everything by the end. She was graphic to the point of embarrassment and my siblings were horrified. Whenever she was alone with me she became animated, convinced I was Lady Celia. My brothers and sisters resented it. I always knew who my father was, but they didn't. My stepfather's redheaded sons made it increasingly difficult for me to visit out of spite and stopped communicating. I only knew Mother died because I had a spy in the camp." Freda's face saddened and Emma watched with horror as a wet tear slipped through the dust on the crinkled face, leaving behind a sludge trail. She swiped it away, beginning to resemble a war painted army commando.

Emma struggled not to interrupt a moment of obvious grief and bit her lip. She stood welded to the spot of broken quarry tile, her hand reaching towards the box. Freda's eyes roved the photograph, pushing away more dust with the side of her hand. When she found what she wanted, she smiled. She sighed in satisfaction and to Emma's horror, leaned forward and placed her lips on the cracked glass.

Freda's face shone with pleasure as she looked up at Emma. "My sister," she said, turning the frame with care so Emma could see. A tiny girl sat in the front row of a class of unsmiling children, her tousled hair blowing around her head. The colour was indistinguishable in the sepia but the face was a less lined, carbon copy of Freda's.

Emma smiled. "How gorgeous. What's her name?"

"Charlotte," Freda said and stroked the glass. "Her hair was mousey blonde like mine and as fly away as a ball of dandelion seed. I loved her the most."

"Not a redhead then? Not like your other step-siblings?"

"No." Freda drew herself up to her full height in the caretaker's battered chair, resembling a princess in her bearing. "Charlotte was my full sister, dear. She was the daughter of my mother and Geoffrey Ayers."

"But you said..." Emma screwed her pretty face up, contorting her features in confusion. "You definitely said your mother married your step-dad and had red-haired babies."

"I did. And she did," Freda said smugly. "But I didn't say she ever stopped her infatuation with my father, nor his with her. Mother was forced to marry to disguise the shame of my birth but she never stopped loving Geoffrey. I always suspected little Charlotte was his, but in Mother's ramblings she admitted it. Charlotte was born just after war was declared in 1939. My stepfather returned so changed from his war experiences he didn't care for his own children, let alone the cuckoos. I raised Charlotte from a baby and took her with me to the Philippines after John and I married. There was nineteen years between us and she was like my own child. She died in her seventieth year and I miss her every day." Freda caressed the glass with fondness. "I don't have this photograph. May I have a copy?"

"Yes," Emma reassured her. "I'll make one for you."

The women worked in relative silence until morning tea time, cleaning the glass on the photographs and removing the worst ones from their frames. They wore white cotton gloves which quickly grew covered in grey dust and the tiny thunder bugs which crept beneath the glass over the years. Freda sat with a pen and paper and painstakingly named the children she remembered, idling over the image of her sister in the 1944 school photograph. Emma copied it and pushed the paper into a plastic wallet, touched when Freda kissed her on the cheek for her pains. "Was she your spy in the camp?" Emma asked and Freda nodded.

"Yes, dear. She flew back and forth when Mother was sick and it was the one secret Mother managed to keep from the others. I was ostracised but she was not."

Emma watched Freda hug the plastic wallet to her breast and ran her hand over her stomach, hoping her children would bond just as tightly.

CHAPTER FIVE

Freda slept in Nicky's bed for the first few nights while the painters finished the guest bedroom along the hall. The rewiring made the walls a mess and the plaster took weeks to dry, but the finished effect was stunning. The men moved the furniture back into the bedroom; the heavy oak double bed and its paired cupboards. They sweated and complained in equal measure. "This furniture's solid!" the younger painter grunted, closing the double doors with his heel.

"Watch that paintwork!" the older man yelled and Nicky bit his lip and hid behind his mother, jumpy around angry males.

Emma stood on a ladder to hang the new curtains and Freda supervised from below. "Left a bit, no, right a bit," she called from the other side of the room.

Nicky held the bottom step, mindful of Emma's pregnancy. "Wow, Mum, it looks amazing," he said, clutching the back of Emma's trousers as she descended. "I bet Uncle Anton would've loved this."

Emma smiled and ruffled her son's hair, tearful emotions rising into her chest at the compliment. She gulped them down, hoping her brother-in-law knew how grateful she felt for him bequeathing the huge estate to her. "I hope so," she said softly. "I did a lot of research before deciding on the colour."

"It's perfect." Freda clapped her hands and executed a graceful pirouette, admirable for a woman in her nineties. "I love the pale eggshell colour. What's it called?"

"Edwardian white. It's a heritage colour and I've leaned towards that period rather than earlier. I know the house dates back to William the Conqueror but I'm not sure rugs on the walls and stripped timber would suit it anymore. I'm glad you like it though." Emma smiled and hid a yawn.

"We're off now!" the tradesmen called and Emma went into the wide hallway to speak to them.

"Are you ok Mrs Freda?" Nicky asked, concerned as Freda stood in the centre of the room with her eyes closed. He touched a pleat of her tweed skirt, his brow furrowed in fear.

"Yes, dear. Thank you, I'm fine." Freda looked down at him, her face a mask of every lost emotion in the spectrum. Emma heard the small exchange from the doorway and glanced back, only half listening to the overall clad man in front of her.

"Call me when you're ready to do the next room," the painter said and Emma nodded, her mind elsewhere.

"Nicky, please could you show the gentlemen out and lock up for me?" she asked, her eyes straying to Freda. Nicky exchanged a wide-eyed look with her and nodded.

"Ok." Relieved of his duty in a feminine world, the six-year-old skipped along the hallway, going ahead of the tradesmen and sliding down the bannister.

Emma heard his palms squeak on the polished wood and cringed, waiting for the cry as he fell off. When it didn't come, she returned to Freda. "What's the matter?" she asked, her tone gentle. "Just memories?"

"Yes." Freda bobbed her head up and down and her white hair moved in delicate waves. "This room was Lady Celia's. She loved being away from her parents and shared the bathroom with her other sister. Her room is so near the laundry, I would sneak out and peek in here while Mother was working. You've got it exactly right, dear, even the pale cream of the drapes."

"I'm glad you like it," Emma sighed with relief. "It proved helpful writing down everything you said, so I'm pleased if it's a good likeness. The men painted the cornice board while I work out if I want curtain fabric over it."

"You've done well. I'll help you make up the bed."

"I'll do it later," Emma yawned. "It's a new mattress but the bedding's still in packets."

"Let me help?" Freda begged, her blue eyes wide. "I want to see it finished."

Emma relented and smiled. "You want to sleep here, don't you?"

Freda bit her lip and her face lit up with an inner glow. "Could I? I'd love to."

"Sure, it can be your room until Ro gets back." Emma knitted her brow and tried not to worry about her husband. Nicky bounced into the room, all blonde curls and enthusiasm. "Is the door locked baby?" Emma asked.

"Yep," he said smugly. "And I let the dog back in. He's lookin' at his food bowl like he wants feeding."

"I already fed him when we came back from our walk, baby. He's teasing you."

Nicky winced. "I gave him some more by accident."

"Nicky!" Emma chastised him. "You'll make him

overweight and he'll get sick."

"Sorry." The child didn't look sorry. "Want me to get the new sheets? Is Mrs Freda sleeping in here?"

"Yes please, she is. But seeing as it's Lady Celia's room, we should call her Lady Freda. What do you think?"

"Awesome!" Nicky laughed. "I'll just get Lady Freda's covers from the airing cupboard. Will you help me change my sheets too then? I wanna go back to my own bed tonight."

Emma disguised her dismay by nodding and turning away. While Freda slept in Nicky's room, he shared with his mother and Emma felt a sinking feeling in the pit of her stomach at being alone in the enormous four poster bed. She tried to stop herself suppressing her child's independence for her own selfish reasons. "Ok," she said lightly. "That's fine."

Emma changed Nicky's sheets first, reasoning he had to go to bed sooner. She left Freda stuffing pillowcases and bolsters. Nicky tried to help Emma, losing himself inside the duvet cover in his attempts to fit it together. "Where've you gone?" Emma asked, poking the lump in the material and making her son squeak. "What are you doing in there?"

"Makin' the bed." Nicky's muffled voice came from a different lump. "Stop poking Farrell."

"Get the dog out of there!" Emma said, horrified. "He's not allowed upstairs!"

Farrell slunk out of the cover and skittered to the door. Emma heard his claws clicking along the hallway towards the stairs. Nicky's voice rose from the remaining lump. "Mummy? Will you be ok in the big bed by yourself?"

"Yeah, course." Emma made her voice sound convincing. "I'll be fine."

"But Mummy, when I was downstairs seeing the men out, the phone did ringing and I spoke into it."

"Who was it, baby?" Emma winced as she stuffed the pillow into its case and braced herself for trouble.

"Harley Man," Nicky said, crawling out with a look of consternation. "I messed the covers up, Mummy. Look, I put it in upside down."

Emma ran a hand over her son's static blonde curls, settling them on his head and feeling them crackle under her fingers. Nicky pressed his face into her stomach. "I know you're gonna tell me Harley Man's not real and I shouldn't be thinking about him like you always say. But it *was* him."

Emma pursed her lips. After years convinced her son invented the motorbike rider who protected him throughout his young life, she was forced to concede his reality last year. Christopher Dolan watched over the little family on the orders of her stepbrother, Anton Andreyev, revealing himself to the child but not to her. Emma sighed. "Ok, baby. What did he say? How did he get our phone number?"

Nicky moved his face across Emma's stomach and pulled back with a grin, leaving a wet stain from his nose. Emma groaned and he smirked. "Harley Man said you won't answer your mobile phone, so he wanted me to give you a message. He said the countess is loosened."

"He said what?"

"The constant is loose."

"No, you said countess."

"I dunno. It was crackly. Can he come round for

tea?"

Emma ran a hand over her face. "What? No?"

"But he *is* real!" Nicky persisted. "You believe me, don't you?"

"Yes, I believe you, Nicky. But he's not coming round for tea."

Nicky pulled a grumpy face and crawled back into the duvet cover. Emma saw his shape moving around as he tried to marry up the four corners. "I'll button you in," she threatened, nudging the child's outline with her toe and he squeaked.

"Ok then. Do it," he giggled. "But you have to lift me onto the bed and flatten me out."

"Don't tempt me," she laughed, biting her lip and tapping her fingers on the bed post in anxiety.

Rohan and Christopher's fight had severed their working relationship forever, after the latter's stupidity put the whole family at risk. "*What are you up to now, Christopher Dolan?*" Emma whispered to herself. "Did he say he'd call back?" she asked, forcing a lightness into her voice.

"Na. He just said to warn you that the controls was open."

"Oh, Nicky!" Emma's patience hung by a very thin thread. "You keep changing the message! Next time, just bring the phone please?"

"You was busy!" he grumbled. "And I was detecting you." He re-emerged from the duvet cover again looking cross.

"Protecting," Emma corrected him. "It's fine. But next time either write it down or bring the phone. Yeah?"

Nicky nodded and turned his attention to putting

his bed back together and Emma worried at the inside of her cheek with her teeth. "Bloody hell!" she hissed and shook her head.

"Swearing!" Nicky chastised. "You won't let me!"

"Sorry," Emma apologised, hauling the duvet onto the bed. At least she knew where the anonymous texts came from.

CHAPTER SIX

"Oh, no!" Emma's colour drained from her face and she reached for the wobbly table behind her with shaking hands.

"Emma?" Sam stopped changing the plug on the staff room toaster, his screw driver poised mid-air.

"What's wrong dear?" Freda stopped itching her shin and pulled her pop sock back up to her knee with a snap. "Is it the baby?"

"Baby?" Sam's eyes bulged in his head. "What baby? Who's having a baby? Are you having a baby?" He glanced at the floor as a screw tinkled across the tiles and shot underneath the desk. "Oh, bloody hell!"

"Young man!" Freda struggled to her feet. "Swearing in front of ladies is so gauche!" There was a hideous twang as part of her whale bone corset settled and the old lady farted. Pursing her lips and smiling with admirable nobility, she sat back in her seat, which emitted a painful creak.

"Stop! Please just stop!" Emma held one hand in the air and covered her face with the other. She squeezed the bridge of her nose between thumb and forefinger and kept her eyes closed against the awful discovery. "I need to think!"

"Are you pregnant then?" Sam asked, banging his head on the underside of the table as he emerged, screw in hand. He jerked his head over his shoulder towards the elderly woman. "I'm guessing it's not her who's expecting." The thought gave him considerable amusement and he laughed like lunatic, sitting cross legged on the floor.

"I think I'm gonna be sick." Emma clapped a hand over her mouth. Freda bent forward and held up a dirty mop bucket and Sam pulled his head back under the table as Emma fled the office and disappeared into the toilets next door. She stood over the sink unit taking deep breaths and peering at her ashen face in the mirror. A few sips of water helped restore her equilibrium and after wiping her lips, Emma went back to the office.

A miserable darkness hung over the school and the high windows offered a view of grey sky. As Emma pushed the door open, Freda and Sam whipped around with guilty looks and Freda turned, pushing something metal along the table with her left hand. Emma's pretty face hardened and she put her hands on her hips. "Stop right there!" she demanded. "Don't you dare."

"But it's a disaster!" Sam exclaimed. "Get rid of it. Nobody will know. I'll take it outside and..."

"No!" Emma slammed the door behind her and stared at the conspirators. "I'm an archivist! My role is to guard history, not destroy it because it doesn't suit me." Emma turned her dark eyes on Freda. "And I'm surprised at you, Freda Ayers! You can't say you're a historian and then pick and choose!"

"Yes, but what will you do?" Freda's crinkled face drooped in misery.

"I don't know!" Emma pushed through and seized the brass plaque from the table. Its pitted surface was distressed by verdigris and Emma's wrist bent backwards with the weight of it. "It's staying!" She cradled the plaque to her breast, smelling the old metal scent as she contemplated her concerned colleagues.

"Let's have another look?" Sam asked, holding out his hand.

"No, I don't trust you."

He huffed and rolled his eyes. "She wanted to get rid of it, not me!" He jerked his head at Freda and the old lady glared at him. "Please, give us another quick peek. It's kinda funny really."

Freda slapped him hard on the top of his head. "It's catastrophic, you foolish little man! It's certainly not funny!"

Emma turned the plaque around so they could read the damaging inscription again. She peered at it upside down, hoping she'd misread it the first five times.

To commemorate the opening of Little Arden School on September 12th in the year 1860 AD by Reverend P. Jameson, Vicar of St Martins, Leicester.

Sam worried at an itch in his scalp and bit his lip. "How could they get so mixed up? They think this year's the hundred and fiftieth anniversary but it's not, is it?"

"No." Emma exhaled and wrapped her arms around the heavy wall plaque. She felt the roughness of the screw holes against her palms and shook her head. "They're five years too late."

Freda stared at the plaque. "I've never seen that. This doesn't make sense." She tapped her grey temple. "There's nothing wrong with my memory."

"Maybe it belongs to a school with the same name, but ended up here by mistake." Sam nodded, trying to inject hope into the awful situation. He pointed at Emma. "Why don't you do some research and see if that's possible?"

Emma grimaced. "Look, we need to keep this between us for now. I'll do some checking with the

Harborough museum, the council and the local library and see what I can find out." She bit her lip. "But we need to face facts. This school might be older than we thought."

Sam held his hands out for the plaque. "Why don't I pop it back in the attic for now? I'll put it behind the labelled boxes so we know where it is. It'd be a disaster if Mr Dalton came wandering in here and saw it. He'd go mental!"

Emma nodded. "Yeah, that's a good idea. But first I'll take a quick scan of it."

"You can't take it out there!" Freda exclaimed as the hand bell rang for morning playtime. "Someone might see!"

"Take a photo on your phone?" Sam's head wobbled like a toy.

"I broke it." Emma's shoulders drooped as she handed the offending artifact over to the caretaker.

"I'll do it on mine and email it to you." Sam laid the plaque on the table and took a few snaps of it. Then he pressed buttons and asked for Emma's email address.

"I don't have one. Oh, this is a disaster!"

"We'll sort it out later," Sam said, slipping his phone into his pocket. "So is one of you really pregnant then? Or was it a joke?"

"Me!" Emma said. "And if you tell anyone about the plaque or my pregnancy, I'll break your legs."

"No, you won't," Sam snickered and then he looked at Emma's intense stare. "Oh, you would."

"I most definitely will!" Emma snapped. She pointed a dust covered finger at his pointy nose. "And I mean it!"

Sam disappeared with the plaque covered in an old stained tea towel, sneaking round the corner like a ninja on a mission. Freda stood next to Emma and stroked her curly hair with tender fingers. "It might not be a disaster, dear. The photos and other artifacts still need taking care of. They'll decay further if we don't get them into the proper wrappers and boxes. I'm sure Mr Dalton will understand that?"

"He won't care anymore," Emma replied sadly. "People only care about history if they can use it for something. Mr Dalton and the committee were only interested in the photos because they needed them. If there's nothing to celebrate, they'll go back into the attic for another fifty years."

"Well, forty five actually," Freda said, giving Emma a hearty pat on the back. "Try not to worry. It changes nothing."

Emma shrugged. "I liked having a job title. Anton left me enough money not to work but I'm used to being independent. It's silly really, I know."

"No, it isn't." Freda bent and kissed the top of Emma's head. "There's nothing wrong with wanting to find your place in this world." She gave Emma's shoulders a squeeze. "Look, darling. Do your research and say nothing for now. I'll pack up for today. I need to visit my apartment and pick up more clothes. Please could you fetch me when you finish here?"

Emma nodded. "Yeah, that's fine." She stood up and hugged the elderly lady. "I'm glad you were here when I found it. It's a relief to have someone to share my burdens with."

Freda winked at Emma as she shrugged on her tweed jacket. "My pleasure, dear. I haven't had this much fun since I was a much younger woman."

Emma smiled, but the expression didn't reach her eyes. "I didn't imagine it would be this turbulent."

"You're doing just fine." Freda grabbed her handbag, stopping at the door in hesitation. "Emma, you'd tell me if I outstayed my welcome, wouldn't you? I've lived at Wingate Hall for over two weeks now and while I've loved every moment, I don't want to become a burden."

"It's been lovely having someone else around," Emma sighed. "It's a huge old place and I've appreciated your advice with the redecorations."

"Very well then." Freda smiled. "I'll give it a few more nights but then I should go home. My poetry recital group have been ringing my mobile phone every day for the last week. I think they're missing me." With a final regal wave she set off, closing the door quietly behind her.

In the empty room, Emma let her head sink into her hands to stave off the groan of misery. She heard Sam walking overhead in the attic. His footsteps were a long way from the mezzanine floor and she picked up the sound of his heavy boots jumping from joist to joist where there was nothing between the insulation and the ceiling. A piece of plaster hit Emma on the top of the head and a shower of white flakes followed it. *Where was he hiding the stupid thing?* Emma sighed and missed Rohan with a physical ache at the top of her stomach. "Where are you, Rohan Andreyev?" she spoke into the emptiness. "Why are you never around when I need you?"

Emma heard Sam moving back along the joists and watched as another cloud of dust shivered through the glow from the bare strip lights, sparkling like glitter. She heaved a sigh of relief that the damning object was once again safely hidden and contemplated the century and a half of trouble it was about to release.

CHAPTER SEVEN

It took hours for Emma to find sleep after her stressful day. The discovery of the mottled, brass plaque filled her with horror and she fretted. It explained the school's classification as Church of England, even though the links with the little church around the corner were tenuous. The local vicar visited the assembly once a month when he could make it and although he was a vibrant and entertaining frocked gentleman, the association went no further. The Church must have commissioned the school, otherwise it made no sense for the Vicar of St Martins to open it. Emma groaned and pushed her face into the pillow. She'd walked the dog for an hour in the dark, hoping to find physical exhaustion conducive to sleep but failing.

The piercing scream woke her, heart pounding and wide eyed as Emma sat upright in her bed and stared into the darkness. She heard the dog bark in the kitchen and panicked.

"Mummy!" Running feet heralded a terrified Nicky barrelling into the room, terror drawing sobs from his slender chest. "Mummy! You heard it?"

"It's ok, it's ok," she repeated, her voice coming amidst gasps of air. "Climb under the blankets and hide. I'll check on Freda." Emma pushed the covers back and patted her son's head, grabbing the cricket bat from behind Nicky's bedroom door on her way past. Her heart pounded, sending blood swishing through her eardrums as Emma ran along the hallway past closed doors, making little sound on the carpet in her socks.

Light came from under Freda's door and Emma heard the low murmur of voices. She pressed her ear against the oak, listening for a repeat of the scream. Her held breath emerged in a rush of recognition and she gripped the knob and flung the heavy door open. "What's going on?"

The man's back was tanned, the flesh scarred with lines which Emma knew intimately. His bare bottom was pert and neat, his arms muscular and defined as he pressed a rumpled shirt over his groin to protect his last shred of dignity. Freda sat upright in the cream bed coverings, her hair sucked tightly into rollers and shrouded by a black hair net. Her wrinkled face was shiny with moisturiser and her lips were in the process of transitioning from horror to pleasure. Her blue eyes bugged in their sockets, crinkled at the corners where the laughter began. "Your husband paid me a visit," Freda simpered, her mouth looking collapsed without her dentures. "But much as I'd love to oblige, I don't indulge in married men."

Emma bit her lip and turned to Rohan. "You came onto Freda?" Her tone sounded incredulous and he shook his head, his face angry.

"No, I bloody didn't! I thought I'd sleep in here and surprise you in the morning. I didn't know there'd be a *staraya zhenshchina* in the spare bed?"

"What?" Freda perked up, rising from the sheets like a flannelette clad ghost. "What did he call me?"

"A guest, Freda. He said guest," Emma replied, not taking her eyes from her husband. She raked his gloriously formed body for injury. Covering for his tactless use of the Russian for *old woman*, her shoulders drooped as she spotted the bruising around his ribs. "I'm awake now, Rohan. You might as well come to bed." Emma turned, waving over her shoulder as she set off towards the bedroom. "Unless you'd rather stay with Freda."

Emma strode along the corridor and placed the cricket bat behind Nicky's door. She heard Rohan shuffling behind her, balancing his clothing in his arms and listing on his prosthetic leg. They met up in the bedroom doorway, Rohan's face flushed with embarrassment and his eyes bashful. Nicky shot up from under the duvet and yelped with pleasure. "Daddy!"

"*Zdravstvuyte, syn*," Rohan replied, dropping most of his clothes as the child hurled himself against the strong, masculine body. *Hello, son.* He struggled to keep himself modestly covered using his underpants and a lonely black sock.

Nicky kissed the washboard stomach and giggled. "You're rudey dudey!"

"Yeah, Dad's tired now, babe. He scared Freda and now he's going to bed. There's nothing to worry about so hop back into bed and go to sleep. You've got school in a few hours." Emma shooed the reluctant child into his room and settled him with kisses, returning to the bedroom to the sound of water running in the ensuite bathroom. Rohan's crutches lay on the tiles near the shower entrance and his prosthetic leg stood abandoned in the corner. A stump sock lay next to it and Emma picked it up, laying it in the washing basket with a sigh.

Steam filled the large room and the slap of water on the glass screen broke into the night, sounding too loud for the hour. Rohan soaped his body with meticulous care and ran his hands over his hair to push the water back from his eyes. He balanced on one leg, intermittently using his hands to brace himself against the walls of the shower. Emma sat on the toilet lid and waited, sleep a long way off.

Rohan pushed the shower door open and balanced on one leg to reach for his crutches. Emma got there first, handing them to him so he could step onto the mat. His body glistened with water and a drip ran off the end of his nose. "Here, let me," Emma whispered, reaching backwards for a towel. With gentle fingers she ran the fabric over her husband's face, patting the soft area around his vibrant blue eyes. Then she smoothed it along his neck and chest. Rohan balanced on his crutches, knitting his brow as he tried to read her expression but Emma moved behind him, stroking the towel over his strong back and patting the shining beads from his shoulders. It was hard work ignoring the pink scar from a stab wound inflicted a few months previously and Emma deliberately concentrated on the ridges of his spine. She bit her lip and hid a smile as Rohan's muscles flexed, sensing his excitement at her touch. She dragged the towel down his ribs with care, seeing the blush of a purple bruise reach towards his backbone. Her lips against his shoulder blade ignited a shiver of desire which rippled across Rohan's body. "I've missed you so much," he breathed.

The crutches made it impossible for him to touch her and Emma played her advantage, trailing her lips down his side to his hip and hearing him gasp. "Did you?" she asked, rising and inflicting a tiny nip on his pectoral muscle. Her brown eyes were full of question, a delicate hint of mischief underlining the fear which drove her to know if her absence affected him.

"Of course I did, *devotchka*." Rohan stared at the floor tiles and his long eyelashes grazed his cheek. "It's strange. I used to feel so alive when I was the Actuary, tracking the risk and planning how to liberate it. This time was different. I wanted to be home with you and my syn."

Emma rested her face against his arm, feeling the hairs tickling her. She closed her eyes and enjoyed the sensation of Rohan's muscles flexing and the changing contours of his flesh against her cheek. "I didn't want you to go," she whispered. "I've hated the last two weeks."

Rohan nodded. "I'm sorry, Em. I shouldn't have gone. It was a big mistake."

"What happened?" Fear lit Emma's face from the inside and her brown eyes flashed.

Rohan shook his head. "No, *dorogaya*, not tonight. I'm tired and I want to be in bed with my wife."

Emma saw the exhaustion in his eyes and the wobble in his stance as he balanced on his good leg and leaned heavily on the metal crutches. She fixed the towel around his waist so he could propel himself across the cold bedroom and drop the crutches next to the bed, falling into the warm sheets with a contented sigh. "You didn't light the fire?" he asked as Emma snuggled into his armpit and stretched her forearm across his damp stomach.

"Couldn't be bothered," she sighed. "Going to bed without you was horrid. It felt soulless like in the old days on the estate, cuddling into my sleeping bag with ice on the inside of the windows."

Rohan kissed the top of her head. "I thought Nicky would take my place. I didn't want to disturb you both so figured I'd shower in the bathroom down there. I smelled paint and wanted to see how the room turned out. I opened the bedroom door and flicked on the light and Freda sat up in the bed like Poseidon."

Emma snorted. "Poseidon with hair curlers and teeth in a glass on the night stand?"

"Don't remind me," Rohan groaned.

"Freda's always telling me this house was a hot bed of affairs and bed hopping in its time. Your nude full frontal was probably the most exciting thing that's happened to her in years." Emma sniffed, her voice sad. "Nicky didn't sleep here after the guest room was finished. Freda moved in there and he abandoned me. She's due to go home tomorrow anyway."

"Nicky's growing up so fast." Rohan shifted on his side and stroked Emma's cheek. Moonlight from the open curtains filtered through the leaded windows and bathed her in a silvery glow. Rohan's fingers strayed to Emma's stomach, feeling the budding swell of his child. "Best he does it before this little one comes along." His fingers drifted inside the elastic of Emma's pyjamas, pushing the fabric away from her sensitive skin. "*Ya lyublyu tebya, Mrs Andreyev.*"

Emma's breath came as a tiny puff as she groaned and whispered, "I love you too."

CHAPTER EIGHT

"Nice of ya to walk yer wee friend home." His lyrical Irish voice made Emma turn sharply on the path through the park, her fright gravitating quickly to annoyance.

"Stop doing that!" she exclaimed. "I'm pregnant, you idiot!"

"Aye so y'are. Didn't I see the test before anyone else, ya stroppy wee mare?"

"Only because you spend your life poking in other people's rubbish!" Emma turned back to her walk and strode towards the school building which rose over the perimeter wall like a sentinel.

"That's not a nice greeting, so," the man grumbled. "I look out for ya and that's how you repay me?"

Emma spun round and faced the tall Irishman, fire threatening in her expression. "Christopher Dolan, your job for Anton is done. I'm safe and happily married to his brother like he always wanted. We're having a baby and I'm renovating the house Anton gifted us. Everything's fine. You can live your life knowing you did a great job. Nicky and I will live happily ever after; thanks to you."

Christopher Dolan's dark brow furrowed and his eyes looked troubled. "Gee, Em! That's rough! A man gives a few years of his life looking after a mate's sister-in-law and that's yer greetin'? I thought better of ya."

"Are you in trouble?" Emma took a few steps towards him, his doleful expression uncharacteristic of the Irish charmer he usually played. She sounded concerned.

"No more than usual." The classic Christopher Dolan smile broke through the sense of rejection and he shrugged with his familiar brand of nonchalance. "But you are."

"Pardon?" Emma eyed him with suspicion and cast around, looking for an assumed threat. The last time Christopher ambushed her in the street she ended up as a hostage.

"No, not from me." He held his hand up to placate her but Emma moved backwards, mistrust in her eyes.

"Sod off, Christopher. If there's trouble, it'll be following you!"

His long strides easily brought him level with her and he pulled on Emma's arm to slow and spin her into his chest. He held her there in a grip she found impossible to break. Her knee in his groin bent him like an envelope and Emma laughed and stepped back. "What? You didn't expect Rohan to give me self-defence lessons after your last little stunt? Ah well, never underestimate an Andreyev."

Christopher muttered something unrepeatable and Emma watched as a line of dribble oozed from his mouth and trailed down to the floor. She had a moment of guilt, quickly extinguished by his next sentence. "Emma, if you won't listen, I'll talk to Nicky."

"You leave my son alone!" She raised her voice to a shout and her face held fury. "You're messing with his head again and I asked you to stop. You promised!"

Christopher stood up suddenly and Emma's eyes widened as she took a step backwards out of range. "I never promised that, Em. Anton asked me to look after youse as long as I could. That's what I'm doing."

"No!" Emma's face screwed up into an unattractive pout and she sounded like a whining teenager. "We have Rohan now. Your job's done."

The Irishman sneered. "That eejit? He'll get youse all killed, so he will."

"Don't be ridiculous!" Impatience flitted across Emma's pretty features. "He's home now."

"Aye, isn't he just! Did he not tell ya where he'd been, Em? Wise up, woman! He didn't come home last night; he's been in town a few days, love. He doesn't keep ya very up to date with his affairs, does he?"

"Affairs?" The colour drained from Emma's face and regret moved across Christopher's brown eyes like a scudding cloud. Her mouth opened and closed again and he moved towards her with care as though approaching a dangerous snake. Emma's body was rigid as the tall Irishman enfolded her in his strong arms and kissed the top of her head.

"Sorry. I didn't want youse to find out like this."

Emma closed her eyes as her jaw worked furiously and she tried to quell the sickness in the pit of her stomach. Her voice was muffled as she spoke into the front of Christopher's jacket. "By 'in town,' do you mean he's been here in Market Harborough for a few days?"

"Aye." Christopher's voice sounded hushed. "Sorry, Em. He's not bein' honest with ya."

The sickness rose into her gullet and she forced herself not to retch. Christopher's words berated her for her endless stupidity in trusting Rohan, when she promised herself at sixteen she'd trust no man ever again. "What shall I do?" She lifted her head to look up at Christopher and her eyes filled with tears which formed a glossy sheen over her huge brown eyes.

"Ach, I don't know, so I don't," Christopher soothed. "He's been at his old place on Newcombe Street. He arrived a few nights ago, a bit banged up. The lights are still on, Em. Somebody's living there with him."

"I feel sick." Emma swallowed bile and clung to a handful of Christopher's coat. "He left over two weeks ago, hardly rang home and now you're saying he's been with someone at his old house for a few days before coming home to Nicky and me?" She took a deep breath. "I'll kill him!"

"Aye well, call me when it's done and I'll get rid of the body." Christopher smiled at her and Emma tried to reciprocate, finding she couldn't manage it. A watery sun chose that moment to warm the park and kiss Emma's cheeks. She lifted her face and closed her eyes.

"I don't know what to do." Her heart felt heavy in her chest, making her feel like she needed to lie down on the muddy grass and sob to relieve the pressure. "Freda wanted to go home today because she felt in the way; I wish she'd stayed." Emma bit her lip.

"Na," Christopher reassured her. "Best do yer dirty washing without an audience. And that auld woman would've killed him for yer, so she would."

Emma nodded. "Probably." She inhaled and ran a hand over her face. "I need to go. School finishes soon." Her legs felt leaden as she took a step back from Christopher's comforting presence. He nodded and let her go. Emma took an uncertain, tottering pace towards the school gate and then looked back, all courage and confidence gone from her eyes. "Christopher, if I need you, how will I find you?"

He smiled and tilted his head sideways. "I'll find ya,

Em. Don't be worryin' about that." His brown eyes narrowed with concern and he shook his head. "Em, I tried to tell ya not to let him leave, sweetheart."

Emma turned away and continued her wooden steps towards the school gate, the memory of the text messages clanging in her head. *'Don't let him leave.'* But she did let Rohan leave and now it seemed she would have to live with the consequences.

CHAPTER NINE

"Where's Daddy?" Nicky's question filled Emma's heart with irritation.

"I don't know, Nicky. Please can you carry your own bag for once?"

"It's heavy. I painted a brick for you. Where's Freda?"

Emma sighed in frustration. "Painting a brick sounds exciting but I need you to carry it, babe, please. Freda's scooter arrived and she wanted to go home and try it out. She might come back at the weekend."

Nicky wrinkled his nose in disappointment and Emma gritted her teeth, feeling all control in her life ebbing away. "Won't I do? I worked at your school this morning, spent the afternoon settling Freda at home and then walked back to pick you up? Isn't that enough?"

Nicky looked up at his mother and bit his lip, nodding his head but keeping his mouth sensibly closed. Emma retrieved the large Mercedes from the car park reserved for staff and set off home, desperately wanting to scrape the expensive paintwork along every bush lining the narrow exit. She resisted only because her son watched through wide eyes, sensing her turmoil without understanding. He touched her leg as she pulled out onto the Northampton Road. "Please may we have take-away food tonight? To celebrate Daddy coming home."

Emma grimaced and gritted her teeth to prevent the

snarky comment escaping. There was nothing to celebrate if Rohan arrived in town days earlier. It made a mockery of her son's easy trust and the notion enraged her further. "Not tonight, baby. I've got microwave dinners in the freezer. Why don't we have one each and snuggle in front of the fire?"

"What about Daddy? He prefers proper food." Nicky's tone sounded petulant and Emma floored the accelerator to avoid answering. She yearned for violent, engine damaging revs but got only the characteristic purr as the heavy car met her needs. "Careful, Mummy!" Nicky's fingers gripped the bottom of his booster seat in fear as the car jerked under Emma's angry grip on the steering wheel.

They conducted the rest of the journey to Wingate Hall in silence, the atmosphere in the car heavy filled with emotional turbulence. Nicky was edgy and frightened and Emma sullen and uncommunicative. She abandoned the car in front of the main entrance, leaving it strewn wonkily across the gravel and slammed the driver's door as though it was Rohan's head in the gap. Nicky got himself out of the car and ran to the front door, ringing the bell and eyeing his mother nervously.

Emma retrieved his bag, leaning into the foot well to reach for the various objects which had spewed out. Winter darkness shrouded her, but in the light from the interior bulb she held his artwork in her hand and fought tears.

Blue paint decorated the house brick, covering its redness with an appealing lavender tone. Nicky had written 'Home' in wobbling script and drawn five distinguishable characters, with large round heads and stick bodies. A huge orange person with sticking up hair was Rohan, a fat green one was Emma, a smaller purple one was Nicky and a blob at their feet was presumably the baby. A large black dog-shaped Farrell was plopped at the other end near the 'H' for 'Home,' looking as though he'd been through a tumble dryer. Emma couldn't stop the tears leaking down her cheeks, wishing they would expunge the orange Rohan with ease. She ran her finger across the surface of the brick, cursing the industrious Mrs Clarke who made the children varnish their artwork and the tears came off in her hand, having done no damage.

Emma wiped her hand over her face and extracted herself from the car. She slammed the door, activated the central locking and skipped up the front steps. "Hi, Farrell." She stroked the dog's fluffy head as he thrust his nose against her thigh, desperate for acknowledgement.

Rohan held the door open for her and bowed his head for the expected kiss, looking hurt when Emma dodged out of the way. She strode into the huge reception hall, dropping Nicky's bags at her feet. The heels of her boots clacked on the polished oak floorboards and without waiting for Rohan to lock up, she bolted for the staircase and ran up it. "I made a roast, *devotchka*," he called up the stairs. "Don't be long."

"I'm not your bloody *girl!*" Emma hissed under her breath as anger replaced the devastation.

A cosy fire burned in the grate and the bedroom felt warm as Emma stripped off her outdoor coat and shoes. The squashy four poster bed which once held the entwined bodies of Lord and Lady Ayers called to Emma, offering comfort and security. The newly renovated walnut wood shone in the orange glow of the fire and she slipped from her clothes and into her pyjamas without considering how early it was. Her tired body sank into the new mattress and she turned on her side and willed herself to relax.

"Daddy maked a lovely chicken wiv roast potatoes and nice things. There's hardly any nasty veggies. You comin' down to the kitchen for some?" Nicky's tiny hand stroked Emma's forehead with gentle motions and he leaned in and put his face sideways on the pillow. "You sick, Mummy? Will I get help for you?"

Emma swallowed and shook her head. "No, I'm fine, baby. Don't worry. I'm just tired. Please tell your father I'm not hungry. I want to be left alone to sleep."

"Ok." Nicky gave her a beautiful smile and kissed her forehead, leaving a wet patch which she left there as a reminder. He skipped from the room in his socks and closed the door behind him, condemning Emma to her misery. The urge to scream and shout and kick everything around her was overwhelming, but she maintained control although it seemed impossible. Hot tears soaked her pillow and she laid trembling fingers over the tiny swell of her stomach, sensing the child within the walls of her womb. Even in her distress she felt the flutter of movement and cried harder, knowing it was an awful moment to experience her baby's first kicks.

Exhaustion released her into sleep despite her attempts to resist it and Emma awoke feeling overly hot a few hours later. The room was in darkness and the fire low in the grate, but she heard Rohan's steady breathing in the bed. As realisation flooded back, Emma stifled a groan of misery and resisted the urge to attack the sleeping man next to her. Questions filtered past her inner vision like a conveyor belt of confusion and she abandoned her marriage bed, padding along the corridor to her son's room.

Nicky snored like a dock worker after far too many pints at the pub and Emma realised she would find only sleeplessness and distraction in his bed. Needing peace, she wandered to Lady Celia's old room, guided by the moonlight which poured through the ornate skylights and lit the upper floor with a silvery glow. Freda stripped the sheets early that morning before school and the duvet looked pristine white in the big bed. Emma smiled at the memory of Freda's childish enjoyment of the room. "I feel like the queen in this bedroom," the old lady giggled.

"You don't have to leave just because Rohan's home," Emma had said, touching the gnarled hand. "You're welcome to stay."

Freda laughed. "Oh, my darling girl. I got a good view of that body he keeps under his clothes and if I stay, I'll feel compelled to seduce him."

The women giggled and stripped the sheets, piling them in the laundry for Emma to wash later. "God help me?" Emma pleaded as the echo of Freda's mirth faded. She begged the deity who surely hated her. "I've screwed up again," she sniffed into the empty room.

The covers were chilly and uncomfortable and the bare mattress unwelcoming as Emma slid beneath the duvet. She pulled it over her head and snuggled down, driven back into sleep by the need to safeguard the health of her unborn child. She woke with the memory of a past conversation in her head, banishing sleep for good. In her mind, Nicky bounced in front of her, repeating the phone message from Harley Man. His garbled case of Chinese Whispers righted itself with awful clarity as Emma unscrambled the real point of the phone call. *The Contessa is loose.*

Emma clapped her hand over her lips and pressed in the miserable moan of realisation. The ethereal Chinese woman floated past her inner vision in her slender, flowy dress as she purred at Rohan through a beautician's trademark lips. Emma accused Rohan of liking her once and he seemed appalled then. But Christopher's message was clear. The Contessa hadn't died in the Scottish fire. She was loose and having an affair with Rohan underneath Emma's gullible nose.

CHAPTER TEN

"Mmmnn, you smell good." Rohan's strong arms enfolded Emma as she wrapped herself in a towel, her body still steaming from the shower.

"Get off, Rohan." Her voice was sharp and she tried not to cringe under his touch.

His perceptive blue eyes narrowed in confusion and he put his hands over her wrists and stopped her frantic movements. "Did I do something wrong?"

Emma snorted with a sarcastic laugh. "How should I know? I'm not your keeper!"

"Why are you being like this?" Rohan took a step back, the metal of his prosthetic leg jarring and ugly against his perfectly sculpted flesh. "Why did you sleep in the guest room?"

"Questions, questions," Emma sighed, pulling the towel tighter around herself. "You expect the truth whilst dishing out lies."

"You're talking in riddles!" Annoyance lit Rohan's face, suspicion oozing from every pore.

"Well, you'd know, wouldn't you?" she snapped. "I'm getting dressed now, *durak*. And you're not watching me!"

"I'm not *stupid!*" He looked so hurt, Emma experienced a pang of regret. It made her spiteful.

"No, but *I* am, aren't I, Rohan? Real stupid!"

"I don't think so." His voice was quiet and full of authority. Emma's husband waved a hand in supplication and he backed away, leaving her to her dissatisfied fury and closing the bathroom door behind him.

Emma rested her forehead against the mirror and watched the condensation run in front of her face. With a sigh she closed her eyes, feeling like a bomb ready to detonate. She needed to talk to Rohan about Christopher's accusation but the words wouldn't formulate themselves properly in her brain. If she tried, she knew her anger would trip the words up on her tongue and make her say things she didn't mean.

Emma dressed in the bedroom, hearing Rohan's voice rumbling in Nicky's room across the hall. When he came in to dress, she avoided looking at the soft tanned skin on his washboard abdominal muscles or the way his boxer shorts nestled along the line of his hips. She fled from the room and busied herself downstairs with toast she couldn't eat and a cup of tea which went down the white, Belfast sink.

Nicky appeared with Rohan and the smile died on the man's lips at her deliberate avoidance of his presence. "Come on, Nicky. I need to get in early today." Emma snatched the car keys from the kitchen table and bounced them noisily in her hand, slipping them into her pocket.

"But I haven't had breakfast." Nicky shot her a look of pure indignation.

"I'll stop at the shop on the corner and get you a pie." Emma stared at her son, willing him to comply.

Nicky's face broke into an innocent grin. "What, like a real pie? In a wrapper and everything?" His eyes lit up and Emma choked back a sob.

"Yes, but we have to go now."

"I've never had one of them pies," Nicky informed Rohan. "I always wanted one but Mum never had enough pennies." He bounced along the hallway to grab his shoes and bag, Farrell running next to him and waving his curly black tail like a flag. Emma heard the wail of dismay. "I forgot to do my homework!"

Breathing through pursed lips, Emma chalked up yet another failure to Rohan and strode across the room. She almost made it through the open doorway before her husband's strong forearm blocked the way, his fingers resting on the doorframe in front of her face. "Talk to me!" His tone was sharp and Emma cringed, feeling the explosion too near the surface to risk opening her mouth. She put her head down and worked her jaw so hard it made her teeth ache. Rohan's presence was a heady mix of masculinity and strength and Emma gripped her resolve and stayed silent. "Fine!" He removed his hand. "This is not like you, Em. Perhaps I will find the answers for myself." Stress made his Russian accent leak through his words like a latent threat and Emma grimaced and made a run for the front of the house.

Nicky whimpered about his forgotten homework, his shoes laced onto the wrong feet as he hopped around on the doormat. "I'm gonna get so done!" he grumbled. "She'll sit on me and I'll never be seen again!"

"Stop exaggerating!" Emma snapped, grappling around in her coat pocket. "Where's the bloody car keys? I had them here."

"You mean these?" Rohan appeared behind them, a look of amusement in his eyes as he dangled the keys from his right hand. Emma looked from the shiny metal to the glint in Rohan's blue eyes and glared at him.

"You stole them from my pocket?" His simple

distraction technique made her blood boil.

"I can't steal what belongs to me." The statement pushed the last button required for Emma's detonation and she stamped her foot in fury.

"Oh yeah, sorry. It's your car, isn't it? Your car, my house. I won't use your car and you get out of my house."

Nicky and Rohan stared after her, aghast as Emma set off through the front door and down the steps, trying not to slip in the heavy frost underfoot. She felt the boys' unease and blew smoke into the cold air, raging inside and swearing to herself like a foul mouthed navvy.

"Mummy!" Nicky called after her, distress evident in his voice. "Come back!"

Emma halted while his pattering footsteps caught her up. Her breath came in shallow hitches, not enough to oxygenate her body and her head swum with a lightness which was eerie in the early morning gloom. "We'll catch the bus," she panted and after a quick glance back at Rohan, Nicky honoured an old allegiance and sided with Emma.

His tiny hand in hers felt cold and Emma bit her lip and tried not to cry. Freezing fog shrouded the tree lined driveway and they reached the end as Rohan pulled up alongside. He wound the window down and matched the car to their walking speed. "Get in the bloody car, Em!"

She turned her face away, her body rigid with pain and stubbornness. "No thanks. I'll buy my own and use that." She heard Rohan blow out through his lips in frustration. Nicky dropped his bag in the tension and Emma bent and retrieved it, glaring at her son as the swear word tumbled from his lips.

"I told you, I'd help you choose a good car," came Rohan's voice again and Emma felt something ping in her chest.

"Yes, but I don't want you to!" she shouted. "You told me a lot of things but none of it was true. I don't want anything from you!" Her lips curled back in a sneer as she pointed back at the manor house squatting on the hill like a guilty eavesdropper. "Please be out of my house before I get home tonight, or I'll burn it!"

"Emma!" Rohan yanked the handbrake on and stepped out of the car. In his confusion he forgot to take it out of gear and it lurched forwards and stalled. The action threw him against the side of the vehicle and a look of pain crossed his face as his leg twisted in the prosthesis. "What's wrong with you?" He spoke through gritted teeth and Nicky looked up at his mother, his face full of misery.

"What's happening, Mummy?"

Emma's poor parenting opened up before her like a void, judging her for involving her son in her relationship mess. Her memory lied to her, telling her it was easier when it was just the two of them, wrapped up neatly in each other without strife. It glossed over her poverty and the awfulness of her circumstances, offering retreat and false security through omission. Emma Andreyev compounded her crimes, heaping on the final indignity as she turned towards her stricken son and unloaded. "Daddy lied to us about when he really got home, baby. He'd been in Harborough for a few days before he deigned to visit us. It appears he has someone else at his old house whom he'd rather spend time with; a certain attractive, well dressed lady. That's what's happening, sweetheart." Her smile was watery and ineffective and Nicky peered round her with a stare of accusation aimed at his father's astounded face.

"Dolan!" Rohan spat his adversary's name with bile and shook his head. "Emma, get in the car and I'll tell you what you need to know. Please?"

"No, thanks!" Emma stuck her head in the air, infuriated with the hot tear which coursed down her left cheek. She swiped it away, registering it as a betrayal and heard Nicky sniffling next to her. She tugged at the child's arm and set off down the last few metres of the driveway.

"Emma! You're upsetting Nicky!"

It was the greatest of insults to Emma's fragile heart and crossed a line beyond which there was no recovery. She let go of Nicky's hand and stalked back to the vehicle, her face ablaze with rage. "Don't you dare criticise my parenting!" she yelled at the top of her voice. "You don't have the *right!*" She screamed the last word and swung the bag in her hand. It hit the passenger door with a deafening clang and a long dent appeared in the bodywork as the brick nestling in her son's homework wrought vengeance for her.

Rohan stood with his hands on the roof of the car and looked at his wife with sadness in his stunning blue eyes. As Nicky broke into a full scale wail, Emma hurried back to him and let them out of the metal gates and onto the wide rural road. They navigated the fast cars of another rush hour and arrived at the bus stop on the other side, both tearful and devastated, gripping each other for comfort.

At school, Nicky didn't want to go into class and Mrs Clarke looked at Emma with a raised eyebrow. Emma's tears hovered so close to the surface, she managed a tiny, pitiful smile and the kind teacher patted her hand and distracted her son. "Right Nicky," Mrs Clarke said, "you can help me wipe the blackboard."

Emma hid in the ladies' toilets and sobbed her heart out, pressing a fist into her mouth to muffle the noise.

"Emma? What's wrong? Mrs Clarke said you're upset. Why aren't you getting the photos ready?" Freda's voice sounded tinny in the worn bathroom and Emma blew her nose without elegance. "Is that you crying?" The old lady tapped on the door with her fragile knuckles. "I rode my scooter here. I want to show it to you."

Emma sniffed loudly and dried her face on toilet paper. It was such poor quality it stuck to parts of her face. It was a puffy eyed and sweaty Emma who emerged from the stall, running her hands over her cheeks to dislodge the tissue. Freda knitted her brow at the state of her and drew her into a gentle embrace. "Dear girl, what on earth's happened?"

Emma shook her head, knowing if she started she wouldn't be able to stop. She inhaled deeply and took stock of herself in the mirror, shocked at what her crying had produced. "Please don't make me talk about it here?" she begged. "Maybe another day?"

Freda smiled. "Of course, dear." She stroked Emma's heaving shoulder and stepped across to the basin, running the cold tap with vigour. "Let's douse those frog eyes with some water, shall we? Or you'll terrify poor Sam." The old woman's ministrations were tender as she dabbed at Emma's face with a wet paper towel. Her easy maternalism spoke to something deep in Emma's heart and as fast as Freda cooled one eye, the other leaked painful tears.

Freda cocked her head like a little bird and smiled

at her, patting her cheek with compassion in her eyes. "You remind me of myself," she crooned. "The day I learned Geoffrey Ayers wouldn't be coming home from the war. I decided when he returned I'd claim him as my father and social rules be damned. I didn't want the grandeur of Wingate Hall or any riches he could offer; just my father's arms around me, telling me everything would be ok." Freda's eyes took on a faraway look, the pupils dilating as she entered another time and place in her mind. "I cried so hard I thought I'd break. Years later I watched a tsunami devastate a small town and it reminded me of that moment of pure sorrow." She looked up and focussed on Emma. "Is that how you feel?"

Emma took stock of herself and shook her head. "No. When my father died I felt like I couldn't breathe and when Rohan went back to the army and left me pregnant with Nicky, it was terrible. My tsunami moment was when Lucya died after taking me in and mothering me. Nicky and I were her whole world and she just dropped dead. I felt abandoned. I couldn't see a way out; everything seemed too dark to see. But now? Now I'm just angry and feel very stupid." Emma swallowed and felt the agonised hitch of her chest as her lungs spasmed. The deep breath got stuck half way and she repeated the exercise. "Thanks Freda, for the clarity. I've been through worse and survived." Emma squared her shoulders and splashed water on her face, running the wetness through her dark hair to tame the rampant curls.

"Good." Freda nodded. "Let's name and scan some photos. I have a date just after elevenses."

"A date?" Emma sniffed and used the bottom of her blouse to pat her face dry. Amusement lit her dark eyes. "I don't think I'll allow it."

Freda simpered and did a wobbly pirouette. "You'll have to run after my scooter to stop me."

Emma laughed, her heart lighter at the realisation she would live to fight another day. Rohan's infidelity was debauched, but not disastrous. Anton made sure of Emma's future security in his clever legal wording which bound everything into a trust. Despite their marriage, Rohan could take nothing financial from her; not that he needed it.

Stepbrother and brother-in-law in life, Anton watched Emma's stubborn poverty with dismay as she shook her head at his offers of help. In death, he provided security, ensuring she always had a home. '*From Russia, with love*,' his will decreed and Emma heaved another sigh, this time of relief.

The women poured over the sepia faces of teachers and pupils long since gone and Emma became engrossed in her task. Time ticked along as Freda filled in names she remembered, writing in her copperplate script with pencil and a notepad. "I can't recall them all, dear," she apologised, using a magnifying glass to stare at a dark eyed face sitting along from her younger self. She pulled on a pair of white cotton gloves and pointed to a name in the register of admission. The binding was fragile and the pages yellowing and age speckled. She tapped her index finger. "I think that's her name. I remember it being an unusual name for the time; Charity Gillespie. Yes, that's sounding right." Freda sighed and leaned back in the rickety seat. Removing her glasses, she rubbed at her eyes. "I haven't been much use, Emma. I'm disappointed with myself."

Emma flipped her hands out of the white gloves

and reached across, running her fingers along Freda's upper arm. "Don't be silly, Freda! I wouldn't have known how old half these photos were without you! Heaps of them aren't dated and nobody else would be able to guess the year by the height of the ivy growing up the building. I think we've got most of them named and dated thanks to you. Hopefully nobody will mind if we've messed up the sequence of a few."

"Probably more than a few." Freda smirked. She turned and gripped Emma's wrist in surprisingly strong fingers. "Have you told anyone yet?"

The colour drained from Emma's face and she shook her head. "I know I should. I just don't know how."

"It has to be done, my love. And soon. Are you afraid they'll end your contract?"

"No." Emma shook her head. "A few months ago it would have been devastating to lose the income but things are different now. Anton's gift changed everything. I could volunteer but it occurred to me, you might be grateful for the wage if I could persuade them."

Freda smiled and her eyes filled with tears. "Fancy you thinking of me. You're such a precious child. My John left me properly provided for, but thank you for your kind thought." She knitted her brow and looked Emma in the eye. "Just because you have security doesn't mean your time becomes valueless, Emma. You deserve to be paid for the hours you do. I'm different. I'm a ninety year old woman with no place else to be and my time is my gift to them. If you want to help them, tell Mr Dalton the truth about his celebration and if they want to continue, perhaps make an anonymous donation to help them get underway."

"That's a good idea," Emma nodded. She looked at Freda, her eyes narrowed. "Why do you say that; about time being valueless?"

Freda rolled her eyes. "Experience, my dear. I once refused payment for something I was entitled to. I worked the hours and then denied the pay. It caused great awkwardness and I sensed an inexplicable loss of status, even though my motives were good. I don't know what they used my wage to buy, but it didn't go where I hoped it might. Somehow I became lesser because of it. When we ran out of supplies, instead of using the unspent salary to purchase them, everyone turned to me and expected another radical act of generosity as though I was their provider and not God. No, Emma. You earn it so you take it. If you give it back afterwards, do so and let it go. Knowing how a donation is used often invites offence."

Emma nodded and let the advice sink into her brain. Freda stood and waited until her old bones settled enough to walk. "I must be off. I want to primp my hair before my date." She winked at Emma.

"Who's your date?" Emma asked, feeling the unquenchable need to know.

"Oh, he's just a lonely old man. He won't get my money and he certainly won't get into my underwear. John was my soulmate and nobody else comes even close. This gentleman's someone new to thrash at Scrabble and that's enough to be going on with."

Emma walked Freda to the front entrance and saw her safely onto the bright red disabled scooter. "What did you do?" she asked as Freda turned the key and the little motor sprang to life. "What wage did you refuse?"

"I taught in Nepal at a poor school in the rural villages. At first they were insulted by my refusal to take their wage and then they learned to take advantage. I became a free resource to be used and abused; my time and skills held no value anymore. When John decided enough was enough and I quit, the little school closed. They enjoyed ten years of my free time and stopped budgeting for a teacher. It meant they couldn't employ anyone after me and I was too burnt out to stay. So I did them great harm with my generosity and ruined something good."

"No, they ruined it, not you!" Emma's indignation made her forehead crease and Freda patted her hand with mittened fingers.

"Emma, remember this, child. The best things in life are not free. Someone always bears the cost and sometimes not willingly. Every action has a consequence." With a wave of her hand she raced through the open front gate, her wavy hair billowing from underneath her woolly hat.

Emma pulled the heavy metal gate closed and heard the catch click shut. She bit her lip and steeled herself to take Freda's advice. *For every action there is a consequence.* "Yes, Rohan Andreyev!" she hissed into the wind. Her mind strayed to the person who hid the plaque and misled whole generations about the age of the school. It was time for Emma to do what she did best; research.

CHAPTER ELEVEN

Rohan didn't come home that night or the next. Twice he tried to see Emma at school and both times she closed the office door in his face. "If you keep turning up here, I'll ask Miriam in the front office to call the police," she stated with her lips pulled thin over her teeth and her eyes flashing with danger. Emma was glad Freda didn't see either altercation, knowing she'd be mortified by their break up.

Freda was away for a few days, razzing around town on her new scooter with the gentleman friend with matching wheels, so fortunately only Sam was present when Emma issued her ultimatum for the third time. "I mean it, Rohan. I've nothing to say to you. Until you're prepared to tell the truth, don't bother coming to see me."

Sam watched in confusion as Emma gave a wooden smile and closed the office door behind her, keeping the men apart and attempting to do her dirty washing without an audience. "You need to leave!" she hissed in the tiny corridor outside the toilets, Rohan's strong chest just millimetres from her face. Emma groaned as a junior class of eight-year-olds trotted past the end of the corridor on their way to a singing assembly, fortunately bouncing straight ahead without seeing the couple standing stiffly apart. "Please go!" Emma repeated, her words hissing through her teeth.

"We're not done, Em. And you know I can't tell you everything about my work, so this isn't fair." His voice was low and deep, rumbling seductively as he leaned against the door frame. Emma felt tiny in comparison, Rohan's body far too close. He reached for a curl. "At least let me leave you the car. The bus takes too long and Nicky hates it."

"That's nothing to do with you!" Emma bit, smiling at an infant who arrived at the sink next to Sam's office and dumped a container of dirty paint water in it.

"Hello, Miss Harrington," the child said, her blonde pigtails swinging as nosiness made her walk into the wall.

"Hello, Keisha," Emma replied. "I hope there's as much paint on your paper as on your face."

The child giggled and skipped off along the corridor, her pleated skirt swinging around her spindly legs. Emma leaned sideways and righted the paint pot, stopping the brown liquid from dripping down the side of the porcelain and onto the floor. It pivoted on the top of a mountain of dirty palettes, brushes and plastic cups, waiting for the classroom assistant to wash them with her bevy of enthusiastic but messy helpers. Emma fought the desire to do it herself, giving her an excuse to turn her back on Rohan.

His strong fingers on the top of Emma's arm swung her easily and she felt her back hit the wall with a tiny thud. Rohan's tall body blocked her from view as he leaned into her. Emma closed her eyes and resisted his scent, which tumbled through her head invoking memories of loving and being loved by him. His breath smelled of mint as it stroked her cheek and lips, his face close. Rohan's lips twitched and his blue eyes danced, vibrant and full of challenge. "Miss Harrington?" he asked. "You've already abandoned the name I gave you?" Rohan overshadowed Emma physically and emotionally and she sensed it was deliberate.

The back of her head bumped the wall as she looked up at him, her brown eyes narrowed in anger. It was pointless telling him she signed her contract as Emma Harrington, penned in the days before Rohan reinstated their marriage. Only Mr Dalton used her married name because only he knew it. "So what?" she said instead, her voice shaking. Rohan's proximity confused her, his sexuality demanding a reaction and her temper readying itself to deliver an alternative. "Married people share things, Rohan. They share their dreams and desires, their troubles and their truths. All we've ever shared is a bed and a son. It's not enough. Go back to your secrets and lies and leave us out of it."

"You knew what I was." His voice was lilting as Rohan's steady hand stroked the soft skin below Emma's bottom lip, soothing her temper despite her need to maintain it. His calculated touch was always timed to reduce her resolve to rubble with little effort. Rohan's eyes never left her face, sparkling like jewels as he sensed her weakness. His lips dropped to hers and Emma turned her face away, feeling the heat of Rohan's mouth on her neck. As he pinched the skin between his teeth she knew that was his target all along, the sacred erogenous zone between her shoulder and jaw.

Emma punched Rohan in the ribs and he snuffed a laugh. "This is a school corridor!" she hissed. "I'm already losing my job, but I guess you'd enjoy seeing me robbed of everything, wouldn't you?"

"No, Em! Of course I wouldn't! Why are you losing your job?" Rohan's fingers reached for her face again but the spell was broken. Emma shoved at him with both hands and her whole body weight, succeeding when he took a step back. "I love you!" he said in English, pointing his index finger at her heart. "Nothing changes that, ever."

"Yeah, except another woman in a house in Harborough. That changes a few things. I'm not into polygamy so it's a deal breaker, Rohan. Go away, leave me alone and let me work out what to do with the rest of my life." Emma exhaled through pursed lips and Rohan's eyes widened.

"You wouldn't sell up and move?" he asked, regaining the tiled distance between their feet. "This will work out, I promise. Don't do anything stupid."

"There we go again; *durak*, that little word which sums up all my dealings with you. I'll do what I like just as you have. Go away, Rohan. Last warning!"

Emma turned and fell through the office door as Sam emerged with his ever present screwdriver and a small coat peg. "Everything ok?" he asked, glancing from her to Rohan. Tears pricked in Emma's eyes as she saw the determination in his soft brown eyes and the fingers of his left hand ball into a fist. Sam's body language spoke of willingness to defend her honour, but the determination in his eyes faded to fear as he contemplated the tall Russian. Rohan's face channelled storm clouds and pure anger.

"Everything's fine," Emma said, touching Sam's arm. She closed the door behind her and leaned against it, every nerve ending in her body giving off distress signals. Her marriage had crumbled at the first hurdle and her job followed it down the same rocky path. "Maybe I *should* sell up and go," she breathed, the idea at the forefront of her mind.

The costly, beautiful plans for Wingate Hall fluttered through her inner vision, the sense of purpose it gave her to restore its dignity pulling her back from thoughts of flight. Emma sighed. "Fine! We'll co-exist in this very small town for now," she muttered to herself, knowing how hard it would be to avoid the Russian.

Sam left his computer logged in and Emma trawled the internet, looking for something to help her research. Her neat script filled the pad next to her, offering directions and places to go next in her quest. When Sam's battered telephone trilled on the desk, Emma jumped and knocked over the dregs of Sam's cold coffee.

"Drat!" Emma exclaimed into the handset, mopping frantically with one of his work cloths. Shoe polish spread across the desk, making a black, muddy mess on the old pine surface.

"Oh, hi Emma. This is Miriam from the office. I've got a lady from a church in Leicester asking for you. Is this a bad time?"

"No, sorry. It's fine. I just knocked Sam's coffee everywhere. Put her through and thanks."

"Did your partner find you?" Miriam asked, her voice tentative. "He left the flowers with me, but wanted to see you first. He's gorgeous."

"Flowers?" Emma's voice sounded flat.

"Yeah, men are predictable, aren't they?" Miriam laughed. "From forgetting to put the bins out to having extra marital sex, they think flowers and chocolates produce instant forgiveness." Emma's silence made the secretary nervous. "Not that I'm suggesting he's had...well, shall I put this woman through?"

"Yes, please." Emma's words came out in a rush. "Thanks. Bloody hell, I forgot it was bin day!" The lack of a vehicle made wheeling the rubbish along the half mile driveway impossible. She shook her head in irritation at herself and waited for Miriam to put the call through.

"Emma Harrington," she said when the connection clicked from the front office.

"Oh, Hi. This is Sharon from the parish council. You spoke to our secretary yesterday about archives held in the diocese?"

"Yes, thanks for returning my call." Emma breathed a sigh of relief.

"Well, we've searched our archives and those of St Martin's. We've also spoken to a local church historian who's familiar with the artifacts held at the cathedral in Leicester. There's no record of the vicar of St Martin's ever opening anything, let alone a school. Because Little Arden is listed as a church school, it possibly had its origins with the diocese, but that's just a title nowadays. As I'm sure you know, the government didn't get involved with mandatory schooling until 1880 but there were grants given after the Education Act of 1870. It's possible the Church grabbed one of those and built the school. There's forty schools I know of which were built under that funding. It's possible yours was one of those projects."

"Thanks," Emma replied, sounding crestfallen and resisting the urge to say too much to the helpful woman.

"Have you come across log books for the school?" The voice sounded tinny.

"Yes," Emma replied. "But the first ones are missing. They don't start until 1865."

"Do the logs mention the school opening in the January 1865 one?" Sharon asked, unable to see Emma's frustrated eye roll.

"No. They mention a delay in opening that year due to sickness. So they're little help in establishing a date. I read somewhere the vicar of St Martin's opened the school building."

"Really? I'd be interested to see that. Was it a newspaper article or an official document?"

"I can't remember," Emma lied, a little too quickly.

"Oh dear. Have you tried the district council and Leicester city council?" Sharon asked, naming sources Emma already tried.

"Yes thanks. The district council had a fire in 1965 which damaged many of their school history records and the main office in Leicester can't find anything. Little Arden was transferred from Northamptonshire to Leicestershire in 1888 and the local council didn't exist until 1894, so the only body likely to have what I need is the Diocesan."

"I wonder why the vicar of St Dionysius didn't open a new school building in his district," Sharon intoned, and Emma felt relieved at the other woman's persistence despite her own ingratitude.

"That's a great point!" she gushed. "I'll check that today. Thank you so much."

"Sorry I couldn't be of more help. Can I ask why you're researching this?"

Emma's pen stilled half way through her doodle and her body froze. "Oh, I'm making display boards for our one hundred and fiftieth celebration and I want to get my facts straight."

"Oh, of course. 1865! Our secretary recorded the year wrong. I've searched 1860 by mistake. I'll go back and look again. That might solve the mystery."

Emma thanked the enthusiastic woman and hung up, knowing she'd condemned her to another wasted afternoon in the annals of the church archives. "But then again," Emma reassured herself, "she might find something to suggest this plaque had the wrong date on it."

Cheered, Emma went back to her research. Unable to rouse anyone in the offices at St Di's by phone, she waited until lunchtime and made her escape. Sam returned just as she pulled on her long coat and sucked his bottom lip as he blocked her exit. "I would've hit him, just so ya know," he said, his thin face sincere.

"I know," Emma said with a smile, not adding he wouldn't have survived the attentions of a trained killer. "You're very sweet."

"So are you married to that Russian guy then?" Sam pressed and Emma focussed on gathering her mittens and stuffing her small purse into her pocket.

"Yes."

"But your baby's not his?"

"What?" Shocked, Emma spun round, almost overbalancing. "What do you think I am, some loose tart?"

"No!" Sam looked sorry and took a step forward, reaching out towards her. "I messed that up, sorry. I just wanted you to know if you need anything, I'm here for you." He smiled and his utter sincerity overwhelmed Emma. She swallowed and nodded, unable to speak. "I talk about you and Freda all the time at home. My missus is right keen to meet ya. We don't have much but if you need anything, you sing out. You're not on your own."

Emma nodded, feeling choked. All the money in Britain couldn't replace the support of good friends. It was an old lesson which came back to her like an electrical pulse, learned on the poverty stricken council estate in Lincoln. "Thanks, Sam," she whispered and beat a hasty retreat.

CHAPTER TWELVE

The beautiful church dominated the centre of Market
Harborough and had done for centuries. The grey
stone spire once stood above the sprawling
Rockingham forest skyline which rambled across the
area unchecked, acting as a beacon of sanctuary in a
tumultuous world. A brochure in the entrance revealed
how the original construction began in 1300 and took
twenty years to complete, the broache spire still the
most striking part of the church.

Emma closed her eyes and breathed in the sense of
the ancients around her. The peace of the building
hummed, its security resting on God and not the
foibles of men. It reminded her of her father's church,
childhood memories invoking feelings of loss which
she wasn't quick enough to dismiss.

Every movement caused a dull, thudding echo in
the cavernous nave and a group of tourists produced a
hum of stage whispers which reverberated around
Emma's head. She opened her eyes and exhaled,
releasing her breath in a controlled whoosh.

"Can I help you, dear?" An elderly woman smiled
at Emma with kindness, a set of expensive pearls
wound around her slender neck and a matching
sweater and cardigan adorning her body. She looked
like the perfect guide for the historic monument.

"I'm the archivist from Little Arden School,"
Emma began, collecting her wits and assuming a
professional air. "I'm trying to find out who the vicar

of St Di's was during the 1860s and whether he might have been invited to open the school."

"Oh yes! It's your big celebration this year, isn't it?" Bright eyes smiled from her crinkly face as the guide held out her hand. "I'm Eva Collins but my married name was Stokes." She smiled at the recognition in Emma's face.

"I've seen your photograph. You went to the school in the 1950s and your father taught the older children. That's right isn't it?"

Eva smiled with pleasure. "Spot on, dear. My, you have a good memory." Her pale skin flushed against her greying hair and she looked ethereal. She waved a hand towards the front of the church. "The vicar during that time was the Reverend Frederick Pigott and he served here from 1856 to 1865. Is that what you wanted to know?"

Emma nodded, the smile wavering on her face. She knew what was coming next and the elderly lady didn't disappoint her. "He died a few months before the school was completed. I believe he was in ill health."

"Did he have regular contact with the school?" Emma tried a different tack, attempting to establish relationship between church and school. "Where would I find that kind of information?"

Eva continued to smile but the confidence in her eyes waned with considerable speed. "I don't know, dear."

Emma pursed her lips and shifted on her feet, hearing the stone floor make a dull shushing sound under her soles. "If he had lived, do you think he'd be the logical choice to open the new building?" she asked, knowing full well the vicar was alive and well when it happened five years earlier.

"But he wasn't, so I don't know." Eva raised her eyes to heaven as though expecting to find the answer written on the vaulted ceiling. "It should have been the vicar of St Mary's in Arden. Do you know who that was?"

Emma shook her head, feeling the visit grow quickly pointless. She gazed at the mediaeval stonework and sighed.

"I'll see if any of the other ladies know," Eva said. With a nod of her head, she clip clopped down the aisle to another white haired lady cleaning the brass at the front of the church. After a whispered conversation she returned, trying not to walk on her heels and producing a peculiar shimmy in an attempt to be less clumpy. "St Mary's in Arden was already in disrepair by then, or at least on its way. Gloria doesn't think it had an incumbent."

"What about the church in Little Bowden?" Emma asked. "It's not very far away, so perhaps the vicar from there attended?"

"Ooh, I think St Di's and Little Bowden have shared a vicar for a very long time." Eva's brow knitted in concentration. "It's only a very small parish, you see. Vicar sharing's been going on for a while."

Emma tried not to roll her eyes at the spurious notion of vicar sharing. "Surely not," she said. "Back in the 1860s they must have employed their own clergy. Arden and Bowden weren't released by Northamptonshire until the late 1880s and the local district wasn't officially formed until the mid-1890s. I can't imagine Leicester taking much responsibility for the area, so that leaves the local churches running everything between them. One vicar couldn't do all of it."

"The Bishop of Lincoln was in charge, dear." Eva felt challenged and her tone became acerbic.

"Lincoln?" Even the name of her hometown filled Emma with a prickling sensation up her spine and her body tensed in response.

"Yes dear, Lincoln. For many centuries the churches of this area were included in the dioceses of Lincoln and Peterborough and under the fee of Lincoln. It was through the clemency of the Bishop of Lincoln that local clergy kept donations from the parish to fund their work."

Emma's eyes wandered around the historical feast, taking in every ancient detail with hungry appraisal. The stained glass windows looked newly restored and the interior stone was clean and free of the usual staining and debris associated with old churches. Eva pointed towards the pulpit, her face crinkling up in excitement as she dropped into her usual tourist patter. "The Sermon on the Mount carving was erected by the Reverend Johnson's brothers as an offering after they returned from India and the vicar himself donated the east window in 1860. They altered and renovated much of the church during his time. He was quite the visionary." Eva smiled and waved at the other tour guide as she bid farewell to her group of Japanese tourists. They bowed and waved with dignity after first instigating a group selfie including her and she hurried across to Eva at the earliest opportunity.

"Hello, nice to meet you. I'm Clarissa Jameson-Arden." The newcomer held out her delicate hand but the smile she offered didn't reach her eyes. Her handshake was limp like a dead fish and Emma withdrew her fingers as soon as she decently could. "I overheard you say you're the new Little Arden archivist." She searched Emma's face with cool interest.

"Yes, that's right." Emma tried not to shrink from her piercing scrutiny. "I'm researching for the display boards. With it being a Church of England school, I want to track down which church commissioned the building."

Something dangerous flitted across the woman's eyes, gone before Emma could properly register it. Her answer was perplexing. "There's no need to waste your time on such small matters. A few photos will suffice on the day. But as you're interested, St Di's commissioned the school when the Education Act came into force and the school pence was removed. Education became free for all after that and children between the ages of five and ten attended compulsorily."

Emma bit her tongue and kept her contradictions to herself. The woman had the order wrong. Something warned Emma not to correct her as the steel grey eyes bore into her face, unsmiling and robotic.

"Oh no, Clarissa," Eva interrupted. "The Education Act was passed in 1870 but school fees were collected until 1891. So for twenty six years, the school collected the school pence in fees. Then schooling became mandatory and free and the age raised to twelve or thirteen, I can't remember which." Eva tittered like a chipmunk. "They seemed to always be fiddling around with leaving ages and new bits of legislation. It gets very confusing." Eva gave a tinkling laugh which set Clarissa's teeth on edge, judging by her painful grimace.

Emma averted her gaze from the hostile stare of the

other tour guide and directed her question to Eva. "The government approved grants to churches around 1870 to encourage school building or extensions to cope with the mandatory attendance. But do you know of any other local schools built under that scheme? Apparently there's about forty according to the Leicester Diocese. Were any others here in Harborough?" A rash of schools built around the same time under the auspices of the same legislation must generate documentation somewhere. Emma just had to find it.

Eva opened her mouth to speak but Clarissa shut her down with little effort. She gathered her expensive lace jacket around her opulent blouse with wooden fingers and set her body in an aggressive stance. "The church built schools when it needed them. It didn't wait for government handouts, not in Market Harborough. That's not how we do things here!" The way she said the name of the town indicated ownership.

Emma fought the urge to bristle and name-drop her ownership of Wingate Hall. It would muddy the woman's jaded opinion of her and force early acceptance into the barred Harborough club, but Emma didn't want it, not that way. She closed her mouth instead, acknowledging Clarissa was right, in part. The church had funded the school a full decade before government legislation released the cash to improve or extend it, but the older woman wasn't to know that.

"Ok, thanks for your help." Emma smiled at Eve but couldn't keep her brow from creasing at the obvious hostility oozing from Clarissa. Feeling awkward and disinclined to explore the architectural magnificence of the ancient church beneath those angry gimlet eyes, Emma left, pulling her scarf tighter round her neck in the icy street.

At Freda's apartment, Emma was subdued and her friend noticed. "Out with it, dear," Freda demanded, folding a pleated tweed skirt into a neat square and shoving it into a plastic supermarket bag ready to go to the laundry.

"How many tweed skirts do you own?" Emma sipped her tea and watched another get squashed into the bag.

"Why? Don't you like them?" Freda paused in her haphazard packing and stared at Emma over the top of her bifocals.

"I don't mind." Emma squeezed her eyes closed and then opened them again. Freda stood with her hands on her hips, an expectant look on her lined face. "I don't. I wondered if they were the same or different."

Freda peered into the bag and pursed her lips. "I love tweed and they're all a teensy bit different. Lots of clothing interferes with one's corset nowadays but these never do."

"You don't need a corset," Emma replied, running her eyes up Freda's neat frame.

The old lady humphed. "Easy for you to say. A young thing like you won't be tripping over your breasts anytime soon!"

Emma looked at the tender swelling buds filling her bra and gave the left one a poke. "I can't guarantee that," she mused, wincing at the tightness under her blouse. "Pregnancy does weird things."

"You still haven't answered my question. Are you distressed about the plaque we found in the attic? Or something else?"

Emma exhaled, putting her tea cup on a coaster. "The plaque mostly," she lied. "I met this officious woman at St Di's. She didn't enjoy me asking questions about the school opening at all."

"Eva?" Freda said. "Little woman, very conservative but delightful? That doesn't sound like her."

"No, not her. It was another lady." Emma concentrated, trying to recall her posh sounding name. "Clarice something. If she could've forcibly ejected me from the church, she would."

"Ohhhh." Freda drew out her reply and rolled her eyes. "Clarissa Jameson-Arden. You've locked horns with the lady of the manor without realising it, dear."

"What manor? There aren't any manors, they were disbanded over a century ago and they weren't secure anyway. From what I've read, the king gifted them and took them back on a whim."

"Quite." Freda smirked. "But Clarissa would've been perfectly happy to go toe to toe with any monarch plundering her heritage."

"Jameson-Arden sounds pompous," Emma scoffed and then her eyes glazed over in thought. "It also sounds familiar."

"St Mary in Arden was the church near the railway station," Freda replied, shoving a bundle of knee high tights into the plastic bag and watching them slither through a rip in the side. "Arden's her husband's side of the family. She's a Jameson from her soles of her nasty bunions to the top of her salon coiffed curls."

"Oh, no!" Emma put her hand up to her mouth and groaned. "She's also the chairwoman for the school's board of governors. I recognise the name from my employment contract." Emma shrugged in resignation. "Ah well, she'll enjoy tearing that up."

"Don't worry about her!" Freda snorted. "She's all *piff nafafa.*" At the look of consternation on Emma's face the old lady laughed and jerked her head towards the front door, indicating she was ready to leave. "It means she's all wind and rain," Freda giggled and Emma swallowed the last of her tea and shook her head.

"You're a very wicked old lady," she told Freda.

"Oh, I know," Freda snorted. "It's what makes me such fun."

Emma hugged Freda outside the laundry room, drawing comfort from the strength of the hug.

Temperatures outside plummeted towards zero as Emma walked through the park and she drew her coat tighter around her slender body.

"Brrrrrr!" Allaine walked up behind her, slipping her arm through Emma's and smiling. "It's freezing! You should be careful walking along here. You can't afford to fall and hurt yourself." She gripped Emma's arm, supporting her as they walked together. "Where have you been? I feel like I hardly see you."

"Busy with the celebration stuff mainly." Emma pushed away thoughts of her failed marriage. "I never imagined they'd left sorting the photos and artifacts to the last minute. Freda's helped me go through most of the boxes stuffed into the attic, otherwise I'd never have everything ready in time."

Allaine pulled a face. "I'll help with displays but I'm rubbish with anything dusty. I'll cover it with snot from my allergy and you'll have to invent tales of green crusty mildew which attacks old photos kept in attics."

Emma smiled, sensing Allaine wasn't fooled by her

downcast eyes and the sad turn of her lips. Her friend eyed her with maternal expertise. "What's really wrong, Em? Rohan's back now, isn't he? I met Freda whizzing around Welland Park on her scooter the other day and she entertained most of the dog walkers with her tale of his glorious, naked return."

Emma wrinkled her nose and shook her head, affording herself a small smile at the image of Freda's storytelling. She trusted her friend not to mention Rohan's prosthetic leg, but imagined most of Market Harborough believing her tales of him being hung like an elephant. "She's a worry," Emma sighed.

"So what else can it be?" Allaine pressed and Emma dismissed the news of her impending divorce with a heavy heart, opting instead for relating her run-in with Clarissa Jameson-Arden.

"Everyone else has been lovely, but she was ripping her nightie all over the place just because I asked a few questions."

Allaine snorted at Emma's description, but agreed. "Oh yes. Our Clarissa likes the town to run as she decrees. She claims her husband's genealogy from the owners of Arden Manor and hers from the Jamesons of Leicester. She's the most stuck up person you'll find here; everyone else is relatively normal."

"Jameson. Is that a common name?" Emma asked, climbing the steps into the playground. "There's been children of that name from the start of the school's history and at least one teacher per decade, including a headmistress."

"That's them!" Allaine punched the air with her mittened hand. "All over the town like a rash. They usually push themselves into leadership roles as if it's their right and Clarissa's no exception. She was a pupil here at the school and then headmistress for a while."

"*She* was the headmistress?" Emma narrowed her eyes. "I didn't realise it was Clarissa in the photos. She had longer hair and it was a different colour."

"Yes, she dyed it red. My older children didn't like her and she wasn't popular; too much 'my way or the highway.' One minute she was retiring and the next getting herself elected onto the board of governors. In no time she'd wheedled her way into the chairperson's role. She's got siblings all over the place and her father taught here for years and his father before him. They're as miserable as sin. Will calls it 'The Jameson Effect.'"

Emma looked confused. "What's that?"

"You'd have to ask him." Allaine shrugged. "They're like a masonic lodge when they get together; all strange nods and funny handshakes. He's run across them a few times as a police officer; they get each other out of trouble and cover their own backs. Think of them as the Harborough Mafia and you won't go far wrong. If you have a problem with one of them, the rest rally around like a parasitic infestation."

"And so sayeth the biologist," Emma laughed.

"Oh, I'm so much more than that!" Allaine said, raising one eyebrow coyly. "Oh, here we go. My rug rat's got a face like a slapped bum." Emma's friend rolled her eyes as Kaylee pressed her face into her mother's coat and insisted on leaving. "See ya," Allaine said, touching Emma's arm as Nicky appeared with a face like thunder.

Emma's son greeted her with a tight lipped grimace and began a steady list of complaints which lasted through the park and onto Northampton Road. It began with his insistence he didn't have a single friend and ended with a generalised grumble about having to walk half a mile and then wait in the icy breeze for the bus. "Stop moaning!" Emma exclaimed finally, tired of the monotone which faded into one continuous bleat. "I'm doing my best, Nicky. Just give me a break for once, will you?"

"I miss Old Mo. Can we visit the estate and see our friends?" Nicky's expression changed to a futile, earnest hope. "Fat Brian would love our new house."

Emma stopped walking and whirled around, keeping hold of Nicky's hand and ignoring the look of annoyance on his face. "I know how you feel, baby. But they can't know we have a big house and money. It's complicated."

"But we shared heaps of things on the estate. We shared furniture and money. Some of the grown ups shared husbands and wives and you didn't have anyone to swap but..."

"Nicky! Sometimes in life we can't go back. We have to keep going forwards and that's how it is, whether we like it or not."

"But Old Mo thought I was only going for a couple of weeks and that was months ago. Now I've got Daddy, a house, you've got a baby in your tummy and he doesn't know any of that. What if he misses me like I miss him?"

Emma huffed and bit her lip, exasperation stiffening her body. "Nicky, I'll say this once. They'll hate us now. If we turn up with all our new stuff, they'll resent us. And worse, they'll think we owe them and they'll take until we have nothing left and we're like them again. Do you understand?" Her warm breath made puffs of smoke in the freezing dusk.

Nicky shook his head. "That sucks. You're wrong."

"Maybe I am." Emma's voice softened. "But I'm

too scared to put it to the test. I know it's horrid, baby, but I want to put that life behind me. It's awful being the poor single mother with holes in her boots and not enough money to feed her son. I'm terrified of ending up back there, Nicky. It gives me a pain." Emma gripped her chest and shook her head, fear making her tremble.

Who am I? Devastation curled Emma's bottom lip and made her chin wobble. *I'm still a single mother but I have nice new shoes and money to burn, an unfaithful husband and an Irishman who won't go away.* Emma sniffed and Nicky stopped trotting next to her, turning to put his hands on her stomach. "Don't cry, Mummy. You've still got me. I won't talk about it again and I'll cheer up, I promise."

Emma swallowed and the groan emitted from her lips too quickly for her mittened hand to cover its escape. "No, it's me who's sorry! You're right and I'm wrong. You shouldn't leave people behind but I don't know what to do." Tears coursed down Emma's cheeks, feeling warm against the Arctic March blast. "I feel like if I go near them again, it'll open us up to trouble. They'll want our money and when it's gone, we'll be back where we started. I know you miss Mo, but I don't know how to fix it." Emma's sobs caused huge clouds of white air to mix in the darkness and Nicky reached his arms around her in misery.

"It's ok, Mummy. It'll be ok, promise."

Guilt assailed Emma's heart. How could she ever think her loyal son would exchange comfort for friendship. The bus approached with lumbering surety and Emma wiped her face on her mitten and fished in her pocket for her purse. They clambered aboard and held hands as the bus headed down the fast

Northampton Road towards the end of their driveway, a few miles out of town. Emma's two lives mixed like oil and water in her mind, the decaying, unfurnished council house and the ornate, opulence of Wingate Hall. The puzzle pieces clashed against one another with no hope of fitting into place.

"Mummy?" Nicky said, squashing himself closer. "Are you thinking about Little Pete?"

Emma nodded and a tear dropped onto her skirt. "Yes," she breathed.

"Oh, I get it." Nicky patted her hand and Emma's heart broke. She swayed with the motion of the half empty bus as her breath caught in her throat. Nicky sighed. "He moved away and got a job and a girl and a baby, din't he?"

Emma nodded. Nicky pursed his lips. "And then when he came to show us, Fat Brian beat him up and took his wallet because he wouldn't let him take his car off him. And the girl called the cops but they wouldn't come onto the estate and Little Pete crawled to the end of the road and his girl cried and his baby cried. Is that what they'll do to us?"

"I don't know," Emma gulped. "I don't know anything anymore."

"It's ok, Mummy," her son said, threading his tiny fingers through hers. "I won't let you be the poor, single mum again. I'll get a job and take care of you just like you always take care of me."

Emma clung to her son like a drowning woman on a life raft, terror washing over her in waves. She felt like a failure as a parent, condemning her son to know things about the world she'd rather he didn't. When the bus driver glanced in his mirror and asked if she was ok, Emma nodded and lied about a fictitious bout of cold.

At home, Emma dished up soup for two at the rustic kitchen table downstairs. The wood grains held traces of the lives of countless servants who looked after the Ayers family and Emma bit her lip and tried not to ponder on their slavery to a social class she found herself thrust into. Nicky reached for his bowl and buttered bread with a knife which looked immense in his tiny hand. He glanced at Emma, deliberately putting too much on. When she didn't react, he goaded her, looking for reassurance. "Mummy, is too much butter bad for you?"

Emma nodded. "Too much of anything is bad for you."

"Like too much money is bad for us? Because it stops us seeing our friends?"

Emma's hand shook as chicken soup dripped from her spoon, the food half way to her mouth. She set the spoon back in her bowl with a clink. "Nicky, I need to tell you some grown up stuff," she said, pushing her bowl away and resting her trembling hands on the table.

"About Daddy? About the other lady and why he doesn't come home no more?" Nicky's face creased in concern and he reached for more bread. Emma pushed the loaf away, the plastic crinkling under her hand.

"Just eat what you've got," she told him and her son looked relieved having finally hit the elusive boundary. He relaxed and Emma fought not to get side tracked. "No, not about Daddy. This is about the council estate."

"And Old Mo?" Nicky looked hopeful.

Emma lifted her hand to silence his questions and delivered the truth as she saw it. "The estate was horrid, Nicky. It was hell on earth and I hated every minute of living there. It was dangerous and terrifying and I always thought Fat Brian looked out for us because he liked us. But he didn't."

"He liked you," Nicky said, dipping his bread in the soup. A chunk fell off and plunged into the liquid and he mounted a rescue mission with his spoon and the butter knife. "Big Jason liked you *heaps*." He stressed the last word and Emma continued before her son became graphic, under no illusions what Big Jason was interested in.

"Uncle Anton paid them to make sure we stayed safe. He gave them cash when he visited so they kept the druggies away from our house. It stopped them asking us for protection money. They might have liked us, Nicky, but mostly it was about what we were worth to them. Everything has a cost, baby and Uncle Anton paid ours."

Nicky stared at Emma in disbelief. "They was paid? Like bodyguards?"

Emma nodded. "But not in a cool way, Nicky. Remember your friend, Elise, who looked like Kaylee? Fat Brian broke her daddy's arm because they didn't want to swap houses with him. Then his men moved Elise's family up the road to the derelict house next to the rubbish dump and it made Elise sick so they left in the night."

"No, Elise wanted to be near the rubbish dump so her daddy didn't have so far to walk with the black bags wiv his broken arm. Then they went to Spain and I cried for a month."

"I know you cried for a month, but Fat Brian made it impossible for them to stay. They didn't go to Spain, baby. They went into a homeless shelter in town until the council moved them onto a different estate. I know because I saw her mummy just before we left and she told me."

"But Fat Brian liked me. He gave me jobs until you stopped him. I earned pennies."

"He used you to carry drugs to his customers." Emma's voice grew hard. "And when I told him to stop, he said I'd be sorry. I didn't sleep for two weeks waiting for him to torch the house with us in it. Then Anton visited and in a moment of weakness I told him the truth. I suspect he paid Fat Brian off. *Again!*"

"Oh." Nicky pushed the remains of his soup around the bottom of the plate, chasing the lump of soggy bread with concentration. "So they wasn't my friends really?"

Emma swallowed. "Some were, but some weren't. The facts are that Anton paid them and they did their job, mostly. Now when I look back, I just feel horrified."

"What about Old Mo?" A tear ran down Nicky's face and bounced off the rim of his bowl. "Was he paid?"

"No!" The emphatic tone in Emma's voice made Nicky's head jerk up. "Never! Mohammed is a dear, sweet little boy who loved you. But if we contact him and he tells anyone that Anton died and left us the house, we'll never be free of Fat Brian and his cronies."

"Mo wouldn't tell, not if I made him promise." The hope in Nicky's eyes unpicked Emma from the inside out.

"So how would you tell him?" Insight made Emma turn the problem round on her son.

"Post him a letter," Nicky said, his eyes growing distant as he drew pictures and wrote facts in crayon on a fictitious piece of paper in his mind.

"Fat Brian intercepts the post." Emma's answer was quick.

"Phone 'im up," Nicky countered.

"Mo doesn't have a mobile phone and his father might answer the house phone. He works for Fat Brian collecting debts and he'd tell him."

"Post Mo a mobile phone and then ring it." Nicky smiled in victory.

"Fat Brian intercepts the post."

Nicky plopped his spoon into the bowl and liquid splatted on the table. He flung himself back in the chair in frustration. "What then? You don't wanna do anything I think of!"

"Do you see my problem?" Emma asked.

Nicky swiped the back of his hand across his eyes and his chin wobbled. "I get it. You don't want them to treat us like they did Little Pete. They laughed about him after the police helped him leave and said nasty things. Fat Brian took the money out of Pete's wallet and burned it on the fire and it was a nice leather wallet from Australia." The child's words caught in his throat. "It's just I maked Mo this." From his trouser pocket he pulled a small plaster shape. It was painted in garish colours and Emma reached out to take it. Nicky handed it over with extreme care. "I chose the car mould because he likes cars. I maked it blue and yellow for him."

"It's beautiful, Nicky," Emma breathed. She turned over to see the back. '*I miss Mo*' was written in paint in a scrawling, uneven hand.

"Me 'an New Mo had an argument." Nicky's voice broke and degenerated into a wail. "He maked one for me because he thought I maked one for him. But I couldn't give it to him because it was for Old Mo. Now he won't talk to me anymore and Kaylee says she's sick of us arguing." Nicky pulled his feet up onto the chair and buried his face behind his knees, his knuckles white as he hugged his shins. Sobs racked his body and Emma paled.

"Nicky, I'm so sorry," she whispered. She covered the short distance between them and plonked herself on the chair next to him. The wooden legs scraped against the tiles as she pulled her son towards her and wrapped herself around his small body. They cried together then, two lost souls in a swirling sea of problems clinging to each other like driftwood. North or south, rich or poor; life held the same barbs for all without distinction. A deep cut to one released fresh, red blood just as furiously as to the other.

The child in Emma's womb fluttered to remind her of its presence and her heart sank further into the mire. There seemed no end to her dilemmas and no solutions to any of them. A black cloud of depression hovered around her head, inviting her to plunge to familiar, comforting depths of darkness and despair. Emma resisted, clinging to her son and teetering on the edge. Her father's deep, gentle voice spoke to her from the grave and the image behind her eyelids refused to be wiped away. The Reverend Harrington stood at the pulpit of his church in long black robes. An ethereal peace shone from his lined face as he held his arms outstretched and spoke the liturgy which he staked his life on. The familiar words washed over Emma's psyche like a gentle caress from the past and then her father smiled. "*Nothing is impossible for God,*" he said and his smile was a reminder to his daughter.

Emma pressed her face against her son's blonde,

sweaty head and kissed it, brushing the damp fringe from his forehead. "I love you, Nicky," she whispered. "If you know nothing else; know that."

He hiccoughed beneath her, the spasm in his lungs forming a loud protest and he nodded without replying. Emma squeezed him. "I've got choc ices in the freezer," she said, knowing food was the last thing to repair a broken heart but sensing it might help. "Want one?"

Nicky nodded and Emma stood. She collected their dirty crockery and dumped it in the old Belfast sink, peering through the window. The darkness outside was intimidating and she shuddered and turned away. "I'll clear up tomorrow. Let's eat choc ices in my bed and watch TV together?"

Nicky nodded eagerly and waited while Emma settled Farrell in his basket and checked the kitchen door. She bolted it top and bottom. "Keep guard, Faz," she said, patting his head. Nicky carried the frozen treats and watched as she set the burglar alarm to cover the downstairs rooms and they went to bed early, finding comfort in each other as they had since the beginning.

CHAPTER THIRTEEN

Emma worked many more hours than she was paid for, throwing herself into her quest to find the truth as an avoidance tactic. Obsessing over the age of the school allowed her a distraction from dealing with her crumbling life and the numbness which thoughts of Rohan induced.

Her husband stayed away and where Emma should have felt relieved, it only made her uncertainty worse, compounding her guilt for not listening to his explanation. She stumbled from day to day, making decent headway with the photographs at school and spending her afternoons in the local museum and library. Emma rushed back to school at the end of the day, collecting Nicky and heading back to their cold, dark home on the bus.

Even Christopher Dolan seemed noticeably absent and Emma sank further into a dark pit of despair, which contained only her son's earnest face as a bright point.

"Miriam, please order more of the special polypropylene wallets for the photos?" Emma asked the secretary, poking her head around the door of the school office. "I need more A3 wallets and another stack of archival boxes too please. Hopefully they'll arrive tomorrow by courier."

Miriam pulled a face. "I don't think Mr Dalton's very happy about the cost," she said, pursing her lips. "He complained yesterday."

Emma closed her eyes with resignation, feeling the lack of support keenly. The previous night's sleeplessness caught her up in a sense of exhaustion. "He buys them and allows me to do my job properly, or I quit." Emma heard the petulance in her voice and detested its squeaky quality. "I told him what I needed before I took the job, so it can't come as a surprise. No good archivist would put those photos back up in the attic in the same state they came down."

"Shall I tell him that?" Mischief lit Miriam's eyes and Emma bit her lip.

"You know what?" Emma turned to leave. "I really don't care."

Freda left mid-morning for a doctor's appointment and Emma finished work and went to her usual spot in the microfiche room of the library. Her stomach growled with hunger as she pivoted on the edge of her chair and peered at old newspaper clippings detailing life in Market Harborough and its surrounding villages in the nineteenth century.

"I bet you could win prizes on a game show by now," the librarian whispered, clearing waste paper from under the desk behind Emma. "Your chosen subject could be the price of eggs and stockings in Market Harborough during the 1800s."

Emma's lips moved into an automatic smile but her eyes channelled fear. She'd been careful not to reveal the reason for her search, but the omnipresent librarian had seen her combing the scanned newspapers. Emma forced herself to answer glibly. "I'm really interested in the reign of Queen Victoria. It's interesting to see what effect educational legislation had on the town and its inhabitants," she gushed. The librarian stared at her with a wooden smile on her face and nervousness made Emma's lips loose. "I'm organising the artifacts and photographs at Little Arden School ready for their celebration later this year."

The librarian narrowed her eyes. "We know who you are," she whispered, leaving quietly on her soft soled shoes.

Emma swallowed and watched the wide skirt bloom around the woman's stumpy legs as she strode across the library floor. Her heart pounded an unhealthy staccato rhythm. She needed to find the elusive clue in the next hour, or not at all. It was clear she wasn't welcome.

Half an hour later, Emma glanced at her watch in frustration, her search unsuccessful. She rubbed at her tired eyes, remembering the thinly veiled spite in Clarissa Jameson-Arden's expression. "What's your problem with me, woman?" Emma whispered into the empty room. She leaned over to turn the computer off, unable to resist one last search. Clicking on the newspaper icon, Emma typed, "Jameson."

The screen blinked and numerous articles popped up, waiting patiently by title. Emma immediately noticed the most recent were accolades and achievements linked to the wider Jameson family but one near the bottom drew her attention, its title consisting of two small words underlined in green. '*Death Penalty.*'

Emma sighed, knowing the red herring was sent to irritate her further and she pulled her coat over her shoulders. Heavy rain slapped the pavements outside and hammered against the windows, filling Emma with misery at the thought of yet another arrival home, soaked to the skin. She pressed her coat buttons closed and clicked on the link as a way of killing another few minutes, curiosity calling her.

The first few lines made Emma's eyes widen and her jaw hang slackly against the collar of her coat. Glancing at the doorway behind her and seeing the librarian shelving books inside the romance section, Emma hunched in front of the screen and read the damning words of the article. She read it four times before the relevance sank into her brain.

'*On this day in 1864, Mr Peter Humphrey Jameson Esquire, of Market Harborough in the county of Northamptonshire was sentenced to death for the murder of Mr Richard Arden of that parish, who died at his home in Scotland Road, Little Bowden. His Honour Mr Justice Aldridge presiding passed sentence, satisfied that Mr Richard Arden was unlawfully killed by the defendant. Suspicious circumstances caused the arrest of Mrs Joy Arden who was found to have had a previous liaison with Mr Jameson, but no evidence was offered against her by the Crown. Mr Jameson, formerly schoolmaster of Little Arden Church of England School was taken to Newgate Prison pending execution.*'

"Jameson," Emma muttered, her brow creasing in concentration. She half stood to peer at the tiny writing on the screen, detailing the date of the article as 12th October 1864. The breath left her body in a whoosh as her proof sat potently before her. Emma used her library card number to print the article, glancing round her like a guilty thief. Stuffing her mittens and purse in her pocket, Emma spied her article sliding gently through the rollers of the copier machine, situated metres away from the librarian's ample bottom as she bent to shelve books.

As Emma took a step forward, the librarian stood in response to a tinkling bell from the front desk. Her eyes locked on Emma's and she scowled. Fixing a wooden smile on her lips, Emma pretended to mess around in her coat pocket, hearing a *thunk* as her purse tumbled to the floor. When she looked up after retrieving it, the paper was gone. "No, no, no!" Emma hissed, moving rapidly across the red carpet squares to the machine. She checked every one of the machine's orifices before being forced to acknowledge her proof was gone. A glance at her watch revealed too little time to start again before Nicky emerged from school, his face raking the playground for her presence. With heavy steps, Emma slunk to the front doors and prepared to accept her dousing by the relentless rain.

"Hey, what's so important about this?" Christopher Dolan's voice sounded muffled under his hood as he ran into the back of Emma. She stood under the porch, psyching herself up to get soaked. With a squeak she snatched the folded paper from his warm hand and stuffed it in her coat pocket.

"What are you playing at?" she demanded, her tone betraying fear and fury. "How did you get this?"

"Just took it, so I did." With casual chivalry he popped open his umbrella and offered Emma his arm. With trembling fingers she seized it and nuzzled close, valuing the covering of the black fabric as the rain pelted it from above. Puddles pooled on the flagstone street as Christopher pulled her south towards the park and school.

"You nearly gave me a bloody heart attack!" Emma chastised the Irishman as she tried to keep up with his long strides over the flooded areas. "I was trying so hard not to be noticed and then you did that!"

"Aye, well you *were* noticed, ya daft wee bint! What're ya playin' at, woman?"

"I'm doing research for work," Emma whined. "I'm

not doing anything wrong!"

"Aye but there's people in this town would disagree with ya. Yer diggin' up dangerous dirt, so y'are."

"Where have you been?" Emma asked, resenting the sound of abandonment in her voice. "You've been gone for days."

Christopher squeezed her arm and smiled. "Man's gotta earn a living, sweetheart. I had a job for a few days."

Emma stopped on the pavement and looked worried. "Christopher, if that librarian turns the computer on, can she see my searches? I never thought of deleting the history. The microfiche is fine but what about the internet searches."

Christopher looked smug. "After I took yer piece of paper, I nipped into the microfiche room and did a little damage."

Emma's mouth hung open in horror. "What did you do? I was the last one in there; she'll think I did it!"

"Ach, Emma! I didn't burn the place down! I just uploaded a wee bug into their system on the computer you were usin'. And yes, anyone can follow you onto a public machine and see exactly what you were searching."

"No!" Emma's eyes widened and she looked like she might cry. "Do you think she'll look? Is that why she behaved so oddly?"

"She?" Christopher's brow knitted in question.

"The librarian who said, '*We know who you are*,' in a spooky voice. I bet she's checking my searches every day after I leave."

"Ach, not her!" Christopher's tone was dismissive. "Not the fat one, the other one."

"What other one?" Emma leaned in to hear him as

pain pelted the umbrella. "There wasn't another one."

"Aye there was." Christopher checked the road before leading Emma across. She trusted him blindly, hanging on his every word. "The one from the big church in town sat in the periodicals section watching every move you made. She rushed into the microfiche room as I came out so she won't be able to see what you were lookin' at. But she'll get the blame when the whole system comes crashin' down, starting with the machine she's on." He smirked with the satisfaction of a job done well.

"So she won't see the article I found?" Emma asked, brushing rain water from her left eye, where it blew underneath the umbrella. She shook her head, hating her technological naivety.

"No, she won't, Em. All she'll see is a message which says, '*You have attempted an illegal login and flooded this machine.*' By the time she's finished panicking, all the machines in the town council will be running a programme which looks like rising water and sending the IT department straight to her machine as the source. With any luck she'll still be sitting there scratching her fluffy head as the techs arrive looking for a cyber-hack." He chortled, unable to resist enjoying his own skill.

"Well, they'll be right, won't they?" Emma shook her head. "You hacked it!"

"Me? Never!" Christopher looked mock offended and Emma laughed.

Her face was sincere as she peered up into his. "Thank you, Christopher. I don't know what I'm onto but whatever it is, someone's gone to a lot of trouble to keep it hidden."

They walked to school in silence, using the

supermarket car park as a short cut and the alley past the back of houses to get to the park quicker. "Don't come this way by yerself," Christopher warned her and Emma nodded.

"Ok, I won't."

Almost at the end of the alley, Christopher turned his back on the entrance to the park, shielding Emma from anyone passing. He brushed drips from her face with warm fingers and she wasn't quick enough to stop him pressing his lips over hers. Emma's brown eyes were wide as he pulled away, holding her breath and refusing to engage in the kiss. Christopher's eyes danced with mischief. "Keep the umbrella," he whispered. "And stop putting yourself in harm's way."

Emma took the curved handle of the umbrella and stopped Christopher as he turned to go back the way they came. "Wait!" she said. "What did the woman look like? The one who checked my computer."

Christopher smiled. "You already know the answer to that."

"Clarissa Jameson-Arden?" Emma asked. "Or the other one, Eve?"

"How about I leave ya with that little mystery, Em?" Christopher asked with a frustrating smile. "Go fetch yer son."

"But are you back now?" Emma asked. "Are you staying?"

Christopher looked confused. "Staying where?"

"With us, at Wingate Hall." Emma's brow furrowed, hating her insecurity.

The Irishman smiled and his face softened, sensing Emma's need to know she wasn't alone. He ran his index finger down the bridge of her nose, a sensuous, slow movement meant to rattle her. "I'll be where I always am, Emma. Takin' care of youse."

"You phoned and spoke to Nicky, didn't you? You told him The Contessa was loose."

Christopher nodded. "Aye."

"Is she coming after me?" Emma asked, her eyes pleading for clemency. Christopher stroked her fringe away from her forehead.

"Yes, Em. Competition, retribution, yeah, she's coming."

A tear rolled down Emma's cheek. "How long's Rohan been sleeping with her?"

Christopher's face paled and Emma watched his jaw work through his cheek, an angular line grinding through his chiselled face. He kept his eyes away from hers and withdrew his other hand from his pocket, revealing Nicky's small plaster car. "I've a long distance delivery to make tonight." He touched the side of his nose and winked, his expression sympathetic. "So don't be waitin' up for me."

Emma exhaled and watched Christopher Dolan's neat butt move along the narrow alley between the houses, the swagger in his stride unmistakeable even from a distance. Turning, she walked the remaining distance to school, jumping over puddles spreading into lakes, glad of friendship and a borrowed umbrella.

CHAPTER FOURTEEN

"Em, can we talk?"

Emma laid the book on the sofa with an angry exhale, tossing her dark head. "Does anyone ever bother to ring the bell in this bloody place, or should I leave the front gates open and the doors unlocked?" She glared at the dog curled in front of the fire. Farrell thumped his tail on the rug and laid his head back on his paws, squeezing his eyes shut. "And you're bloody useless," Emma grumbled.

"Don't be like that, Em. I'm still your husband and we have a son together." Rohan closed the door and stalked across the vast room, hands rigid by his sides. He eyed the empty grate with a wrinkle of his fine nose and observed his wife swaddled in the blanket. "When are you gonna learn to light a fire, *devotchka*?"

"I'm fine," Emma lied, rolling her eyes and hoping Rohan didn't see the hairs standing up on her chilled arms. "The dog thinks it already is."

Rohan's blue eyes twinkled as he sat next to her and Emma's heart squirmed. A dart of desire shot from navel to groin and she tensed and looked away. "What do you want?" she snapped, her tone hard.

"Why did Dolan drive to Lincoln?" Rohan asked, distracted by the blanket sliding apart to reveal Emma's slender, creamy thigh.

She chuckled. "You're the spy, Ro. You tell me. And if you're here, it means someone else is watching him."

"I'm not a *spy!*" Rohan's eyes narrowed and his brow creased with indignation. "I'm an actuary."

"Ah yeah, *the Actuary,*" Emma sighed, recalling the bruises on her husband's body and the healed stab wound on his back. "Well, I don't love the Actuary; I thought I loved Rohan Andreyev but they're the same man."

"I'm so sorry, Em." Rohan's eyes glittered like diamonds in his tanned face and he pursed his lips, shrouded by sadness. "It's one reason I didn't look for you; the two halves are difficult to reconcile."

Emma pursed her lips and stared at the rug on the polished floor, tracing the intricate patterns in the period weave. She focussed on that instead of her husband, sitting too close for comfort. Rohan leaned forward and brushed a strand of long hair behind her ear. "What, no biting retort?" His voice was soft and he searched her face with his eyes. His fingers began a steady massage of the back of her head, a gentle, soothing action.

Emma closed her eyes, enjoying the physical contact and an interlude in the pervading loneliness which haunted her. Rohan moved closer, edging his way across the sofa until their knees touched. Emma felt the supple casing of the leg brace through his trousers, another reminder of her husband's addiction to risk. His magnetism hauled her in with a delicate pull, so light she didn't react. It enveloped her in Rohan's aura of safety and intoxicated her with his musky scent, reassuring and solid in its heady mix of perfume and maleness.

Rohan's fingers brushed Emma's dark hair from her shoulder and continued massaging, squeezing and releasing the tense muscles in a steady, calming rhythm.

When his lips grazed her temple, Emma pressed her eyelids closed and knitted her brow, fighting the dart of need which began again. His stubble against her jawline and neck made her tense, shivering as though electrified with each subtle touch. Rohan sought the soft skin where collar bone met shoulder, teasing the softness between his lips and tugging. Emma registered the tightness as he sucked, branding her with his signature. She knew he must stop, but stayed frozen in position, her body thrilled with the pleasure-pain reflex.

Rohan finished and moved up the tendons of Emma's neck, smoothing and grazing as beard alternated with lips. Her mouth quivered as he found it, settling his lips with teasing kisses. When Emma opened her eyes she stared straight into his, the pupils dark voids in the vibrant blue irises. Rohan's stealthy fingers stole inside the blanket and his lips parted over Emma's as he drew in an appreciative breath. Her night attire comprised one of his old work shirts, stolen from their shared wardrobe and the fabric fluttered apart to show a pair of battered knickers. Rohan slipped questing fingers inside the frayed elastic to cup her buttock and Emma held her breath as the reminder began a steady throb in the back of her brain.

"You have another woman!" She pushed at his chest with force, overbalancing him. The surprise on his face mixed with hurt.

"Oh, *Emma!*" Rohan pressed his fingers against his eyelids and shook his head, his body stiffening in anger. The bulge pressing against the groin of his trousers looked painful and Emma glanced away, knowing if he tried again she'd give in. Loneliness and disappointment made poor lovers and Rohan's sexuality offered fulfilment and the promise of companionship in the empty bed upstairs.

"Is it because of *him?*" Rohan asked, his voice hardening with every syllable. "Dolan?"

Emma stood with an angry huff, the exhalation full of irritation and injustice. The blanket fell from her lithe body revealing slender, athletic legs and the beginnings of a pregnancy bump. She saw Rohan swallow, his Adam's apple bobbing as he appreciated her loveliness. When she put her hands on her hips, the shirt front parted to show the front of her underwear and the bare flesh of her belly. The wide shirt cuffs hung over her hands as she postured, narrowing her eyes at her husband. "I'm sick of this!" she hissed. "It's tiring being the piece of meat you two *sobaki* fight over! Why won't you both just leave me alone?"

She strode from the room, her anger warming her up the stairs and along the cool corridor to her bedroom. Nicky slept on Rohan's side, his delicate face cast into shadow by the lamp he'd lit. *They're like dogs*, Emma raged in her head, proud of her use of the Russian word which caused Rohan's eyes to widen. Emma turned the key in the bedroom door with a click to prevent other disturbances. She climbed into bed, curling her body around the child next to her, guilt robbing her of sleep as she punished herself for giving and then taking away a precious father figure. "Sorry, Nicky," she whispered. "I'll try to be enough for you."

CHAPTER FIFTEEN

Emma sat in the darkened office, pouring over the school logs. Her gloved fingers moved over the tattered leaves, ruined by damp so only the first few pages were legible. "Bloody shame," Emma complained to the empty room.

Her lips moved as she read the copperplate script documenting Freda's mother's last year of school. She became a class monitor on the first step towards earning a teaching qualification and Emma suppressed sadness at the knowledge by the end of the year, poor Mary Clarke would be a lady's maid.

1923

January 9 - Mary Freda Clarke commenced this day her services as paid monitor.

January 10 - Paulie Arden absent due to farm duties.

January 11 - Clarice Dawlish absent due to sickness.

January 12 - Sid Beetham, Ingrid Arden, Patricia Jameson late due to flooding.

Emma sighed and walked to the photocopier, hoping not to damage the fragile log as she scanned and copied its delicate pages.

"I was hoping to find you." The woman's voice sounded clipped as she accosted Emma.

"Hello." Emma's body ached and she sighed, emotionally spent with no energy for a robust discussion. "How can I help you?" she replied, smiling as sweetly as she could muster and halting the copier's frantic paper flinging.

"I want to talk to you somewhere private," the woman demanded, taking a step closer to Emma and adopting a menacing stance. Her delicate pearls tinkled around her neck, belying the gentle-old-lady image. The tiny, dark eyes bore into Emma's face with a piercing quality.

"There is nowhere, sorry." She smiled, the hairs standing up on the back of her neck. The woman oozed threat. Emma turned back to the photocopier, grateful for its corridor location. "We can chat here though, Mrs Jameson-Arden, as long as you don't mind me continuing."

"I wondered how it was going," the woman replied, studying Emma with gimlet eyes trained to miss nothing. "How did your research go?"

"Oh, good thanks," Emma gushed. "It's an amazing church. I'd love to have a more thorough look one day."

Clarissa Jameson-Arden's face puckered as though lemon sucking was on the menu and her face pinked in frustration. Emma's hands trembled over the log book but she daren't stop and face the woman. *As long as I don't mention the library, nor can she*, Emma reassured herself.

"Where else have you tried to find answers?" Clarissa asked and Emma's heart sank.

"Oh, the usual places." Emma shot her an I'm-trying-to-be-helpful face while exuding an air of extreme busyness. Her hands sweated in the cotton gloves protecting the book from the acid on her skin, tight and itchy. Emma's long dark curls tumbled sideways, covering her flushing cheeks as stress soared through her body. Danger hung around the women like an oppressive shroud.

Emma inhaled as Clarissa Jameson-Arden took a long stride towards her, the hem of the older woman's jacket brushing Emma's arm. Her breath was warm on Emma's overheated cheek, smelling faintly of peppermint. With a valiant effort, Emma turned to meet the flashing grey eyes in Clarissa's angry face. Emma put a haughtiness in her stance and raised herself up to her full height, which didn't equal her opponent's but made her appear less cowed. Clarissa's voice was a low hiss. "It took Mr Dalton a long time to convince the board we needed an archivist for this celebration." Her voice dripped bile, burning holes in the air between them. "I'm still not convinced we do." Clarissa's smile was wooden and her tone laden with threat.

Irritation burgeoned in Emma's breast and something of her old self revived, meeting the other woman's suggestion with newfound confidence and the knowledge she no longer needed a job so desperately. Anton's gift, *from Russia, with love*, made it so. "You must do what you think best," Emma said, scorn building and spewing from her eyes. "I needn't work; I'm doing this because I love it."

"Nice bluff!" Clarissa leaned into Emma's face. "I've spoken to your old employer and he thinks differently. He ended your contract and you couldn't keep hold of your council house. He figured you were homeless until he heard you washed up here!"

Warm spittle landed on Emma's cheek and something inside her snapped. She laughed, a deep forbidding cackle low in her chest which frightened even her. As Clarissa took a step away, Emma moved into her space, enjoying seeing the woman lose ground. "I suggest you ring him again," Emma jeered. "Ask him why my contract ended. Go on, ask him!" She leaned closer to Clarissa, seeing the grey strands peeking through the bleached curls. Emma lowered her voice to a whisper. "Ring him again. Remind him that telling the truth is a good idea because I have the luck of the Irish."

With flushing cheeks and a temper waging war inside her body, Emma seized the log book from the copier and pressed the button to send the scans to Sam's computer. She made the long walk back to the office with dignity, despite her pounding heart. Clarissa's eyes bored holes in her back with every step taken and by the time she parked her bottom in the rickety office chair, her stomach had churned her breakfast into ash.

"You gonna throw up again?" Sam asked, handing her the dustbin. The sight of a browning banana peel alongside sandwich remains growing their own fungal experiment, made her want to heave and Emma clapped her hand over her mouth and moaned. Sam jerked the dustbin towards her again and she kicked it in an attempt not to touch it with her hands. "I'll take that as a no," he grumbled. "Just trying to be nice!"

"Ugh! By showing me things which make me wanna puke?" Emma squeaked. "That's not helping!"

"Who's puking?" Freda tottered into the office and whipped off her woolly hat. Static sent her hair towards the ceiling, giving her a frightened look. "I thought you'd stopped the morning sickness?"

"So did I. There was a spat with Clarissa Jameson-Arden and it made me unwell. She spikes my blood pressure even from the other end of the corridor."

Freda balled her fists up next to her ears. "Where is she? I can take her!" She pushed her scrawny arms through the air like a boxer and nearly flipped herself onto her back.

"Steady on there!" Sam took her flailing weight and stood her upright. "You'll end up beached like a turtle."

"Turtles don't beach, young man!" Freda straightened her skirt with a delicate shimmy. "God designed them with the right geometry for self-righting and he doesn't make mistakes."

Sam shook his head and sat on his chair. Emma groaned. "God doesn't, but I do! Making an enemy of the chairwoman of the board is my dumbest mistake yet!"

"I'd have to agree with that one," Sam sighed. "She marched in here on my first day and said she'd put me on a verbal warning if I didn't stop salting the front pavement in the ice."

"But I want you to salt the pavement," Emma said, poking her face out of her hands. "If I slip over, I could hurt myself and my baby. And what about Freda? She'll break bones."

"She had these special boots, see. They cost a fortune and the salt was eating away the soles. She went mental."

Emma groaned and pushed her face back into her hands. Freda got her fists ready again. "I'll deal with her," she said. "Where is she?"

"It's ok now!" Sam jerked upright. "I salt and then put sand on top. It neutralises it and she doesn't realise. Please don't ruin it for me?"

"Stop bibbling man!" Freda snapped. "I'm defending Emma, not you! You're ugly enough to fight your own battles."

"This is no good." Emma stood. "I can't do this.

My life's a mess and I don't have the energy for her bullying tactics. At the library I found..."

There was a sharp rap on the office door and its three occupants jumped. When Mr Dalton bounced in like Tigger on cocaine, he found startled faces and frozen bodies. "Ah, here we are," he intoned with his usual brand of effervescent happiness. "Have you met our board chairwoman? This is the lovely Mrs Jameson-Arden."

Sam's head whipped round to the padlock on his desk and Freda's lips curled back in a snarl. Emma's breakfast roiled in her stomach again, but the room remained dead silent. For once Mr Dalton seemed wrong footed as awkwardness descended. "She's interested in the progress of our archives," he said, stumbling over his words.

"What would you like to see?" Emma plastered the smile to her lips and held her hand out, encompassing the large photographs laid in date order on the work bench.

Freda reached for a sharp blade and held it in front of her, a manic look in her eye. "There's always room for another helper, isn't there, Emma?" she said.

Emma's smile wavered as every nerve ending in her body screamed a contradiction, but Freda stepped towards Clarissa brandishing the blade. "An idiot put Velcro sticky dots on the back of the original class photos. You can help me slice them off." She grinned, slashing the air with her blade and her top set of falsies clacked onto the bottoms, giving her a ghoulish appearance. With her other hand, Freda reached out to touch the floaty chiffon of Clarissa's expensive dress. "You might need an apron though. Look how dirty we get."

Clarissa's eyes widened in horror as Freda's blackened fingers dropped the fabric, leaving a streak of dust along the floral print. She lurched towards the open doorway. "Oh, no...terribly busy...jolly good...I'll leave you to it." She exited backside first and her boots clacked along the corridor at speed.

Freda's cackle split the air and with a look of mystification, Mr Dalton left and closed the door behind him. Sam snorted and held his mirth until the headmaster's voice could be heard chatting to a child in the corridor, then he exploded in a mist of spit and tears. "You're wicked!" he spluttered, jabbing his finger at Freda. "Nobody's ever dealt with her like that before."

"I don't understand what you're talking about," Freda said, shrugging and plonking her bottom in her seat.

"You just got me fired," Emma grimaced and Freda put her nose in the air and refused to be drawn. Emma pushed a photograph with care into its acid free wallet and added it to the pile. Then she turned to Freda as her friend chewed the end of her pencil and pondered the name of long forgotten faces. "What's the story with you and Clarissa? Why don't you like each other? She was born while you were abroad and you've only been back a year."

Freda pushed her spectacles to the end of her bulbous nose and jerked her head at Sam. "Young man, kindly get the ladies tea for two."

"What?" Sam's face shot out of his mending. "Who do you think I am? The bloody butler? Get it yourself."

"Ok." Freda got to her feet and hobbled towards the office door. She gripped the work surface in gnarled hands and heaved herself along. Emma's mouth dropped open at the realism of her performance. "I may be a while though," Freda said in a wavering voice, bending her body from the waist as though bearing a turtle shell on her back. "Ninety's not the most agile age and I tend to slop when I'm carrying liquids. I'll try not to spill in the corridor. Is there any particular cloth you'd like me to use when wiping up after myself?"

"Oh, stone the bloody crows!" Sam exclaimed. "I'll do it!" He stomped from the room and slammed the door behind him.

Freda stood upright and shimmied back to her chair. Emma shook her head. "For a Christian lady, you're diabolical!" she laughed.

Freda grinned. "God's got me covered. Every time my poor decrepit guardian angels think it's time for a lie down, I get them hopping to attention." She burped and put delicate fingers to her lips. "Ooh, pardon."

"So, what's the secret?" Emma asked. "You must have sent Sam out for a reason. What's with the eyebrow war between you two ladies of the manor?"

"Well, back when we were girls, Clarissa's grandmother, Annie, had her eye on climbing the ranks and marrying John Ayers. She was in my class through school and her parents had a loose connection with the Lord's family, so every story she wrote involved her life as a future great lady. When poor John came back from the war scarred she didn't hide her horror. He maintained he always knew her desire for him stopped at his title, but her behaviour was still hurtful. After he and I eloped, poor Annie married a Jameson who left her destitute after a rotten hand at cards. Clarissa's father was an unambitious Jameson who taught here and she married an Arden. The problem with that family's always been bitterness and pride. It's all about the family image and the riches which go with protecting it. I mean look at Clarissa with that dirty mark. She'll be harrying the dry cleaners in town even as we speak." Freda knitted her brows. "Perhaps it was mean of me."

"Here!" Sam barged into the room and set two mugs of tea on the desk. "It's playtime and Muriel's doing tea leaves. She's gonna do mine so I'll be in the staffroom if anyone wants me." He slammed out in a huff.

"Ooh that's bad news," Freda muttered. "Never be tempted to mess with that rubbish."

Emma shook her head. "I won't. Dad was clear about occult stuff, even the things which seem harmless. He always said there was a cost to it but I didn't understand what he meant. I wish he was here. There's so many things I still need to ask him. He was such a knowledgeable man." Emma sipped her drink, her face downcast.

"Did you still believe it was Rohan's fault your father died?" Freda asked and Emma gasped at the unexpectedness of the question.

"What? I've never blamed him!"

"Haven't you?" Freda's bright eyes conveyed a perception which Emma found hard to bear.

"No! I've never blamed him." Even the words had a false quality on her tongue. "How can I blame him? Maybe it was all our faults; Ro just happened to be the eldest."

"But you've told me you tried to protect each other from his mother's poisoning. None of you would think to protect a grown man."

"Anton protected us." Emma's teeth ground in her

jaw making her whole face ache. "He flushed Alanya's food down the toilet and gave us his."

"But Rohan was older than both of you, wasn't he?" Freda asked. "Wasn't it his responsibility?"

"He didn't *see!*" Emma's hands became fists. "*He never sees!*"

Freda nodded and continued with her pencil list, leaving Emma with the damaging revelation. She licked her dry lips and sipped her tea, a knot of something nasty stirring in her breast. When she scraped her mug on the desk and put her head in her hands, Freda crossed the tiles between them. "There, there," she soothed, her fragile arms like tiny bird's wings around Emma's torso. She offered no judgement or condemnation, but Pandora's Box left its debris suspended in the air molecules around their heads.

"I *do* blame him," Emma confessed. "It's why I don't trust him. He wants to protect me but when he tries, I can't let him in case he gets it wrong and somebody dies. Last time it was Dad; this time it could be Nicky. I have no one left to lose."

"You need to remember he was a boy, a boy who loved his mother and didn't want to see what she was doing. *Munchausen syndrome by proxy* is a manipulative illness. They're like magicians performing tricks for an audience. You can't blame him for being fooled by a skilled practitioner. There's no wonder as an adult, he deals in facts and figures and hard won analysis of risk. Can you blame him for needing proof for every move he makes? He wants it weighed and measured before he takes a single step forward. I think under the circumstances, it's understandable."

"What kind of risk am I?" Emma sniffed, the heady aroma of Freda's floral perfume providing a shroud of safety around her head.

"I think you're an unpredictable one," Freda said, her voice low and soporific. "He can't plan or chart your explosions because the fuse moves every time you open your mouth. You don't trust him and he can't trust you."

"You make us sound like an accident waiting to happen," Emma snorted.

Freda smiled into her face, her eyes sparkly and young in the crinkled face. "Oh, my darling," she crooned. "You're the best firework display I've seen in years!"

In the staffroom, Freda handed Emma her mug to load into the dishwasher and turned towards the knot of excited bodies crowded around Muriel in the corner. She waxed lyrical over something in the bottom of the Year 4 class teacher's mug. As Emma shut the dishwasher and turned round, her heart quailed at the sight of Freda ploughing her way into the centre of the group and leaning over the mug. "That's a tea bag!" she said with disdain. "You can't do a tea leaf reading with tea bags; it's cheating!"

Emma groaned and ran her hand through her hair as a few staff members lost faith with surprising speed and left. Freda raised an eyebrow at Annabel, the Year 4 teacher and cocked her head like a sparrow. "Why do you want to see what tomorrow has for you, when getting through today's such a struggle? God sends the good and the bad when we're ready to cope with it. Knowing the bad things in life early causes unnecessary worry and getting the good things early is like ruining Christmas."

Muriel tutted and heaved herself out of the chair. "It's a bit of fun. Why do you have to ruin it?"

"Fun?" Annabel's voice rose a few octaves. "It's not fun for me! You're meant to be telling me when I'll get pregnant!" Her words spluttered out around a growing barrage of tears. "My husband's desperate for a baby and you said this would help!"

At the hysteria in her voice, Muriel slunk away, dumping the sacred mug and remaining grounds into the dishwasher, as though demonstrating their irrelevance in the grand scheme of things. "I wanted a baby!" Annabel wailed, folding forwards so her elbows rested on her knees. Huge sobs emanated from her slender frame. Emma bit her lip and pulled her cardigan around her growing secret, keen not to cause offence.

"A baby? Is that all?" Freda exclaimed. "Stand."

The shaking woman got to her feet and Freda seized her shoulders and bowed her head. "What are you doing?" Annabel whispered.

"Praying for you, dear. Not much else will work; the Lord gives and He takes away. So why go asking a few tea crumbs in the bottom of a mug for something they aren't able to give? Now shush."

Annabel poked in her sleeve for a tissue and dabbed her nose as Freda lowered her hand and raised her eyes. "We've tried everything and I can't seem to get pregnant," Annabel sniffed. "Every month is such a disappointment."

"Well, next month won't be." Freda smiled and patted her on the arm. "You should go, there's a riot in your classroom."

Annabel's eyes roved towards the open staffroom door as her ears picked up a high pitched shriek. "Oh, goodness, yes I can hear them. Little monsters!"

Emma watched Freda with eyes of suspicion as the

staffroom emptied, leaving the two women and Sam. Freda straightened the magazines on the coffee table and stood upright. "Come on, missy, out with it."

"You promised her a baby!" Emma exclaimed. "She'll be devastated when she doesn't get one."

"*God* promised her a baby and *I* facilitated the prayer reaching her. She won't be disappointed."

"How can you be sure?" Emma wrung her hands, her dark eyes filled with pain. "My dad believed everything in the bible, even as his wife slowly poisoned him. Where was God for him? Why didn't He heal my father and stop my life turning to misery?"

"I don't have the answers, Emma; this silly old woman's not God. I only know what I know. And He was with you through your worst nightmares; He never abandoned you."

Emma nodded and sniffed, eager to end the conversation. She pulled herself together with an effort of will. "Come on, let's finish these 1930s photos and start sorting the ones with names." Before she left the room, Emma glanced back at Sam. "You coming?"

He followed, his face set in a dark glower and closed the office door behind him with his foot. Then he paced around the room. "Why didn't you tell me you could do that?" he spat.

"What?" Freda settled herself in a chair next to Emma, ready to pour over more photos.

"Make people have babies. I want a baby. You never did that thing for me!"

Freda looked at Sam as though he was a small boy. She dragged her words out. "You can't have babies, Sam. You're a man."

He balled his fists by his side. "My wife's been trying to get pregnant for the last two years and can't." He jabbed an angry finger at Freda. "My sex life rotates around temperatures and calendars and positions that might make it easier for..." He stopped and rubbed his hand over his face. "And all the time you could've helped."

"I can't help if I don't know," Freda said with gentleness, standing and approaching the angry young man. She placed her hands on his shoulders and closed her eyes. Emma watched the angst leave Sam's face and peace take its place. "There," Freda said and kissed his cheek with a light touch. "That's in repayment for the times you've pulled my scooter out of the rain and left the gate open for me. I always notice."

Sam's face creased into an embarrassed smile. "Yeah, I do. That's cool." His face became eager. "So, do I rush home and do it now?"

Freda clutched her chest. "Ooh, if you're hoping to get graphic with me, young man, please remember my old heart."

Sam nodded and reached for his jacket and phone. "I'm nipping out to...to...get supplies," he said. Emma smirked as she heard him dial his wife. "Yeah, I'll be home for lunch in five minutes. No, we're not eating."

"You're a woman of many talents," Emma said, the half-smile not reaching her eyes. "Don't suppose you could fix my life too?"

Freda scooted her chair closer, the castors making a strange noise on the tiles. Her spindly arm around Emma's shoulder offered comfort. "Once you've worked out what you want, everything else will fall into place. Find out the story behind this celebration and make your stand. Decide whether you want the gorgeous Russian in your life; then ask him back."

"Or not."

"Oh, you want him, dear, but your head won't listen to your heart. Don't leave it too long. There's plenty out there would be glad of his attentions." Freda kissed the side of Emma's face. "Now, I have a game of Scrabble waiting and you've already worked your paid hours. I suggest you do some thinking and tell me what you decide." Freda pushed a stack of photographs in front of Emma. "There you go, dear. All the 1930s named as best I can. Those records of admission helped jog my memory. Frank Jameson taught me." She tapped a gloved finger over the greyed face of a nondescript man standing to attention next to the gathered rows of children.

"Clarissa's grandfather?"

"Great-grandfather. Not a kind man; abusive in the classroom and at home. That's his son, right there above me. Silly Annie married him after the war and regretted it. I wouldn't have touched the family with a bargepole after being taught by old Frank; drunk most of the time and fathering cuckoos in other nests for the rest of it. He had eleven sons, poor dribbling wrecks of boys and none of them veered very far from their father's path. You didn't in the old days. A bad reputation was a terrible thing and stuck from one generation to the next."

"Clarissa knows you married into the Ayers family, but does she know you're one by blood?"

Freda's face creased into a knowing smile. "I'm saving that one up for the perfect moment. It's the stuff of fantasy and I can't imagine when it'll be, but it will come. Everyone will enjoy watching her face change from disdain to agony when she realises she should have been getting on side with me, instead of slamming the doors of Harborough society in my face."

Emma sighed. "Wait until she realises I own Wingate Hall."

Freda snorted. "Maybe we should break both bits of news at the same time and see what happens?"

"You're a wicked woman." Emma allowed herself a smile. "Now play Scrabble with your oldie. When do I get to meet him?"

"He's a Scrabble partner, my dear; nothing more. You take care." Freda kissed the top of Emma's head and left, taking the lightness from the room with her. Emma sighed in her wake and laid her head on her forearms, peering at the photo from close range. Frank Jameson looked stern in the photograph, his unsmiling eyes staring through the ages without compassion.

Emma moved it out of the way and peered at the same view in an older photograph, the children wearing clothes from the late 1800s. Emma's eyes almost crossed as she spotted something in the background over the male teacher's left shoulder. She reached for the magnifying glass Freda used for identifying children's faces. The corner of an object looked familiar and Emma gasped.

The last four letters of the plaque's top line were almost readable, hanging next to the rear doors of the main building. Emma raked the sea of sepia colours looking to identify more of the surroundings and then she left the office, powering along the corridor at a trot. A little boy sidled towards her, his fingers entirely covered in glue. "Om er, miss. You're not allowed to run," he said, scandal lacing his squeaky voice.

"It's a fast walk," she answered. "Aren't you meant to be washing that off?"

He nodded. "Yep, but I want it to dry before I peel

it. It's more fun."

The teaching assistant from the reception class in which the four-year-olds were sequestered, appeared in a rush, closing the door behind her against the cacophony of noise. "Robert Powell!" she announced in a voice of steel. "Get that washed off now."

"Nooooo," he began and Emma smiled at the long suffering assistant and continued on her mission.

It was icy outside and a breeze blew leaves into a whirl in one corner. Emma stood in the playground and stared at the building, mentally placing the rows of children and the schoolmaster. The red brick grimaced back at her as the weather battered its surface for yet another season and Emma saw nothing. Clambering onto the railing which surrounded two sides of the steps, Emma ran a shaking hand over the bricks. Her fingers found what her eyes could not and the two little indentations revealed themselves. Filled over decades by dirt and dust, the holes were unnoticeable to the naked eye. But their presence betrayed the telltale drill sites for two large screws which once held the plaque in place. For a few years, the school displayed its true date of inception but at some point before 1900, it was stripped of its history. The question was why? And by who?

CHAPTER SIXTEEN

Sam's computer yielded the missing link between the disgraced school master and the opening ceremony. The 1841 census revealed the delightful occupants of the home of the Reverend Peter John Jameson, incumbent of St Martin's Church in Leicester. His seven children included the eldest son, Peter Humphrey Jameson. Emma rested her chin on her forearms and peered at the screen, sighing when the expected sense of victory didn't come. The vicar of St Martin's was the guest at the opening because his son was the new school master. Four years later the same family reeled as their son hung from the neck until dead in a stone walled courtyard in Newgate Prison. "I wonder if he died or if his sentence was reduced to life imprisonment," Emma muttered to herself.

"What?" Sam dropped the cable he was working on and swore, darting a nervous glance at Emma. "Who died?"

"Oh, nobody," she said, watching the screen flicker under the strip lighting. "But I've solved the mystery of the school opening. Mr Dalton and his team of merry widows are definitely five years too late."

"Bloody hell!" Sam exclaimed. "That'll eff their plans up." He chuckled. "I'm not bothered. Less work for me."

"That's the spirit, Sam. Now I have to find a way of telling Mr Dalton." Emma laid her face sideways on her arms, tiredness creating a weight in her chest.

Nicky spent the last three nights in her bed, clinging to her in between bouts of tossing and turning. It was exhausting when added to the extensive walk and bus ride to get anywhere. "Isn't it holidays yet?" Emma sighed. "I think I've had enough of this celebration; I should just leave."

"Brave lady," Sam chortled. "Drop your bomb shell and run, why don't ya?"

"Yeah, I guess it's cowardly. Come on, hurry up man! Get into the attic and fetch boxes. And I need your muscles to carry that delivery of supplies from the front office, please?"

"You're so bloody demanding, woman!" Sam smirked. "Yeah, I'll get it. Just let me finish this repair. It's Mr Dalton's computer lead. The cleaner ran the vacuum over it. I think it's buggered." He picked up the squiggly cable and opened the door.

"Take your time. I'll have a nap." Emma closed her eyes, lulled by the false sense of peace in the office.

The lunchtime hand bell rung by a junior school child, made sure Emma didn't relax for long. A knock on the door heralded Nicky, looking much happier. "Hi, Mama," he said, poking his face into the gap. "Can I 'ave a cuddle?"

"Yeah, sure baby. I don't think Sam will mind."

Nicky pushed his way in and closed the door behind him, bouncing across to Emma and putting his head on her lap. Emma stroked his hair, drawing comfort from his nearness, gratitude burgeoning in her heart. "Did you see Daddy at playtime?" Nicky asked, his voice muffled in her skirt.

"No." Emma felt a sickness in her stomach that he hadn't sought her out. Her sense of reason asked why he would after their last conversation. "Where was he,

Nicky?" She kept her voice level.

"He was walking past. One of the junior classes went to the museum, so as a very special treat, my class went to the ball courts to play soccer. I waved to him and we spoke through the fence. He said he loved me and he'll see me soon."

"That's nice," Emma replied, keeping the circular stroking motion going on her son's back although her body was tense. A gnawing ache yawned in her heart and she fought to close it, changing the subject. "Don't you need to get your lunch?"

"Yep. But it's cabbage today, I hate cabbage. I can smell it from here."

Emma sniffed. "Ah well, eating cabbage stops you behaving like one."

"Is that true?" Nicky's head shot up and he searched her face. "I'll go get some then." He reached his little face up to hers for a kiss on the lips and offered a stunning smile. "Love you, Mummy."

"Love you too, baby," Emma replied, smiling for the child's benefit.

Nicky battled with the door handle and turned back to her as he squeezed through the gap. "Anyway, it's not Sam. It's Mr Arden to me." The door closed behind him with a click.

"Bloody hell!" Emma groaned and laid her head back on her forearms.

CHAPTER SEVENTEEN

"What are you saying?" Mr Dalton paled, the colour draining like a chemical reaction. He reached behind him for his chair and pulled it nearer so his bottom sank into its folds with relief. "Explain again."

"It won't help," Emma sighed. "I've been over and over it and the school is 155 years old. The Church of England built it in 1860. The bell was added five years later and if I could get up there, I might find another inscription relating to its dedication. We don't have all the photos from that time but a very faded print of the building dated 1865 doesn't show the bell or its housing. It wasn't there."

"It has to be a mistake!" Mr Dalton balled his fists and his colour returned. "The bell was mended four years ago and it definitely said 1865 on it." He glared at Emma and she felt pity for him as he postured and tossed his head in an attempt to regain control of the situation. "The celebrations are booked! Past pupils are flying in from overseas. The committee's been working on this for years!" His eyes bulged and Emma winced, anticipating a medical emergency. "We can't call it off now. Who'd know if we put away this damn plaque and pretended it didn't exist?" His eyes glinted with a peculiar diamond hardness as he contemplated the unthinkable.

"I'd know!" Emma let him hear the shock in her voice. "And I've taken digital scans of everything I've uncovered so far." *Except the plaque*, she reminded herself. "Do it right, or don't do it at all." She pursed her lips and hoped he didn't ask to see the plaque. Sam called in sick and Emma squashed the urge to give him hospital-worthy sickness of the kick in the nuts variety. A feeling in the pit of her stomach told her the plaque was in danger.

Mr Dalton's shoulders slumped. "I don't believe this."

"I'm sorry," Emma said. "A parent doing this mightn't have dug so deep into the history. They'd slap a few pictures on a display board and watch everyone spill coffee over the originals. But that's not what you employed me for, is it? The remit you gave me from the Board of Governors was; *to fully investigate, catalogue and digitise your archives, storing them in such a way as to ensure longevity for the generations to come.*" Emma quoted straight from her mandate, written as a wordy and noble nod to history which would now damn and derail their plans. "That's what I'm doing," Emma said. "I'm preserving your history for future generations. If you want me to stop, I will. It can all go back into the attic and be forgotten for another 145 years. But the next person who looks through it will end up right back where I am."

"I feel sick." Mr Dalton put his head on his forearms and took a few steadying swallows. He popped his head up and looked expectantly at Emma. "I'll call an extraordinary meeting of the Board and celebration committee members. You can come along and talk to them and explain what's happened."

Emma stood up and shook her head. "No thanks. I'm happy to write a timeline and give you a statement of what I found, but it's best if I'm not there when you make your decision. At some point after the 1884 school photo was taken, someone removed the plaque from the wall and hid it. The 100th anniversary subsequently occurred five years too late, which is probably why everyone assumed this year should be the 150th. I believe in the truth and I can't work with anything less. Let me know what the board says." She stood and left the room, closing the door behind her and leaving the headmaster to his devastation.

Emma dropped the timeline and supporting documents on the desk of the new school secretary an hour later, smiled and left. Outside the school gate she paused, contemplating the bus ride home only to repeat it an hour later to fetch Nicky. On a whim, Emma turned left and walked through the park, enjoying the kiss of the watery sunshine on her face. The journey west took ten minutes and Emma felt the day's stress losing its hold on her.

On Newcombe Street she paused, hoping Allaine didn't mind having her afternoon gate crashed. The street felt familiar and Emma looked wistfully towards Rohan's house at the other end, remembering her arrival in the market town as his guest a few months ago. She paused at Allaine's front gate, curiosity getting the better of her. In a few short minutes, Emma had ducked down a lane between two houses and walked behind the row. Long gardens stretched out towards the lane and Emma's footsteps shortened as she realised the futility of her mission. Only the upstairs windows were visible, too far away to allow her to snoop. She didn't bother walking towards the back gate of Rohan's house, turning on her heel and dragging her feet back up the lane to the street. She skirted the puddles and kicked at loose stones, pondering her spoiled relationship with a heavy heart.

Emma hopped around on Allaine's front porch before ringing the doorbell. Her boots were filthy and she slipped them off, struggling with the left one. The sound of a baby crying drew Emma's attention and she stood up in her socks and peered up the street. A redhead stepped onto the pavement and Emma recognised the click of Rohan's gate as it closed behind her. The baby had white blonde hair and kicked legs clad in a blue sleep suit; his cry pitiful. Emma watched as he screwed up his little face into a grimace and rubbed his eyes, the relationship to Nicky overpowering. Her breath caught in her chest as Rohan strode down the path, unlocking the dark Mercedes as he let the gate close behind him.

Emma inhaled like a balloon on a fill setting, unable to release. She heard the moan issue from her lips and felt the world shift on its axis as her pulse rate increased. The redhead slipped into the back of the Mercedes and closed the door as Rohan started the engine, nosing the vehicle from between parked cars. Emma's gasp exhaled in a whoosh of misery and she pressed a hand to her mouth as the expensive car slid past, still sporting the brick's ugly dent in the passenger door. Rohan glanced up once as Emma galvanised herself and turned, hammering on Allaine's door with her fists. She saw the dismay in his face and screamed for her friend. "Allie, help me," she sobbed without dignity. "Allie, please!"

The sound of screeching brakes filled the street as the door opened inwards and Emma tumbled into her friend's arms. "Close the door," Emma howled. "Close the door! Don't let him in, please."

Allaine slammed the front door as Rohan shouted, his voice carrying through the glass panel. "Emma, please. Listen, *dorogaya*. Let me in!"

Emma's complexion was white with shock and she slid down the wall in agony as Allaine stared from her prone body to the front door. Rohan knocked on the glass, his voice sounding panicked and full of distress. "Emma, talk to me."

"No!" Emma's friend defended her with loyalty and defiance. "Go away, Rohan. She clearly doesn't want to see you. Get off my property or I'll call the police!" Allaine swished the door curtain across the glass and threw herself on the ground next to Emma. "Sweetheart, what's happened? What did he do?"

Emma couldn't talk. Her voice was strangled by the sobs which wrung from her chest until she felt she couldn't breathe. The sound of a vehicle honking its horn at Rohan's abandoned Mercedes drew him away from Allaine's front door and she heaved a sigh of relief. "Shall I get Will?" she asked. "Is Rohan violent?" She didn't seem reassured by her guest's shake of the head. "Emma, you're scaring me," Allaine said, feeling the intensity of Emma's hold on her arms. "How can I help you?"

"I don't know, I don't know," Emma repeated, over and over again. She clutched her upper abdomen and groaned. "It hurts so much. I can't bear it."

"I'm calling Will." Allaine stood up.

"No," Emma moaned. "You don't understand." She pushed herself sideways and lay on the beech parquet floor, her face white and her shoulders heaving, tears dripping off the end of her nose. "I think I'm gonna be sick." The hand clamped over her mouth prevented the immediate action but as Allaine ran back with her washing up bowl, the sight of food stains and a piece of chunked up carrot stuck to the side were enough to seal the deal. Having eaten nothing, Emma threw up a cup of tea and a glass of water, Allaine rubbing her back with tender fingers.

"There's nothing left now," she said eventually, taking the bowl away and washing Emma's hot face with a wet tea towel. "Come outside and get some fresh air. We'll sit on the bench and I'll fetch you a drink of water."

Emma's body trembled with involuntary spasms and she moved like an elderly woman. Allaine steadied her as they walked through the house and emerged from the back door like two octogenarians out for a stroll. "Sit here," Allaine said with authority, tucking Emma's coat around her knees. "It's freezing but take deep breaths and it'll help. I won't be long." She returned with a strange purple looking mixture fizzing in warm water. Emma pulled a face.

"What's that?"

"Rehydration powders. You can take them while you're pregnant, I checked. Kaylee had a dreadful bout of the squirts a few months ago and I had packets left."

Emma took a sip and tasted blackcurrant. She swallowed and struggled to hold the liquid in her stomach.

"Keep going slowly," Allaine urged. "You've clearly eaten nothing today and not drunk enough. It's after lunchtime, Emma. You need to take better care of yourself for the baby's sake." She looked at her friend with maternal concern and stroked her forearm through the coat material. "Now tell me what happened earlier?"

Emma lurched through her sad tale, beginning with Christopher's bombshell about Rohan arriving in town but staying away, to the little family emerging from

Rohan's house further up the street. Allaine knitted her brows. "So, you think he's got another family holed up at his place?"

Emma nodded and took another sip of the drink. "The baby was identical to Nicky; white blonde hair and facial features. He even grizzled like Nicky used to. Rohan put them in the car and drove off and they're the reason he stayed in town before coming home."

"So, how old did the baby look?" Allaine asked. "Maybe Rohan was involved with this other woman before you came on the scene and chose to stay with you after she discovered she was pregnant."

"The baby looked about a year old," Emma sighed. "I only arrived four months ago. Rohan told me there was never anyone else, which means he lied."

"Will charged a guy with bigamy the other day," Allaine said conversationally. "He lived two completely separate lives in different houses. There were four children in one and two in another. They literally lived within a couple of miles of each other. He only got caught out because a teacher moved from the school at the top end of town to that new school over near the industrial estate and he turned up for parents' evening with a different family. She asked him about his son and the wife looked stunned. After that it detonated like a bomb and the wife went to the police. Will said he wouldn't have the energy; the poor guy looked knackered and said he was pleased to be caught. Crazy hey?" Allaine looked sideways at Emma's devastation and bit her lip. "Sorry, Em. I'm sorry. That was really unhelpful." She put her arms around her friend as Emma dissolved into tears again.

"What will you do?" Allaine asked later as the women sat in the kitchen. Emma pushed a biscuit round a plate in rigid, triangular motions and frowned.

"Buy a car."

Allaine blinked and put her hand over Emma's to stop the irritating movement. "Eat it, Emma. If not for you, then do it for your baby." She watched as Emma took the smallest bite and chewed. "I meant long term. What will you do? Although I suppose you do need a car now, but that's fine. You hated Rohan's anyway."

"Yeah." Emma swallowed. "Where do people buy cars round here? I haven't noticed any garages in town."

"There aren't many. People go to Leicester or buy privately."

"I can't risk private sales. I don't know enough about cars and Leicester or Northampton are a bit out of the way unless I go car shopping on a bus which seems ridiculous."

"Will's selling his Ford if you're interested. It's a year old but probably too expensive."

"The little SUV with the wheel on the back? Why's he selling it?"

Allaine smirked. "Everyone at the police station calls it 'The Girly Car' and he's had enough. He wanted it because it's higher than a saloon but they've done nothing but make fun of him for the past year."

"The red one?" Emma took another cautious bite. "I like it. I'll buy it."

"Hang on, you haven't even driven it!" Allaine laughed. "And Will bought it new so I've no idea what he wants for it."

"It can't be worse than Rohan's big car and I like the look of it. Ask him what he wants for it and I'll buy it. I'll have to get insurance sorted though. I drove Lucya's old car in Wales and it crapped out on us just before she died. I was on her insurance so never had my own."

"Ouch, that'll cost you," Allaine mused. "And you're under twenty five."

Emma shrugged. "Anton left me enough."

"And you've got your little job at the school."

"Yeah." Emma rolled her eyes. "I don't want to talk about that right now."

Allaine looked worried. "You sound like someone whose world is unravelling before her eyes."

Emma bit her lip and swiped away another tear. "That's how it feels. Text Will and ask him and I'll sort it out as soon as possible."

Allaine fluffed around on her phone, sending a text to Will and watching Emma fight the biscuit. She pushed a glass of water towards her. "Drink that too. And I'll be cross if I see you treating your body like that again. You must eat and drink properly when you're pregnant; it's irresponsible."

"Yes, Mum," Emma replied and reluctantly took a sip of the water. "Allaine," she said, the glass half way between her lips and the table, "When the baby comes, would you be its godmother?"

Allaine blinked as her phone vibrated on the table. "Really? Me?"

Emma nodded. "I know it seems a bit inappropriate now, but I really want to know there's someone lovely there for my children if anything happens to me. You've proved yourself over and over and I can't think of anyone better. Would you consider it?"

Allaine shook her head and Emma's shoulders drooped. "Of course I don't have to think about it, idiot. Yes, I'd be honoured. Where would you have the christening?"

"I don't know. Your church?"

Allaine pulled Emma into a firm hug and kissed her on the temple. "If you want. We don't call it a christening and we don't dunk or flick water. We pray over the children and call ourselves prayer-parents. Then the child decides when they're older if they'd like to be baptised and we do full immersion. But I'll go anywhere you want me to, it's up to you."

"Your way sounds nice," Emma sighed. "Poor Nicky didn't even get one."

Allaine gave her a squeeze. "Christen them both at the same time."

"Can you do that?" Emma said and smiled for the first time since she arrived. "My dad was an Anglican vicar and wore robes and stuff. It always seemed very formal and a little false. He blessed baby after baby and then never saw them again. At least everyone at your church knows Nicky from the times he's been with you and Will."

"They love him," Allaine snorted. "He stands on his chair and plays air guitar during the singing. He's hilarious!"

Emma nodded and ran her hands over her stomach. Her lips turned upwards in a tiny smile. "The baby's moving again; just little flutters but I can feel it. At least I have Rohan's children, even if I don't have him." Emma pressed lightly on her stomach, connecting with her child. Allaine put her hand over the top.

"Then promise me you'll take better care of yourself? If you've made me godparent then I'll make it my business to tell you off when you don't. I take my responsibilities very seriously!" She shot Emma a stern look and the other woman nodded.

Allaine's phone buzzed in a continuous frenzy on

the table and she picked it up and winked at Emma. "It's Will," she said, standing. "Hi, love. Emma's interested in your car." She pulled a face and rolled her eyes at Emma. "Sorry, I didn't see your text; we were chatting. Ok, I'll ask her. Yes, I'll ask her now." Allaine turned to Emma and named the price he paid for the new vehicle a year ago and the price he'd accept. Emma nodded. Allaine went back to her call and grabbed a pen and paper from the side, scribbling frantically on it. "Ok, I'll look it up now. Yes, I'm sure she'll let you know soon." Allaine ended the call and fired up her laptop. "He wants me to check the retail price of that make and model online for you."

"Why?" Emma shook her head. "I trust him."

"He doesn't want you to feel ripped off, I guess. Look." Allaine spun the screen around and Emma peered at the pictures of cars, scrolling through myriad prices and bits of information intended to help potential purchasers. Allaine pointed at a picture of a blue SUV like Will's. "That's the same make and model but it's got less mileage on it. Are you sure you wouldn't rather go to a garage? I can drive you there tomorrow if you like."

"No, it's fine. I want the red one and Will's set a good price. But what will he do if I buy his?"

"Give me my little car back hopefully!" Allaine snorted. "I've had this old ute for years, since before we sold the farm and Will joined the police. He's running around in that instead to avoid embarrassment. I use his red one or walk and last time I drove Kaylee to Brownies, he complained I made it dirty and he had to wash it again for the advert photograph. I haven't used it since."

"So it's here?" Emma looked interested. "I didn't

see it on the street."

"It's at the back. We don't keep our cars on the road. We drive down the lane and in the gate at the bottom of the garden."

"Yeah, that's what Rohan did when we lived up the road," Emma said, her face taking on a wistful look. "If he'd done that today I'd never have known what he was up to." She finished the glass of water and pressed the last bite of biscuit into her mouth. "Come on. I want a test drive and then I'll ring my solicitor and get him to transfer the money straight into your bank account. Please can I use your phone to get insurance?"

CHAPTER EIGHTEEN

"Mum, why are you driving Kaylee's 'Girly Car'?"

"I bought it." Emma took the book bag from Nicky's hand and put it on the back seat. The weight of it betrayed the brick still inside. "Kaylee's daddy let me take it today but the money will go into his bank account tomorrow morning. I've got my own insurance policy now." Emma smiled and looked pleased with herself. "Would you like to go to the shops before they close and choose a brand new booster seat?"

Nicky shrugged and climbed into the back of the vehicle, the red paint shining under the lamp light in the growing darkness. "Can Daddy come?"

"Not tonight," Emma said brightly. "I don't know what he's doing."

"He's probably at home," Nicky said, with hope in his voice and Emma raised her eyebrows.

"I doubt it." She afforded herself a small smirk at the success of her busy afternoon. Organising the insurance policy on Allaine's phone was a relatively quick affair, helped by the use of her new credit card. The other call was to the company who maintained the security system at Wingate Hall. They rung her as she waited in the playground to advise her of the new gate and alarm code.

Nicky was quiet as he chose himself a bright red booster seat to match the car. His brow knitted as Emma paid at the checkout and she pulled his head in to her waist to comfort him. "It's ok, baby," she whispered. "Uncle Anton made sure we wouldn't have to worry like we used to."

"I think I'll always be bothered," he said. "It's not naughty, is it, to worry about not having enough pennies?"

"Course not, sweetheart." Emma took the carrier bag from the cashier with a smile and handed it to her son. He hefted its bulk outside even though it reached almost to the ground. Emma squatted next to him before unlocking the vehicle, getting eye contact and making sure Nicky understood. "Nicky, I behaved badly this morning towards your father because he hasn't been honest with me about some important things. I know how much you love having him in your life and I promise not to get in the way. I'll organise things where you can be with him by yourself, but just for now, I don't want him at the house or near me. Do you understand?"

Nicky shrugged in the darkness, his face oozing misery. "Not really. I love you being together like a proper mummy and daddy. It's what I always prayed for."

Emma stroked his cheek. "I liked it too, baby. I thought we'd be happy forever but sometimes things don't work out like we want them to."

"What did Daddy lie about?" Nicky's vibrant blue eyes fixed on Emma's face, searching for answers. She swallowed, spite making her want to tell him but wisdom advising her not to.

"Some important things. I'll explain when you're older, I promise, but at the moment we need to concentrate on putting our lives together and enjoying the lovely things Uncle Anton left for us. I've bought a car now which means we can go places and explore and we'll keep renovating Anton's house and make it into a beautiful home. But I can't do any of it without you, Nicky. Nothing matters without you in my life."

"And the baby?" Nicky asked and Emma nodded.

"Yes, definitely. We've got heaps to look forward to and things will work out; they always do."

"Ok. Love you, Mummy."

"I love you too, baby." Emma kissed Nicky's forehead. "Let's put your new booster seat in the car and go home."

Nicky stared out of the window as the dark countryside whipped by. Emma indicated and turned left into the driveway, almost rear ending Rohan's Mercedes. He unwound his long frame from the car as Emma sat rigidly in the driver's seat with her hands clamped around the steering wheel. "Daddy!" Nicky squealed with excitement and started unbuckling himself.

"No, Nicky! Sit still!" Emma got out, locking the vehicle with the key fob. Rohan walked towards her and they met in the space between the vehicles, back lit by Emma's powerful headlights.

"You borrowed a car?" Rohan said softly, jerking his head towards the vehicle. Emma gritted her teeth and didn't answer. He licked his lips and thrust his hands into his pockets, keeping his legs slightly splayed to brace himself. Rohan towered over Emma without meaning to and she tilted her head back to watch his face. "I need to explain things to you," he began and Emma shook her head.

"No, you don't Rohan. I thought you loved me but you don't rate me enough to be honest with me. You have this whole other life I know nothing about and I can't live like this anymore. Please move your car. Nicky and I want to go home."

"You changed the gate code." Rohan's voice was laced with hurt.

"I don't want you here, Rohan. I'll gather your gear up and drop it at your other house in the next few days."

"But I don't want this, Emma. I just need to explain..."

"No, Rohan, I'm done. Your sordid love life doesn't interest me, thanks. I thought the problem was your double life as the Actuary but it's clearly more than that."

"Sordid? Love life?" Rohan screwed his face up and shook his head. Emma flicked her long curls over her shoulder and squared her shoulders.

"I've spoken to Nicky and when we've got our separation amicably sorted out, I'm happy for you to see him by agreement. Until then, stay away from us."

"I don't want to stay away from either of you!" Rohan's eyes flashed in the headlights and he took a step towards her.

Emma stepped out of range and raised her hand to stop him following her. "I mean it, Rohan, don't touch me!" Her voice cracked and she felt the sob well up into her throat. "Just go!"

"Em, I know about the messages Dolan sent you," Rohan said, lowering his voice so Nicky couldn't hear.

"I didn't know they were from him!" Emma snapped. "You can't hold that against me. Don't try using that as an excuse for your behaviour!"

"I'm not, Em, I promise. This isn't tit for tat, *dorogaya*."

"Don't call me that, I'm not your girl!"

"Shh, Em, please. Nikolai's watching us." Rohan took another step towards her and gripped her wrists. "Stop!" Rohan hissed as Emma struggled. "This isn't fair on him!"

"You should have thought of that!" Emma snapped. "You've lied to me!"

"Emma, my new tech traced the messages. I can't tell you the truth about anything because of him; because of Dolan. I couldn't ring you or tell you where I was because of *him*."

"So you're keeping another woman and a baby because of Christopher Dolan texting me?" Emma sneered. "You have to be kidding! That's the best excuse for infidelity I've ever heard!"

"Infidelity!" Rohan spat, anger surfacing. "*Ya ne veryu etomu!*"

"I don't care what you *believe!*" Emma stormed. "Let go of me and move your car or I'll call the police. I'll tell them everything, Rohan. I'll tell them about the Actuary and everything you've ever done which has crossed the line. So *don't* push me!"

Rohan let go of Emma's wrists as though she was contaminated. He stepped back and took a deep breath. Steeling his face into a smile, he walked to the side of the car and put his palm against Nicky's window. Nicky placed his tiny hand against it and Emma turned her face away, her eyes pricking with tears at her cruelty. The car key in her hand prevented Nicky winding the window down and she heard him crying from her spot between the cars.

"I love you, *syn*," Rohan called to the sobbing boy. With a stiff posture and a face filled with anger, Rohan left his wailing son and stepped in front of Emma. "Get rid of Dolan!" he told her forcefully. Then he dipped his head and covered her cold lips with his. Emma inhaled his familiar scent and tried to suppress the need in her gut to plunge into his safe, strong arms. Instead she turned her face away and felt Rohan's warm breath in her hair. "*Ya lyublyu tebya*, Emma Andreyev," he whispered and stroked her cheek with the back of his hand. *I love you.* "Don't believe everything you hear."

He revved the powerful engine and swung the car around in the small space with skill. Rohan smiled and waved at Nicky but ignored Emma, leaving her on the dark driveway facing the equally dark, chilly manor house high on the hill.

Emma climbed back into the red car and started the engine, keying the new number into the gate lock through the open driver's window. She drove up the driveway in silence, hearing Nicky's hysterical sobs in the seat behind her. Her heart constricted in her chest and by the time they reached the front door, both were sobbing.

CHAPTER NINETEEN

Emma slept late the next morning, waking stiff and tired despite the eight hours of sleep. She groaned as her eyes opened to the grey light filtering through the thick drapes. "I think someone rolled a steam roller over me in the night," she hissed, bending her joints to test them.

"Aye, you look like it too, so yer do."

Emma shot to a sitting position, her dark hair curled around her face and her tee shirt clinging to her. Christopher Dolan smirked and shifted uncomfortably. He sat on Rohan's side of the bed, one hand resting on the foot board. "Don't you fancy a quick tumble with me instead of that great Russian eejit?" he asked, his voice soft. A few strands of black hair slipped into his eyes, giving him a seductive air.

"No!" Emma folded her arms to cover the obvious outline of her breasts and raised her knees. "How did you get in?"

Christopher lifted the bunch of keys in his hand and slipped them back into his jacket pocket. "Mind you," he smirked, "I didn't need them. I could've gotten in anyways."

"I changed the codes and set the alarm downstairs. How did you get past that?" Emma's face showed panic. If he could get in, so could Rohan and anyone else he'd upset.

"Aw, steady on, Em. You set the alarm when I was already in and I know the override for the gate code

161

anyway."

Emma exhaled and closed her eyes. "Please go away. You've done enough damage."

"Aye, sorry about that." The smirk gave him away, lifting his handsome features into a jovial expression which infuriated Emma.

"You're not sorry at all. Get out before Nicky wakes."

Christopher pursed his lips and Emma lost her temper. She slid from the bed and stalked to the bathroom, the tee shirt exposing her shapely legs and the bottom of her knickers. Christopher watched her progress across the room with intense interest and stood as though to accompany her. Emma's eyes flashed in warning and he sat down again.

Emma sat on the toilet with her head in her hands, ruing her sudden change of fortune. The flush covered the sound of Nicky's pounding feet and he burst into the bathroom as she dried her hands on a towel. "Mum!" His eyes were wide and full of fear and Emma panicked.

"It's not what you think," she began, raking the bedroom with her eyes but seeing no sign of Christopher through the partially open doorway.

"Mum, there's cops everywhere! Outside the front gates. I seen 'em from my window!" Blonde hair stuck up on his head and his pyjama bottoms were askew, showing a pale hip under the flannelette fabric. Nicky grabbed her hand to drag her into the bedroom. "Come and look!"

Emma followed her excited son, staring around her empty bedroom with surprise and watching for signs of the Irishman. Nicky ran ahead to his bedroom at the front of the building. "Hurry, Mum!"

"Yep, coming." Emma bobbed down to look under her four poster bed and heard a snort of derision from the walk in wardrobe.

"Look, Mummy, look!" Nicky tugged her hand and yanked his curtains back to reveal a grey wintry Saturday swathed in low overhead cloud. In the distance beyond the trees were a series of blinking red and blue strobes. "Can we go and look?" Nicky begged, excitement dancing in his eyes.

"A traffic policeman probably pulled someone over in front of our driveway," Emma groaned. "They'll be gone before we get there and staring at people in their misfortune is mean, isn't it? That's not what we do." Emma ruffled the white blonde hair and listened to a muffled bark from downstairs. "I can't believe it's after eight in the morning." She yawned. "Poor Farrell probably needs the toilet."

Nicky tore around his room, decimating drawers as he searched for clothes he could pull on at speed. He settled on a pair of tracksuit pants which were too small and an old sweater with hard glue stains on the front. Emma exhaled and shook her head. "You haven't had a shower and you're not going down there by yourself!"

Nicky halted half way through pouring his bottom into a pair of briefs and eyed his mother in horror. "But you'll be ages! Can't I just ride my bike and take a little look? I'll pretend I'm getting the post from the box." His blue eyes looked eager and filled with enthusiasm. Emma remembered the bereft, quiet little boy who ate his microwave meal in her bed, only half watching the movie she put on the TV. She felt grateful for his new focus and relented.

"Fine! But Nicky, I'm warning you, if you open those gates there'll be bigger trouble than you can handle."

"I won't." The child hopped around the room pulling on his socks, his face all eagerness. "Where did Daddy put my skateboard?" He stopped in front of her, his little face tilted upwards to read her expression.

"It's in one of the stables, I think," Emma replied. "The first one on the left."

"Thanks!" Nicky tore down the long hallway to the stairs and Emma shouted after him, "Wear your elbow pads!"

She heaved a huge sigh and stared at the commotion beyond the gates. A plain black van pulled up, just visible through the trees and was joined by another strobing police car. "It looks like more than just a traffic offender," she mused to herself, turning to find herself inches away from Christopher's strong chest.

"Aye, bit of a crime scene outside yer gate, then?" he stated, as though he knew the answer. "I wouldn't have let my wee boy go down to stare at a dead man's body, but I'd be a shite parent anyway, so who am I to criticise?"

"A body?" Emma's voice sounded flat, even to her. "There's a dead body outside my property?"

"Well, technically it's *on* your property, because that wee piece of driveway belonged to Anton, so I'm sure it belongs to you now." Christopher smirked at the horror in Emma's face. He smoothed an index finger across her brow, pushing her fringe out of her eyes. Emma slapped his hand away and took a step back, wedging her thighs against the hot radiator and releasing a hiss of pain. She had nowhere to go but forward into his body. "And I don't hide under a lady's bed, Em. It's not dignified. I believe in hiding in plain sight, love."

"You Irish idiot!" Emma gave him a hearty shove and Christopher stepped back, openly laughing at her. "What did you do?" Emma pointed a shaking finger at the scene through the window, a scene towards which her six year old son currently skated, trailed by an excited, barking black spaniel.

"I was waitin' to tell ya," Christopher snorted, thoroughly enjoying Emma's horror. "But you looked so beautiful, so ya did. It was just a wee accident, Em. And not entirely my doing. Maybe you'd like to send them the Actuary's way. That'd be a mighty fine revenge, so it would. Then he'd have to tell everyone who the wee family at his place belonged to, wouldn't he?"

"You killed someone on my doorstep to flush Rohan out?" Emma sounded appalled and her eyes widened in anger. She set off towards the door. "I'm going down there right now to turn you in!"

Christopher snatched at Emma's wrist and spun her round so she cannoned into his chest. "That'd be a very bad idea, sweetheart." His fingers were unyielding on her soft flesh, biting into the bone and hurting. Emma struggled, but it was pointless.

"Are you threatening me?" Her voice sounded hushed and strained.

Christopher shook his head. "No, Emma. It's a promise. That wee dead guy out there came here after you. Your husband brought his crap home and he didn't even realise. There's nothing to tie that body to me or you, but now's your chance. If you want rid of Rohan and the Actuary, now would be a great time to follow through. Once he's out of the way, the Contessa's men will have no need of you. It's him or you, Em. Choose."

Emma broke free and pushed Christopher's chest hard enough to take him by surprise. His strong body moved back a few steps, giving her passage. "You don't know, do you?" Her terrified eyes searched his for an answer, her bottom lip trembling and her fingers unclenching and clenching into fists. "You don't know who the woman and baby are, do you? For once, Christopher Dolan, even I know more than you." Emma turned and jogged from the room, running a hand through her unruly hair.

In her bedroom she threw on underwear, a jumper and a pair of tracksuit pants. Grabbing her wellington boots from the built in cupboard next to the front door, she pushed her bare feet inside. The clatter of a skateboard hitting the stone steps heralded a puffing Nicky and a black dog, both equally thrilled to meet Emma coming down the steps. "Get down, Faz, don't jump up!" Emma chastised the bouncing hound and turned to Nicky, trying to disguise the shake in her voice. "What's going on, baby?"

"The policemens want to see you, Mummy. There's heaps and heaps of them. They had a dummy under a blanket. They're doing practices and want to know if they can come in. There's a van with dogs in it though and they did barkings at Faz. He didn't like it so I came back." Nicky's face looked troubled as he fondled a sleek, black ear. Farrell looked up at him in doggy adoration.

"Ok, keep Faz here and I'll walk down and see what they want." Emma smiled at her son, hoping she offered reassurance and not what she really felt; a mixture of trepidation and doom.

"But I wanna come too!" The whine in Nicky's voice penetrated Emma's nerve endings and she gritted her teeth and huffed.

"You just said the police dogs scared Farrell! Why would you want to take him back there again? Poor dog. Take him into the kitchen and give him breakfast. There's a new sack of biscuits in the pantry but only one scoopful! I don't want him having health problems."

"Ah, yeya! Fazzy I can feed you today. Come on, then." Nicky patted the side of his leg and the dog smiled and let his tongue loll out the side of his lips. They trotted up the steps into the reception hall, leaving the front door wide open.

Emma closed it, stepped over the temporarily discarded skateboard and set off down the driveway at a brisk walk. The air was icy, moisture hanging in it and bathing Emma in tiny, uncomfortable droplets. By the time she reached the gates, her hair hung limply down her back, her fringe swathing her face in glittering curls. The police dogs in the back of the van set up a racket and Emma hung back from the entrance, waiting.

A man in a suit approached the ornate filigree rods and peered through. "Hello, madam. My name's Detective Paul Barker." He held up a pocket sized, black folder and flipped it open, revealing a replica of his face on a police warrant card. Emma peered at the picture and then back at its owner.

"How can I help you?" She kept her tone formal, as though merely interested and not desperately frightened. "My son came down for the post and said you wanted to see me."

"That's right. I'd like to come in."

Emma eyed the barking Alsatians with obvious fear and then looked back at the detective. "I don't want them in." She pointed a cursory finger in their direction. "They frightened my dog."

"It's fine. Just me." The detective smiled, revealing perfectly aligned white teeth and a handsome smile. He was dark haired and shaped like an athlete, his tight suit fitting snugly over one of nature's better male bodies. Emma nodded and pressed the release for the gate, situated a few metres inside the driveway. The gates moved inwards with a faint mechanical whine and the detective stepped into the gap.

Paul Barker walked up to Emma and offered his hand. Hers felt tiny and cold in comparison and he frowned. "You're freezing. I'll walk you back up to the house." He touched Emma lightly on the shoulder and she tensed as a reflex. Panic bit at her heart and the urge to spew everything out to this man was overwhelming. His persona was kindly, but Emma detected shrewdness beneath the gentle veneer.

"What's going on?" she asked, hearing her teeth chatter. "My son said it was a practice for something."

"Mmnn," the man tutted and turned stunning green eyes on Emma. "I told him that because he appeared just as my colleagues were erecting that white tent over the body. I didn't want him to have nightmares."

"Body?" Emma's voice sounded flat and she stopped abruptly on the gravel. *Damn you, Christopher Dolan.* A dreadful thought snaked terror into her heart as it occurred to her that the victim might be Rohan. "Who is it?" she asked, her fingers rising to cover her lips. "Was it someone coming to see me?" A hitch caught in her chest and her other hand sought the tiny mound forming underneath her waistband.

Concerned, the detective reached out and clasped her wrist in strong fingers. "Steady, madam." He eyed the unoccupied ring finger and changed his address.

"Do you need to sit down, miss?"

"Who's the body?" Emma persisted, her voice emerging with a strangled undertone. "Is it a woman or...a man? Please tell me?"

"It's male." The detective watched Emma carefully as she bent double, trying to control the light-headedness. "Were you expecting anyone last night? Someone who didn't turn up, perhaps?"

Emma shook her head. "No. Nicky and I were both home, but we went to bed early. It's been a hard week and we were both tired. We chilled out and watched TV and he went to his room about nine o'clock. He's only across the hallway. What did the dead person look like?"

"Chinese." The detective watched her carefully and seeing no recognition, relaxed.

Emma stood up and moved slowly, trying to control the rising bile in her gullet. The detective stopped at the sight of her new red car parked haphazardly in front of the front steps. "This your car, miss?"

She nodded. "Yes. I bought it from a friend yesterday. We did the documentation online and posted hard copies of everything. It probably won't be processed until Monday but it's definitely mine." Emma rested her palm against the solid, wet metal, using the vehicle to steady herself.

"Would your friend be a policeman, by any chance?" The detective smirked.

Emma nodded. "Yes, Will. And I know this is, 'The Girly Car.' Now it actually belongs to a girl, so I guess that's ok."

Paul Barker laughed openly. "So he caved in and sold it! Some people just can't take a joke, can they?"

"Bullying isn't funny!" Emma eyed the detective primly, succeeding in wrong footing him enough to cover her own difficulties. They reached the steps and she climbed them slowly, buying time and hoping Christopher was back in hiding, wherever that was. The thought he might have been in the house the whole time filled Emma with a sense of sickness. Her physical relationship with Rohan was exciting and not always confined to the bedroom and it made her stomach churn until she remembered it was not likely to be repeated.

The front door flew open and Nicky stood behind it, wide eyed. He clutched a tub of chocolate spread in his streaky fingers and a large, brown grin began at his mouth and covered most of his face. Farrell stood next to him, licking his lips. Emma exhaled loudly. "What are you doing? You know that's naughty!"

"It's breakfast." The child's voice sounded foggy and the brown stuff swilled around in his mouth, making Emma want to throw up. She swallowed and kicked off her wellies, stuffing them into the shoe cupboard without looking.

"If you've given that to the dog, it could kill him." Emma looked at her son with a sternness which caused him to wither before her.

"He licked up a splash of it, but not much. He won't die, will he?" Nicky looked from the police officer to Emma and back again. "Will he, Mummy? Will it be my fault?"

Emma pointed behind him to the corridor and the kitchen. "Chocolate can kill dogs, Nicky. Hopefully he's not had enough. Go and put that on the table, wash your hands and put the dog outside. If he pukes, you're cleaning it. Then get upstairs and have a proper shower and if I find chocolate marks on any of the walls, you're in big trouble!"

Nicky sloped off and Emma relaxed. "I can make you coffee?" she offered and the detective bit his lip and then declined.

"No, thanks. I've got a few questions but I might need to come back another time. Maybe the offer will extend to then?" He smiled again, a blaze of elegance in a handsome wrapper. Emma nodded and returned his expression of cordiality, glad not to have to face the mess Nicky must have made in the kitchen.

"Ok, but it's cold in this big room. Do you mind if we go into the sitting room?"

"No, that's fine. Should I take my shoes off?"

Emma looked at the neat brogues on the detective's feet and shook her head. "No, you'll be fine. The Persian rugs are being cleaned." She laughed at the man's expression, her face becoming solemn as she remembered a man was dead outside her gate. "We don't really have expensive rugs," she said, her face earnest. "It's just floorboards."

Detective Paul Barker followed Emma along the corridor and past the ornate staircase. He glanced upwards at the viewing gallery and saw the small blonde child peeking through the balustrade. In the sitting room, Emma jerked her head towards a cream sofa and reached above the mantelpiece for a box of matches. "I'll just get this going. It'll take the edge off the chill." She fluffed around on her knees, lighting the newspaper which Rohan had set in place days ago. It caught and flames licked at the grey surface, turning it black and chewing through it without conscience. *Like my marriage*, Emma thought sadly, watching as the kindling smoked and sent tiny distress sparks into the chimney.

Paul Barker cleared his throat. Emma turned to see him seated on the edge of a sofa, notebook and pen already poised in a slender hand. Emma exhaled and sat on the fluffy cream hearth rug, banishing memories of Rohan's naked body wrapped around hers in front of the fire, satiating their passion for one another. She clasped her hands together around her shins and rested her chin on her knees, presenting a serene smile to the man in front of her. "Can I ask your full name?" he asked.

"Emma Katharine Harrington," she replied. "My married name is Andreyev but my husband and I are separated." She swallowed and stared into the flames which ran riot as a sad reflection of her charred heart. The detective wrote that down, struggling with the spelling of her married name and getting it wrong despite Emma spelling it for him phonetically.

"This is your house?" Barker asked, his eyes seeming incredulous at Emma's confirmation.

"Yes, my brother-in-law left it in his will last year."

"All of this?" The policeman sounded doubtful and it pressed a dangerous button in Emma's psyche.

"Yes! All of this. I don't see how it's relevant but my solicitor is David Allen of Allen, Holdsworth and Bowes. I'm happy for you to check it's all above board!" Her tone was snippy and she gritted her teeth, thinking she might have got the order of the names wrong but deciding she didn't care.

"I didn't mean anything by it, Miss Harrington," the policeman countered.

Emma ignored him, getting to her feet and striding across the room. She pulled back the huge wooden shutters, latterly painted a clean shade of white and allowed the grey daylight further access to the large room. She stared at the circus beyond her gate and sighed. "I can assure you, I'd rather have Anton back here, alive, than any of this." Emma waved her hand around the room and thought of his bright, happy smile. In her mind's eye, Anton threw his head back and laughed at some small, private joke which he'd refuse to share with her. Emma's lips twitched and she closed her eyes against the tears which pricked behind them. *I've messed up already, Anton Stepanovich*, her heart wailed.

"How did he die?" the policeman asked, all pretence at tact lost in his inquisitive nature.

"Bowel cancer," Emma sighed. "He left it too late. He was my best friend growing up in a very difficult home and he had nobody else to leave it to."

"How was he your brother-in-law?" the man pressed. "How were you related? Was he a sister's husband or...your husband's brother?" Barker seemed way too interested in the intricacies of Emma's relationships.

She turned. "My ex-husband's brother. And before you ask, Rohan didn't need Anton's money, so it was left to me and Nicky and he's happy with that. This has absolutely no relevance to a dead Chinese male found outside my property. Please get to the point or leave!" Emma sat on the plush cushion which graced the window seat and folded her legs elegantly beneath her.

Paul Barker nodded and feigned an apologetic stance. Emma could recognise an act in progress and humoured him. Anton would have been impressed with the detective's ability; he might have offered him a part in his latest theatrical venture.

The man moved through Emma's last address and

employment in a monotone, becoming frustrated as he failed to make a link between her and the dead man at her gate. "Do you know anyone of Chinese origin in Market Harborough or anywhere else?" he asked in desperation.

"Probably, but only in passing!" Emma scoffed. "I've been in the town just over four months. My friends comprise a policeman's English wife, a ninety year old ex-missionary who's also English and an Afro-Caribbean woman who just moved out of a shelter for battered women. I don't know anyone else! I've been working at the school for exactly five weeks and when I'm not there, I'm here. The estate I lived on in Lincoln was inhabited by purely racist individuals and nobody of alternative persuasions would voluntarily live there." Emma touched her stomach as the fluttering began in her groin, closing her eyes against Rohan's child and its constant reminder of the pleasure he took in her body.

"Are you alright?"

Emma's eyes snapped open, surprised at the concern in the policeman's face. "I'm three months pregnant and alone. Of course I'm not alright." She instantly regretted her barbed tone and sighed. "Now there's a dead person outside my driveway and you clearly think I killed him."

"I didn't say that." Paul Barker left the sofa and sat by Emma on the window seat. He sat so close, their legs touched. "I'm just trying to collect the facts. I don't want to miss anything which might be important later." He gave a wry smile and his dark eyelashes swept upwards in a graceful arc. "I shouldn't tell you this, but the medical examiner thought it looked as though his neck was broken. Unless you're a secret judo expert, I doubt very much you'd have the strength to do that.

He was built like a brick privy."

"What a horrible way to die," Emma breathed. "Could he have been hit by a car? It's a fast road." *Christopher Dolan said it was an accident, but not what kind of accident.*

"Possibly," Barker said with confidence. "He's quite bashed up. It's the broken neck that's confusing, unless it was done at the time." Emma grimaced and closed her eyes and he sidled closer, offering comfort through his masculine proximity. "Sorry, too much information. He must have driven here but there's no sign of a vehicle."

"The buses run until eleven," Emma suggested. "Try the bus company."

The policeman nodded and wrote it down in a slanted shorthand.

Emma glanced out of the window. The fire in the grate fogged up the glass and the proximity of their breathing exacerbated it. The lights from the police vehicles outside were dimmed by the condensation and Emma pretended they didn't exist. They sat in silence, but it was companionable and the moments extended as the grandfather clock in the corner ticked in a relentless, comforting rhythm. Its loud chiming of the hour made Emma jump and the policeman drop his notebook.

They both laughed. "Sorry," he said, retrieving it and Emma smiled with her eyes.

"When can I get out of my driveway?" she asked.

"Not sure. Isn't there another way out?"

Emma shook her head. "No. We're pretty fortified here. Anton had six foot wire put around the entire perimeter. There's another gate a few miles away, but I'd need a Landrover to get across the fields. It's padlocked and I've never worked out which is the right key to open it."

"Bummer," Barker replied. "You could give 'The Girly Car' a go and take some bolt cutters, I suppose. Want me to come with you?"

Emma snorted. "I'll tell Will you said that. He'll be impressed you thought it might make it. You know it's only a two wheel drive, don't you?"

Barker nodded. "Yeah. Poor bloke. We thought he'd sold it months ago when he stopped driving it to work."

"Hmmmn." Emma stirred and put her bare feet on the floor. Her toenails sparkled with the polish she persuaded Nicky to slap on and she stared at it wistfully. Her head snapped up with realisation. "That child's been ages up there. I should check on him. If he's taken the dog in the shower with him again, I'll kill him!" Emma's expression changed from annoyance to horror in a few muscle movements and she stared at Barker in dismay. "Obviously, I won't literally kill him," she ventured.

The policeman laughed. "Yeah, I knew what you meant."

Emma led him to the front door and explained how to use the gate release panel from the inside. He thanked her, holding onto her fingers a little too long in the formal goodbye. "I'll be in touch," he said, his eyes bright as he processed some inner turmoil known only to him.

Emma closed the front door and listened to the dog barking gleefully down the driveway with the policeman. At least he wasn't in the shower with Nicky. She watched as Barker walked around her car, checking for signs of damage or hasty repair. Turning to go upstairs, she found Christopher Dolan behind her. He smirked. "Another conquest, Emma Andreyev," he said, his dark eyes studying her with intensity. "Every man who sees ya falls in love."

Emma shook her head and looked away from his dangerous gaze. "Whatever, Dolan."

"Aye, but we all do," he whispered, wrapping his arms around her slender frame and pulling her in close to his warm chest. "I meant it before Christmas, ya know."

Emma shook her head. "I'm off men for life. The only man I ever wanted was Rohan; look how that turned out."

Christopher tutted. "Ach, he loves ya alright. He's just an eejit."

"Yep." Emma's flat tone housed bitterness. She pushed Christopher away from her, needing space between them, knowing her loneliness and disappointment made her vulnerable to his charms. Emma saw the heat flare in his eyes as he remembered the stolen kiss in the wrecked Scottish manor house, given and taken when both felt the touch of death on their lives and had nothing left to lose.

"It was a good kiss. I can't get past it." The bold Irishman stared at her lips and Emma felt her colour rise.

She fought to change the subject. "The man who died was Chinese. That policeman said."

"I could've told you that," Christopher snorted.

"Well, why didn't you then?" Emma furrowed her brow, emotion making her cross.

"Because you wouldn't have been convincing!" he retorted and Emma sighed, seeing his point.

"Well, someone died and they need justice. Did you

kill him?" She faced the Irishman with a determined stance, her hands squarely on her hips. Christopher looked at the budding pregnancy and his eyes momentarily channelled regret.

"No, I didn't kill him."

"Did Rohan?" Emma's voice wobbled at the question and Christopher shook his head.

"No. I wish he did, but he wasn't here." Mischief back lit his dark eyes. "I'd have framed him like a shot. We still could."

"I'm not framing Rohan! Who did it?" Emma demanded. "I want the police off my driveway, so if it wasn't either of you, let's save them a load of trouble and just tell them."

"No way!" Christopher's voice rose. "You've no idea what yer messing with here! That guy was a Triad and he came after you, woman!"

"Me?" Emma's colour paled and she took her hands off her hips. "Why would they come after me?"

"You make me tired, Emma!" Christopher ran a hand over his face and Emma noticed the dark shadows under his eyes. She felt a wave of sympathy. "The Contessa got out of that fire. She's burned but very much alive and extremely pissed at Rohan. I tried to warn you, you eejit! His new tech guy's a waste of time and yer stupid husband went off on that last job and walked right into her little trap."

Emma's rosebud lips formed a little 'o' of dismay. *Don't let him leave.* "I couldn't stop him," she protested. "He wouldn't cancel the job."

"I know." Christopher placed soft lips against Emma's forehead. "Don't worry. It's not yer fault."

"He said there was a reason he didn't come straight home," Emma said quietly. "Was that it? I thought he was with her."

Christopher shrugged. "No idea. He detoured at the end of the job and I thought so too. But then he reappeared after a flight to Moscow, taking out of the way flights. When he arrived home, he had house guests."

Emma's back stiffened at the reminder of the other woman and the baby who resembled Nicky so closely. They had to be family. Her lips pursed in pain and she gritted her jaw. "We both know why he didn't come home," she said, her voice sounding wooden. "Let's not kid ourselves."

Christopher reached out and stroked Emma's cheek with rough fingers. "Don't fret, Em. I'll stick around and make sure you're safe. I need to grab some sleep now though. Obviously the danger periods are at night."

"Where are you staying?" Emma asked, as realisation blossomed in her eyes. "In the apartment above the stables? You cheeky git!"

Christopher Dolan grinned and shrugged. "Aye. It's empty, so."

"How long have you been there?" Emma's face clouded. "Were you there all the while Rohan was home?"

The Irishman nodded. "Aye. I never left. He's a fool, Emma; giving up you and this *teaghlach*."

"What does that mean?" she whispered. "Is it Gaelic?"

"Aye." Christopher's face came closer to hers and she felt his warm breath on her face. "It mean's *family*, Em. He's got the one thing I've always wanted and he's risking it all for something he doesn't understand." Christopher jumped back as Emma dodged his clinch and he looked hurt. He eyed her through narrowed eyes. "One day, Emma, you'll give in to my charms," he prophesied and she shrugged and shook her head.

"I told you, I'm off men for life." She scurried up the stairs, glancing down as she stepped past the first dogleg.

"Hey!" Christopher's hissed admonition halted Emma's flight and she peered over the bannister. "I'm offended you think I'd hide under a bed. It's against my personal code to lie down for any woman."

Emma snorted but there was no mirth in the action. She leaned further over the hand rail. "Maybe that's where you're going wrong, Christopher Dolan." She skipped up to the next level and stopped to weigh the Irishman's reaction. The space where Christopher stood was empty and once again he had melted into the surroundings with apparent ease, like a ghostly fog dissipating without trace.

CHAPTER TWENTY

"What did that policeman want?" Nicky looked up from the task which previously engrossed his attention.

"To ask questions; he's gone now." Emma watched her son attack his underwear with her nail scissors. "What are you doing?"

Nicky's brow furrowed as he worked with a pink tongue poking from between rosebud lips. "The new pants you bought me have itchy tags. I'm doing snipping."

Emma tutted at the pile of white threads on the floorboards and ran her hands over her face as Nicky gave an involuntary shiver. She waggled her fingers. "Give them here. You're freezing!"

Emma's son held out the underwear and she took it, allowing him to hug his naked self and rub his shivering arms. Emma stripped out the tag with expert precision, removing the tiny stitches and pulling the whole thing away from the seam. "You don't have to sit here stark naked, you know. You can put on a sweatshirt."

"Oh, yeah." Nicky's face brightened and he ran to his tallboy and wrenched out a tee shirt and warm sweater. Emma sat on his bed with the scissors in her hand and the pants resting across her leg, observing her son with maternal interest. At nearly seven, his body was lengthening, losing the puppy curves which formerly managed to align his body, even though poverty kept them both from overindulging. Since coming to Harborough he showed signs of earning his father's impressive height, needing new shoes again as his feet grew. Emma sighed and pitched backwards into the soft duvet, already fearing the day when he banished her from his room and rejected her affection.

"Fanks, Mum!" Nicky snatched the pants from her knee and pushed his feet through the holes, overbalancing and face planting into the mattress. "Oof!" He laughed at his own antics, sitting to add socks to his ensemble. "Ain't your feets cold?" he asked, stroking her bare instep with gentle fingers.

"Yeah." Emma nodded, hearing her dark hair swishing against the covers. "But I got dressed quickly, like you did." She peered sideways at her son as he pulled clean tracksuit pants up his thighs. "You've put the undies on backwards, you wally." She smirked and pointed to the bright red briefs which touched his belly button at the front and left a builder's crack on view at the back. "That's why the tag's helpful."

"Oh." Nicky spun round trying to see his error and then started again. "Sorry about the chocolate. Farrell won't die, will he?" The boy hopped around negotiating his pants and Emma shook her head.

"Not from a little but don't do it again. There's lots of things dogs can't have."

"Sorry, Mummy." Nicky looked contrite as he pulled his tracksuit bottoms up for the second time. "Daddy bought me chocolate spread when we went to the shops together. I said I'd never had it before and he got me a whole tub to myself. It's only for treats. I thought I could eat a whole one and he said it'd make me sick and he was right. You can't have too much of nice things, can you? They make you poorly."

Emma closed her eyes against the sudden thought

of Rohan's lips over hers and his fingers tugging up her shirt to gain entrance to her secret places. She sighed. "Yeah, Nicky. Too much of a good thing does make you sick." *Heartsick.*

Nicky clambered onto the bed and lay next to her, shuffling close so he could rest his head on her shoulder. "What will we do, Mummy? How will we cope without Daddy?"

Emma stroked the soft downy hair and kissed Nicky's temple. "We'll cope just fine, baby. It was you and me for six years before Daddy found us, so we'll manage again. Uncle Anton left us this house and lots of pennies to run it. He also owned a theatre company which I must see sometime soon. It's in Northampton and having a car will make it easier to visit. A few more weeks and then it's half term and we can go exploring."

"Yeah!" Nicky's enthusiasm warmed Emma's heart and she squeezed him close.

"It'll be exciting to see what Uncle Anton built," she mused, her mind filling with memories of the vibrant Russian actor.

"Did he build it wiv his own hands?" Nicky sounded incredulous and it was endearing and cute.

Emma snorted. "We'll find out, won't we?" She sighed. "I might get a shower to warm up and put clean clothes on. I should probably eat breakfast too." Emma ran a hand across her abdomen and sighed. The child inside produced a fluttering of tiny arms and legs. Nicky's fingers strayed across and touched Emma's sweatshirt and on impulse, she placed his fingers over the butterfly signals under her skin. The communication was faint but discernible and Nicky's eyes widened, his jaw growing slack with childish wonder.

"That baby's talkin' to me!" His eyes filled with tears. "She's sayin' hello. Does she know I'm her brother?" he gushed.

Emma smiled. "Probably. But it might be a boy. What will you do then?"

Nicky shook his head emphatically, his blonde curls spinning around his face. "Nope, she's a girl called Stephanie."

Emma gulped and clamped her top teeth over her bottom lip to stem the pain. Her voice was a whisper. "Why that name?"

"Because Uncle Anton's special gift name was Stepanovich and he's got nobody left to take it. I have Nikolai for Daddy and Nana Lucya's family, so Stephanie will carry Anton's for him." The earnestness in Nicky's glittering blue eyes and the sincerity of his words forced Emma down an emotional road she usually avoided. Pressing the heels of her hands to her eyes, she struggled to stem the unwanted tears. They bubbled up and over, running up her wrists into her sleeves and making her cheeks slick as the salt water dripped into her ears.

Her son stroked the soft skin of her wrist and laid his head on her shoulder. Nicky was quiet as Emma cried for Anton's loss and the gaping hole he left in their lives. "I miss him too," Nicky whispered when she finally came up for air. His face was blotchy and the rims of his eyes red from his own grief. Emma kissed his forehead, leaving wet tear stains on his soft, peachy skin. "Every time I cry for him, Mama, it feels better. It's like the tears wash something bad out." He smiled at his mother, the wisdom of a child forcing the adult towards reckoning and Emma rewarded him with a watery smile.

"Whose child are you?" she whispered, cradling his face in her hands. "Because you're way too clever to be mine."

Nicky turned the moment to humour, wiping his wet cheeks on her sweater and giggling. "Can I watch TV?" he asked. "It's Saturday cartoons."

"Yeah." Emma stroked his face. "Go in the sitting room; I've lit the fire. Farrell went to the gates with the policeman so let him back in with you and he'll lay in front of the fire. Make sure he sits on the towel by the back door for a minute though to dry his feet. I don't have the energy to clean dog-prints off the floors today."

"Ok, Mum." Nicky kissed the tight, salty skin of Emma's cheeks and slipped off the bed with a soft thud.

"No more chocolate spread," Emma said, waving a tired hand in his direction. Nicky rolled his eyes.

"Na. I threw the pot away," he said with emphasis, putting his hands on his hips and mimicking Emma's serious pose. "If it kills dogs then I don't want it. It must be poisonous. I'm glad we never afforded it before if it's that bad for you." He sauntered off along the corridor and Emma heard him slide down the bannister. She shook her head and huffed crossly. It was pointless shouting at him from that far away, he wouldn't hear. Emma held her breath until she heard his feet hit the oak floor at the bottom and then exhaled in relief.

The powder blue of Anton's old bedroom shrouded Emma in a gentle peace as she laid on her back and soaked up the sense of his presence. Her vicar-father would have told her it was fanciful; the dead didn't return in God's careful order. "No," Emma sighed.

"But the living can leave a powerful trace in the world before they go." If she closed her eyes, she smelled his scent, a faint waft of masculine musk and cologne which eked out from the heavy drapes and lavender rug next to the bed. Grief bit again at Emma's chest and she pushed it away, sitting up and busying herself with the child's messy bedroom.

With the clothing stored away, the bed made and a handful of tags snipped from Nicky's pants in her hand, Emma closed the door behind her to allow the radiator to spread its ineffectual heat into the huge room. She padded barefoot across the hall and cleared up her own bedroom, changing her sheets to rid herself of Rohan's distinctive scent and bundling it down to the laundry. Emma set the washing machine going and closed her bedroom door against the cool of the house, putting fresh clothes over the radiator for when she emerged from the shower.

Emma let the water tumble into her mouth, the toothpaste nulling any other taste as she desired to be washed inside and out. The shampoo added a heady scent of apple and coconut and Emma smoothed her hands over her body, following the budding line of her womb as it distended with the passing weeks. *Stephanie.* It felt right. All feelings of sadness were banished from her brain as the fluttering began and Emma felt a knowing in her heart. She ran her hands over breasts which swelled with the pregnancy and imagined what it would be like to have a daughter.

Emma performed her ablutions with regimental precision and leaned against the tiled wall, allowing the water to pound her head and press her dark curls into thick lines against her breasts and shoulders. The water was intoxicating and held her there, avoiding the chill of her bedroom while she wasted hot water. *Get out, Emma!*

The internal decision and the action were divided by a moment's delay, but Emma fumbled the switch to end the watery cascade. She sighed as cool air assailed her body, winding itself around her stomach and thighs like an unwelcome cat. The shower cubicle offered a modicum of cocooned warmth and she huddled there for a moment, watching drips run down the glass creating a domino effect as they merged and parted. The dark shape on the outside moved a fraction, enough to bring realisation with it. What Emma mistook for her dressing gown hanging on the back of the bathroom door became the outline of a man. "Get out!" she snapped with anger. "How dare you?"

"I needed to check you were ok." Rohan's unwelcome presence hit Emma like a train and she almost slipped on the tiles in her fury.

"Really?" she snapped, her anger doubling at the knowledge that two men roamed her property without restriction. "I told you to get out and I meant it!"

"Are you sure you weren't telling Dolan to get out?" Rohan's voice dripped with mix of acid and sadness, like oil and water.

Emma blushed at his astuteness and struggled to come up with an answer. "Well, at least you know I'm not interested in him!" she retorted after a few seconds of thought. "Pity you don't have the same scruples, isn't it?"

The cubicle door swung open and Rohan's dark shape filled the gap. "I have never been unfaithful to you! I didn't see you for six years and I never touched another woman!"

The revelation shocked Emma. "You're lying!" she

shouted. "You touched Felicity!" It was a low blow and Rohan's pupils dilated, almost obscuring his blue irises. Icy air wrapped itself around her nakedness and Emma tried to cover herself with her arms.

"That's cheap!" Rohan hissed, stepping into the cubicle fully clothed. His shoes left dark marks on the white tiles underfoot. He ran his fingers over the slight bump at the back of Emma's head, the ridge from Felicity's attack lumpy under his pads. "You throw a stalker in my face? A stalker who's locked up?"

The sleeves of his jacket felt rough against Emma's cheek as Rohan's fingers massaged the back of her head and roved down to caress the muscles in her neck. "What about the blonde baby?" she countered, thinking of the hidden child at the Harborough house.

"My family, but not my *syn*," Rohan breathed, resting his forehead against Emma's.

A truce flag hung in the air over them but Emma felt too conflicted to grasp it. She wanted details and answers before she could understand or forgive Rohan's deceit. She opened her mouth to speak and his lips found hers, filling her with his probing tongue. Emma gasped and inhaled, smelling his hair and the essence of Rohan Andreyev superseding the shower fragrances she'd filled her tiny world with. "Nobody else?" she whispered as he broke the kiss, demanding truth from his blazing eyes. Rohan shook his head, his blonde fringe sticking to her wet face.

"Never, Em. Never. I want nobody else." His breath countered the cool air swirling around her and the fabric of his outdoor clothing felt coarse against her skin. "I love you, Emma. I don't cheat." Rohan's eyes burned with emotion and Emma's chest felt tight. Her breasts pushed against the cool zipper of his jacket and she gasped as he pressed closer, forcing her against the condensated tiles. Emma shuddered and widened her eyes with the sensation of the icy smoothness on her spine.

Rohan ran his fingers lightly down Emma's neck, letting them trail along her shoulder and arm. His thumb brushed the sensitive skin of her ribs and his fingers linked through hers as they fluttered at her side. "Emma," Rohan breathed, settling his lips against her neck and running them across the butter soft flesh. "*Ya lyublyu tebya, moy dorogaya.*"

"I know." Emma's words came out as a quiet snuff, silenced by Rohan's groan of appreciation as his teeth nipped lightly.

The douse of cold water made them both jump and Rohan laughed, his full lips turning upwards. He leaned past Emma and released the corner of his sleeve from the shower handle and accidentally set it off again. Emma inhaled and bit her lip, her husband's proximity making her feel irrational and charged with desire as the cold droplets coursed down her flesh. She shivered and Rohan's brow creased. His arms pulled her close, the jacket rustling. Emma closed her eyes against the droplets sitting on its dark surface, watching them blur and mist through her eyelashes. Rohan's hands on her body supercharged every nerve ending and Emma felt the pressure of his fingers through her back as an electrical pulse. Rohan's desire was hard against Emma's groin and she pushed herself forward in eager anticipation. He released her and Emma gave a small squeak of shock as the cold draught whipped between them.

Rohan turned and stepped from the shower, holding onto the door as he took care with his footing.

He offered Emma his open hand and she shook her head and covered herself, feeling rejection as keenly as a graze. Her eyes searched his in confusion, not understanding why he pulled away. She looked at her feet, seeing the water drain through her toes and onto the tiles, bypassing her glittering toe nails.

"*Idi syuda*," Rohan said. He motioned with his fingers, bidding Emma to obey him and turning his head quizzically when she pursed her lips and shook her head. "Emma?" His voice was soft and cajoling. "I want you, *devotchka*. I want you more than anything but right now, I need to talk to you and it's more important."

"You're messing with my head." Emma's fingers fluttered with stress as she put her hands over her ears. "You always do this and I can't live like it anymore." She pushed her body into the corner of the shower cubicle and turned her back on Rohan.

"Emma!" Rohan's breath was hot on the back of her neck as he bent at the knees, turned her and scooped her into his arms. He struggled to balance himself as he carried her through the wide shower doorway, sending Emma through feet first. She kept her hands over her ears, banishing her husband's sweet words and persuasions. Tendons and sinew stood out on Rohan's neck as he carried Emma from the bathroom, grunting and leaning his weight on his prosthetic leg as he snagged a warm towel from the rail.

Emma poised her body, readying herself to run as soon as he set her on the floor but he didn't. Rohan sat on Emma's side of the bed and folded her into his lap, wrapping the towel around her shoulders and maintaining a tight grip. He pulled her left hand away from her ears and let her struggle for a moment. "Em," he whispered. "I didn't come here for sex; I needed to make sure you and Nikolai were ok. A man died outside the gate, Em and it's possible he was a Triad. Nobody knows why he came here."

Emma gulped, her eyes widening in horror at the very real and present danger overriding her emotional turmoil. "He came to hurt you, or us?" Her face paled and she rubbed a shaking hand across her eyes. "Even Nicky?"

Rohan cuddled her closer and kissed Emma's damp forehead. "The Triads don't care, Em. They're after me because I left the Contessa to die in the house fire. I knew all bets were off and you and Nikolai would become collateral damage once they found out about you. I thought I'd been more careful than that."

"Is that what Christopher meant? *The Contessa is loose?*"

Rohan spoke through gritted teeth, his expression thunderous. "*Da*, well, he would know, wouldn't he? It was all under control until he got involved! His interference blew the whole thing out of the water."

Emma slumped into Rohan's chest as her disjointed memories of the terrible night caught up with her, reducing her resolve to rubble. "I heard you tell Frederik to burn the house with everyone in it." Her words came in gasps and Emma swallowed hard as orange flames licked a Scottish house in her inner vision. Drugged and insensible, she remembered the night as a series of disjointed snapshots and images.

"*Da*," Rohan nodded.

"Christopher too?" Emma's brown eyes contained accusation.

Rohan's jaw stiffened again and he shook his head. "Absolutely, Em. He betrayed me and allowed the

Contessa to get close enough to hurt me. He knew the score and made his choice. Dragging you into it was his last mistake."

"But killing him?" Emma screwed her face up, not understanding. "That's massive!"

"*Da*, Em. But one of the crew must have let him go and look what he did? He took the Contessa with him and led her straight to us!"

"He wouldn't do that!" Emma protested. "Anton asked him to..."

"To what, Em?" Rohan's anger bubbled over into his voice, already betrayed in the stiffness of his legs and the tight hold on Emma's body. "To look after you? Maybe you should ask him the wording of his task because it's very different to his claim. Anton asked him to take care of you until you reunited with me and were safe in this house."

"How do you know that?" Emma asked, doubt in her face.

"I've seen the terms of my brother's will," Rohan replied, his expression one of pain. "My tech hacked into the solicitor's system when I sensed Dolan was still hanging around. He found the emails for me and now I know how much that *durak* was paid by my brother." He balled his fists. "I knew the Contessa was loose but never expected her to track me right to our front door. There's only one way she could've found me, Em and Dolan's the logical answer."

"But why would he?" Emma pleaded. "He always maintains he's protecting me. He loved Anton. I don't even think he's being paid anymore, the money must've run out by now."

"Emma." Rohan turned her face towards him with his index finger under her chin. The motion was half pressure, half caress. "Who knows how that man's mind works? I couldn't come straight home because my tech intercepted noise from the Triads which suggested they were following. I made the drop in Paris a few days after I left." He paused and bit his lip at Emma's look of incredulity.

"But you were away for two weeks." Her eyes flashed with accusation.

"I took another job, Em. It was unexpected, *dorogaya*. I booked my flight home and then took a call from Moscow. There was a problem and my new risk turned out to be human."

Emma shook her head and began to struggle on his knee. The towel around her felt damp and itchy in the cool of the bedroom and she braced herself against Rohan's chest. "Don't you dare pass that child off as a business deal. He's the image of my son, Rohan. Don't take me for a fool!"

"I won't, I promise." Rohan seized Emma's hands in a firm grip and held onto them. "I want to tell you everything, but I can't, Em. Dolan's here; I know he is. If he thinks so little of my family that he'll give you to the Contessa, he'll enjoy handing over someone else I care about. I'm upset the Triads have come here, Em; I won't risk anyone else."

Emma shook her head. "I don't understand." Her body sagged on his knee. "I want to be left alone to live my life; is that too much to ask?"

Rohan shook his head. "It's because of me and I take full responsibility. But Dolan's the problem, Em. He brought the Triads here."

"What shall I do?" Emma's huge pupils made her brown eyes look black. "How can we make it go away?"

"I don't know," Rohan shrugged. "For the moment, stick to your routines and I'll keep living elsewhere. Let Dolan think we've separated for good."

Emma pursed her lips. "Who says we haven't?" Her eyes flashed and Rohan looked saddened.

"I wanted you to get rid of Dolan but on second thoughts, if you ask him to leave, I suspect he'll give you up to them. It's possible he's using you for leverage at the moment and hasn't told them everything." He shook his head. "Why the hell Anton trusted him, I'll never understand." Rohan bit his bottom lip and sighed. "Wherever Dolan goes, trouble follows."

"How did you get onto the property and into the house?" Emma asked.

Rohan smiled and kissed the end of her nose. "You should pay more attention to the blueprints of this house, Em. Don't worry, nobody else can get in that way. I'll come and go when I can, but Emma; I'll always be watching."

Emma nodded, feeling exhausted. She was surrounded by men who painted themselves as heroes and yet exposed her and Nicky to danger. Two years on one of the worst housing estates in Britain proved less fraught. "Oh, Rohan, what a mess," she sighed. She ran her index finger down his cheek and around the line of his strong jaw. She added her thumb and turned it into a grip containing Rohan's chin. Her eyes narrowed as her fingers tightened and Emma stared him in the eyes. "Swear that baby is nothing to do with you." Her gaze was intense, her teeth gritted.

Rohan shook his head. "I can't do that, Em. He is something to do with me, but I'm not his papa, I promise."

Emma closed her eyes and weighed her options. "I

have to believe you, don't I? I'm running out of choices." She acknowledged Rohan's nod. "But who's the woman, Ro?"

"Emma, no." His voice was soft as he released her hand from his face. "But I'll tell you one truth, so you know. I'm not living with her. I've been sleeping at Mama's apartment for the last few days, contrary to whatever Dolan's told you. The child needed a doctor the other day and his mother couldn't cope. Maybe the flight caused it, but he has an ear infection. That's what you saw, Em. I promise. *Obeshchaniye*. I tell the truth."

Emma lowered her eyes and the towel slipped from her shoulder. Chilly air kissed her skin and she shivered. Rohan's blue eyes followed the line of the fabric as it caressed her and he raised a finger to touch her exposed shoulder. "Where's Nikolai?" he whispered.

"In the sitting room watching TV," Emma replied. "The dog's with him."

Rohan nodded and a small smirk touched his lips. His index finger trailed down her breast, following the line of her body until it rested on the small bump underneath her navel. "You're so beautiful," he breathed. "It's killing me not waking up next to you; I miss you." His eyes coveted her shapely body and his pupils dilated, betraying his desire. His fingers strayed to Emma's thigh, running along the contours of her buttocks, his feet shifting in discomfort as his neat trousers constricted his hardened interest.

Rohan hauled himself to a standing position, still cradling Emma in his arms. She reached around his neck in fear as he balanced precariously and stripped the sheets back with his hand. The scent of fresh laundry assailed their noses as Rohan lay Emma on the plush mattress and covered her body with his.

He devoured her with his fingers and lips and Emma fought his clothing with ferocious need. Rohan's buttons popped and skittered across the floorboards as she pushed his shirt backwards over his shoulders and exposed his muscular frame. Rohan swore as he fumbled with his zipper and underwear, Emma's lips caressing the soft skin between his neck and shoulder. She nipped and Rohan gasped. "Hold me," Emma begged as Rohan settled into his rhythm and he pressed his lips over hers and enfolded her tightly in his arms.

CHAPTER TWENTY ONE

"I don't want you to leave." Emma voice dripped with sadness and Rohan kissed her temple and drew her closer.

"I need to go back to Mama's," he whispered. "Let them track me in and out of there; it's better than being seen here."

"It's an old peoples' home," Emma said in disbelief. "How do you manage to live there when you're not even thirty?"

"Skill," Rohan scoffed and Emma sighed.

"Nicky will come looking for me soon. Do you want to see him?" She leaned up on her elbows and picked at a loose thread on the pillowcase. "I'm sorry for what I said before. It's been hideous believing you cheated on me with another woman and fathered a love child I knew nothing about. I'd never stop you seeing Nicky but didn't like you very much for a while there."

"You're beautiful when you're angry," Rohan snuffed, pressing his face into her soft hair. "I couldn't help kissing you outside the gate when you turned up in your bright red car."

"Were you play acting?" Emma asked in a small voice and he shook his head in reply.

"*Net.* I felt devastated. I saw how easily I could lose you over this."

Emma's long lashes brushed her cheeks as she picked at the thread and concentrated on the mundanity of the task. "Why does this woman, the Contessa, hate you so much, Ro? Who is she?"

Rohan exhaled and rolled onto his back, his blue eyes raking the ceiling. "Dolan!" he sighed. "And it's really *slozhnyy*."

"What does that mean?" Emma trailed a finger lightly over Rohan's chest muscle, noting with satisfaction the red welt from her lips at the bottom of his neck.

"Complicated, for sure." The deep rumble of his voice comforted her and Emma walked her fingers down his defined pectoral and brushed his nipple. Rohan's strong fingers stopped her roving and he turned to meet her eyes. "There's a few of us out there, Em, liberating and eliminating risk. There's enough work for everyone. No self-respecting company or individual ever employs two professionals to work on the same job; we work alone and we get the job done. We have backers who fund our expenses and take a cut of the profit at the end. Dolan likes to play games. Anton recommended him as a tech and I trusted his character reference, which turned out to be a big mistake. Everything's a game to him and he gets people killed. A Triad group in Auckland back the Contessa; she's the niece of the Che family who run that operation so it's tight and family based. Dolan used a trip to New Zealand to flush her out and get her into bed. She was on her way back from collecting a database stolen by a disgruntled employee and spent two days holed up in a hotel instead of delivering the risk to her uncle. Dolan stole it."

"Ohhhh." Emma pursed her lips and shook her head. "That sounds like him."

"Yeah, he couldn't resist. He tried to pass it off on

me and I wouldn't take it. I wasn't stepping into the centre of that, not for some dumbass Irish idiot who treats everything like it doesn't matter."

"What happened?" Emma tried to release her fingers from Rohan's hand but he gave her a knowing look and kept hold of them.

"He found out who my backer was and took the database direct to them. They arranged the alternative drop and the Triads were discredited. Dolan started a war and I got caught up in it."

"Is that why she stabbed you last time?" Emma shuddered at the memory of the wound on Rohan's back and how the white flesh gaped open under her pathetic attempts at first aid.

He nodded. "*Da.* I heard you make a noise in the hallway and took my eye off her for a second. She aimed for Dolan and I got in the way. One of my men shot her and Dolan knocked him out. I'd had enough of Hack to last me a lifetime. I hit him and he went down and didn't get up again so I figured they could both burn. I should've waited around to make sure it happened." Rohan released Emma's fingers and ran his hand over his face, his brows narrowed with frustration. "This will go on and on until one of us dies. Unfortunately, my backer enjoys the game and periodically leaks my jobs to Che. He sends the Contessa after me and so it goes on, like an endless quest."

"Do these Triad people know your real identity?" Emma's fingers fluttered nervously at her throat.

"Only if my backer chose to tell them," Rohan said quietly. "And if they've turned up here, it's possible he or Dolan already has."

"Who's your backer? And why would he do that to

you after all this time? You've been the Actuary for years."

Rohan blew out a breath and turned on his side. Emma heard the metal of his prosthetic leg clank against the zipper of his trousers, snarled up in the covers near his feet. "My backer is a family member who lives in Moscow. He's my mama's brother and isn't happy about her being in prison right now. Once he discovered she was on remand, the game became nasty."

"Oh, no!"

"*Da, dorogaya.* Dolan's nasty game just turned on me."

"But she's guilty! She poisoned both our fathers, your baby sister and countless others at the residential home, not to mention she made our lives a living hell, you, me and Anton!"

"I know, Emma!" Alanya's guilt still bit at something deep within her son's heart. "She's mentally ill; she thought she made people better. I don't want to talk about her; I have other problems."

"But can't we make your uncle understand?" Emma's face was earnest. "I can talk to him."

"No!" Rohan's reply was a reprimand, an order and Emma pulled back. "They don't know about you and Nikolai yet and it stays that way."

"Of course they know about me and Nicky! They came to our front gate!"

"No, they knew I visited here and followed me. I'm not staying here anymore so that takes you out of the firing line. Keep Dolan on side and then he won't tell them."

"You're happy for him to stay here?" Emma screwed her face up and her tone was disbelieving.

"I'm anything *but* happy, Emma! Don't let him in the house and lock the bedroom door at night; I don't trust him but he seems to have enough regard for you to protect you and my *syn*, for now. Who knows how that man thinks, but I'll be watching him. If he comes any closer than a room's distance from you I'll kill him. Then when I sort this out, I'll kill him anyway!"

"But it'll never end!" Emma hissed, her eyes widening in fear. "I don't understand this world you live in. I'm the daughter of an Anglican vicar, for goodness sake." Emma bent her knees and leaned forward to hug them. The ridges of her spine showed through her soft skin, her ribs standing out like the construction arms of a bridge. Rohan splayed his fingers along the lines and Emma shuddered at his touch.

Rohan sat up and the white sheet slipped sideways, exposing his naked hip. He pulled her into him and kissed the side of her neck. "It'll be ok," he whispered. "Somehow."

"Would you like to spend time with Nicky?" Emma asked softly. "Or must you stay away from him too?"

"Yeah, I'd love to. I'll talk to him and explain why we need to meet inside the house. It's probably best if he goes with the story that we're separated."

"You're asking my son to lie?" Emma sounded incredulous.

Rohan snorted. "No, Emma. I'll treat him like an adult and explain the problem. Nikolai's smarter than you think. He didn't survive on that housing estate by being *naivnyy*, naïve."

"Yeah, well you'll have to explain that Harley Man's possibly a baddie then." Emma rubbed her palm across her nose roughly and Rohan pulled her hand away from her face.

"What?"

"He thinks Christopher Dolan is Harley Man, a hero action figure. Dolan's been talking to our son for years and I thought it was his imagination until a few months ago when I saw him on..."

"Anton's old Harley! *Krovavyy ad!*" Rohan lay back on the pillows and groaned.

"Was that a swear word?"

"*Da*, but not the first one which came to mind!" He ran his palm across his bristly chin and Emma heard the shushing sound it made. She wanted to feel it sweeping across her bare neck and shoulders again and smirked, distracted.

"You think it's funny?" Rohan's brow creased and Emma shook her head.

"No. I was thinking of something else."

"As long as it's not Dolan!" he spat and Emma snorted.

"Ooh, touchy, touchy. Of course it's not him. Stop being an idiot." Emma slapped his muscular bicep playfully and shrugged herself out of the sheets. The floor boards felt cold underfoot as Emma strode towards the ensuite, feeling Rohan's desire stretching across the distance between them.

"Come back to bed, *devotchka*," he begged, his voice gruff.

"No," she replied with a forced calm. "Make the bed and then see your son." She closed the door and locked it.

Emma leaned her forehead against the glass as she showered again, soaping away her husband's lascivious kisses and banishing the feel of his persuasive fingers on her skin. "I'm so confused," she whispered to her reflection in the mirror opposite. "I don't know who to believe anymore." She heard the bedroom door close as Rohan left and heaved a sigh of relief. She felt trapped between the plausible Christopher Dolan and the convincing words of her husband, not knowing which of the strong men spoke truth and which didn't. Emma towelled herself dry and dressed in the warm fog of the bathroom, putting off the moment for braving the chilly bedroom. The icy blast was no less unpleasant from having anticipated it, but a small fire burned in the grate, taking the edge off and crackling happily with its feast of kindling and dry logs.

Downstairs Emma sought her son, holding her breath as she stepped into the sitting room. Farrell gave a doggy yawn from the hearth rug and Nicky sat with his back against the sofa, sucking his thumb as his eyes followed animated figures on the screen. "Did Daddy come and see you?" She glanced around the room in confusion, expecting Rohan to appear from behind a piece of furniture.

"Yeah," Nicky replied, his eyes glassy from his involvement with the colourful action in front of them. Emma deliberately put herself between the boy and the TV.

"What did he say?"

"Just stuff." Nicky leaned sideways so he could peer around her legs. When Emma moved again he gazed up at her in annoyance. "Mum!"

"It's rude to ignore me, Nicky."

"It's more ruder to stand in front of the telly when someone's watching it!" he scoffed. He gave an exaggerated sigh and removed his thumb. "I saw Dad. Everyfink's good. He told me secret man-stuff and it's fine."

"Where's he gone?" Emma asked, opening her arms wide and looking around the room.

"He had things to do."

"Who put more logs on the fire? Not you?" Emma studied the glowing embers and the fresh wood being licked by the orange flames. "I don't want you playing with the fires, you could get burned."

"Course not." Nicky moved his whole body to the right to watch a cartoon figure climb a building and do a forward roll onto the roof. "Dad did it. He left something on the mantelpiece for you."

Emma stepped over the dog and reached up to the high shelf. Unable to see, she felt around with her fingers until they contacted something small. Drawing it carefully between thumb and finger, Emma pulled it towards her, knowing what it was by touch. The wedding band lay in her palm, vulnerable and stunning as the heat from the fire enveloped her legs. The gold shone and inset diamonds sparkled at intervals along its surface. Tiny wording wrapped itself around the outer edge, skirting the expensive stones and acting as a border along the bottom edge. '*навеки мой*'

Emma turned to her son, disturbing him again as she asked, "Nicky, what does this mean?" She held the ring towards him and he crawled over, caressing her fingers as he turned the metal in her palm.

"It's Russian," he concluded, seeking approval with his blue eyes.

"I know that," Emma replied. "But what does it mean?"

"How should I know? I can't read proper Russian; I'm just a little boy." Indignation spoiled the innocence of his childish face and Emma relented.

"Fine. But I don't know what it means."

"If it's from Daddy, it'll be 'I love you,' or something sloppy," Nicky giggled.

"I know what that looks like and this isn't it." Emma's shoulders drooped and she looked sad.

"Look online?" Nicky suggested and Emma shook her head.

"I think Dad took his laptop, so I can't."

"Oh." Nicky stroked his mother's fingers with tenderness, his warm breath on her skin acting as a balm. "Can I put it on you, like a proper wedding ring?"

Emma shook her head. "Not at the moment." She reached up and placed it gently back where she found it, glancing down at the devastation on her son's face.

"But Mummy, if he's givin' you a wedding ring it's 'cause he wants to stay married. Don't give up, Mum. Please give him another chance."

"Baby, this is so complicated..." Emma began and Nicky broke contact with her and took a step back.

"Wear his ring, Mama. Do it for me!"

Emma opened her mouth to argue, feeling the energy sapping from her body as though quick sand sucked her down. "Ok," she heard herself say. "But only for now."

The ring fit perfectly, the mathematician's accuracy on target as always. Intricate and beautiful, it caught the light and sparkled against the orange flames. Nicky's face lost its haunted look and he relaxed.

"Everyfink's gonna be ok, Mum," he said with surety. "It's all gonna be ok."

CHAPTER TWENTY TWO

Emma sighed and pulled herself from sleep, feeling the mattress rise and depress near her feet. The heat from the bedroom fire pressure cooked one side of her body and a faux fur blanket felt heavy over her shoulders. "Nicky?" Emma's voice sounded dull and filled with confusion as she struggled to sit up. "Sorry, baby. I only laid down for a second."

"Aye, well that's how it happens." Christopher Dolan's voice sounded wistful and Emma's consciousness level snapped her fully awake.

"What're you doing in here?" she gasped, yanking the blanket around her neck and keeping the fingers of her left hand hidden. "Get out of my bedroom. Where's Nicky?"

"He's fine. He and the wee dog made a sandwich and then fell asleep in the sitting room watching a movie."

"What's the time?" Emma yawned and fought the need to stretch, keeping her wedding band safely out of sight.

"It's after three o'clock," Christopher replied. He eyed the bed with proprietary interest and Emma's brown eyes flashed.

"Don't even think about it, Dolan!"

He shrugged. "It wouldn't be the first time, Em."

"That's true. We spent a night on the same dirty mattress, huddled underneath your jacket, as I remember. Nothing happened because we were both waiting to die."

"Ach, you know how to spoil a memory," he replied, his long lashes brushing his cheek as he stared at Emma sideways. "The cops are still outside the front gate."

Emma groaned at the memory of the dead Chinaman on the roadway, his battered body now the source of a criminal investigation. "You know who did it, don't you?" She leaned up on her right elbow and studied the Irishman. "Did you see it happen?"

Christopher raised his dark eyebrows and then nodded. "Aye. I watched him get out of his car and walk towards the gates. He tried to work out how to get in without buzzing the house and I realised there was another vehicle I hadn't noticed. Its lights were off and it started moving from about a mile away. The moon was almost full and picked up a flash of metal. I don't know how long it sat there before it began rolling but it kept coming. The guy went back to his car and reached inside the driver's door for something and as he stepped back out and closed the door, the other car side swiped him."

"So it was on purpose?" Emma asked, her eyes wide. "They meant to do it?"

Christopher pulled a face, contorting his features in thought. "I think the cops will go for a hit and run but then why would the other car just sit there watching, before running him down? It was definitely deliberate and really sloppy workmanship."

Emma winced at the professional appraisal of a tragedy. "You said he had a car, so where is it now? Did the police take it away?"

"No. After the impact, the car stopped on the road and the passenger got out. He checked the body and snagged his keys from the dead man's trouser pocket. Then he got into the car and followed the other one towards Northampton. The Chinese guy slammed into the back of his own vehicle so it would've been damaged."

"Did he check to see if the man could be saved?" Emma's naivety made Christopher smirk.

"Oh, he checked alright!"

Emma's eyes widened. "He left him to die?" Bile rose into her chest and the banished morning sickness made a bid for return. "That's awful." She clapped a hand over her mouth, waving away Christopher's concern with the other one.

"No, Emma. He made sure he died."

"I can't do this!" she panicked. "It's too hard, I'm pregnant, I've got problems at work and now this!"

Christopher's brown eyes widened at the sight of the ring on her finger and he wrenched her hand free. "Andreyev's been here!"

"He left it with Nicky!" Emma heard her voice go up an octave and grew afraid at the rage in the Irishman's eyes. "He begged me to wear it."

"The Actuary?"

"No, Nicky! Nicky begged me. This is none of your damn business. Stay out of my marriage. In fact, stay out of my life. Wherever you are, there's death and destruction. Just go, please? Let me have my life back."

Christopher's gimlet eyes hardened into a penetrating stare and Emma held her breath. Inwardly she punished herself for already disobeying Rohan, who told her to keep Dolan on side. Then his body relaxed and he smiled at Emma, the good-natured expression returning like a slow tide. "Don't be daft, Em. I promised Anton I'd look out for ya, so I will."

"I think that contract's long since finished," Emma risked and Christopher smiled.

"Is it?"

The smile disappeared from Emma's face at his reply and with a wink which belied his oversized ego and revealed far more of himself than he intended, Christopher Dolan turned and left the room, closing the door behind him. Emma sat up and hugged her knees, feeling her heart sink with each thud of her pulse. The strange buzzing drew her attention to Rohan's pillow and she started, expecting a large wasp, sleepy from the wintry weather to crawl out. When nothing moved, Emma stretched out tentative fingers and lifted the pillow, scenting her husband's musky shampoo ingrained in the clean fabric. The shiny red mobile phone repeated its buzzy dance, jerking itself around the mattress in an excited movement.

With dread snaking around her breathing muscles, Emma reached out and picked it up, feeling its shiny newness under her fingers. Recognising a superior model to the one she smashed, Emma pressed buttons to isolate the message, finding one unread text in the empty cache.

'*Naveki moy*,' it said, the phonetic Russian looking strange on the screen.

The door handle moved and Nicky's face peeped through the widening gap, his blonde hair on end and his cheeks flushed. When he saw Emma sitting up, he beamed and pushed his way through the door bearing a tea plate and a battered-looking sandwich. "I maked you this before," he said, prodding at the dry, crinkled corners of bread. "But you was asleep and then I fell asleep waiting." He crinkled his nose and looked sheepish. "There were two more, but I tripped in the hallway and Farrell gobbled them up."

Emma smiled and reached for the plate, grateful for the thought behind the flimsy feast. "Thanks, baby. Cheese and pickle, my favourite." She took an obliging bite and despite the hardness of the bread, her stomach growled in anticipation of more. "Nice."

"You're still wearing it." Nicky pointed to the ring, looking smug and Emma nodded.

"I think Dad left me a new phone too." She handed it to her son and pointed to the message. "Can you read what it says?"

Nicky shook his head. "I told you, I can't read Russian, only speak it. You read it to me and I might know."

With her mouth full, Emma read the words as they appeared, spitting breadcrumbs over the pretty duvet cover. Nicky cocked his head like a bird, smiling as recognition came. "Oh, yeah," he said, grinning. "I know. It's 'forever *mine*'. Look." He laid the phone down and seized Emma's hand, hauling her fingers into his lap. "I bet that's what these words mean. Dad wanted you to know. It's Russian for that." Rohan's blue eyes smiled out from the face of his son as Nicky turned his vibrant gaze on Emma. "He won't let you go," he declared with confidence. "And he means it."

"This sandwich is really nice," Emma said, trying to distract her son. "That's so thoughtful. Sorry I nodded off."

"It's ok. I love lookin' after you." Nicky plopped his bottom on the bed. He pressed buttons on the phone and knitted his brow, engrossed in something on the screen. "Mum," he said, looking up at Emma. She grimaced and pulled a dog hair out of the corner of her mouth, trying to pretend it wasn't there.

"I'm full up now," she concluded, laying the plate on the bed. "What, baby?"

"If I tell you something what Daddy told me, can you keep a secret?"

Emma's body stiffened and she stroked her son's hair back from his forehead. "Course."

"There's a bug under your car," he said, matter-of-factly. "Harley Man put it there. It's how he wants to keep track of us."

Emma swallowed. "I don't think so, baby. That's the stuff of spy movies and..."

"There is!" Nicky protested. "Daddy said. But I'm not to tell Mo or Kaylee."

"Or me?" she asked.

Nicky stuck his chin out. "He didn't say not you. But I don't think Daddy likes Harley Man. Is it because he put a bug under your car?"

"Oh, I think it runs a bit deeper than that," Emma soothed her son. "And I'm not going to pretend to understand those two."

"Ok." Nicky pressed his head into Emma's arm, seeking comfort. He held the phone up to her face. "You have to keep this phone with you all the time."

Emma winced. "No, I don't. I've lived quite happily without one all these weeks. It's just something else to worry about."

"No! You have to!" Nicky's blue eyes widened and flashed Rohan's characteristic expression of annoyance. "Dad said!"

Emma sighed. "Fine!" She shoved it into the pocket of her sweatpants. "But there's no numbers in it. Who will I call?"

"You call Daddy," Nicky replied. "If another plastic dummy gets lost at the bottom of the driveway, you call my dad."

CHAPTER TWENTY THREE

The police finished their investigation on Sunday morning and Paul Barker walked up to the house after buzzing the gate. Emma stood up to greet him, her hands covered in dirt from weeding the border at the edge of the huge front lawn. "You need a gardener," he said, turning her hand over. "And you should wear gloves."

Emma shrugged. "I don't have any."

"Mum said I could buzz you in." Nicky looked proud of himself. "But only when she says."

"That's very sensible," the policeman answered, smiling at the boy.

"Can you ride a skateboard?" Nicky asked, clattering his toy onto the driveway.

The detective looked back towards the road and seeing the last police car move away, nodded and smiled. "Yeah. But not on here. You can't do it on gravel."

The child's eyes lit up. "I do it in the stables on the concrete or on the stone curb. Wanna try?"

Emma bit her lip and her brow knitted in an involuntary reflex action. The unassuming policeman might find it easy to get things out of her son if they were left alone. She eyed her little red truck with nervousness, wondering where Dolan put the bug intended to track her movements. "I'll come with you," she said, keeping her tone light. She flung the small trowel onto the loose border and followed the excited males around the corner and past the coach house.

"This is an amazing property," Barker said, matching his pace to Emma's and letting Nicky skate off ahead.

"Yes." She nodded in reply and turned her face away.

"You mentioned you were renovating. How far have you got?"

Emma smiled and slid easily into talking about the enlivening of the old property. "Oh, not very far. My stepbrother did one of the bedrooms so I've picked up where he left off. We did the master bedroom and bathroom before we moved in and the downstairs sitting room. The upstairs hallway needed plastering, so we did that next. I urgently need to do something about the kitchen as I'm sure half the appliances aren't safe."

"Isn't it a listed building?" Barker appraised the back of the coach house and squinted against the watery sunshine.

"Yes," Emma replied. "But bizarrely it wasn't listed until the late 1990s which was possibly what made it harder for the Ayers family to keep. I got in touch with the Heritage Office and have someone I can go to for help. He's been quite supportive but I have to apply for consent every time I want to hang a picture."

"I bet that makes it expensive." Barker gave a low whistle and rolled his eyes.

Emma shrugged. "Anton left me the money to do it properly. I suppose the planners are helpful because I approached them before I started renovating. Apparently they're used to fighting home owners after they've already taken out walls and destroyed heritage features." She smiled. "I don't have any interest in doing that."

"So, is the type of paint different to what you buy from regular shops?" Barker asked.

Emma nodded. "Yes, it's got different properties and its application can be complicated. I've taken some of the rooms back to the 1950s because a local historian remembers exactly what the house was like then and she's been very helpful. During that era they used pastel colours with vibrant accents. Obviously prior to that they used lead based paints and I can't replicate that. In the library downstairs we pulled off the wallpaper and found a complete mural on one of the walls which I'd like to have restored. That dates back to the turn of the century, about 1895."

"This whole place is beautiful. I love what you've done with the room we sat in." Barker nodded with approval, jerking his head back towards the house. "How did you know the colours would work?"

"My friend told me." Emma smiled. "Freda Ayers."

Barker bit his lip and widened his eyes. "Did she used to own this place, then?"

"You don't know your Market Harborough history very well, do you?" Emma mocked, narrowing her eyes and nudging his elbow. "It's complicated. She's directly related to the late Lord Ayers but no, sadly she never owned Wingate Hall." Emma looked at the weeds wreaking havoc between the layers of cracked concrete as they entered the courtyard around which twenty stables stood empty. "You're right though. I do need someone to help me with the grounds; they're a mess."

"One can never get good help nowadays," Barker commented and Emma laughed at his mock accent, mimicking the nasal expressions of a bygone age.

"I've never had to try before," she mused. "It's been

me and Nicky forever. Where do I start?"

Barker cocked his head on one side and looked at her. Then he took a step forward, so they stood close, his green eyes serious. "I shouldn't be telling you this..." he paused in obvious confusion. "It's not professional." He bit his lip and fought an internal dilemma. "My dad just lost his job. They were all made redundant at the paint works in Leicester and now he's in his fifties he can't find anything else. He loves gardening and I know he'd work hard for you." Paul Barker swiped a nervous hand across his top lip and stepped back. "Sorry, sorry, I shouldn't have told you that. Forget it. I'm taking liberties."

"What can you do?" Nicky called, flipping the board with the toe of his trainer and failing in his bid to make it right itself. "I can't do very much."

Barker hurried over to the child and bent to his level, explaining something about the dynamics of the skate board. Emma watched his interaction with her son, pondering on his hastily imparted words. A feeling of discomfort worked its way forward in her brain, making the hairs stand up on her arms and giving her a strange sense of foreboding. She glanced over her shoulder and felt the eerie sensation of someone watching. The stable block had apartments overhead and Emma's eyes moved upwards to the tiny panes of blown glass rimmed by decaying wooden frames above the old office. *Dolan.* Emma couldn't see him but felt his eyes boring into her, encroaching on her privacy and space. Rohan didn't trust him and that should be enough to make her send the Irishman away, but Emma acknowledged a deep sense of mistrust in her husband. Again she felt trapped between the two men, a pawn in a game she would never understand.

As she watched, Barker's perfectly shined shoe flipped the edge of the skateboard and it executed a perfect arc and landed in his outstretched hand. Nicky's eyes lit up with admiration and Emma smiled at his childish excitement. Barker bent and explained something technical. Nicky looked up at him and then at the board, communicating his enthusiasm through wide blue eyes and an eagerness to try again.

"I did it, Mum! Look at me! I did it!" Nicky's voice held an edge of hysteria as he flipped the skateboard from the concrete into his hand with the flick of his toes. "Fanks, Mr Policeman!" he said with a glance across at Emma. Then he ruined his nice behaviour. "I know you're not all bullies. Fat Brian said the pigs are fascists but Mummy said..."

"Nicky!" Emma was too far away to perform her usual trick with her hand over his mouth, but the boy read the angry communication in her eyes and had the decency to look guilty. "Apologise!" she exclaimed, tiredness creeping into her voice.

"Sorry, Mr Policeman," Nicky said. "Next time I see Fat Brian, I'll tell 'im I've met two good pigs, you 'n Kaylee's daddy. He'll think it's amazing!" The child drew out his adjective to a point way past decent and Emma gritted her teeth and glared at him.

"I'm going in now, it's too cold. Let Detective Barker go and you come in too." She eyed the blank windows of the apartment and shivered.

"I can just stay here in the stable yard," Nicky began and Emma shook her head.

"No. In. Now." She held her arm outstretched to indicate her final decision and Nicky's shoulders slumped. "Don't argue with me!" Emma insisted, looking up at Barker's throat clearing.

"Hey, Nicky, do as your mum says," he stated. "I'll come back and show you another trick soon, but not today. There's stuff going on around here at the moment so you can't be on your own outside. Get it?"

Nicky put his head down and grumbled under his breath, picking at a loose sticker on the board. "You probably don't know any more tricks anyway," he muttered and Emma exhaled, opening her mouth to chastise her son.

"Do actually." Barker seized the skateboard from Nicky's fingers and slid it along the ground with a fluid movement. He let the board run ahead of him before taking a long, running stride and landing square on its length. He weaved a few times and turned the whole thing in a wide arc before stopping sharply and flicking the board into his outstretched fingers.

His indignation forgotten, Nicky ran to him, eyes wide and mouth already begging for a lesson. "I wanna do that too," he protested.

"I'll show ya next time," Barker said with a smile and handed back the board. "But only if you've done what your mum says. I'll ask her."

Nicky nodded and looked back at Emma, suspicion in his eyes. Then he ran off towards the house. She shook her head at his retreating back and smiled at the detective. "Thanks. That was nice of you."

"Hey, it's hard on your own," he replied, sympathy in his voice. Emma closed her eyes and looked away, sensing something poignant in the detective's words. "My dad brought me up by himself," he said, lowering his voice to dignify the shared confidence. "My mother suffered from depression so he was practically a solo parent. He gave up a good career to take care of me and my brother. He's a good bloke, but you don't have to give him a job; I shouldn't have said anything." He ran his hands through his dark hair, hating himself. "It was unprofessional of me."

"Hey, it's fine. You're a loyal son." Emma touched his arm as they continued walking back to the main house. She stopped at the red car near the front steps and rested a hand against its cold, metallic surface "I'll buy him a coffee after work tomorrow and see what I think. No promises though. I never wanted to get a job out of pity and he won't either."

Paul Barker nodded and held out his hand towards Emma. She clasped it in hers and they shook on it. "I'll meet him at the Baptist Coffee shop at one o'clock. You can explain what I look like to him so he can make himself known."

"Thanks. Thanks so much. Dad's called Ray."

Emma smiled and hugged her arms tightly round herself as she walked up the front steps. She felt the detective's eyes watching her and the misgivings began to flow as soon as she closed the front door behind her.

CHAPTER TWENTY FOUR

Ray Barker sat at a table in the coffee shop, twirling an unopened sachet of sugar. His physique was slender like Paul's, but a line of muscle poked through his shirt as he wiped his brow with his sleeve in a nervous action. Large hands used to physical work shook as he played with the sugar. Emma watched him suffer, her heart softening. She went to the till, smiling at Freda's friend and ordered an herbal tea and coffee for her guest.

The dark haired man jumped up as Emma approached his table and offered his hand. "Thanks for meeting with me, Miss Harrington. Paul said you need a gardener."

"Call me Emma and yes, a handyman who gardens would be awesome."

Ray's eyes flitted up as the elderly woman placed drinks on the table with a shaking hand. His lips parted in dismay. "Oh, but..."

"My treat," Emma said quickly. "Please may we have scones for two, Edna? We can call it lunch."

The lady smiled and patted Emma's shoulder, moving off on her painful hips to fetch the food. "Freshly baked today," she said with enthusiasm calling behind her.

Ray watched Edna's progress with sympathy. "I've never been in here," he admitted, poking at the Christian literature on the table. "I assumed they'd jump on me and convert me." His eyes were battle weary.

Emma shook her head. "They've never done that to me. A good friend works here. It's voluntary and the profits go to charity each year. Freda says it gives her a focus and a reason for getting up in the morning."

"Really?" Ray looked impressed, the admiration fading on his face as Emma shook her head.

"Not at all. She loves a good gossip and it's the pulse beat of Harborough. It's heaven for a retired lady in her nineties and a way of being useful whilst getting up Mrs Jameson-Arden's nose."

Ray snorted. "Yeah, I know that woman. Her family bought the factory in Leicester I worked at and ruined it. They sold out to a group of Americans who stripped the assets, crushed the competition and sold the land. Bye-bye loyal workers."

"I'm sorry," Emma said. "Tell me about yourself so I can get an understanding of how we might work together. I'm worried it could bore you. Mowing lawns, mending fences and fixing random bits that fall off the house doesn't sound much fun. And it'll be rather lonely; often only my son and I are there."

"I'm fine with that, miss; the chance to work again would be enough. There's not much to tell about me really; I joined the British army at seventeen and came out after my twenty two years finished. It would've been great to stay on but it's a hard life for families and my wife wasn't keen, not with the lads being at secondary school age by then." He paused as Emma's face fell, her mind cast back to being a dewy eyed, pregnant teenager, secretly married to an army communications officer. "You ok, miss?" he asked, his brows knitted in confusion.

"I'm fine," Emma smiled. "You should probably

know I'm pregnant and due in August. My husband isn't living with us."

"Oh, sorry, miss." Ray swallowed a mouthful of coffee and thanked Edna as she arrived with the buttered scones.

"Just call me Emma," she said, hiding her misery with a smile. Ray nodded and Emma waited for Edna to stumble back to the counter and leaned closer. "This will sound terrible, but I need someone trustworthy to work for me. I don't want my affairs broadcast the length and breadth of Harborough for others' entertainment and I don't know how to ensure that happens." Emma felt encouraged by Ray's sympathetic nod. "Not many people in town know I own Wingate Hall yet and I'd like to keep it that way as long as possible. Do you understand?" Emma worried at her bottom lip and Ray put his knife on the plate with a calculated movement.

"You're also aware my son's a police officer and you don't want that kind of attention either?" Ray's question stunned Emma, but she nodded in silent agreement.

He offered her a hand covered in callouses, a working man's hand. "You have my word," he promised. "I won't perjure myself but I won't go looking for trouble either."

Emma heaved a sigh of relief and let her slender fingers disappear into Ray's bear-like paw. "Then I just hired myself an employee," she said with a smile.

He laughed and gripped her fingers. "I have a strong back and a good head. You plan it out and I'll make it happen."

"Awesome!" Emma exclaimed. "What do you know about ride-on mowers?"

Ray winked. "Always try before you buy, miss."

They ate with appreciation, warm butter slipping onto their fingers from the delicious scones. "You mentioned you had lads," Emma asked between mouthfuls. "What does your other boy do?"

Ray shook his head, sadness descending over him. "Hugh died."

"I'm so sorry." A mental image of Anton's vibrant face danced in front of Emma's eyes and she closed them, fresh grief biting her again as the old wounds of Lucya and her father's deaths bit at the periphery. "Losing someone's awful," she sighed, placing the remainder of her scone on the plate.

Ray observed her through keen eyes and nodded. "It is. I can see you know that." He covered her hand with his paw and smiled. "I think we'll get along just fine," he said, pledging fealty to the vulnerable woman with pain in her eyes.

They parted outside the coffee shop and shook hands. "It'll be dark by the time I get home," Emma said with regret. "Come to the hall tomorrow after I finish work and we'll look round in daylight. I haven't explored more than the house. I'll start your contract from tomorrow and we'll sort out hours, pay and things like that."

"Righto. Thanks, miss," Ray replied, his face made youthful by his happiness. He set off towards the Commons Car Park with a spring in his step and Emma chewed on her bottom lip.

"He has a car then," Rohan's deep voice rumbled in her ear and Emma smirked.

"I saw you, Mr Actuary," she said, turning slowly in the small entrance to the coffee shop. "Did you enjoy your chocolate cake? I thought you'd freak out, having the father of a cop on your doorstep."

Rohan pushed his face into Emma's long hair and slipped his hands under her coat. His fingers threaded around her waist, making Emma shiver. "Anyone could be watching, Ro," she hissed. "You said we'd to stay apart."

He nodded, his blonde fringe touching his eyelashes before he scooped it back with long fingers. "*Da.* I did. But it's killing me."

"Did I do anything wrong?" Emma asked, narrowing her eyes in concern.

Rohan wrinkled his nose and shook his head. "You don't know if he can landscape or whether he's honest. You don't have a CV or references or know if he's a drunk, gambler or drug taker. He might beat his wife or be a pedophile. What then?"

"Oh." Emma's face paled and her eyes darted after her new employee as she gulped. "Damn." Her eyes flicked to Rohan's smiling face as she glared at him. "Why do you look so bloody happy about it then?"

"Because you have me to take care of your interests," he said with a sexy smile. "Nikolai told me you offered to meet with the policeman's father so I checked them both out. Good men. Ray Barker has an unblemished work record, in the army and at the factory. He doesn't drink, smoke, gamble or whore, so he'll be fine. If he steps out of line I'll kill him and bury the body." Rohan's fingers strayed to Emma's curls, twirling a length with interest.

"How can we be separated if you keep touching me?" Emma asked, her brown eyes laughing.

"I think we should get back together again," Rohan mused. "Mama's place is depressing! Someone died in the lift yesterday and I had to give mouth to mouth and prop them up once they were breathing."

Emma cringed and put a hand over her mouth. "Did they have false teeth?"

Rohan pinched her bottom and she squeaked. The door clattered as a group of elderly customers exited the cafe. "Ooh, hello Mr Andreyev," a woman simpered, patting his muscular shoulder. "How're the renovations going with your mother's flat? A friend of mine was asking when it would be for sale. I mean, it's not like Alanya's coming back, is she? If she gets off those murder charges, it'll be a miracle. Pop by for a cup of tea later; you read poetry much better than anyone else in the apartments."

"It's that gorgeous accent," another octogenarian commented, her back so bent she stared at her own sturdy shoes. "Can I come?"

Rohan fixed a wooden smile on his face and waited until the cackling group passed. Then he heaved a sigh of misery. Emma touched his cold cheek with her fingers. "Poetry?" She smirked.

He shrugged. "They make me do stuff. *Please can you carry my shopping, Mr Andreyev? Please can you open this jar of pickle?* But I can't stay there forever. They'll get suspicious eventually."

"Was it one of them you kissed?" Emma asked, peering round his burly body and watching the assorted grannies waddle towards the residential home's minibus.

Rohan put his palm on Emma's cheek and forced her to look at him. His blue eyes were wide in his angular face. "It wasn't kissing, Em! It was resuscitation. And no, it wasn't any of them. That poor woman's still in hospital."

"Yeah, your kisses can do that," Emma snorted.

Rohan pushed his face into her neck and nipped the soft skin beneath her hair. Emma groaned and sought his lips in the shadow of the porch.

"We need to stop," Rohan breathed, pulling away from the kiss, his eyes shrouded with reluctance and his pupils dilated with desire.

"You started it," Emma grumbled, straightening her blouse. "So, how do you get in and out without the warden seeing?" Emma asked. "Freda says that woman has eyes in the back of her bum."

"It's ok in the daytime," Rohan confessed. "I've painted a few walls and wandered in and out with tools. Night time's harder. Freda lets me in the fire escape and I wait until late and sneak along the hallway. We watch TV together and she makes me dinner."

Emma's lower jaw hung in a surprised expression. "You're sneaking *into* an old peoples' home. That's hilarious! Don't people usually try to break out?" She snorted.

Rohan narrowed his eyes and glared at her. "It's not funny!" he retorted.

"Oh, it really is!" Emma giggled. She sobered. "Her comment about Alanya wasn't though. What will you do with her apartment?"

"Sell it," Rohan said. "I just don't know what to do with all her things. Some of the furniture is antique Russian as much my father's as hers. And her clothes and ornaments. Where do I put it?"

Emma grasped his cold fingers. "Bring the furniture to the hall. I don't want her clothes or ornaments, thanks. It'd bring back terrible memories, but for you, I'll house her furniture."

"Thank you, *devotchka*," he whispered and bowed his head to knit their icy lips. Every facet of her husband was intoxicating and Emma sighed into the kiss, wanting to be consumed in their intimate meeting of souls. Rohan pulled back first with a ragged inhale and cleared his throat, amusement in his tortured eyes. "I need you," he whispered. "I'll come and see you tonight."

Emma bit her lip and her brown eyes flashed like coals, betraying her craving. She nodded. "Ok."

Rohan turned to leave. "Emma, tell Dolan about your gardener. Ray Barker lives on his son's sofa so he might like accommodation. Make sure Dolan knows he's a policeman's father. It won't make him leave but he'll at least stay out of your way."

Emma heard her husband's low chuckle as he walked down the street, his limp barely detectable. He blew on his hands and thrust them deep in his pockets, pulling his jacket tight across his neat backside. Emma admired his physique, excited about their tryst later.

The sleek black car slid from the Commons Car Park behind him and pulled over. A man with Oriental features slipped from the rear and closed the door with a quiet click. He gave the driver a barely imperceptible nod, thrust his hands in his pockets and blended into the growing crowd of mothers pushing prams to fetch older children from school. He weaved in and out of the group heading for St Joseph's school and kept his eyes fixed on Rohan's back, matching his pace once he was free of buggies, women and grizzling babies.

"No!" Emma hissed, panicking. In the shelter of the doorway she fumbled in her pocket for the red mobile phone. She texted the only number in her contacts list and pressed to send. Rohan made no sign he'd received the text, strolling up the street towards town. '*A Chinese man is following you*,' the message declared.

Rohan's body kept walking, his back straight and his hands jammed in his pockets. Emma fretted and considered running after him. She planned scenarios where she pushed the man into the busy afternoon traffic or caught him up and screamed her head off as though he'd done something to her. "Just wing it!" she told herself, launching off the porch steps and into the throng of bodies.

Her phone throbbed in her pocket and she stopped, a pram and a toddler cannoning into her legs. Emma extracted herself from the mess and took refuge in a jeweller shop, eyeing gold necklaces and letting her heart rate settle. Her hand shook as she pulled the phone from her pocket and unlocked it, reading the text twice before it made sense. *'I know. It's fine.'*

"How did he do that?" Emma said aloud, her eyes wide.

"Pardon?" the shop assistant answered in confusion.

"Nothing, sorry," Emma said, embarrassed. "Just a text." She peered at the necklaces to cover her nerves and felt the phone vibrate again. She read the next text and her face broke into a smile. *'Ear piece and voice text, baby. Don't worry about me. I love you.'*

She glanced up to find the assistant smiling at her. "I'd like a necklace," Emma said with confidence. "It needs to be strong enough to keep a ring close to my heart without breaking and fit under my blouse out of sight."

CHAPTER TWENTY FIVE

"Just wait here for me, Nicky? Don't come in please."

Nicky pouted and watched Emma disappear through the half door leading into the storage area. "What are you doin' in there, Mummy? Why are you grunting?"

Emma walked over the first part of the flooring, crouching to avoid the roof joists above her head. She daren't look upwards, knowing she'd encounter spiders of all shapes and sizes and didn't want to scream and scare her son. "It's small in here," she called back. "I have to bend and it's making me nauseous."

"I'm small, I can help!" he shouted back with enthusiasm.

"No!" Emma said, loud enough for him to hear. "I need you to guard the door. Mr Dalton might not realise we're in here and lock it. Then we'll be stuck up here until tomorrow."

"Ooh, fun!" The child's imagination saw it from a different perspective and Emma rolled her eyes, any sense of amusement evading her. The celebration committee's decision to continue with the event despite the evidence, made Emma nervous enough to contemplate a rescue of the plaque.

At the end of the false flooring, a puzzle of wooden joists stretched out before her, the single bulb near the door hardly stretching its light beyond Emma's feet. "Oh, great!" she sighed.

Wishing she'd thought to bring a torch, Emma stared at the dark space ahead. She estimated the distance to the void above her office, remembering the sound of Sam moving overhead when he hid the plaque. Emma stepped from joist to joist, holding onto the wood crisscrossing overhead, for balance.

"Ok, Mummy?" came Nicky's voice, sounding distant and muffled.

"Yep!" Emma called back, hoping he remained in the library where she left him.

"Mum!" he shouted again, an edge of fear in his voice. Emma sighed, guessing he could no longer hear her.

"It's pointless shouting!" she muttered, sweating from her exertions. She paused for breath, aware of the fragile ceiling boards either side of the joists. One slip and she could plunge herself into a room below. Noticing the open cold water tank which serviced the staff toilets ahead, Emma dropped to her knees and crawled across the next long joist, desperate to finish her mission and get to safety. She groaned as a splinter stung the soft skin of her left knee. Rubbing at the sore spot, she almost overbalanced and panicked, feeling more shards enter her fingers as she gripped and waited, expecting to fall.

"I can't do this," she wailed, but sheer bloody-mindedness drove her. Self-motivation comprising a continuous rant about Clarissa Jameson-Arden meant Emma finally reached the water tank, sitting cross legged on the only suitable patch of floor boards sharing her small space with four dead cockroaches and a mouse trap. "What now?" she hissed, catching her breath and detaching a multitude of cobwebs from her face and hair.

Without her crawling figure blocking it, the dim light reached further and Emma peered around the water tank. It seemed the perfect place to hide something. She crawled around, searching with her fingers, jumping and squealing as a mousetrap activated and almost caught her thumb.

"Mummy!" Nicky's voice became a whimper, sounding like he stood at the end of the boards, peering into the darkness. "I can't see you," he wailed. "You've disapparated."

Emma groaned. "I told you to stay in the library by the door to the computers."

"What, Mummy?"

"Stay there, Nicky!" Emma shouted, seeing his delicate features in shadow. "I'm fine. Two more minutes. Guard the door!" She watched him turn and plod back to the doorway with reluctant, slow moving feet.

Emma crawled around the water tank like a child playing hide and seek, finding nothing but dust and fluffy pink insulation. "No wonder it's so bloody cold downstairs," she grumbled. "There's not enough fibre glass up here." The pathetic swathes of of pink filler drifted like light snow, barely filling the loft against the chill penetrating from beyond the slate tiles above. Emma felt her way along the side of the tank, reaching into the space between its condensating bulk and the eaves, wide enough only for her arm. She inhaled a mouthful of dust in excitement as her fingers closed around a cloth and she lifted it to her face. The patterned tea towel was still recognisable despite the filth covering it but as Emma held it up, she knew the weight of the plaque was absent. She felt around on the joist and the ceiling board next to it, baffled when her hands returned empty.

"No!" she groaned. Dragging the tea towel with her, she traversed the water tank and searched the other three sides again. Nothing. Emma back tracked, covering the ceiling over her office and beyond, searching by touch, desperate for her fingers to find the cold brass beneath them and disappointed with every questing reach.

Nicky's concerned face stared back at her from the edge of the boards as Emma heaved herself to a crouch and balanced. "I'm scared for you, Mummy." His voice held tears and Emma measured her tired breaths and nodded, remembering he couldn't see her properly.

"I'm fine, baby. I'm nearly there." She stepped her way across the narrow wooden struts, relieved to feel the boards under the soles of her boots.

"What's that?" Nicky pointed at the tea towel. "Is that your special hidden thing?" he asked, tears still in his voice.

"No, it's gone, baby." Exhaustion consumed Emma's body and she brushed at the mess on her skirt and blouse. "I need a shower."

Nicky pressed his face into her stomach and Emma kissed the top of his head. "I can't touch you, baby. My hands are filthy."

"I don't care." Nicky wrapped his hands around her waist and sought comfort in her nearness. When he coughed they both laughed. "You stink of old stuff!" he said and wrinkled his nose.

Emma closed the door to the storeroom and examined herself in the fluorescent lighting of the library. Nicky let out a hoot of laughter. "You've got grey hair, Mummy," he giggled and Emma detached cobwebs from her hair with a groan. The school was silent as they crept from the mezzanine floor, careful on the stairs to the ground level. The cleaners buzzed around the junior classrooms with their vacuums and Emma left through the playground door, scooting across the concrete and using the park gate.

"Don't you have the car?" Nicky asked as they ran through the park and Emma stopped.

"Oh, yeah. Well done, Nicky!"

They took a circuitous route to the staff car park and Emma settled into the driver's seat with a sigh. She threw the incriminating tea towel on the floor at Nicky's feet as he climbed onto his booster seat and clipped himself in. The dark felt eerie and Emma activated the central locking and drove home, feeling confused and upset. She took a long, hot shower in her ensuite and pitched her ruined stockings into the dustbin, emerging to find Christopher Dolan sitting on her bed. "Bloody hell! Don't you ever knock?" she shrieked.

He shrugged with exaggerated nonchalance. "No."

Emma clutched the towel closer to her body and felt her soaking hair drip between her shoulder blades.

"So, where's all the blood from, Emma?"

Her lips parted as she stared down in alarm, seeing the towel speckled with red. Her heart gave a skip of fear until she saw how her hands increased the mess on the towel and turned them over. "I cut my hands and knees," she said, feeling faint with relief. "It's not the baby." A heady faintness overwhelmed her and she sat down, clutching one of the bed posts in her left hand. "I feel sick."

With a grunt, Christopher rose and went into the ensuite. Emma watched his body disappear into the cloud of steam through a haze of nausea. He emerged with a glass of cold water and pressed it to her lips. "Drink," he said with uncharacteristic softness. "Let me look at yer knees." He parted the towel to reveal a series of gashes and scrapes. "This looks nasty, Em. Where'd ya go?"

"In the attic at work," she said between gulps. "I crawled along the joists."

"You could've fallen." The reprimand was clear and Emma pursed her lips.

"But I didn't."

"Still bloody irresponsible!" he chided and Emma looked away.

"You need to leave. Nicky might come in."

"At least let me dig the splinters out," Christopher said, looking up at her with his intoxicating brown eyes. Emma nodded and pointed to a drawer in the dressing table, which he raided without care. She hissed and complained for the next five minutes while he relieved her flesh of shards of wood and sizeable splinters which had gouged her knees and palms. Then he cleaned the areas with fresh water and cotton wool. "You're a worry, woman!" he said finally, sitting back on his haunches. "What was so important?"

"An artifact that changed everything," she sighed. "It doesn't matter anymore."

"You need an early night," Christopher said, his tone soothing. Emma glared at him with suspicion and he laughed. "No, seriously ya do."

"I'll feed Nicky and then maybe he'll come in here with me," she replied, gazing at the empty grate and wrinkling her nose.

"I'll light the fire," Christopher offered. "You feed your son and yourself!" He left the room, allowing Emma to pull clean pyjamas on, after raiding the first aid kit Rohan kept in his top drawer. She needed four large plasters to cover her weeping knees and another two on each hand. In the kitchen she discovered her son using the toaster whilst standing on a chair.

"I'm makin' you tea, Mummy," he said with enthusiasm and Emma cringed.

"Thanks, baby, but it makes me nervous to see you playing with electrical things."

"I always used the toaster at Fat Brian's," he said with a smile. "But we didn't always put toast in it."

Emma opened her mouth to ask the inevitable question and then closed it again. "Don't you want something more substantial than toast?" she asked instead and her son shook his head.

"Na. It reminds me of when we were poor and we shared a slice. But now it's a happy memory because I can have six."

Emma stared in horror at the toast mountain next to him. "Nicky! Stop! I hope you're going to eat all that!"

"Yep!" he assured her, clambering down and seizing the knife and margarine.

Emma shook her head and sat in the seat next to him, accepting the nearest slice adulterated by a glob of slippery yellow stuff. Farrell snuggled next to her leg, resting his head on her thigh and sighing. "You've been feeding the dog at the table, haven't you?" she said and Nicky squeezed his face and looked guilty.

"He said he was very bored today."

"Nicky!" Emma's eyes widened in annoyance. "He ran around the garden all day!"

"Ah, yeah." Nicky winced. "But he misses me."

"He's perfectly happy. He's got the whole grounds to run around in. Don't feed him rubbish, please."

The dog's black tail thumped on the tiles and Emma rolled her eyes at him, knowing he'd been prowling with Christopher Dolan. The red clay on his legs said they'd been as far as the boundary.

"Mum? Do you think there's secret passages in this house?"

Emma's eyes widened and she choked on the piece of toast in her mouth. "I never thought about it. Why do you ask?" Rohan's statement about the blueprints of the house came back to her. The main house predated William the Conqueror's invasion of Britain in 1066 so it was highly probable.

Nicky swallowed his mouthful and wiped his lips with the back of his hand. "The other night when you ran upstairs to put our electric blankets on before bedtime, Farrell kept looking at the wall and wagging his tail. He did his smiling thing with his face, like this." Nicky pushed his face into his mother's, beaming like a maniac and allowing her a close up of the margarine on his cheeks and chin.

"Lovely," she said, frowning. "I know the smile. Sometimes animals do silly things; I wouldn't worry."

"But do you think there are some?" Nicky pressed. "Like on the television. Can we find them?"

"There won't be," Emma reassured him, standing up to grab a cloth for his face. "After you've eaten, would you like to have a hot shower in my bathroom and snuggle with me for a while? We can do homework in bed."

"Ok, but I'll sleep in my bed tonight if you don't think you'll be scared. What about Farrell?" Nicky pointed a slice of toast towards the dog who obligingly lurched for it, devouring the bread in a single gulp.

"No!" Emma replied and glared at the dog. Farrell

slunk away with his tail curled between his glossy thighs and Emma narrowed her eyes. *Secret passages. And she bet the Russian and the Irishman were using them.*

CHAPTER TWENTY SIX

"That is so hot!" Rohan moaned, slipping the fragile straps of the silky nightdress off Emma's shoulder.

"The nightie or the necklace?" Emma giggled.

"Both," Rohan breathed. His fingers caressed the gold links nestled over Emma's breast, the ring resting close to her nipple. "I'll never get this image out of my head now." He kissed the supple flesh, feeling it bounce under his lips and groaned. The ring clinked against his teeth and he gathered it into his mouth and then used his tongue to place it over the other breast. With a tug, the shimmery nightdress material slid to Emma's stomach, leaving her exposed to his ministrations. His breath was hot on her neck and his kisses insistent, broken only when he sat up to part with his trousers and shirt.

The metal shin of his prosthetic leg shone in the flickering firelight and Rohan uncoupled it from his knee. He left the sock over his stump, rolling backwards and hauling himself up the bed towards Emma. She looked into his eyes as he settled over her, tracing his lips with soft fingers. "This was my honeymoon nightie," she whispered, indicating the wine coloured silk with a crooked finger. "Do you remember?"

Rohan nodded, his eyes narrowed and sultry. "I remember everything."

"Every time you tried to slip it off me, I was so scared I giggled," Emma whispered. "And then I cried because I thought I'd disappointed you."

Rohan shook his head and kissed the end of her nose. "I was frightened," he admitted, his Russian accent lacing his speech in the darkness. "Terrified I wouldn't be enough for you."

"You were," Emma said. "But you're getting better with practice."

Rohan snuffed and bit the soft skin on her neck, following a line to her breast. "You're not still scared, are you?" Emma asked.

Rohan inhaled and sighed. "Yes, Emma; I'm still terrified."

Emma ran her lips along the underside of his jaw, feeling him tremble above her. "Why?"

"I have a stump where there was a leg and a body so scarred I hardly recognise it. I'm not the same man; not the excited nineteen year old with a new wife and a world of sensuosity to explore. I'm damaged goods, Em. One day you might want a man with two legs and no scars and I'll have to live with it."

Emma rolled her husband over so she straddled his prone body, staring into his deep blue eyes. His pupils dilated so she could hardly see the azure irises and she smiled. "It won't happen, Ro."

"Nicky tells me the nice young policeman shows him skateboard tricks and impresses him. What if he impresses you?"

Emma crossed her arms over her chest and seized the sides of her nightdress, hauling the satiny material over her head. Her hair covered her shoulders in ringlets and the necklace settled the wedding ring between her breasts. "He's impressive," she agreed. "But he's not for me. The first time I slapped him or grabbed a stranger by the balls because they annoyed me, he'd die of shock. He didn't braid my hair when I was six or hold my hand when Alanya shouted at me for not calling her 'Mama'. He didn't climb into the toy box with me and hold me when I cried and he didn't make love to me when I was sixteen and sobbing. He'll never know Anton and he won't see the real Emma." She put her arms above her hair and plaited her dark locks, her breasts trembling with the action as she made Rohan wait, feasting on her sexuality like a starving man.

"You were there, Ro. You're my history and my future. I bore you a son and I'm carrying your child." Emma splayed her fingers over her stomach and he stared at her, the pregnant nakedness intimate and secret. Her fingers moved lower, splaying across her thighs. "It's ok if you're not up to it," she teased, squirming over him and feeling the heat.

Rohan's eyes lit with laughter and he growled, pulling her on top of him and burying his face in her neck. "I love you, Emma Andreyev," he whispered.

Emma kissed him, feeling the urgency of his fingers as he pushed into her dark places. "Stay with me," she begged. "Stay all night."

"Ok," he whispered, groaning as he bit his bottom lip and felt her sacred warmth enfold him.

CHAPTER TWENTY SEVEN

"Emma, don't scream!" Rohan's voice pulled her from sleep, his hand clamped over her mouth. "I need to go." Rohan slipped from the bed, jamming his knee into his prosthesis and completing the seal. He stood, boxer shorts already in place as he made the metal leg secure.

"No, stay; you promised!" Emma objected.

"I fell asleep," Rohan hissed. "I missed something important. Just trust me."

Emma turned on her side and smirked at her husband in the firelight. "Did I wear you out, soldier boy?"

"Too much, *devotchka*. I agreed to be somewhere an hour ago."

"You promised you'd stay with me." Emma's voice held accusation. "You said!"

"And I did!" Rohan hissed. "But I need to go now."

"Why? Where're you going?" Suspicion laced her tone and she screwed up her face in a sulk.

"Someone's in the house, Emma. I heard them. I need to go." Rohan paused at the door.

"It'll be Christopher moving around," Emma grumbled, still sleepy. "Nicky keeps his door locked and so do I normally. It's fine. I thought he wasn't meant to know you were here so don't go running out there in your underwear. Just lock the door."

"It's not just Dolan!" Rohan spat the Irishman's name. "He's got trouble with him."

"Well, what about Nicky?" Emma sat up and Rohan put his finger to his lips.

"He's ok," he mouthed in the light from the fire embers. "They're not interested in Nicky. But someone's coming so keep still." He shifted his muscular body behind the door, the metal leg joint making the faintest squeak in the darkness.

With terror growing, Emma stuffed the sheet into her mouth and lay on her side, her body rigid as she narrowed her eyes enough to see in the darkness.

The door opened and a shape entered the room with stealthy precision. Emma held her breath as another followed. She heard Christopher Dolan's whispered voice. "You're just talking to her, right?"

"Where's the boy?" a heavily accented voice asked and Christopher replied.

"Along the corridor. That's not the deal."

The taller shape turned to leave, flicking on a flashlight and moving towards Nicky's door across the hall. Emma gulped as the remaining outline reached the end of the four poster bed and took another step forward. She pressed the sheet into her mouth as a dull thud sounded in the silent room, followed by the sound of something heavy being dragged across the boards. The bathroom door opened and then clicked closed.

"His door's locked," Christopher's voice hissed, stress making his Irish accent stronger. "But that's not the deal. The Actuary said he'd talk. It doesn't need to involve his kid. Where are you? Stop mucking around!"

There was a prolonged groan and a thud and Christopher fell silent.

"Rohan!" Emma whimpered and heard him immediately.

"It's ok, *dorogaya*. I'm here."

"Can I turn the light on?" she stage whispered. "I'm scared!"

"*Da*," he replied with confidence and Emma flicked the lamp next to her bed with shaking fingers, bringing the room into soft light and shadows.

"Ah, shite!" Christopher groaned, his voice groggy. "You weren't supposed to hit me."

"Really? Sorry, I forgot that part of the plan."

"Aye, well you weren't meant to be in here. Youse agreed to meet in town."

"Got waylaid," Rohan said, a nasty edge to his voice. "Get up. Double cross me again and I'll finish this for good."

"Where's the Chinaman?" Emma hissed, holding the sheet up to her chin to cover her nakedness.

Christopher glanced across and his eyes darkened at the slender outline behind the fluttering fabric. "Oh, right; that kinda busy."

"Turn around!" Rohan snapped and Christopher gave a heavy sigh, turning his back towards Emma. She darted from the bed and pulled the slinky nightdress over her head, her eyes widening as Rohan raised an eyebrow and gave her a wink of approval. Emma dragged track pants and a fleecy top from a nearby drawer and pushed her feet into slippers.

"Where's the Chinaman?" she asked again.

"What's she on about?" Christopher snapped, turning to face her. "What feckin' Chinaman?"

Emma pointed to the bathroom door and the groaning coming from behind it.

"That's no Chinaman, that's my wife!" Christopher joked, silenced by Rohan brandishing the poker in line with his throat. "Aye, ya would too, wouldn't ya? Want me to bend over so youse can do it right?"

Rohan narrowed his eyes. "That's your specialty, Irish, not mine."

"I'm not gay!" Christopher grew animated and waved his arms. Rohan threatened him with the poker again and he grew quiet. "Fine!" he said angrily. "I'm on your side so feckin' behave like it!"

"Well, I'm never entirely sure!" Rohan answered, his teeth gritted.

"Why is there a strange man in my bedroom?" Emma yelped, desperate to get to her son.

Rohan shook his head and glared at Christopher. "Good question."

"We were trying to sort things out," Christopher said, sounding doubtful.

"We?" Rohan snorted.

The groans increased from the bathroom. Christopher glanced at Emma. "He needed to talk to yer man and the Actuary won't see him, so he came for you."

"I don't believe this!" Emma hissed, pinching the bridge of her nose between finger and thumb. "I thought you were my friend! You brought him to my house and let him in my gate and my front door. I'm guessing you turned the alarm off too?"

"Of course I turned the bloody alarm off. I always do at night when I'm checking up on youse all! I'm not superhuman!"

"But you let someone nasty in!" Emma raised her voice in anger and Christopher shook his head.

Rohan put his finger to his lips and Emma sank onto the bed in defeat.

The groans from the bathroom were accompanied by shuffling and Rohan turned to Christopher, sticking the sharp iron edge of the poker beneath his Adam's apple and pressing. "Last time, Dolan. You're either with me or you're not. Make your choice. If you double cross me again, I'll find you and kill you whatever the result of tonight. *Da?*"

"Aye, I'm with ya," Christopher conceded. "All I wanted was for you to take me back."

"Bloody hell!" Emma snapped. "What is this? Aunt Cissy's agony page? There's a man in my bathroom!" The end of her sentence was a wail and the men nodded to each other in a hurried truce.

Rohan stood on one side of the bathroom door and Christopher the other. Rohan seized the door handle and opened the door with force, contacting the person on the other side. There was an almighty smack as the man went down onto the tiles, backwards.

"Up ya get," Christopher grunted, pulling the stranger to his knees and hauling him into the bedroom. Emma gulped and backed towards the wall, eyeing the newcomer with fear. Christopher dropped him onto the floor boards, his back against the wall and a long gash bleeding into the man's eyes.

"Em, meet Uncle Mikhail," Rohan said, his teeth gritted. "My backer and Mama's brother."

The man was old, once blonde hair turned ash grey and the familiar blue eyes narrowed in a crinkled face. "You need to get her out of dat prison!" he yelled, galvanised by mention of his sister. Spit sprayed from his lips as he raged and waved gnarled fists.

He wasn't the only one motivated by the woman's name and Emma stepped away from the wall, taking long strides towards the prone male. He looked in his sixties, lithe and ferocious, his crinkled face and staring eyes familial and disturbing. "Why are you in my house?" Emma hissed. "Why do you keep trying to hurt us?"

"I vant to talk to him, *to him!*" Mikhail blustered, waving his arms towards Rohan. His eyes strayed from Rohan's scarred torso to the prosthetic leg and he baulked and grew silent. "What happened to you, *syn?*" he asked, his voice sad. "I didn't know."

"Why do you want him?" Emma stepped again, resting her foot on the man's ankle. She kicked his foot inwards and then pinned it there with her weight on one leg. "Why do you want him?" she repeated and pressed.

"I vant to get Alanya from prison!" he gushed. "But instead he take boy. I want to see boy!"

Emma eyed Rohan and Christopher in turn, knowing as her eyes settled back on Rohan, he alone knew what the old man wanted. Emma pushed on the joint again. "Why here? Why my house?"

"Triads follow him here," he groaned. "They want to make deal. I need to see him." He jabbed a gnarled finger at Rohan.

"No more deals, Uncle," Rohan replied, hefting the heavy poker across his thigh. "My collateral's too precious nowadays to play your games. I told you in Moscow; I won't work for you again."

"Please, *syn*, please?" the old man begged. "I'm in trouble."

Rohan's smirk reached his eyes. "Too bad, Uncle."

Emma took a step back and released the man's ankle. "Is he alone or are there more like him outside? More Chinese people?"

Christopher's mouth opened in annoyance, his brown eyes flashing. "What's with the Chinese people?" he snapped. "Are you obsessed or something?"

Emma blinked. "Aren't the Triads Chinese?"

"Aye, but they're not here!" Christopher sneered. He waved a finger at the collapsed Russian on the floor. "Does he look Chinese, ya eejit?"

"Hey!" Rohan pushed the poker into Christopher's throat and swore in Russian. "Watch your mouth, *da*? You don't talk to her like that!"

"But the Triads *are* here," Emma pressed, frustration putting a whine into her voice. "The man who died outside the gates was Chinese. Today I saw a man following Rohan and he was Chinese too."

"What?" Rohan's face paled. "No. You saw Uncle's men. They were across the street and followed as I walked away. It's why I stopped you in the porch, out of sight."

"No!" Emma insisted. "A car passed me and a Chinese man got out. He walked behind you in the school crowd." She stamped her foot on the rug. "I texted you and you said you knew they were there. Bloody hell, Ro! What kind of spy are you?"

"Spy?" The Russian man on the floor bridled, shifting his feet and trying to stand. "You are spy, Rohan Andreyev? *Der'mo!*"

"No, I'm not a spy, I'm an actuary!" Rohan glared at Emma. He pushed the old man on the shoulder and forced him back to a sitting position. "Tell me about the Chinese man."

"I need a drink!" Emma snapped. She pointed at the prostrate male. "And I want him to stop bleeding on the floor."

"Vodka?" Mikhail said hopefully, his blue eyes widening as he ran a bloody hand through his hair.

"No!" Emma replied, her jaw tensed. "Tea!"

CHAPTER TWENTY EIGHT

"What's happening, Mummy?" Nicky stood in the kitchen doorway rubbing his eyes and staring at the room full of people. His eyes widened at the sight of Christopher and he gave a small smile of victory and raised an eyebrow in Emma's direction. "Mummy. Why's Harley Man in our kitchen?"

"He brought a friend, baby," she replied, filling the tea pot and glaring at Christopher.

"Hey Daddy." Nicky skipped across to his father and wrapped his arms around Rohan's scarred stomach, squeezing and kissing the smooth six pack. Rohan stroked the soft blonde hair and kissed his son on the top of his head. "You're rudey dudey," Nicky giggled and pointed at Rohan's boxer shorts.

The old Russian seated at the kitchen table knitted his brow and eyed Rohan with suspicion. "What is dis, *syn*? You have family and say nothing to your own uncle?"

"Are you surprised?" Emma sneered, thumping the teapot on the table. "We nearly died in Falkirk a few months ago, while you had fun with a Triad boss. Why would he give you more ways to hurt him?" Emma added mugs and a milk jug. "You can manage without sugar; there isn't any," she told the man.

"Mummy, did you nearly die in Forkip?" Nicky's eyes were wide and his bottom lip turned down. "Why, Mummy?"

Emma clicked her fingers and the dog moved off

his blanket, appearing by her side like a sylph. She pointed at Nicky. "Farrell can take you to the sitting room while the grown-ups have a chat. Put a nice film on, baby. Don't watch the channels this late at night."

Nicky nodded and patted his thigh. The dog rushed to him and they pitter-pattered from the room. Emma poured four mugs of tea and pushed one towards the old man. She reached behind her and dragged kitchen towel from the roll and dropped it on the table. "You're bleeding," she said and pointed to her own forehead. Glittering blue eyes watched her movements as though their owner waited to pounce. Emma took a step back, finding Rohan's hands on her shoulders.

Behind the Russian, Christopher withdrew the knife he'd hidden from Nicky and held it against the man's neck in threat. "Just give me a reason, old man," he breathed.

Rohan sighed and pulled out a chair, the wood scraping across the tiles like an intrusion into the forbidding silence. "Speak, Uncle. I'll give you five minutes and then my friend here will drop you on a lonely road and call the Contessa."

Emma felt too disturbed to sit, despite her husband's sense of calm. Rohan lay back in his chair and folded his arms in a casual guise. Emma saw the telltale vein tick in the side of his neck and sensed the pent up aggression waiting to be unleashed, a paradox to the small smile on his lips. She leaned her bottom against the counter and sipped her tea, deciding the hot liquid would make a ready weapon if required.

The Russian pulled a mug towards him and added milk, sipping the liquid and smacking his lips in a way which seemed habitual. Emma watched as his eyes flicked towards her and back again. His suit material had an expensive plushness to the way it lay on his shoulders, stained by blood along the wide lapels. His eyes burned into Emma's face, sizing her up and weighing her value as collateral. She gritted her teeth. "Tick-tock," she said, raising her eyebrows. "Time's running out."

His eyes widened in surprise and Emma saw Rohan smirk, dimples appearing in his cheeks as he tried to hide his amusement. Emma shook her head, not enjoying the game. "Stop staring at me and put some effort into your excuses," she said. "This is my house and I don't want you in it."

The man sneered and Emma lost patience, setting her mug loudly on the counter. "Fine then," she snapped. "Police it is." She reached into her pocket and drew out her mobile phone, waiting for the icons to appear on the screen.

CHAPTER TWENTY NINE

"I told you, I won't work for you again," Rohan said, his voice calm.

"Please, *syn*, one last time," Mikhail begged, patting his cut with Emma's tea towel.

"He said no, idiot!" Emma spat, casting frightened glances towards her husband and pleading with her eyes. "He's got responsibilities and we already agreed." She made her tone sound confident and brave, feeling neither as she watched her husband's interested expression and the way he cocked his head wanting to hear more.

"I already accepted." Alanya's spiteful brother smirked as though he still possessed the power to make demands and enjoyed Emma's reaction of badly veiled devastation. "It's a final wager with the Triads," he said with a smile, not realising the irony as he nodded to the deal with another peddler in human misery, the faceless Che. "It's local." Mikhail's wrinkled face lit with enthusiasm. "If we neutralise the risk, we get paid and they leave us alone. If not, Che will unpick all of us, piece by piece." Mikhail's face collapsed in misery, pointing a gnarled finger at Christopher Dolan. "This is because of you! The Contessa is his niece and you defiled her. Now, we will all be punished."

Christopher shared only two words of infinite wisdom. "Ah shite!"

Mikhail tapped keys on his mobile phone and read in halting English from a contract, detailing both the risk and payment for its neutrality. Rohan sighed in frustration and snatched the phone from the old man's fingers. "The client's offering half a million sterling to recover a historical artifact belonging to..." Rohan stopped, biting on his bottom lip and staring at Emma with wide blue eyes. "It's a brass plaque belonging to Little Arden Church of England School, Market Harborough, which has the potential to defame a prominent local family. The item and any evidence of its existence must not be destroyed, but returned to the client. The handover must be no later than midnight..." Rohan looked at the digital display on his wrist. "Tomorrow."

"You are *not* serious!" Emma whirled on the spot and faced Rohan, a grimace budding on her lips. As the men stared at her as a collective she realised the futility of her situation and fled from the room. She was half way along the corridor towards the sitting room when Rohan's ungainly tread sounded behind her and she bit back a smirk of victory. Rohan Andreyev belonged to her, not the sour Russian at the kitchen table.

"What's funny?" Rohan pushed her against the wall of the hallway, preventing her reaching for the sitting room door handle. His hands straddled her hips, strong and protective as he pushed himself close. "It's dead easy, but they don't know that." He lowered his lips to her neck and nibbled at the soft skin. "It's awesome."

"No, you promised no more actuary jobs. And there's something wrong with this; it's not right!" Emma pushed her husband away, her brow furrowed in confusion. "It's a fix! Another of Mikhail's games."

"Just because it's easy, doesn't mean it's fake," Rohan said, clasping Emma's flailing hands and drawing them into his stomach. "I've done jobs round the corner and the profit was mine to keep. Backers don't care how you do it as long as you get the job done cleanly."

Emma felt the coolness of her husband's skin and snapped at him, distracted. "Put clothes on, Ro! You don't usually wander round in your boxers and it's freezing!"

"It's rattling my uncle and I intend it to."

"Why?" Emma pressed her lips against Rohan's bicep and inhaled his musky scent. "Are you playing the sympathy card?"

"Emma Andreyev!" He faked horror, his blue eyes wide and the expression ruined by his amusement. "I didn't have time to put clothes on, but he didn't know about my injuries; I want him to see how hard he made my life for his sport."

"He's a wicked old man!" Emma hissed. "Why leave him alone with Christopher? He's about as reliable as a chocolate teapot!"

Rohan laughed and his comforting tenor carried along the hallway. "He wants the chance to work with me again. I believe he'll remain trustworthy, for now."

Emma snorted. "Yeah, whatever!" She trailed kisses over the downy hair on Rohan's chest and then pushed him away. "I'd still feel better if you were in there with the nasty uncle. Check on Nicky and I'll run up and grab your clothes." She set off towards the stairs at a jog and halted as Rohan called her name.

"Emma!" She turned and he smiled. "I love you, *zhenshchina*."

"Yeah," she replied over her shoulder. "You'd better!"

Emma sat on her four poster bed with her head in

her hands and Rohan's shirt draped over her knees. A lipstick stain on the collar reminded her of their frantic tryst a few hours earlier although the blush of sex left with the entrance of Mikhail and Christopher. "What am I going to do?" she murmured, experiencing waves of panic interspersed with frustration. The simple task stretched before her like an impossible quest, the grail unattainable. Emma cradled her husband's shirt and pressed it to her nose, knowing he waited downstairs for her but not able to face his enthusiasm with her catalogue of errors.

"Nicky's asleep on the dog," Rohan said, stilling Emma with a hand on her shoulder as his voice made her jump. "Didn't mean to scare you, *devotchka*. I thought you'd got lost." He teased the shirt from her fingers and shrugged it over his muscular torso, grabbing his trousers from the floor and sitting on the bed to push his feet into them. Emma pointed wordlessly at a knife attached to the metal of his prosthetic and her husband grinned as he stood to close his zipper. "There's a clip welded onto the shaft. It's difficult to get off, but there if I need it."

"Can't you put a magnet on the knife and it'll stick?" Emma said, her voice sulky.

"*Net*. Carbon fibre isn't magnetic." Rohan glanced up at her as he fixed his left shoe over his foot and tied the laces. "Somebody didn't concentrate in physics class."

Emma snorted. "That's because you had English next door and all I could think about was the kiss you'd give me on the way home."

Rohan smirked and leaned across, pressing his lips over hers. "Then I ruined your education and I'm truly sorry." He put his palm over his heart in a noble salute and Emma laughed.

"Idiot!"

"So, about the job." Rohan sat next to her and pressed his palms over his knees. "You know where to find this brass plaque at the school? It should be the easiest job yet and it's the one to end this feud with the Contessa." He looked thrilled and Emma chewed her bottom lip and exhaled in desperation.

"It won't," she conceded. "I know everything about the plaque and even why someone would like it hidden for another century or two. I had it in my hands, catalogued and ready to scan. When I realised the problem it might cause, I got Sam to hide it but when I went looking last night, it wasn't there."

"*Der'mo!*" Rohan swore and lay back on the mattress with force. "This is bad, Emma, really bad."

CHAPTER THIRTY

"Why does the horrid Russian keep asking for his *syn*? Isn't that what you call Nicky? *Son*?"

Rohan nodded. "*Da*. His son's hiding in my house on Newcombe Street."

Emma shook her head, her eyes narrowed as she hunted for lies. "No, you're hiding a woman and baby." Her face fell. "A baby who looks like Nicky."

"Ah, Emma," Rohan breathed. He pulled her into his chest and kissed the top of her head. "You're too sharp for your own good, *devotchka*."

Emma swallowed and waited for him to break her heart, surprised when he chuckled. "Except in physics. You suck at that."

"Just tell me!" she bit, her tone heavy. "Who does the baby belong to?"

"The boy's my nephew."

Emma looked up and stared at her husband sideways, doubt shrouding her expression. She opened her mouth to speak and Rohan placed a gentle finger over her lips. "His father, Sergei Romanov is my younger brother and Artyom is his son. The woman you saw is Sergei's wife, Bella."

Emma gaped, the absence of words an unusual curse. Her brow knitted as she thought of Anton being replaced and nausea roiled in her gut. "How can he be your brother?" she asked, her voice a whisper. "There was only Anton and you."

Rohan ran a hand over his eyes and kept his other

arm around Emma's shoulder. "After my sister died, Mama conceived again. She grew sick at the end of her pregnancy with fever and swelling and the local doctor hospitalised her. The child died in the womb and was removed by Cesarean section. We grieved and it prompted my father to apply for the diplomatic role in England. We left Russia for London and never spoke of the baby again."

"That's awful!" Emma shuddered. "But it doesn't explain how Sergei's your brother."

Rohan paused, his face ashen. "While I was away last time, I completed the job and headed home as usual. I knew Hack watched so took detours. When I reached London, I received communication through my tech from a Russian in Moscow who used our coded email address. He fielded it and passed it through as I reached England. Before he died, Anton became obsessed with finding family members. I wasn't interested, but it was a passion for him. Dolan helped and they identified numerous cousins and a few uncles we hadn't known." Rohan stopped and sighed.

"You were young when you left Russia," Emma said, her tone soothing. Impatience made her want to demand answers but wisdom told her to wait. "It's understandable you don't remember everyone."

"I didn't want to know, Emma; I have my reasons. But apparently Anton found Sergei and made contact with this supposed cousin. They met in Moscow last summer and Sergei said they both knew immediately something was wrong and made discreet enquiries through the Russian authorities, finding nothing. There was no record of Sergei's birth or documents relating to his mother's pregnancy."

"What do you mean, '*they both knew something was*

wrong?" Emma's brow furrowed.

"They were identical, Em; like twins. When you meet him, you'll understand."

"Oh." Emma lay back on the bed to process the tale.

Rohan nodded. "Mama's baby didn't die. Her sister-in-law took him and raised the child as her own."

Emma shook her head. "How? Weren't there doctors and nurses to stop that happening?"

"You have no idea how corrupt Russia was then. A bribe could secure anything."

"But what about your uncle? Or was he in on the deception?"

"Obviously not, judging by his behaviour recently." Rohan wiped his lips on the back of his hand. "My uncle was a soldier in communist Russia and when the government changed, he was considered a violent dissident. Six months before Sergei's birth he was sentenced to five years prison in Siberia. It was entirely probable the child was his. There was no family contact with prisoners and he arrived home to find a blonde haired child who looked like him. My family left Russia two months after Mama gave birth and she disliked Mikhail's wife and had no reason to see her. She doesn't know Sergei's alive and I don't know how to tell her."

"But Anton must have told you this. Why does it seem like you only just found out?"

"He tried." Rohan sighed in exasperation. "I didn't hear him out. Apart from Mikhail, I wanted nothing to do with the family. It was just one of the conversations he tried to have with me in the hospital before he died."

"The other one was about me and Nicky, wasn't it?"

Emma said, stroking his arm. Rohan nodded. "*Da*. I was always good at avoiding the truth." Regret filled his expression, his head drooping and his eyes closed. "I'm a fool, a *durak*."

"Daddy said you can't hide from truth," Emma said, remembering her father's gentle teaching. "It always gets you in the end."

"Well, it sure has," Rohan mused, shaking his head so his blonde fringe bounced on his eyelashes.

"This is sick," Emma whispered, clutching her stomach. "They stole Alanya's baby?"

Rohan nodded. "*Da*."

"But without documents or witnesses, how could Anton prove it?" She sat up, intrigued by the tale, cocking her head to hear Rohan better and resting her cheek against his shoulder.

"DNA tests," Rohan replied. "By the time he returned home, Anton knew Sergei was our brother. It was around the time he discovered he was dying."

"Does Sergei know Anton died?" Emma asked. "You wouldn't have known to contact him."

Rohan shook his head. "No. He'd been trying to speak to Anton for months before he found me."

"So why did Sergei need to contact you? Did he hear about Anton another way?"

Rohan shook his head. "Anton figured it was best to leave Sergei in the life he created for himself and maintain regular contact, but recently something happened. Uncle discovered he had leukaemia and needed healthy bone marrow to survive. With only one son as a blood relative in Russia, Sergei was tested. His blood group didn't match Uncle's and raised suspicion for the old man."

"But Nicky might have my blood group instead of

yours, or be a cross between them. That's not a red flag for anything; Sergei might be a match for Mikhail's wife."

Rohan rolled his eyes. "Sergei was born while Uncle was in prison, remember. My aunt died when Sergei was fifteen and her medical records showed an unusual blood group. The matter perplexed Mikhail enough to do DNA tests without Sergei's knowledge."

"How can you do it without someone knowing?" Emma asked and Rohan shook his head, balling his hands in frustration.

"Hair from a comb, saliva on a glass; anything, Emma. What's relevant is when the results came back, Mikhail became furious enough to take Bella and the baby to his compound and hold them at gunpoint."

"How could he hold Sergei responsible?" Emma complained and Rohan raised an eyebrow.

"You've seen him, Em. He's hardly rational, is he?"

"What happened?"

"The old man had a seizure and Bella escaped. They left Russia in a panic, getting as far as Kiev. When Sergei couldn't reach Anton, in desperation he used the email address Anton gave him before he left. He told him it was only for emergencies and would cause upset. Sergei knew nothing about me only that I was a viable contact in time of trouble."

"What a shock for you," Emma whispered.

Rohan nodded. "*Da*, to receive a request for help from my dead brother wasn't what I expected from a business email marked as urgent."

"But you helped him." Emma pursed her lips, ruing her own misery for jumping to wrong conclusions.

"*Da*. My tech organised passports and visas for the UK within a few days and I met the family at Heathrow for the first time."

"Genuine passports?" Emma asked, her face earnest and Rohan stroked her cheek with tender fingers.

"Of course not, *devotchka*."

"So, they're illegals?" Emma exhaled and bit her lip.

"Their documents will pass reasonable scrutiny, but *da*, they'll be imprisoned and deported if discovered. The trip to the doctor was fraught with danger in case the documents weren't accepted. Decent ones take time."

"Sorry." Emma cuddled harder into her husband and wrapped her arms around his rigid torso. "I bet they think I'm an idiot for my scene in the street." She sighed.

Rohan kissed the top of her head. "Bella was devastated. She doesn't speak much English but knew you were important to me. She tried to get out of the car to explain but I couldn't risk it. Dolan would use the family as leverage against me and I felt caught between losing you and risking them."

Emma bit back her pique that Rohan didn't throw his family to Dolan to save his marriage. She knew it was unreasonable but the fact stung. "Is that why your uncle keeps asking for the boy?" she asked instead. "He wants Sergei. What will he do to him if he finds him?"

"I don't know," Rohan replied. "He's staring death in the face and can't take it. Maybe he wants a tearful reunion or to rid himself of a scam he wasn't part of."

"So he's still sick?" Emma said and Rohan nodded.

"*Da*. And furious about Mama being in prison. Last time I saw her she rattled on and on about Mikhail so I suspect he visited recently. I've begun to wonder if losing two children was the final straw for Mama. She keeps trying to give me an herbal recipe for vitamins and telling me I have to take care of Nicky or he'll die."

"Whatever!" Emma scoffed. "Final straw? She killed your little sister and two husbands, plus a heap of defenceless old men in the apartments. Why do you always make excuses for her?"

Rohan shook his head to clear it and changed the subject. "How do we get the plaque back? It's the key to ending all this. Uncle will hand it to the client and return to Russia. The client claims to have influence with Che and the Triads and will agree a truce on delivery. Mikhail doesn't know for sure I've met my brother and I can keep bluffing him. He's making wild assumptions, so if I keep playing dumb, he'll look elsewhere in whatever time he has left."

"So this sort of risk elimination is genuine?" Emma asked, still sounding doubtful. "You've fetched things this small before?"

"*Da*, I told you. I don't care what the job is as long as the money's good enough. In this case, there's more at stake than that. Mikhail accepted the job, Em. You know what that means. I have to follow through."

CHAPTER THIRTY ONE

"Did your uncle kill the Chinese person at the gate?" Emma whispered in the hallway.

"*Da*," Rohan replied. "For sure."

"Why?" she asked and Rohan halted, his slender fingers on the door knob.

"What do you mean?"

"Why would he kill him? It seems an odd thing to do and why would the Triads negotiate when he wiped out one of their foot soldiers? He's behaving like he didn't know about me, Nicky or this house. He wouldn't agree to meet you elsewhere if he knew he could just show up here, would he? It doesn't feel right."

Rohan nodded slowly. "You're right. Perhaps the Triads owe the client a favour." He worried at his bottom lip with his teeth and pondered on Emma's question. Then he shrugged. "It's all academic, Em. We're caught now; we have to retrieve the plaque and make the deadline. Then we'll see how it pans out."

"You're an actuary!" Emma said, her eyes wide in disbelief. "These are significant risks which it's your job to weigh."

Rohan stroked her cheek with the back of his hand. "And sometimes, Em, despite the best endeavours, you still have to fly by the seat of your pants and hope it turns out ok."

Inside the kitchen he questioned the old man in Russian, receiving a slow head shake and denial in

English. "*Net*. Not me," Mikhail maintained. "This is first time I come to this house." He waved a casual hand to indicate the old fashioned kitchen. "Is impressive. You do well with my backing." His blue eyes glinted spite and Emma recoiled and opened her mouth to claim ownership of everything he saw. Rohan stopped her with a look of warning and a slight shake of his head.

Emma saw her husband glance in Christopher's direction and the Irishman nodded in affirmation. He'd watched the murder from a distance and denied it was Mikhail. To her surprise, Rohan left the matter alone, sending Christopher to the gate with his uncle. "Don't come back," he told Mikhail with authority. "We won't meet again. I don't know where your son is so look elsewhere. Uncle, our business agreement is over."

"What about this job?" Mikhail asked, his eyes wide. "Don't you need my help?"

Rohan shook his head. "*Net*, Uncle. Go back to your hotel and return to Moscow. I'll sort it out. We're done."

Mikhail gulped. "But what about Alanya? I want her out of prison."

"Leave her," Rohan instructed. "She's sick and they're giving her help. She kills people, Uncle. Leave her alone where she's safe. Don't go to see her again!" Rohan's eyes flashed with danger and the nasty old man allowed himself to be led down the driveway towards his waiting vehicle outside the gate. Rohan closed the front door and turned to Emma. "Now we find that trophy and you're gonna help me."

Emma didn't sleep. Rohan carried Nicky upstairs and laid him in bed, returning to the kitchen to plan. When Christopher came back, they debated the issues.

"So, Mikhail didn't kill the Triad at the gate?" Emma asked, shaking her head in disbelief. "Nothing makes sense. Who's the client, why does he want the plaque and how can this last job end a feud with the Triads?"

Rohan shook his head. "I agree with everything you've said. What are we missing?" He strummed his fingers on the kitchen table in an irritating beat.

Christopher poured himself a large brandy, sloshing it into a mug. Emma screwed up her face. "Don't drink that! It was here when we moved in; goodness knows how old it is."

"It's mine." Christopher closed his eyes and savoured the burn at the back of his throat. "I often drank with Anton. Brandy helped him after chemo."

Emma saw Rohan's body stiffen in misery and reached for his hand. Rohan threaded his fingers through hers and Christopher rolled his eyes. "Stop it!" Emma reprimanded the Irishman. "Get used to it or get out!" She shook her head and her mind worried again at the problem. "Why believe Mikhail when he says he didn't kill the Triad? Does it make more sense if he did? Could he be deliberately making things worse and setting you up?"

Rohan nodded. "Absolutely. Ok, let's assume he did it and lied. Now solve the rest of the problem. Who's the client and why does he or she want an artifact from a tiny school in the Midlands? What's his connection and how would it present a risk worth half a million pounds?"

Christopher pulled out his iPhone. "Mikhail sent me a job number. I'll track it backwards through the server." His fingers flew over the keypad, pressing buttons and logging into a powerful device elsewhere.

Emma turned back to Rohan. "How far would the

Triads take this grievance and what would call them off? How bad is it?"

He sighed and ran his free hand through his blonde hair, leaving it sticking up at the front. Emma resisted the urge to mother him and pat it flat, gripping his fingers and waiting for his quick brain to solve the equation. "Che lets the Contessa run her own course. He gives her backing, but he's only offended because she is. It's not so much the Triads who are a problem, but her."

"Offended?" Emma cocked her head.

"Yeah." Rohan flicked his eyes towards Christopher. "A weekend of debauchery with our Irish friend didn't work out as planned for her."

Emma saw Christopher's face twitch and hid the smirk which pulled at her lips. "So he stole what she was carrying and took it to Mikhail?"

Rohan nodded. "Yep. Che wasn't happy because as backer, he looked a fool and the industry lost faith in him. It was a reputation issue. But for her, it was more than that."

"And financial?" Emma asked. "You told me you accepted an advance and once you did that, you had to deliver. Like now."

Rohan stroked her fingers and offered an appreciative smile at her understanding. "*Da.* The advance becomes repayable, but the compensation outweighs any profit the actuary would have made if successful. Compensation is intended as a painful penalty. Our business doesn't tolerate mistakes or failure because the cost to the client is always high. If they don't get the risk returned or destroyed it can be game over for them. Usually when you screw up you don't work again, but the Contessa is protected by Che being her guarantor. He indulges her because she's his heir. She came after us more out of revenge than to recuperate her losses; she doesn't need the money." Rohan looked at Christopher. "Who are they, Hack? Who's the client? We find the client, we find the reason."

Christopher stood up and scraped his chair under the table. "I can't do this here; I need my tech stuff. The server's working on it." He unlocked the back door, pulling the bolts from their housing and leaving the kitchen in a blast of cold air.

"What's he talking about?" Emma asked, knitting her brow. "What server?"

CHAPTER THIRTY TWO

Emma clutched Rohan's phone in her hand as he led her across the stable yard. She raised it to her ear and listened. "Are you sure it works?" she asked, anxiety in her voice. "And you locked up properly?"

Rohan rolled his eyes. "Yes, it works and yes I locked up, Em."

Daylight pricked the dark sky in growing streaks of red and gold, heralding the coming dawn. "Is this what people use as baby monitors nowadays?" Emma asked, raising the phone to her ear again.

"I dunno!" Rohan scoffed. "You wanted to see the server but we can't leave our son in the house alone. This is the solution but we need to hurry."

"I didn't know my phone could be a listening device." Emma put Rohan's phone to her ear again, listening to her son's steady breathing. Her phone lay on the pillow next to him. "It's so clever."

Rohan shook his head and opened the door to the apartment over the derelict stable office. "Woman, you're a worry," he snorted.

"I couldn't afford proper things!" Emma reminded him as she faced the rickety stairs to the upper level. "I'm trying to forgive you for neglecting us, but it's hard."

Rohan heard the mocking in her voice and pinched her bottom as she climbed the stairs in front of him. "Get up there!" he chastised. "And stop putting the bloody phone to your ear! The volume's as high as it goes. Knowing your luck, you'll turn mute off by accident and wake Nicky up yourself!"

"Oh." Emma stopped on the stairs and Rohan ran up the back of her in the gloom. "Could that happen? Maybe you'd better hold it." She held the device out to him with a look of distaste. Rohan took the phone from her outstretched palm and pushed it into the top pocket of his shirt. It made the material sag and he saw Emma's eyes widen in concern.

"It's fine," he reassured her. Rohan fixed his blue eyes on Emma's face, reading her latent mistrust like an open book. His index finger traced the line under her bottom lip. "When this is over Em, we need to sit down and talk properly; about everything."

Emma felt the protective wall go up over her heart, sheltering her from further pain. She swallowed and knew Rohan saw her withdraw. "What will that mean for us?" she asked, hovering on the step above her husband. "Seeing you pick the lock into Nicky's bedroom was a bit of an eye opener."

Rohan stroked her cheek and pushed his hand into the long curls at the back of her neck, using the leverage to ease her lips onto his. The kiss was tender. "It means no secrets. I want to spend the rest of my life with you, Emma Andreyev. It means I tell you everything."

"Will I want to know?" she asked in a whisper, feeling his breath on her skin as Rohan's lips hovered over hers.

"Probably not," he muttered, his pupils dilating. He grazed her lips with his, jumping back in alarm as the door at the top of the steps propelled open, banging against the wall behind it. Rohan scrabbled for the handrail, finding nothing but empty brackets and struggling to stop himself falling backwards down the stairs.

"Are youse doing this on purpose?" Christopher shouted. He jabbed a finger at a point above Emma's head and she looked up, seeing nothing.

Rohan smirked as he regained his balance. "Just keeping you on your toes, Dolan."

"Aye, well, necking on my security monitor's not cool. I don't want to see youse getting it on in front of my face while I'm trying to work!"

Emma kept her face skywards, raking the ceiling for a camera. Rohan rested his head next to hers and pointed a long arm into the corner above the open door. He waved his hand and the movement triggered a tiny sensor which emitted a dull flash of white light. Emma's lips parted in wonder. Rohan nudged her, urging her wordlessly up the stairs and turned his attention to Christopher. "You need to stop it flashing. It's a dead giveaway in the dark," he said.

The Irishman sneered and pulled a nasty face. "*You need to stop it flashing!*" he repeated childishly, parroting Rohan's words.

"And hence why we never worked as an effective team!" Rohan snapped.

Christopher's attitude changed with frightening immediacy. "Sorry," he said, with contrition. He glanced across at Emma, naked jealousy in his eyes and her look of surprise chastened him. Her pity made it worse and Christopher gulped. He waved his arm, encompassing the large open room in his gesture. "Welcome to my place," he said with a wry smile. "Anton let me keep my gear here and I'm hoping the new owner doesn't mind."

Emma stared around the scruffy apartment. Old

furniture lined the open space, a sitting room with dilapidated sofa and chairs gathered around a high spec TV and theatre system. The theme was grunge-meets expensive technology and the image was jarring and incongruous. An unmade double bed huddled behind the sitting area, the sheets rumpled and the duvet half on the wooden floor. A wall of windows graced the living half of the apartment, overlooking the stable yard and shrouded by blackout blinds which hugged the windows snugly. A glass partition divided the two halves of the room long ways, keeping personal and business separate. Emma stood with her nose pressed to the glass in wonder, staring at the amassed technology lining the apartment's back wall. Lights flashed as information passed through the myriad racks of servers, blinking from one to another with regularity. Emma understood none of it, fascinated only by the aesthetic wonder of the sight. "Wow!" she breathed. "*Those* servers. There's more than one."

Next to her with its back to the glass stood a high spec computer, the monitor frozen flashing a trail of information, temporarily halted by its creator's absence.

"This is yours?" Emma turned to Christopher, her eyes wide with amazement. "These computers belong to you?"

He nodded and ran a hand through his dark hair. "Aye. It's why I couldn't leave. Anton let me set up here and I've nowhere else to put it. I know I must leave but I can't find anywhere suitable."

"Why isn't that computer in there?" Emma asked, her face innocent as she pressed a few keys on the keyboard in devilment.

Christopher rolled his eyes. "Server rooms are

freezing, like fridges. Besides, it needn't be. Do you know what you just pressed? I never had youse down as a terrorist."

Emma pulled her fingers away and gulped, seeing Rohan smirk and bite his bottom lip. She gritted her teeth and refused to admit to the pounding heart of fear Christopher deliberately caused. "I hate you both," she grumbled. Her attention wandered towards a bank of power sockets on the far wall. "Is this why the power bill's so high?" she demanded, narrowing her eyes at the Irishman. "I've turned half the bloody radiators off in the main house!"

He had the decency to look guilty. "Aye, probably. I'll reimburse you," he offered. "But your heating's gas and this is electric."

Emma's fierce expression wiped the smirk off his face. She shook her head. "My son's still cold because I couldn't work out the reason for the huge bill. And the person causing it's offering to pay only now I've found out. Why couldn't you be honest with me from the start?" She glared at both men. "Why couldn't you both be honest?"

Rohan shrugged. "Nothing to do with me; he's your house guest."

"That's no excuse! You should've told me! You were happy for him to use it to bug my car and follow me everywhere!" Emma put her hands on her hips. "The stuff you're doing here, Christopher, is it legal?"

He took a moment to formulate his answer under her piercing scrutiny. "The equipment itself isn't illegal. Anyone could own this system."

Rohan snorted. "What, with a glass partition, insulated walls and air conditioning? I guess Microsoft and Google have something similar." He shook his head and folded his arms.

Christopher took a step towards the Russian, his face angry. "No! Any medium sized corporation in the country has something like this. I know youse don't want me here and the moment this job finishes you'll throw me out yerself. I'm sorry for everything, Rohan! There, I've said it! I shouldn't have seduced the Contessa or stolen the risk and I shouldn't have kissed your wife. Everything I've done since your uncle went to war with Che was my way of tryin' to put things right. It's been my dumb assed way of restoring things back to how they were before I screwed up. I'm sorry, Rohan; Anton told you I was someone I can't be. I don't know why he thought I was this wonderful, trustworthy friend; I look in the mirror and I can't see the man he saw." Christopher turned and thumped himself into the squashy sofa, all signs of his classic arrogance gone, replaced with self-doubt and a sense of failure. He shot a sideways look at Rohan. "And no, I wasn't his gay lover."

He ran a hand dusted with dark hair across his forehead, his handsome face downcast. "Every time I tried to get us back to where we were, Mikhail double crossed me again and again. He told Che about Falkirk, not me. The Contessa was all over that long before you neutralised the risk and her guys jumped me. I thought I could limit the damage by luring them to the house in Falkirk but I didn't expect them to take Emma. I thought I'd scammed them out of it." The Irishman sighed.

"That's why you tipped me off and arranged the earlier drop at Heathrow?" Rohan said, his face softening at Christopher's nod.

"No." Emma interrupted, shaking her head. "*You*

kidnapped me not the Contessa's men. You told me to get in the car." Her brown eyes raked the Irishman's face for deceit. "And they weren't Chinese."

Christopher frowned. "You have an obsession with Chinese men." He examined a ratty nail with distraction. "They told me at the club they'd found out where Rohan lived. The Contessa paid them for a hit on both of youse and I persuaded them to wait. She slipped up by using common thugs and I couldn't stop them killing you, but I convinced them it made more sense to do it in front of the Contessa. They assumed she was a man because she used Che's name to employ them. I played on their egos and made them believe he'd reward them if they presented youse as a gift. Then I changed the drop location and directed Rohan to the Falkirk house. I knew he'd suspect trouble, bring Frederik's crew and get us out."

"So, why did you help the Contessa out of the fire?" Rohan spat. "That's not the work of a sorry man!"

Christopher stood up, his fists balled by his sides. "Youse left me there to die!" he shouted. "Everything I did was for you and *her!*" He jabbed a finger at Emma. "You left me in an inferno like I meant nothing!"

"You double crossed me at every turn!" Rohan spoke through gritted teeth, his blue eyes blazing like blue agate in his face.

"Not on purpose!" Christopher's body looked deflated, his desperation showing. "I just wasn't smart enough to outwit Mikhail and the Contessa combined." He sighed and pressed the ball of his thumb against his full lips. "I'm not an actuary, I'm just a tech." He waved his arm towards the glass partition. "This is my world and I couldn't cope in yours." He stood in front of the angry Russian, his eyes begging for mercy. "Look, I don't blame youse, Rohan. I've been one big stuff up from start to finish just like my daddy said I'd be. I got meself chucked out of Oxford University for hackin' and the only reason the Air Force kept me on was because I hacked what they wanted. What a bloody mess!" He rubbed his eyes and looked so downcast, Emma felt pity rise in her chest.

"Let's deal with today's problem," she said, speaking reason into the argument. "We'll sort everything else out afterwards."

The men turned their faces towards her, accepting her direction. Christopher gave a watery smile. "Ok, we'll do this one for old time's sake."

"Bloody better not be!" Rohan snapped. "You try one dodgy move and I'll kill you." He drew his index finger across his throat and Emma watched the Irishman pale.

"I won't let yer down," Christopher promised. "I promise youse this time."

"Who's the client?" Emma directed her question at Christopher, pushing her question through the haze of testosterone. "Are you any nearer to finding out?"

Christopher nodded. "He used an email account with false details to list the job, but I've traced it back through IP addresses. He's good at what he does, but not with anything technical; it's not his field."

"What is his field?" Rohan asked, relaxing his posture. He thrust his hands into his pockets.

Christopher licked his lips, happier to see Rohan's strong hands move out of sight. "He's a very successful plastic surgeon. He's got offices in Harley Street and an international reputation on the line."

"Why does he want an old plaque from a primary school?" Emma asked, screwing up her face. "How is it a risk to him? It makes no sense."

Christopher stood up and walked to his computer. Emma watched the tall Irishman's back as he pressed keys and glanced at the large screen. A printer kicked out a single sheet of paper and he grabbed it, turning back to his rapt audience. A faint smirk lit his lips as he handed the paper to Emma.

"Oh." Emma sighed and handed it straight to Rohan. He perused it quickly and shrugged.

"Means nothing," he said, looking from Christopher to Emma.

"It does to you though, doesn't it Emma?" the Irishman said and she nodded.

Emma reached out and took the sheet of paper from Rohan's fingers, shaking her head. A basic internet search on the name Christopher gleaned from his complicated tracking, revealed the portrait photograph of a sixty-five-year old man from his clinic profile. "Fantastic!" Emma said, anger in her voice. "Adam Jameson must be related to Clarissa Jameson-Arden." She glanced up at Rohan's blank face. "Clarissa's the chairwoman of the board of governors at school. I found the plaque weeks ago and started investigating the school's history. I stupidly alerted her when I visited St Di's and she guessed I knew something. She's been watching me ever since, according to Christopher and she threatened me."

"Threatened you?" Rohan's eyes widened and fury lit a flame in his irises.

Emma waved her hand, realising too late she'd dismissed his concern. "She tried to blackmail me with lies from my former boss, but I sent a message back to him that might stem his bile permanently. I said I had the luck of the Irish."

Christopher laughed and Rohan's eyes flashed danger. "What?"

Emma regretted the look of isolation in her husband's face as Christopher enjoyed her little joke and she gave him a shortened version. "Christopher beat him up."

Rohan glanced at the Irishman. "Was that before or after I got you to plant porn on his office computer and get him investigated by the Ministry of Education."

Christopher looked duly contrite. "After."

"Nice," Rohan bit. "Real nice. I didn't realise it was a competition."

Emma groaned. "Should I carry on or just tell whoever survives your dog fight?" Her tone dripped with intended sarcasm and the men continued an eyebrow war with intermittent glaring.

"So, Clarissa definitely didn't want me to find out the family secret, but I'm not sure she knew there was a plaque. Someone in the distant past removed all school logs dating from 1860 to 1864, although the 1865 one mentioned nothing about a grand opening, which is odd in itself to an archivist. When I told Dalton about the plaque, he would have informed her as chairperson straight away."

"Explain the relevance of the plaque," Rohan asked, his face betraying his confusion.

Emma sighed in frustration. "Over a hundred and fifty years ago, a Jameson killed an Arden over an affair and was hanged for it. I couldn't find definitive proof he actually died or had a reprieve, but it was the crime of the century in this small community. He was the original schoolmaster and caused a huge local scandal. Someone removed the plaque from the wall which gave the original date of the school opening, destroyed or removed the log books and waited for the dust to settle. I've checked and the one hundred year celebration was held five years too late. The Jamesons seem determined for this event to go ahead on the wrong date again and the plaque and me are the only things standing in the way."

Rohan shook his head and opened his arms wide in front of him. "That's it?" He looked disappointed. "Half a million sterling for this?" He turned to Emma. "If you were a Jameson, what would you do?"

"I don't know." She shrugged. "If I was the headmaster, I'd use it for publicity. It'd make a fantastic media opportunity. The public love a story like that and whoever went to all that trouble to hide the real dates is long since dead. A bit of newspaper coverage would draw amazing crowds and raise enough money to fund whole new buildings." Emma gnawed on the inside of her cheek. "But if I was Clarissa Jameson, I'd probably be mortified. Anyone else would take it in their stride, but she's set herself up as the queen of Market Harborough, so it'd be a painful, public humiliation."

"And awkward," Christopher added. "Her ancestors killed a member of her husband's family generations ago. Maybe he doesn't know."

Rohan sneered. "This is stupid!" he exclaimed. "The risks I recover for that kind of payment are hard drives which can destroy corporations or high ranking officials who have more to lose than reputation." His Russian accent made his disgust seem more brutal. "This is *melochi!*" He waved his arms. "Trivia!"

"Not to Adam Jameson maybe," Emma countered. She peered at the sheet in front of her. "Look, he's a justice of the peace and acts as patron to a victim support charity. If he's anything like Clarissa, it's all about social standing and garnering respect. I suppose the descendant of a murderer might feel awkward as the patron of a charity for victims of crime."

"Especially as his ancestors went to such lengths to cover it up," Christopher mused.

"So, what's the link to the Triads?" Rohan asked.

Christopher gulped. "When I pulled the Contessa out of the fire she was unconscious. The burns to her face and hands weren't pleasant. We came out through a front window and she sustained bad gashes as well. I was coughing and she was a dead weight..."

"How did you get away?" Rohan's jaw worked in his face and Emma looked for signs of guilt, seeing nothing.

"One of her men was outside checking the perimeter. I suspect he hid while youse left because he was only a wee lad, about nineteen. He helped me carry her to the nearest house. We hid from fire vehicles and cops and she didn't wake up. At the first farm I hotwired a car and drove to the nearest city. We parted company and I don't know where they went. I let them keep the car and made my way back here."

"Why was she so badly hurt and yet you weren't?" Emma asked. She remembered the night Christopher met her in Allaine's garden and pictured the cuts and bruises on his face.

Christopher snuffed, his short laugh full of sarcasm. "I *was* hurt, Em." He stared at Rohan, his face full of accusation. "But not as badly as her. Yer man here knocked me out and left me to die. I woke up as the Calor gas heater in the corner of the room exploded. I hoped it had a natural leak because it only takes the smallest amount to create an inferno, doesn't it

Rohan?"

Emma's lips parted in horror. "Are you accusing my husband of turning the gas on?" She put her hands on her hips and stared at the Irishman, her lovely face a vision of righteous indignation. She took a step towards Christopher. "I remember the explosion because it brought me out of unconsciousness. Rohan was outside, loading me into his hire car with the soldier who knocked me out. I'm sorry you were left there, Christopher, but the house was completely ablaze when Rohan gave the order to leave you. He wouldn't do something like that, would you?" She glanced at Rohan, horrified at the time he took to answer.

"I would," he confirmed. "It was a good idea and I wish I'd thought of it. You double crossed me and I didn't care if you became collateral damage in your own foolish game. I'm sorry Hack, but you brought it on yourself."

Emma closed her eyes and held her breath. When she opened them again, she found Rohan and Christopher shaking hands. Her jaw dropped. "What the hell?" she exclaimed.

Rohan smirked and Christopher shrugged, neither offering an explanation. Emma huffed in anger. "I'll never understand men; I give up." Her brain returned to the problem. "So, the Contessa and Adam Jameson could have a link through her need for plastic surgery?" she asked. "Or maybe she's had surgery and feels indebted to him? She's an actuary, so why doesn't she recover the plaque and wipe you two out at the same time? That'd work."

Christopher shook his head, his eyes narrowed as his brain worked. "It was only a few months ago and that girl's gonna be havin' surgery for a very long time. The side of her face melted, Emma; it was beyond bad. And she'll need reconstructive surgery to her jaw after Rohan shot her in the face."

"I didn't shoot her in the face!" Rohan looked affronted, his gaze fixed on Christopher as he jutted out his chin. "I didn't use my gun." His fingers reached towards the back of his trousers and then stopped and he shot a quick glance in Emma's direction. Her eyes widened.

"You carry a gun?" she asked. "How come I've never noticed?"

"Maybe you don't touch the right places," Christopher said, the snarky comment lighting up his face.

"You'd know!" Rohan snapped and Emma saw the argument beginning again.

"So, who shot her in the face?" she demanded. "If it wasn't either of you, could it have been one of Frederik's men?"

"No. They inventoried their rounds and accounted for every shot, just like they always do. Fred told me afterwards when we talked. Besides, our men were elsewhere when it really kicked off." Rohan's eyes narrowed. "The only other person in the room besides us was..."

"The Contessa's bodyguard." Christopher finished Rohan's sentence, ignoring the other man's flash of irritation. "Bloody hell! What's going on?"

"It's irrelevant right now." Rohan stood up straight and touched the phone in his top pocket. "My *syn's* waking. We'll talk after we get the plaque back." He turned to Emma. "Get ready for work as normal and we'll see if your caretaker friend's there. If not, we need to find him."

"I'll keep searching," Christopher said, running his hand through his hair. His dark eyes looked tired and a growth of stubble covered the lower half of his face. He dismissed the Andreyevs with an uplifted eyebrow and they left his loft apartment with the basis of a plan.

CHAPTER THIRTY THREE

"What did you do?" Emma snarled, appearing from behind Sam's car as he cleared frost off the windscreen.

"Bloody hell, Emma!" he squeaked. "Don't jump out at me." Sam clutched his heart and paled as Rohan stepped around the brick corner of the house. The Russian's blue eyes watched Sam like prey and the caretaker lost his nerve within seconds. "What do you want?" he asked, his voice cracking in fear. "My wife's inside; she'll call the police."

"That's funny." Rohan withdrew his hands from his pockets and stepped towards Sam. "Because we watched her leave." He towered over him and Emma watched her colleague gulp, caught out in his lie.

"Inside," Sam hissed, jerking his head towards the house. He unlocked the front door of the semi on Stuart Road and waved the couple in. The house looked meticulously tidy as though someone took great pride in appearances. In the kitchen at the back of the house, Rohan took up position blocking the back door, folding his arms across his massive chest.

Emma followed Sam into the room and prodded him in the back. "Where is it, you little weasel? I trusted you!"

"Why aren't you at work?" he squeaked.

"I was at work!" Emma snapped. "I went looking for you and had to pretend I felt ill. Where is it?"

"Where's what?" Sam asked, his eyes straying towards Rohan's inert form, his jaw working frantically.

"Don't bother, Sam!" Emma snapped. "You know what I'm talking about. Where's the plaque?"

"How did you find out?" Sam groaned. "You couldn't climb up there; you're pregnant and it's dangerous."

"Well, I did!" Emma replied. "Why did you go back for it?"

Sam cringed and cast around him, settling his backside into a dining chair. He eyed Rohan with nervous glances. "They said they'd pay for IVF," he whined, running a shaking hand through his sparse hair. "My marriage is on the line here."

"Where's the plaque?" Emma said, gritting her teeth and resisting the urge to slap Sam's stupid face.

"I can't tell you!" the man groaned. "Please don't take this chance away from us."

"Freda prayed for you; you don't need IVF," Emma snapped. "Have you no faith, man?"

"No!" Sam shouted. "You don't understand what it's like. My wife's desperate. I can't take anymore and it's our last hope. I'm the problem, Emma, *me*. She can leave and get pregnant by someone else anytime she likes!"

Emma glanced at Rohan, giving her husband a look of frustration. Rohan stepped in, seizing a chair, pulling it out and sitting his neat backside on its wooden surface. "If you give me the plaque now, I'll fund your first two rounds of IVF."

Sam gaped. "Two rounds? They only offered me one. That's like..." He counted on his fingers. "Twelve thousand pounds."

"Where's the plaque, Sam!" Emma shouted. "You have no idea how important this is."

"It's safe," he breathed. "I promise." His eyes strayed to Rohan. "Two rounds of IVF?"

"You won't need them!" Emma fumed, surprised by her own vehemence and belief. "Freda prayed for you."

"If my wife's right and you don't need the treatment, I'll just give you the money. You can have it today." Rohan's face hardly changed and Sam gulped.

"For real?"

"He doesn't break his word!" Emma broke her pacing to slap Sam around the back of the head. "Why aren't you at work?" she chastised him.

"You're not my bloody mother!" Sam complained, grimacing as Emma slapped him again. "I'm sick," he conceded.

"Rubbish! You look fine!" Emma snapped. "What's going on?"

"It's a sort of sickness," Sam whined. "I've been having sex every waking moment. I'm knackered. Sal's just nipped out for more baby oil but I don't think I can keep this up."

Rohan smirked and Emma slapped Sam again. "That's disgusting!"

"You asked!" he complained.

Rohan cocked his head and muttered, "Sounds like fun actually."

"Where's the damn plaque?" Emma yelled, pushing her frustrated face into Sam's.

"Alright, alright," Sam groused. "I hid it upstairs." He glanced at Rohan. "If I give it to you now, when will you give me twelve thousand pounds?"

Rohan pulled his phone from the inside pocket of his jacket. "As soon as you give me your bank details," he said, punching the password into his phone. "And after you tell me who else wants the plaque."

"Oh." Sam's face paled. "That part might cost extra."

Emma whipped round, her long coat flapping around her shins and almost tripping her. "Not bloody likely!" she raged. Her face changed to one of calm vindictiveness. "Actually, don't pay him anything, Ro. I'll just go back to work and report a theft. You wait here and don't let Sam move and I'll send the police right round to turn his house inside out. I've heard they leave an awful mess once they get going. They're like teenagers looking for the other sock in the pair. Lend me your phone." She held out her hand and Rohan smirked, putting his device into Emma's palm.

"No! No!" Sam shrieked. "Please don't! I'll lose my job and Sal will kill me. She can't stand mess. I'll get it, I promise. Twelve thousand pounds is more than enough."

"Go with him," Emma ordered her husband as Sam stood. "Don't let him out of your sight." She turned to Sam. "Be quick, love. I'm feeling restless and I might not be able to help myself if I'm left alone too long. I love looking in other people's drawers and getting everything out."

"Don't touch anything!" Sam's tone betrayed his fear. "I'll be quick!"

Emma put her hand against her chest as she heard footsteps overhead. Rohan's light tread followed Sam's frightened stomping and Emma tried to calm her pounding heart and concentrate on lowering her blood pressure. "Bloody men!" she hissed to herself. She ran a gentle hand over her swelling belly. "I hope you are a little girl," she sighed. "It'll be lovely to have someone who knows what I'm talking about."

The men returned within minutes, Rohan looking disgruntled. Emma panicked at the look on his face. "What's wrong?" she demanded.

Her husband handed over the rectangular shape, wrapped in an unfortunate covering. Rohan wiped his hands down the side of his smart trousers. "He wrapped it in his knickers!" he complained. "It was in his knicker drawer."

"They're not knickers!" Sam protested. "They're Y-fronts!"

"Bloody weird," Rohan muttered. He waved his hand at Emma. "Check it's there and then I'll pay this *sheister*."

Emma heard the thud of the heavy metal as she laid the object on the table. She smiled at her husband. "You've been listening to Christopher. It's his favourite word."

"Who's Christopher?" Sam asked, shifting on his feet in a fit of nervousness.

"Shut up," Emma said, at the same time as Rohan.

CHAPTER THIRTY FOUR

"Did Dalton believe you were sick?" Rohan asked and Emma nodded.

"Yes, it wasn't a complete lie either. I'm exhausted. Nicky wasn't happy about me not staying at school though."

"Was Allaine ok with Nikolai staying at her place tonight?"

Emma shrugged. "She was, but he wasn't. Nicky and Kaylee aren't such good friends now Mo's gone."

"Gone where?" Rohan placed the mug of tea next to the plaque on the kitchen table.

"Not sure," Emma yawned. "He disappeared in the night which was weird. Mel seemed happy in Harborough and I know she loved her job at the coffee shop."

Rohan sat at the table next to Emma and rested his hand on her thigh. "Get Hack to look for her. He'll tell you if everything's ok." He smiled as Emma nodded and covered another yawn with her hand. "Go to bed, *devotchka*. Get some rest."

She shook her head. "I won't sleep, Ro. There's too much going on in my head." She nudged the plaque with her hand. "Where do you hand this over? Do you have a location yet?"

Rohan shook his head. "*Net*, but that's not unusual. The client often leaves it until the last minute to arrange the drop. It's too risky otherwise."

"Will Adam Jameson come himself?"

"I doubt it, Em. He'll send someone else. Clients remain anonymous but they arrange a designated collector; sometimes another actuary. I've done jobs like that, simple pickups."

"It sounds complicated." Emma stroked the plaque with loving fingers. "Such a small thing to cause so much trouble. I don't want to part with it really; it goes against my responsibility as an archivist."

"To protect artifacts for future generations?" Rohan asked softly, his fingers lingering on her thigh.

Emma smiled and felt her heart soften. "Yes. I didn't think you listened when I talked about my work," she said. "It can sound rather boring compared to your job."

Rohan sighed. "I listen, *dorogaya*. I'll try harder at the husband thing, I promise; I'll do better from now on."

When Emma yawned again, Rohan ordered her to bed and walked her up the wide staircase. "Just lay down," he said, kissing her cheek. "Christopher hasn't texted for a while and I need to see how he's getting on."

"What's he doing?" Emma asked and Rohan pressed his lips over hers.

"Sshh, *devotchka*. Let me take care of things and prove I can be trusted."

Emma nodded and laid her head on the pillow, expecting sleep to allude her. She woke up three hours later, groggy and disoriented, nursing a monster headache. "Ugh!" she exclaimed, wiping saliva from her cheek and sitting. The fire burned low in the grate and the room was darkened by the thick curtains which Rohan must have pulled across the windows. "There was nothing refreshing about that nap!" Emma complained, stumbling to the bathroom to wash her face. "Daytime sleeping sucks!"

A glance at the bedroom clock made her eyes widen in horror. "No! Ray Barker's due now!" She slapped her cheeks and ran wet hands through unruly curls before running down the stairs.

"Steady on!" Rohan caught her on the last step as Emma tripped in her hurry, landing in his strong arms. He used the opportunity to kiss her, his lips cold from outside.

"I'm meant to be meeting someone," Emma gushed and Rohan's eyes narrowed.

"Should I be worried, *devotchka?*"

"My new gardener's due here at one o'clock to take a look around," Emma said, rubbing her eyes with the heel of her hand.

"Ah." Rohan did the infuriating uplift of the head and made no other comment, leading Emma by the hand into the reception hall. He enfolded her in his arms and kissed her neck. "Be quick," he said. "I've something to show you." The lilting Russian accent sounded sultry, muffled by Emma's hair and she turned her face to nip the soft skin at the edge of Rohan's shirt collar. He moaned and pulled her into him.

The sound of the gate intercom made them both jump and Emma gave a nervous laugh. She broke free from her husband's muscular arms and skittered over to the box near the front door.

"*Ray Barker to see the lady of the house,*" her new gardener said, his voice sounding crackly and disjointed in the cavernous hallway.

Emma giggled and pressed the button. "Come on up, Ray." She turned to Rohan biting her lip. "He called me the lady of the house," she said with a smile.

Rohan shook his head. "Well, you are, *koroleva*."

"Queen?" Emma said, biting her lip and simpering. "Your queen?"

"*Da*," Rohan replied slowly. "Always, Em."

Emma opened the door to greet Ray Barker with a regal smile. He made no comment on her dress sense, the baggy track pants and scruffy sweatshirt adorned by a slinky nightdress which had worked its way out of the back and hung past her knees. "Hi, miss," he said with a smile, entering the wide front door and shaking her small hand in his huge paw. "Wow, this is some place you've got here."

"Thank you," Emma replied graciously. "We're part way through renovating but it's a long job. And call me Emma, please."

"I'm sure it's been a labour of love, miss." Ray said, looking around him. Feeling Rohan's eyes on the back of his neck, Ray turned and his face paled, his eyes widening as his lips parted. Emma saw him gulp as a dark look crossed his face and he took a moment to collect himself at the sight of the big Russian. "Captain Andreyev!" he said, his voice wavering.

Emma looked from one to the other, her expression showing surprise. Ray's colour looked deathly, but Rohan was as composed as always, nodding once to the stricken man. "Mr Barker," Rohan said.

Ray Barker floundered and Emma reached for him in concern, catching hold of his forearm. "Would you like to come to the kitchen for a hot drink?" she asked, widening her eyes at Rohan in question.

"Yes. Yes please, miss," the man answered, allowing himself to be led along the corridor to the kitchen.

Ray sat at the table, his face ashen and his giant hands shaking. He remained silent as Emma brewed strong tea and lay mugs and a milk jug on the table. "Sugar?" she asked and Ray nodded and muttered an unintelligible reply. He glanced at the kitchen door a number of times but Rohan didn't follow.

Emma sat next to him and poured tea into a mug. She pushed it towards him and he nodded his thanks. "Rohan's my husband," Emma said softly. "I didn't mention his name because I had no reason to think you might know him. I'm sorry you're upset." She gulped, knowing it would be impossible for Ray to work in the grounds if he suffered such a negative reaction to Rohan's presence. Curiosity burned in her breast but she suppressed it, needing to ask her husband for the truth first.

"It's fine." Ray reached for the milk jug and slopped the white liquid in the mug and down the sides to pool on the table. Emma waved away his apology and fetched a cloth, mopping at the mess with the calm skill of a mother used to frequent disasters.

"How many sugars?" she asked, loading the spoon and sparing Ray the embarrassment of adding granules to the damp table.

"Four, please," he said, oblivious to Emma's surprised blink.

She loaded them in and left the spoon for him to stir the sweet mixture, sipping at her own drink and waiting for him to calm. "I understand if you're not interested in the job anymore," she ventured, her voice sad. Ray referred to Rohan by his army rank and Emma recognised her impotence against army issues.

"I *do* want to work here," Ray stuttered. "It was just a shock seeing Captain Andreyev standing there. I haven't seen him since..." His voice shook and he took a fortifying gulp of the hot mixture, spluttering as it hit the back of his throat. Emma reached for the box of tissues in the centre of the table and slid it towards him. Ray snatched two and pressed them to his lips. "So much for making a good impression," he sighed.

Emma noticed the neat shirt and smart suit trousers and compassion flooded her heart. It touched her that he wanted to work for her badly enough to show up for a gardener's job in neat clothes. She cast her mind back to the meeting in the cafe and saw then the effort he'd made, overlooked by her as she fumbled through the foreign process of engaging employees. She reached out and put her slender fingers over his, surprised when he clasped them in his giant hand. "You have no idea how desperate I am for this job," Ray said, his voice wavering. "Now I've messed it up." He removed his hand from Emma's, pressing his fingers either side of the bridge of his nose.

"You haven't," Emma reassured him. "But I don't know how to fix this."

"You don't have to." Ray rubbed his palm across his entire face and stood. "I've nothing against your husband, miss. It was just a shock." He straightened the patterned tie at his neck and took a deep breath.

Emma stood also, horrified to notice her nightdress trailing on the seat. She bit her lips, her eyes wide. "Oh. Talking of good impressions!" She snorted and attempted to stuff the fabric into her pants, giving herself a tyre around the middle. "I'm so sorry."

Ray smiled for the first time. "It's fine, miss."

"You're not going to call me Emma, are you?" she asked, shoving the nightdress further into her pants to create curious wedges in front of her thighs.

Ray shook his head. "Just don't feel right, miss."

Emma shrugged. "Fair enough," she said, wincing

as the silky fabric worked its way down to her knees. "Why don't we go for a wander around the property and you can take a look at what needs doing?"

CHAPTER THIRTY FIVE

"I see why you need help." Ray stood at the end of the rutted track and surveyed the vast estate. A cool breeze attacked the lapels of his hurriedly donned suit jacket. "How much land is there?"

"Lots." Emma's hair blew back from her face, flapping behind her like a dark flag. The escaping nightdress obeyed the tug of the breeze and Emma pressed her hands against her waist to stop it taking flight. "I can check exact number of hectares on the deeds when we get back."

"No matter," Ray said. "As long as you have a plan for it."

Emma shrugged. "I'm open to suggestions," she replied, sounding hopeful. "The adjoining farms lease some of it for grazing but that was an arrangement Anton honoured. I haven't seen any money for it yet so I'm not sure what's going on there."

"Anton?" Ray asked, his words thrown around by the wind.

"My stepbrother," Emma said, sadness cloaking her with its dark kiss. "He died and left me the house and land."

"Lucky," Ray muttered and Emma nodded, not offended.

"Very," she replied. She turned to face him, stunning with her pink cheeks and dishevelled hair. "I know what it's like to have nothing, Ray," she said and he studied her, his gaze one of assessment.

Finally he nodded. "Yes, miss. I think you probably do."

"Will you work for me, please?" Emma asked, shivering in the icy air.

Ray nodded. "Love to, miss."

Emma sighed with relief as they climbed back into her car and made the bumpy journey to the sprawling house nestled in the valley. "I'm glad," she said, clumping her foot on the brake to avoid a rut. "I need help to formulate a plan for the land as well as the house; it's overwhelming when I'm awake at night worrying. You'll spend lots of time on the phone talking to the heritage people from the council and they'll be partly helpful and partly obstructive. Will you be ok with that?"

Ray nodded and smiled sideways. "Can I ask about your marriage to Captain Andreyev?" he asked. "You can refuse to answer."

"I'm happy to talk about it," Emma said, negotiating an open gateway. "Rohan's my stepbrother and we grew up together. We fell in love and married without his mother's knowledge when I was sixteen. He went to Afghanistan and I discovered I was pregnant with our son. There were reasons I needed to leave home for my own safety and Anton made me promise not to see Ro again or tell him about Nicky. He told Rohan on his death bed to find me but he didn't know about Nicky until we met again at the end of last year."

"Oh." Ray's silence made Emma glance sideways at him. "It sounds like a novel," he said eventually, flicking at a speck of mud on his trousers. "Like one of those sad love stories. You called him your ex-husband at the cafe. Is there any likelihood of you both finding what you lost before it's too late?"

Emma bit her lip and swallowed. "We already have," she said, struggling to answer such a personal question from a comparative stranger. "It's just proving harder to translate that into real life after such a long time apart." Emma felt tears prick behind her eyes. "Things get in the way and we're not teenagers anymore."

"Sorry," Ray said. "You didn't have to be so honest, but I appreciate it. I've got nothing but respect for Captain Andreyev after what happened. I'd love to think he was happy."

Emma slammed on the brakes and the car skidded to a halt. "I thought you hated Rohan!" Emma exclaimed, her fingers clenched around the steering wheel.

Ray's jaw dropped as he turned to face her. "No! Absolutely not! Your husband was my son's commanding officer on their last tour in Afghanistan. They were injured in the same blast and Captain Andreyev pulled Hugh to safety." Ray ran a shaking hand over his face and Emma waited, holding her breath as a hidden window opened into Rohan's life. "Hugh died at a military hospital but at least your husband tried to give him a chance. He didn't leave him there for the bastards to finish off. The captain was messed up so bad himself, it's a miracle he dragged him as far as he did. It's why they gave him the Conspicuous Gallantry Medal and he deserved it. Only five of them made it home and most of them banged up like your husband."

"I didn't know." Emma fixed her eyes on the roof of Wingate Hall in the distance, tracing the apex angles and seeing smoke winding skywards from the chimney stack above her bedroom. "Rohan won't talk about it."

"Yeah, well, he's a bloody hero." Ray sniffed and Emma kept her eyes averted to give him dignity. "He spoke at Hugh's funeral. They wheeled him in but he insisted on standing to give the eulogy. Miss, he looked so sick and bashed up, but he stood there and said his piece. He knew my boy, right down to Hugh's dry sense of humour. The words he spoke in Russian sounded real special and it touched us; my wife and me. He said it was from a song his father taught him." Ray stared into the distance, his voice trailing off as he contemplated his tragic memories.

Emma bit her lip, knowing the other reason Rohan looked sick. He returned home, injured and desperate for comfort, arriving to hear the lies of his mother and Emma's conspicuous absence. "Rohan was blown up the day I gave birth to Nicky," Emma said, a catch in her voice. "We were both hurting, neither knowing what the other was going through right at that moment. It's Nicky's birthday in September and he'll be seven. It'll be a strange day for both of us." She wrinkled her nose. "Nicky won't have a clue. He's asked for a party; he's never had one before."

"But you'll make it work now?" Ray pressed. "You and the Captain?" Emma nodded.

"We'll certainly try." Emma pushed the vehicle on and rode the last hundred metres back to the main driveway, hating the jarring trip across a cattle grid. "I heard somewhere, maybe from Paul," she said, "you're sleeping on his sofa."

Ray nodded, his cheeks flushing with shame. He lowered his eyes and wrung his hands together. "Yeah. Council doesn't really care about a single man with no job and places round here are too expensive for someone on unemployment benefit. There's no council houses spare but I'm on the waiting list for a flat."

"You mentioned your wife," Emma began. "It's just..."

"Died," Ray interrupted. "Five years ago. Hugh's death broke something in her and she gave up on life. She'd had cancer before, but it came back and this time she didn't bother fighting. She suffered from depression our whole marriage; I often thought it was my fault." He glanced at Emma, his eyes red-rimmed with grief. "Sorry," he said. "What were you gonna say?"

"The job comes with accommodation," Emma said. "The coach house might be too big for one person, but take a look at the other apartments. There're three more above the stables and four on the top floor of the main house. Have a think about it and come back tomorrow. I've something else to sort out this afternoon, but I'm happy to negotiate wages and living arrangements then. Your salary can start from today; I just need Ro to help me sort the documentation out."

Ray bit his lip as Emma pulled the car up behind Rohan's Mercedes. She turned the engine off and pushed the driver's door open, her eyes widening as Ray grabbed her forearm. "I don't deserve this," he whispered, emotion crumpling his face like putty.

Emma smiled in sympathy, her brown eyes soft as she patted his hand. "Ray, I wake up every morning and look around me feeling exactly the same way." Her gaze strayed to the enormous house filled with history and untold stories and Emma sighed. "You know, I think you and I will work well together. We both know extreme hardship and won't take anything for granted." She held out her hand, her face serious. "Welcome to Wingate Hall. You're our first employee, so I guess that makes you my manager."

Ray grinned and the years dropped away from his face. "Thanks, miss," he said. "I won't let you down."

CHAPTER THIRTY SIX

Emma stood on the front steps and smiled at her new employee. "Bring your gear tomorrow lunchtime and put it wherever you choose," she said. "I'll be home from work by then. You'll need keys and codes for the gate and burglar alarm and after that, you can come and go as you please. My son found an equipment shed the other day but I've no idea what's in it. We'll check after you've settled in; maybe there's something salvageable."

Ray nodded, still looking overwhelmed. "Thanks, miss. I'll see you tomorrow."

Emma pushed the front door open, disappearing inside and cursing the flapping nightdress which leaked over the back of her track pants. "Bloody thing!" she hissed, an embarrassed flush creeping across her cheeks. "I bet he noticed and didn't mention it."

"Em!" Rohan limped towards her, his face filled with excitement. "Come and look at this." He seized her hand and pulled her along the corridor towards the kitchen.

Emma gripped the flapping material and ran to keep up. "Where's the fire?" she grumbled.

"In our bedroom," Rohan replied, his face serious. "I got it lit again, but the surprise isn't up there; it's in here." He stood outside the kitchen door, excitement lighting his blue eyes like rare diamonds. "Close your eyes."

Emma felt his large palm covering her sight and

wriggled in annoyance. "Rohan, stop!" she protested.

"Shh," he insisted, pinching her bottom as he pressed her forward into the room.

Emma flapped at Rohan's impertinent hand, indignant at his distraction technique. She jerked her head and blinked in the light of the kitchen, seeing Christopher's lithe shape standing by the table. "Hey, Em," he said, sounding pleased with himself.

"What's so important?" Emma whined. "It better be good." Her gaze drifted to the table, searching for the plaque and not finding it. "Where's it gone?" she panicked, raking first Christopher's face and then Rohan's. "Where's the plaque?"

"I told ya she'd flip!" Christopher said with satisfaction. "Ya should've shown her afterwards."

"Shown me what? Rohan, that plaque cost you twelve thousand pounds; where is it?" Emma fanned her face with her hand and staggered to a chair. "I feel sick," she gasped.

"It's in the oven," Christopher informed her and Emma stared at him.

"What?" she snapped, convinced she heard wrong.

"In the oven. Look." The Irishman pointed towards the cooking range which occupied the old fireplace. The closed doors of the gas Aga kept its secret.

"You put an irreplaceable artifact in my oven?" Emma whispered, shaking her head to clear it. "You just put it in the oven; a hundred and fifty five years of history...in the oven. To cook?"

"Aye," Christopher confirmed.

Emma closed her eyes and blew out through pursed lips. "So, the oven's on?" she asked, pressing her fingers to the aching bridge of her nose. "And you're cooking it like a big biscuit?"

"Aye."

Emma's eyes snapped open and her cheeks blushed in anger. "Why?" she yelled at the Irishman. "Why would you do such a dumb thing?"

"Is everything ok, miss?" Ray asked, his voice sounding concerned as he poked his head around the doorframe. Christopher and Rohan adopted a fight stance and Ray looked past them to Emma.

"Who're you?" Christopher asked rudely and Emma laid her forearms on the table and buried her face in the soft material of her sweatshirt.

"You're cooking a valuable artifact?" she groaned. "This isn't real; I've fallen asleep and there's a moron in my dream."

"Mr Barker," Emma heard Rohan say.

"Captain Andreyev," came the reply.

"Who is he?" Christopher asked again, his voice laden with threat. He advanced past Emma and she reached out and grabbed at the bottom of his shirt.

"Don't even think about it, Dolan! He's my new park manager," she hissed, making up the title on the spot. She sat up and turned around, not releasing Christopher. "What's the matter, Ray?"

"Left my car keys," he said, indicating the fruit bowl in the centre of the table. Emma nudged it with her free hand and it shifted, revealing a set of keys with a battered cuddly rabbit hiding under a fallen banana.

"Let go, woman!" Christopher strained against Emma's hold on his shirt.

"Do you want me to stay, miss?" Ray asked, ignoring the room's more formidable occupants.

Emma let go of Christopher's hem and turned to look at Rohan before answering. Her husband stood with his backside leaned against the counter, arms folded and eyes narrowed. Emma opened her mouth to dismiss Ray with unconvincing platitudes, beaten to it by Rohan's heavily accented voice. "Stay, Mr Barker," he said. "We could use the help."

Emma shook her head in amazement and let out a sigh which deflated her body. Christopher froze on the spot. "What? Don't be an eejit! We know nothin' about him!"

Rohan fixed his penetrating blue eyes on the Irishman. "I know plenty about him and he's a good man." He raised blonde eyebrows at Christopher. "He stays."

Christopher stomped back towards the Aga, swearing under his breath. Ray ventured further into the room, choosing the chair next to Emma. He pocketed his car keys and leaned back in the seat. "What's going on?"

"I found an artifact," Emma began. "It proves the school's five years older than first thought and puts in jeopardy the one hundred and fiftieth celebration later this year. Unfortunately, a number of people don't want me to reveal it. This morning, Rohan and I retrieved it after it was stolen." Emma slumped in her seat. "But it's all pointless as we're due to hand it over to someone else at midnight tonight and don't have a choice." She glanced at Christopher and pointed a shaking index finger at him, her voice wavering. "And my Irish friend's solution is to bake it like a cookie."

"Why all the fuss?" Ray shrugged. "Can't you go public and get the newspapers on board; then it can't be hushed up?"

"Oh, guy's a genius!" Christopher muttered in his Irish brogue. "Why didn't we think of that?"

"*Zatknis'*, Hack!" Rohan snapped, telling him to

shut up. Christopher grumbled like a sulky teenager in the corner and watched as the Russian turned his attention to Ray Barker.

Emma scraped her chair back and stood. "I'm going for a shower and change of clothes." She held the bottom of her nightdress up in her left hand. Her smile for Ray was gentle. "I'm sure my husband will be happy to explain everything for you." Emma jabbed an index finger at Christopher. "And if that plaque's not out of the oven before I get back, *you're* in big trouble."

Upstairs in her bedroom, Emma sat on the bed for a moment to disgorge from her unusual attire and woke an hour later. The back of Rohan's hand stroked her warm cheek. "Emma, it's four o'clock, *dorogaya*. We need your help."

"Nicky!" Emma sat up with a start, making her head swim.

"He's fine, I promise. He went home with Allaine; she texted me. Kaylee's father wants to take them to a soccer game so Nikolai sounded happy. Kaylee's his best friend again, so all's well in his world."

Emma nodded and sank into the pillows, her heart pounding in her chest. She placed a shaking hand over it. "I'm not sure what happened. I only sat down to take my socks off."

"You're tired." Rohan stroked her hair back from her forehead. "And pregnant." He pushed his hand underneath the slinky nightdress and ran gentle fingers over the delicate skin of her abdomen. Emma groaned.

"I can't believe I've been walking around like this all day." She wrinkled her nose at the sight of her grey track pants shrouded by the silky claret nightie.

"I quite like it." Rohan bit his bottom lip, his eyes sparkling.

Emma couldn't help herself and tinkling laughter escaped her pink lips. "Does nothing spoil your libido?" she giggled.

"Some things." Rohan smiled, but a dark cloud crossed his eyes and Emma reached for his hand, sorry for her throwaway question. "I need to go back downstairs, Em. Can you meet me in the kitchen in ten minutes? It's important." He looked tired, dark circles creeping under his stunning eyes and Emma nodded, sensing her husband's tension.

"Ok," she promised.

"Up then," Rohan said, standing and offering his outstretched hand. "I need to see you actually moving around before I trust you enough to leave."

Emma heaved her unwilling body off the bed, shucking her sweatshirt and aiming it loosely in the direction of the door. She missed and it landed on the hearth. "Oops," she sighed as Rohan retrieved it, brushing off the fine layer of ash. "I'll take it to the laundry with the rest of this," she said, shimmying out of her track pants. Her eyes sparkled with mischief as Emma slipped the thin straps of the nightdress over her shoulders, letting it ripple over her soft skin and pool in a puddle at her feet like merlot.

The crow's feet at the corners of Rohan's eyes creased as he enjoyed his wife's nakedness, conflict creating a furrow in his brow. "I should go downstairs," he breathed, his voice wavering as doubt gnawed at him.

"Ok," Emma grinned, turning her back on him. She felt the pressure of his eyes raking the curve in the small of her back before her flesh plunged over her delicious buttocks, thrilled by the power which his insatiable need for her offered. "Off you go," she commanded, the wicked glint in her eye not dimmed by the deliberate swing of her hips as she closed the ensuite door on him.

Emma turned the water on and waited for the spray to heat as she listened to Rohan's phone chirp and his rude retort to the caller. "Shut it, *durak*! I'm coming now," he spat. She heard the bedroom door close and felt the vibrations of his footsteps through the floorboards. In the shower, she leaned her forehead against the tiles and closed her eyes, allowing the water pressure to pound the aching muscles at the back of her head.

Emma kept her promise, arriving in the kitchen dressed, with her wet hair tumbling from a clip and her jeans open at the zipper. She rolled her eyes at Rohan's curious expression. "They won't do up anymore," she grumbled, hauling her sweater down to cover the gap.

"About bloody time!" Christopher complained, turning from the sink. Emma's jaw dropped in amazement at the white powder dusted over his chin and cheeks. His jeans bore large, white handprints and his fingers were coated in a thick, white residue. A glance at Ray's guilty face next to him revealed one white eyebrow and a smudge which stretched from ear to chin.

"I'm glad the male bonding's going so well," she said, looking to her husband for assistance.

"Well, youse ran out on us!" Christopher protested. His face creased into a smile. "But we've had us a lot of fun, actually."

Emma shook her head. "So you turned from destroying precious artifacts to manufacturing cocaine?"

Rohan snorted with laughter but the Irishman

bridled with indignation. "No! We had to do it without youse, but Ray's good at this crap."

Ray ran a powdery hand across his forehead, leaving a line and creating a snowstorm of the white stuff. Rohan pulled out the chair next to Emma's and sat down with a sigh, slipping an arm around her shoulder. "Hack and I decided this job doesn't feel right. We talked it through and came up with a solution. Who, apart from you, Sam and Freda know what the plaque looks like? Did you show anyone else?"

Emma shook her head with a slow movement, considering the question. "No," she concluded. "Just we three and whoever hid it in the first place, added to anyone who's moved it around since. The mezzanine floor for the computer suite was added twenty years ago according to Sam, so it may have been disturbed during that period."

"But if someone saw it and knew what it was, they would either have destroyed it, or waved it around and made a big fuss?"

Emma nodded. "Exactly. A Jameson would have destroyed it for sure, but anyone else would draw attention to it because it tells a different story from popular belief."

"So we can conclude only three people have seen it in the last few decades?"

"Yes." Emma nodded her head with certainty. "I'd say that was a fair assumption."

Christopher took up the story. "Seeing as youse seemed so upset at parting with the plaque, we decided not to."

"What do you mean?" Emma said, sitting up straighter. "If you don't hand it over, you forfeit the job and pay a penalty. Then the Triads come after all of us."

Christopher shook his head and looked at Rohan, who interjected. "See, *devotchka*, that's where it doesn't feel right. The Triads played with us for over a year and yeah, the Contessa's mad at me for the fire, but something's wrong with this job. The Triads take what they want. If Che wants revenge, he gets it; they don't bargain over tiny jobs like this in the back of nowhere."

"But you gave the order to burn her," Emma whispered, glancing nervously at Ray. Her new employee raised a white hand in a modest wave.

"I know everything, miss. You explained there might be things I'd see which I couldn't tell my son and I accepted the job anyway. I'm in, miss."

"I condemned her to the fire but Hack pulled her out," Rohan said. He concentrated on Emma's hair, running his index finger through the centre of a damp, escaped curl. "It's business and the Triads know that. Everything made sense until Mikhail factored them in; then it fell to pieces."

"If you don't give the client the plaque," Emma said, her brown eyes wide, "what will happen?"

"We *will* give him a plaque," Christopher said with a smirk. "We just won't give him the real one."

Emma squeezed her eyes shut as she digested the riddle. Ray spoke. "We've made a duplicate, miss."

"How?" Emma asked, her face screwed up in disbelief. "It's made of bronze!" She glared at Christopher. "Or are you going to reveal you're really a master sculptor underneath that Irish-James-Bond exterior?"

Christopher preened himself at the backhanded compliment and Rohan sighed. "No. He bought polymer clay in liquid form from the art shop in town.

That's what he was baking."

Emma turned in her seat to look at Rohan. "But it'll come out backwards and instead of indented, the words will stick out, *in reverse*. That won't fool anyone."

"Duh!" Christopher postured, moving out of the way so Ray could wash his hands in the Belfast sink. Emma watched the white splashes pool on the metal draining board, wrinkling her nose at the mess.

"The clay formed the mold," Rohan said. "We baked it in the oven on a low heat to let the mold dry and now they've filled it with plaster of Paris."

Emma couldn't prevent the smirk which lit her rosebud lips. "So you've had a craft afternoon together," she said. "Was it fun?"

"Ha bloody *ha!*" Christopher retorted, glaring at Rohan. "I told you she wouldn't appreciate it!"

"Oh, I do," Emma said. "I just don't understand how something made of plaster can look like a bronze plaque from the late 1800s."

"Paint effects," Rohan said and looked at Emma with expectation.

"Me?"

"*Da*, your art at school was amazing. You won that trophy for your competition entry in Year 11. Remember?" Rohan leaned forward, his face earnest.

Emma ran a tired hand over her face. "I don't believe this."

Christopher spilled the contents of a plastic bag over the table. Paint pots, tubes of colour and brushes clattered in front of Emma. "Here you go," he said with enthusiasm. "The Actuary said you're great at that kinda stuff." He waved a hand in the general direction of Emma's chest as though she contained a blueprint on counterfeiting artifacts.

The three men watched her with such absolute faith in her abilities, Emma found it hard to breathe under the pressure of their expectation. She reached out a tentative finger to stroke the bristles of a short stippling brush and the men gave a collective sigh of relief. Emma turned to Rohan, worry etched into her furrowed brow. "I didn't say I'd do it," she protested. His scratchy bristles felt rough against her cheek as he leaned in to kiss her temple, his blue eyes radiating pride.

"You're brilliant," he confirmed. "What happened to the art work?" he asked. "They displayed it in a gallery for a while, *da?*"

Emma shrugged and swallowed the lump in her throat. "Lost," she replied and Rohan looked disappointed. Emma blinked back a hideous memory of his mother's wrath as she spotted the likeness of her own wickedness in the witch who patrolled the candy house.

Rohan turned to the other men, expounding on the parts of the oil painting he remembered. "It was Hansel and Gretel," he said. "The sweetie house was so real, you could taste the sugar." He nodded, his eyes soft. "You promised I could have it," he said, frowning at the memory.

Emma floundered, tears rising like floodwater behind her eyes. Her blood pressure hiked as her mind revealed the image of Alanya smashing the canvas to pieces in the back garden and lighting the incinerator. The wooden frame crackled as the flames licked along its length and her stunning artwork melted in the heat, the oils merging into one hideous colour. "*Don't move!*" Alanya screamed as Emma took a step backwards, her sobs audible even over the hissing, crackling fire. "*You did zis!*" She stabbed a crooked index finger in Emma's direction. "*You mock me and now everybody sees.*"

"*Sees you for who you are!*" Emma hurled in reply and her stepmother moved quicker than she anticipated, delivering a sharp slap to the girl's cheek. The skin stung and Emma touched her face, feeling the heat rise. Her legs buckled and she found herself on the back door step, grappling behind her with her hands for balance as another slap followed.

"*After everything I do for you!*" Alanya stood over her, eyes bulging in their sockets as anger poured out. "*You show my syn!*" she screamed and there it was; the reason for her anger. Rohan's last weekend visit home before deployment was a magical farce of homemade dinners and joviality. Emma nursed the secret of her pregnancy, waiting for an opportunity to talk to her husband of a few months and beg him not to leave.

Stress over the deployment made him snappy and in the only hour they had together, they went to bed and then argued. Emma ran from the house in distress and when she returned, he'd already gone.

"Emma?" Rohan's concerned expression brought her back to reality from the miserable annals of her past and Emma jolted forward in time with a heaving sob.

"I can't do it!" she hissed, shoving her chair back with her legs. It skittered across the tiles with a jarring scrape. "I don't paint. I can't." Her breath came in short gasps and she turned and ran from the kitchen, her socks pattering on the floor as her mind replayed her winning canvas melting before her eyes.

"Emma!" The kitchen door slammed as Rohan followed. Emma kept running, slipping on the wooden floor as her socks failed to gain purchase. "Don't make me run, please!" Rohan pleaded, throwing his prosthetic leg out sideways to get the complicated joints to move faster.

Compassion made Emma skid to a halt at the bottom of the stairs and she stood rigid, her body heaving in a mixture of embarrassment and misery at the memory of the three stunned male faces in her kitchen. She detested the drama of female hysterics and Emma covered her face with her hands, livid with herself. Rohan spun her round and cradled her into his body, showering kisses on the top of her head. "What happened, *devotchka*? Tell me."

"I don't want to do it," she sniffed. "Please don't make me?"

"Not back there," Rohan breathed into her hair. "Before. I saw in your face the agony of something dark. Tell me about that."

Emma swallowed and the memory surged in front of her face again, Alanya's fury and the blows from her fists raining on the sixteen year old's head. "Your mother was the witch in the painting," Emma panted. "She burned it and beat me."

Rohan swore in Russian and crushed his wife to himself. "I didn't know," he whispered, his voice thick with emotion. "Em, I didn't know." He lowered himself onto the stairs, high enough to straighten out his prosthesis. Emma slumped onto his good leg, nestling into his breast like a child. She breathed the scent of his deodorant, masculine and safe as it enfolded her and gave her enough security to calm. "So much I didn't see." Rohan rocked her, massaging the back of her head and pressing kisses into her hair. "Forgive me?" he whispered and she raised her tear streaked face and studied him.

"What for?" she asked, her voice croaky from the

tears.

"For leaving when you needed me," he replied. "For believing Mama when she said you cheated and ran away. But mostly for not protecting you." Rohan swallowed, devastated in a way Emma had never seen.

She panicked, their roles reversed. "It's ok," she urged. "Don't go back there in your head." Her brow furrowed as she watched her husband sift through their childhood, torturing himself. "Don't do it, Ro. I love you. Protect me *now*."

Rohan nodded. "Ok. Don't paint the plaster cast. I'll hand over the original and see what happens. It's fine." He pressed his lips over Emma's, tasting the salty tears as he upped the tempo, slipping his tongue through the seam and sighing with pleasure as she gave him entry. Emma put her arms around her husband's neck and kissed him back, channelling her distress into something safe and familiar.

The click of the kitchen door sent them skittering apart and Emma wiped her face on the shoulder of Rohan's shirt before nestling into his neck. Christopher's quick footsteps echoed along the corridor. "What're youse doin'?" he demanded. "I've spent all day makin' this feckin' thing! Somebody just paint it, I don't care who. Except Ray, he shakes like a bloody junkie." Exasperation oozed from Christopher's flailing arms and his expression of ultimate irritation betrayed an Irishman in a funk.

Emma sat up and turned, her hair tumbling into Rohan's face and making him splutter. "I'll do it," she said, using the bottom of her blue sweater to dab her eyes. "I'll paint it now."

"Fine!" Christopher snapped and strode away. "Then I'll go set up the tech, which is actually my proper job."

Emma swallowed and brushed her long curls out of Rohan's face. His blue eyes glittered with sorrow. "Don't do it," he said, his brow furrowed. "We'll manage."

She shook her head. "I'll do it for you," she replied, forcing a smile onto her lips. Emma stood and offered her hand to Rohan, allowing him to haul himself up with her help.

"Did she burn the trophy too?" he asked, his pupils dilating with fury as Emma nodded.

"Everything," she replied. "All my art stuff too; everything. As punishment for putting her in my picture."

"Even the art set your father bought for your last birthday before he died?" Rohan's eyes narrowed in disbelief as Emma nodded. He shook his head and closed his eyes, biting his lower lip. "I'm so sorry, Em."

"She took everything from me, Rohan," Emma said, her face taking on a determined hardness and her eyes flashing. "But piece by piece, I'm taking it all back; my education, Nicky and now you." She reached out a shaking hand and seized her husband's strong fingers. "I think today I'll take back painting."

"My brave girl." Rohan's thumb across Emma's cheek offered a soft caress, infusing her with strength and courage. "*Istrebitel*."

Emma smiled, acknowledging the compliment. "Fighter?" she translated. "Yes, maybe I am."

CHAPTER THIRTY SEVEN

"That's amazing!" Ray breathed, peering at Emma's finished work.

She leaned back in her chair and surveyed the mess on the kitchen table; various mugs filled with dusky water and opened paint tubes jockeying for position in an ice cream tub. "I think I'm done," Emma said with a satisfied sigh. "The verdigris isn't the right shade of green, but hopefully they won't have anyone there to verify it."

Ray leaned back against the kitchen counter and yawned. "Captain Andreyev thinks they won't," he replied.

"Will you always call him that?" Emma asked with a smile. "How come he gets a posh title and I get, 'miss'?"

"He's earned his." Ray smirked. "And he doesn't have green acrylic paint on his face."

Emma sighed and face planted onto her forearms. "I could use another sleep," she said, her voice muffled. "How long do we have left?"

Ray checked his wristwatch. "Hack said they meet at midnight in the middle of Market Harborough. The message said inside St Dionysius Church."

Emma's head rose slowly, her eyes widening as her head shook from side to side. "Then Rohan mustn't go!" she said, her tone disbelieving. "It'll mess everything up."

"Like what?" Ray stood up straight and observed

Emma through narrowed eyes. "What's wrong, miss?"

"If the exchange is in the church, Clarissa Jameson-Arden will be there." Emma stood. "This is a disaster. She's the chairwoman of the school governors and she might have seen Rohan at the nativity last year; he's quite distinctive and there was a bit of a scene at the ticketing desk. But even if she missed that, what if she sees Rohan at another time with Nicky and me? She'll know I handed the plaque over and took money for it. She might even be suspicious of the copy because I can't remember if I told the headmaster it was a *brass* plaque, or just a plaque."

Emma shoved her chair under the table and paced in the space behind it. "This is terrible," she hissed. "*I'm* terrible! Archivists don't sell history to the highest bidder!"

"It's hardly like that," Ray interjected. "The Triads' involvement makes it much more complicated. And how do you know this woman will be there?"

"She's a guide at the church and we think Adam Jameson is her brother. It's the most obvious place and she'll have a key. How else could the exchange be made in a church at midnight?"

Ray ran his palm over his bristly chin. "The Ardens left me with nothing to show for years of loyal service in that damn factory. Bloody family." He turned to Emma. "I'll make the drop," he said. "Leave Rohan out of it."

"Where is he?" Emma asked, reaching for the door handle.

"With Hack," Ray answered, following close on Emma's heels as she ran to the front door, shoving her feet into trainers on the door mat. "Lock up!" he warned her sternly. "You don't know who's around."

Emma pointed a stubborn finger towards the front gate, opening her mouth to deny the danger. She withdrew her hand at Ray's raised eyebrow. "You're not my father!" she bit petulantly and Ray snatched the keys from her hand, locking the front door behind them.

"Lucky for you, miss!" he retorted with a smirk. "Do your shoelaces up."

Emma obeyed, pursing her lips in amusement. Her gentle father's face moved across her inner vision and she missed him with a deep ache. Ray's teasing revived a desire to be cosseted and Emma beat it down with scorn. At twenty four years old, something in her soul responded to Ray's paternalism and it left her conflicted and confused. She reminded herself he was her employee and stood up from her ministrations, her face fixed into a stern expression. "They'll be in Christopher's apartment," she said, all gentle femininity replaced by a businesslike demeanour.

They breached the stairs to the apartment in silence. Emma waved at the camera and wasn't surprised to meet the Irishman already at the door. "What's up?" he asked, picking up Emma's angst.

Ray explained while they sat around the scruffy lounge, Emma quenching her thirst with a mug of water. She grimaced at the chipped rim but drank anyway, sensing her husband's blue eyes studying her.

"Na, youse can't go," Christopher said with a definitive nod towards Rohan. "Em's right. Hell of a risk if this woman sees you later. What about yer wee boy? She could make his life a misery."

"And would!" Ray confirmed, nodding his dark head with certainty. "I said I'd go."

"But then she'd see you around town later too."

Rohan scratched his chin, staring at the ceiling in thought. "That puts you at risk of reprisals down the line."

"I'll do it," Christopher offered. He sat on the arm of the sofa next to Emma and she felt the whole thing sag sideways, bracing herself with her feet on the dusty floorboards. "She doesn't know me and I've nothin' to lose if she sees me again."

"What about wearing a balaclava?" Emma asked innocently. "If Clarissa's in the church but doesn't know you, she'd never recognise you again if you covered your face."

"It's a good idea," Ray said, silenced by Christopher's scornful scoff.

"I'm not coverin' my face!" he snapped. "That's not what we do! I'm a businessman, not a bloody gangster!"

Emma stood up and took her mug to the outdated kitchen. She pushed it around on the counter and looked at the elderly oven and cracked sink. It seemed incongruous against the pristine computer room. Emma shook her head and turned to catch her husband's eye. "What do we do, Ro? What's the answer?"

Rohan leaned back in a dilapidated armchair and raised his arms above his head. Emma watched his shirt part, revealing his smooth stomach and the start of one of the long scars. The urge to touch him and sense his fingers on her soft skin felt overwhelming and she closed her eyes, opening them to find his blue irises caressing her face. He communicated strength and leadership in the single smile he gave her and Emma's body relaxed.

"Can you handle it, Hack?" Rohan asked, his voice

sounding lazy.

Christopher's eyes flashed with excitement. "Aye. Sure!" His expression sobered. "But what about the tech stuff? Who'll do that?"

"I will," Rohan answered and Christopher nodded with enthusiasm.

"Ok, I'll run you through the new stuff I've added. I'm already linked into the cameras around the church so you can watch out for the Russians and Triads. There's a lot to monitor though." Christopher's enthusiasm waned and doubt crept into his voice.

Rohan nodded. "I've done it before, remember?"

"In the army?" Emma asked and her husband smiled.

"Slightly different technology but yes." Rohan looked at his watch and yawned.

"Slightly inferior technology," Christopher smirked and Rohan raised a blonde eyebrow.

"We'll go into town early and set up," he said. "I'll need at least two hours to check the surrounding area and be ready for any surprises." Rohan rubbed his eyes. "I need to sleep. Ray, can you help Hack set up so I can get my head down for an hour, please? That'll be enough, then I'll finish running the checks while Hack sleeps."

Emma expected Christopher to protest out of machoism but he didn't. Their forces training dictated they sleep when possible and Ray nodded his agreement. "I'll help wherever you need me," he said and Rohan and Christopher smiled their acceptance.

"What should I do?" Emma asked, hopeful of inclusion. "Can I do something?"

Christopher raised an eyebrow and left it to Rohan to break the bad news. Emma's husband stared indulgently at her. "You're pregnant, *devotchka*. You stay here with Ray."

"That's not fair!" Emma protested. "I can't sit here doing nothing while you two get yourselves killed. You wouldn't really expect me to do that, would you?"

"*Da*," Rohan said, standing and raising his arms above his head. Emma glimpsed the tiny patch of gorgeous midriff and the sight made her angrier.

"I'm not happy with this!" she chuntered as her husband took her upper arm and led her from the apartment. Emma glanced back to see Christopher and Ray grinning at each other, which enraged her further.

Emma bitched and complained all the way down the stairs and across the broken concrete yard to the main house. "I don't think I like Ray," she whined, her petulance wasted on the Russian. "He's not gonna do anything I tell him, not while you're around. He works for me and naturally defers to you. It's not fair!"

Rohan unlocked the main house and stepped over the threshold. A black shape hurtled towards him and sneaked in the gap. "Farrell loves it here," Rohan smiled. "It's home for him. He can play for hours and come home when he's hungry, just like he did when Anton lived here."

"He sounds a lot like you," Emma muttered, pursing her lips at Rohan's smirked response.

The wind had tousled Rohan's blonde hair and given him a windswept sexiness which made Emma pout in annoyance, as though he didn't deserve his good looks when he wouldn't include her in his intrigue. Farrell pattered along the corridor to his bed in the kitchen and Emma listened to the sound of him lapping water from his bowl. Rohan sat on a sofa in the reception hall and took off his outdoor shoes, wincing as he rubbed at his right thigh. Emma felt herself softening. "Is it hurting?" she asked.

"*Da*," he said softly. "I've been awake for hours and standing too much. I'm too old and banged up for this life."

Emma felt hope blossom in her heart and suppressed the excitement bubbling within at the thought he may decommission the Actuary forever. "Lay on the bed and I'll take the prosthetic off and give your leg a massage," she offered.

Rohan held out his hand and Emma hauled him to a standing position. "You're beautiful, Em," he breathed, kissing her temple. He released Emma at the bottom of the stairs in exchange for the handrail and made his way up to the first floor. In the bedroom, Emma waited for her husband to remove his trousers and release his stump from the prosthetic sleeve. He snoozed on the bed with his eyes closed while she pulled off the stump sock, huffing at the creases in the material.

"You put it on in too much of a hurry," she chastised him. "It's rucked up and you've rubbed a mark next to the scar."

Rohan nodded and Emma found some lotion, rubbing it into the stump. Her fingers were tender and her husband sighed with pleasure and said something complimentary in Russian. Emma massaged the tender skin, no longer seeing the scar tissue from an operation carried out under battlefield conditions to seal a leaking artery and severed leg. She saw a two legged teenager who played tennis and rugby with abandon; a serious academic boy who walked her home, held her hand and showered her with secret kisses. She ran her creamy fingers over Rohan's knee, feeling the blonde hair under her hands, closing her eyes and starting in surprise when the shin ended abruptly beneath her palms. Emma sighed and kissed the stump, tasting jasmine and vanilla on her lips and feeling the lotion's scent billow over her face.

"Don't do that, Em," Rohan said, his voice husky. "I'm meant to be sleeping otherwise I'll be a liability tonight."

"Ok." Devilment lit Emma's eyes and she pushed her fingers through the slickness of the cream and brushed the bottom of Rohan's boxer shorts. She felt his strong thigh muscles tense and saw his excitement grow.

"Are you trying to get me killed?" Rohan said, his voice descending into a moan.

"Nope," Emma replied, moving her right hand over the top of his thigh and letting her fingers contact the smooth skin of his hip beneath his shorts.

"You're still not coming out with us tonight," Rohan said, as much a threat as a resolution.

"Ok," she replied, her eyes glinting with dark mischief as she massaged the inside of his thigh, studying his face for lack of control. When she saw the giveaway vein pulse in Rohan's neck, she gave a smirk of victory.

"Bloody hell, woman!" Rohan grunted, sitting up using his strong abdominal muscles. "I'm glad you weren't on the battlefield!" He seized the tops of her arms and hauled her across the bed, shifting his body on top of hers with alarming ease. "Something bad might've happened." He rained kisses on her face, staying away from her tempting lips and making her wait. "I might have blown my damn leg off!" he joked, pain absent from his eyes for the first time as he mentioned the life changing event.

"I'd still love you," Emma whispered, clasping her hands around his neck and feeling the starchy shirt collar under her wrists.

Rohan pushed questing fingers under her sweatshirt, caressing the budding pregnancy and sensing the nearness of his unborn child. He tugged at her jeans with urgency and kissed her exposed neck. Emma kept eye contact with her husband as she unbuttoned his shirt and pushed it back, exposing defined shoulder muscles and rippling pectorals. "I don't want to compromise you by making you more tired," Emma said, smirking. "Maybe you should just go to sleep."

Rohan snorted. "I can't sleep now!"

Emma squealed as he tickled her sides, making her squirm and writhe underneath him. Seriousness descended like a blanket as Rohan pressed his soft lips over hers and used up valuable rest time on other exhausting activities.

CHAPTER THIRTY EIGHT

Rohan lay on his back sleeping deeply as Emma crept from the bedroom. Fresh logs on the fire and a light blanket over his naked form ensured he wouldn't wake prematurely through discomfort. She closed the door with a gentle click and wandered down the long hallway to the main staircase.

Christopher leaned over the counterfeit plaque, nodding his head in admiration as Emma walked through the kitchen door. "Not bad, Em," he complimented her, glancing over his shoulder. "Even together they're almost identical."

"Almost?" Emma asked, pouting. "What's wrong with it?"

"Nothing." Christopher furrowed his brow. "Youse did good. Don't be sensitive!"

Emma sighed and checked the wall clock. "I'll wake Ro soon. Then you can get your head down for an hour. You both spent the night chasing Mikhail around the house."

Christopher shook his head. "I don't sleep much anymore. Not since..." He bit his bottom lip and gave her a wavering smile. "Don't wake the Actuary. Everything's ready to go, so he only needs a quick run through on the monitors and we'll head out. Will you be ok here with Ray?"

Emma nodded her head with a grimace. "I don't have much choice," she grumbled.

Christopher observed her through narrowed eyes.

"Aye. Home's the best place for ya, Em." He pointed at her belly. "Especially now."

Her fingers rested over her bump in a subconscious movement and Emma rolled her eyes as she saw the smirk touch the corners of Christopher's lips. "Sod off!" she retorted and he laughed. "I painted the back of the plaster version," Emma said, changing the subject and pointing at the fake. "But I'm worried. What if the Jamesons know it's counterfeit and come looking for revenge? And what do I do with the original afterwards; I can't produce it as evidence to put the story straight, can I? It'll stay hidden forever, so what's the point of subterfuge? They've employed an actuary to neutralise the risk so they can go back to running the town and playing royalty. Half a million pounds is a lot of money to lose when it turns out to be a scam." Emma's brow knitted. "I'm scared. It makes me want to run away and start again somewhere new." She gnawed on the inside of her cheek and Christopher's frown contained sympathy.

"I know it's hard, Em. Trust us; we do this all the time."

"I can't live like this," she sighed. "I hate it." She wiped her lips with the back of her hand and Christopher sidled across to put his arms around her.

"It'll be ok," he whispered. "I won't cock it up, I promise."

"Ok." Emma nodded against his chest. She pushed him away with a guilty backward glance at the doorway. "How do you usually package this stuff?"

Christopher shrugged. "You got any bubble wrap and a padded envelope?"

Emma grinned. "Scared you might smash it before you get there?"

"No!" Christopher sneered. "Course not!"

Emma fetched bubble wrap from a storage room in the cellar, unable to resist popping the delicious air filled bubbles as she handled it. Christopher fiddled with parcel tape, his big thumbs becoming entangled in its stickiness as he wrestled with the scissors. "Stop doing that!" he snapped as Emma enjoyed another series of satisfying pops.

"Get out of the way," she laughed, pulling the tape from his wrist.

"Ow!" he squealed as hair clung to the glue. Emma giggled as she unintentionally waxed his wrist and part of his forearm.

"Big baby!" she snorted.

Ray's presence brought with it an awkwardness which made Emma feel irrationally guilty. It translated as a fit of giggles and communicated itself to the Irishman. Christopher possessed the uncanny ability to enjoy himself whilst maintaining a convincingly straight face, leaving Emma weeping tears of genuine mirth like the resident moron. Ray seated himself at the kitchen table to watch their antics, making the atmosphere worse.

"Please go!" Emma snorted. "I need to do this by myself. You're making it harder."

Christopher pulled a face at his hairless wrist and set Emma off again. "Fine!" he said, faking anger and winking at her behind Ray's back. "We'll do the final checks. Wake the Actuary when you're done and ask him to meet us at the van. Tell him to put some clothes on first."

Emma gulped, reading the expression in the Irishman's eyes and wondering if he had her bedroom bugged. "What van?" She dried her damp cheeks on her sleeve.

Exasperated, Christopher glared at her. "Just do it, Em!" He followed Ray from the kitchen but poked his head around the doorframe, deliberately startling Emma. "Hey, use that tape to do your moustache," he advised, jerking his head towards the parcel tape. Emma raised her fingers to her top lip, her eyes wide with embarrassment as she felt for hairs.

"There's nothing there," she replied, mystified. She huffed as Christopher's dark head disappeared and she heard him chortling along the corridor. "Idiot!" she grumbled, irritated by his ability to ruffle her so easily. She ripped off a strip of tape and stuck it over her top lip.

"What're you doing?" Rohan's blonde hair stuck up like a crest and a pink line bisected his cheek from the seam of the pillow. He wore neat slacks on his bottom half and fumbled his buttons into their holes with fingers which operated like sausages from tiredness.

"I'll do it," Emma offered. She pressed the buttons home and ran her fingers down the strong chest. Rohan's eyes crossed as he stared at the sticky brown tape over Emma's top lip and she stepped back and ripped it off on the way to the dustbin. It hurt enough to make her wince. "Christopher said I had a moustache," she said, sounding sulky.

Rohan smiled and bit his bottom lip. "Come here," he ordered. Emma sashayed across to him, feigning shyness and he took her in his arms and ran his smooth face along hers. He smelled of aftershave and Emma sighed.

"You smell lovely," she whispered. "Let's go upstairs and forget about all this."

"I wish," Rohan replied. "I need to find Hack."

"He said they'd be at the van," Emma said and Rohan kissed her and retreated from the room. She heard his heels clicking along the hallway in his smart shoes. "Don't mind me," she muttered crossly. "Don't bother telling me what van you're talking about. Even Ray knows more than me!"

She surveyed the identical plaques, both damaging with the truth they carried. Emma shook her head and touched her counterfeit with a tentative graze of her finger. Apart from its plaster composition, it looked realistic sitting next to the real thing. She fingered the bubble wrap in her other hand and popped a few of the plastic bobbles in concentration. Emma reached for the scissors and spent the next few minutes sealing the plaque into layers of protective wrapping and slipping it into the padded envelope. She placed the other one in the library safe, following the instructions memorised from Anton's will. It nestled on top of her and Nicky's birth certificates, hidden even from her husband. Emma closed the safe with a click of metal on metal, twisting the ancient dial and sealing the space behind the bookshelf. She pushed a faded copy of *The Complete Works of Edgar Allan Poe* upright again and the structure swung back with a hiss, resuming its place as a solid bookcase.

Emma spun on the spot, her eyes raking the floor to ceiling shelves, some glass panelled and others openly displaying their literary wares. Her fingers ached to touch them all and sense their history through the fragile spines.

"Miss?" Ray's low tones made her jump. "You ok?"

"Yeah, thanks," Emma replied, facing the doorway and searching his face for signs he might have seen her sleight of hand. "I need to catalogue everything in the house, including the books in here. Some are terribly old." She sighed. "It's a huge job. I feel tired just looking at this house sometimes."

Ray ventured into the room and touched Emma lightly on the shoulder. "I can fetch and carry for you, miss. It's no bother to do whatever you need; I know this job's more than just a grounds-man, for now."

Emma smiled. "Thanks, Ray," she said, gratitude making her brown eyes twinkle. "I will need help. I should get more staff but it's impossible to know who to trust." The task overwhelmed her and it showed in the pallor of her face as the colour drained away. "I don't suppose you've got a trustworthy sister?" she asked, smiling at the futility of her own joke.

"Sorry, no." Ray shook his head in sympathy. "Someone will come along, miss; like I did. Have faith."

Emma nodded. The grandfather clock in the library chimed the ninth hour and her blood pressure increased, sending an unhealthy surge of blood to her head. "Christopher hasn't slept," Emma panicked, desperate to delay the men's departure.

Ray smiled a sad, tight lipped expression. "Some men don't, miss. War ruins it for us." His dark eyes flashed and Emma saw into his soul for a fraction of a second, viewing the darkness of loss and human misery. It shocked her into speechlessness and she recognised the black thing which stained her husband's heart often, making him uncommunicative and sombre as he receded into himself for restitution.

"Falklands?" she asked softly and Ray nodded, adding a shrug to shroud his emotions once again.

"Amongst others." He jerked his head towards the door. "You coming to wish them luck?"

Emma gulped and fought the tears which pricked behind her eyes. "They're leaving already?"

Ray nodded and walked with Emma to the front steps. Farrell followed, his claws clicking on the floorboards and his nose batting Emma's thigh to remind her he was there.

Rohan and Christopher had morphed into the Actuary and Hack, businesslike as they said their goodbyes. Emma kissed her husband and hugged her friend, her heart leaden in her breast. She wrapped her arms around herself and watched as two vehicles moved down the long driveway in the darkness, brake lights pausing for the gates and then moving onto the main road. The dog kept pace on the lawn, barking happily as he chased the vehicles to the gate, the cattle grate making it impossible for him to follow them onto the main road.

Market Harborough created a semicircle glow against the black sky, its night lights reflecting like a dome of safety. Emma moved back over the threshold to her mansion, sickness working its way up her gullet in a flurry of terror. *And guilt.*

CHAPTER THIRTY NINE

"I switched it." Emma's brown eyes flickered with a heady mix of guilt and fear and her fingers beat a nervous tattoo on the front of her sweatshirt.

"You did what?" Disbelief stamped its mark on Ray's face and his jaw dropped open, revealing neat, straight teeth underneath his moustache. "After all that work to replicate it, you switched it back?" He stood up, placing his mug of tea on the table with care.

Emma mentally questioned the rationale behind the ex-soldier's anger. "Are you angry because we got stuck with the fake, or because you wanted to see if the Jamesons fell for it?" Emma chewed her bottom lip and looked at the floor. "Or is it because all that hard work is wasted?"

Ray shook his head and grabbed her by the shoulders, his grip firm. "Neither, miss! It's because you changed the rules of the game and your husband and Hack have no idea!"

"I know," Emma said, her voice wavering as she struggled to keep her feet still. "We have to stop him."

"Why did you do it?"

"I love history and it's a sacred job being a guardian of the truth. It's also a terrible responsibility sometimes." Emma's words caught in a sob and her eyes sought the clock over the mantel. "But I love Rohan more. I couldn't risk someone checking and realising it's fake. What if the client has an archivist or art expert standing by before he accepts it? Things went wrong last time and Rohan got stabbed in the back." Emma's wide, tearful eyes blinked up at Ray and she watched his resolve crumble. "I can't lose him again," she pleaded, the memory of his blood pooling in the bottom of the shower driving her to act.

"I get it," Ray said gruffly. "I get it." He snatched Emma's car keys from the table and ran for the door. "Although why the bloody hell you didn't say something two and a half hours ago, I'll never know!"

"I'll get the fake," Emma shouted, running for the library and skidding on the floorboards.

Outside the front door, Emma gripped the plaster replica wrapped in her jacket. She dropped the door keys repeatedly, fighting with Farrell who seemed keen to join their night time adventure. Exasperated, Ray seized the keys and let the dog out. "Let him go," he insisted. "Guard!" he told the spaniel and Farrell gave an excited woof and stuck by Emma's leg.

"Not me, the house! He wants to come with us," Emma wailed, standing on the frozen gravel in her socks, trainers in hand.

"Well, he can't!" Ray snapped, pressing the key fob and jumping into the driver's seat of the 'Girly Car.' "Get in!"

"It's raining!" Emma protested, opening the boot. "I need my umbrella."

Ray fired up the car with a few choice swear words as Emma put her finger to her lips and let Anton's faithful dog into the boot. She touched the carpeted floor with her forefinger and the dog leapt in and buried his nose to the surface in obedience. Emma shook her head and pressed her lips again as Ray shouted at her. Farrell became a statue, so still even the metal links on his collar made no sound.

"Steady!" Emma wailed as Ray gunned the engine. She banged her forehead on the dashboard lacing her trainers, feeling the grittiness from the gravel under her toes. "I haven't got my seat belt on!" She kicked the umbrella further into the foot well.

Ray acted furious, tearing into the Northampton Road and fighting the vehicle out of an accidental skid. His moustache covered his tight lips and he shook his head numerous times, glancing sideways at Emma and swallowing his rebuke.

Emma's heart beat like a drum in her chest and sickness pooled in her gullet as the car blasted through the southern gateway to the small town. "Slow down!" Emma gasped, clinging to her seat belt to keep it from tightening against her belly and locking. "You'll attract attention."

Ray slowed to the legal speed limit and it felt as though they walked the last few miles to the epicentre of Market Harborough, their urgency crippled. Emma fidgeted, wanting to see Rohan, but terrified at the same time. The ex-soldier's eyes darted left and right as he looked for hazards Emma couldn't comprehend. "He's gonna kill me," Emma groaned.

"I damn well would!" Ray snapped and she pouted and watched darkened houses spin past the car window.

Emma tipped sideways to peer at the clock on the dashboard, groaning as the digital display tipped onto eleven forty-five. Ray took side streets and skirted the old church, raking the parked cars with his eyes. St Dionysius stood like a beacon in the centre of town, snuggled next to the old schoolhouse which teetered on its mediaeval stilts. Floodlit from every angle, the church glowed against the night sky, offering a deceptive sanctuary. The empty streets were deathly quiet but for the sound of raucous revelling in a nearby pub.

"Look for the van!" Ray hissed, slowing to a crawl.

"What van?" Emma wailed and he shook his head in disappointment.

"It's a white transit, kinda like a painter's van. I can't remember what it says on the side but Hack's got the tech set up in it."

"I didn't know he had a van," Emma whispered, searching wide-eyed for a large, white vehicle.

"There's a fair bit you don't know, miss," Ray said, his tone softening. "Me and you are gonna comb that place and inventory every nook and cranny in it."

Emma nodded and clutched the counterfeit plaque to her chest, feeling the seat belt cut into her neck. "I don't see a van," she said, surveying the darkened street on either side. "Do you?"

Ray shook his head, concentrating on cruising along Adam and Eve Street and keeping his speed low. "No. They can't be far away." He drove towards the start of Roman Way and past the rear of Church Square.

"The lights are on inside the church," Emma breathed. "That's not normal."

"Ok, don't panic," Ray reassured her. "Captain Andreyev can't be far away."

"There, look!" Emma squeaked and Ray jumped and swore, following the line of Emma's finger with keen, dark eyes. "It's the Chinese people's car!" She turned to Ray with terror in her face. "They'll kill him and Christopher. It's a trap!"

"Calm down!" he hissed, keeping the car moving and grabbing Emma's arm with his left hand to stop her hurling herself from the moving car. A line of slender, black-clad bodies slipped from the parked vehicle and morphed into the darkness. "Don't be a fool!" Ray snapped. "What can you do against all of them? I counted four and they move like they know what they're doing. You're no good to your husband dead, woman!"

Ray moved the car back towards Church Road, circling St Di's and taking them left onto the main road. Emma became frantic, engaging in a tug of war with Ray and begging him to release her forearm. A low growl issued from the boot of the vehicle and Ray's jaw dropped open. "You brought the bloody dog!" he squeaked in amazement swerving over the centre line.

"Get off me!" Emma wailed. "You're fired!"

"Shut up!" Ray's words contained urgency and silenced her with immediacy. "Who are they? Look, that group over there."

Emma stared through the windscreen, at first seeing nothing. Ray kept the car rolling and Emma gasped at the sight of Mikhail's spiteful face lit up by the headlights. "Look away," Ray hissed and Emma bowed her head, preventing the small knot of pedestrians identifying her in the darkened car. Mikhail raised his hand to limit the glare of the headlights as he crossed in front of the moving vehicle with his customary arrogance.

"It's Rohan's uncle," Emma panicked. "He's got two men with him." She tried to twist in her seat to get a better look and Ray growled at her.

"Turn round!"

"But Christopher!" Emma wailed. "We have to help him!" Her eyes widened in horror as Ray gunned the gas pedal and the car sped forward. "No!" she demanded. "Go back!"

Ray stopped the car at the junction with the main street and glared at Emma in the reflected light from the church. "We do this my way, miss, or I drive you home right now!"

"No!" Emma whimpered. "You're meant to do what *I* say!"

"No, I don't; you fired me remember?" Ray shrugged as though he didn't care and turned left, driving past the front of the church and sending Emma into a paroxysm of misery. Unable to obey any longer, Farrell leapt over the back seat, nosing his way from under the parcel shelf and scrambling free. He shot through the centre, over the gear stick and hurled himself into the foot well by Emma's feet. His wet nosed kisses caressed Emma's fingers and his furry head felt comforting on her thigh. The guttural growl warned Ray to mind his manners. "This is a disaster!" the man breathed. "A total bloody disaster. Women in combat is a horrible idea."

"Go back," Emma begged. "Please go back to the church?"

"Where's the damn van?"

"I don't know, I can't see it," Emma panicked, fondling Farrell's long ear to calm her frenzied fingers. He whined and licked his lips, sensing her turmoil and fixing his deep brown eyes on her face. "There!" she screamed and the dog barked. "There's Rohan's Mercedes!"

Ray swerved and swore. "We're looking for the bloody van, miss!" He indicated and turned left into St Mary's Road and circled left into Adam and Eve Street again.

"Try Factory Road," Emma said, her voice urgent. "It's a dead end which leads to the theatre. They might have parked there."

Ray nosed the car into the road and spotted the inconspicuous van parked in a bay near the end. "Bingo!" he exclaimed. "Don't you dare!" Ray grabbed at Emma's arm as she grappled with the door handle. "If you go blasting out and attract attention to them now, *you'll* be the reason they die. Hack diverted the street cameras onto a feed into the van and replaced it with a loop back to the council. If Rohan's in the van, he'll see you."

"What will he do?" Emma whispered, glancing sideways at the van with the windows blocked out. "Will he come out?"

Ray shook his head, barely holding his temper. "Yep, sure. He'll come bouncing out in a clown suit and do a bit of magic and then they'll shoot Hack as the grand finale."

"I've gone off you," Emma whined, folding Farrell's thick scruff in her fingers.

"Likewise, miss," Ray sighed. "You're a bloody liability."

"So what can we do? How do I get Rohan's attention?" Emma hissed.

"Text him." Ray jerked his head towards Emma's fleece pocket and she nodded and handed him the plaster cast.

Emma felt the sinking feeling in her gut as she searched first one and then the other pocket. Her words caught in her throat and she choked on them. "I don't have it," she gasped. "It's at home."

Ray heaved out a huge breath and shook his head. "Do you know his number?" He glanced at the distress on Emma's face, seeing her wide-eyed terror and groaned, running a hand across his face. "Don't tell me;

he put it in the phone and you just press a button?"

Emma's sob broke into the tension as she pressed her fingers over her lips to prevent more following. Ray relented. "Hey, don't do that. It's ok, we'll sort it out." He tutted and ran a comforting hand up and down Emma's upper arm. "Don't cry, miss. I can't think straight when I see tears. Just give me a minute and I'll come up with something." He clasped her shaking hand in his and squeezed.

Farrell laid his head on Emma's knee and his brown eyes glinted in the streetlights. She closed her eyes and concentrated on her breathing, praying Ray would think of a solution. He didn't let her down. "Stay here," he told her, flicking the interior light switch, so it stayed off when he opened the door. He slipped from the car, making minimal sound as he pressed the door closed. Emma cuddled Farrell's soft ruff as she watched Ray hurry to the back of the van and knock. She held her breath as he waited, his ear next to the rear door.

With a shake of his head, he strode back to Emma. He opened her passenger door and ignored the dog who was eager to be out.

"Something's gone wrong," he declared, urgency in his voice. "Captain Andreyev's not in the van. He's locked it and followed Hack. I'll get into the church; you stay here." He glared at her through narrowed eyes. "I mean it, miss. You stay here!"

Emma opened her mouth to protest, closing it again in response to the warning look in Ray's green eyes. She fondled Farrell's soft ear and nodded. "Please can I have the car keys?" she asked, holding her hand out. Ray placed the keys into her palm and winked, the comforting gesture lost in the eerie night glow. Emma watched him stride away, heading for the main door facing the high street.

"Well, that won't work, will it?" she murmured, talking to Farrell. "He thinks he can just walk in and say hey to everyone." Emma glanced around her, worrying as a police car cruised by on Adam and Eve Street. She peered at the white van, fear gnawing at her insides. "I can't sit here doing nothing," she grumbled, rewarded by Farrell's faithful blink of agreement.

With shaking hands, Emma slipped the collar over Farrell's head. She let the chain slither to the floor, feeling the dog's wet nose against her fingers as he traced its journey. "I know," she whispered. "But I need you with me and they'll hear you coming wearing that." Emma wagged her finger in Farrell's face. "You stay to heel though, Faz. Ok?"

Farrell licked his lips and smiled, blowing dog breath into Emma's face. She waved her hand and crinkled her nose. "You can stop that too!" she complained.

Taking a deep breath, Emma looked around her at the empty street. As the world crossed the line over which midnight hovered and pitched into the next day, she made her choice.

CHAPTER FORTY

The central locking made a dull clunk as Emma closed the door and pressed the key fob. She ambled as though walking her dog late, checking around her for danger and half expecting Ray to appear and make her scream. The dog's claws clicked on the cobbles surrounding the old schoolhouse and Emma sneaked beneath the giant stilts and hid, catching her breath. Reaching a hand down, she found the loyal, furry head and Farrell licked her fingers. "Quiet now," Emma told him and surveyed the church. All was silent. Light glowed from the leaded glass windows, dulled by the floodlights outside. She moved soundlessly, using her expertise at creeping up on Nicky's misdeeds to reach the side wall of the church, puffing from fear and exertion. A camera on the high ramparts stared straight at her and Emma gulped, trusting Rohan to have rerouted the feed as he promised. "Where are you when I need you, Andreyev?" Emma mouthed. Farrell glanced up and wagged his tail.

Emma crept along the side of the building, grazing her fingers on the roughened brick as she stuck close. The front doors of the church faced the main street and saw most foot traffic from tourists and visitors. Reaching the black, metal gates protecting the side door into the nave, Emma enjoyed a momentary flashback of Nicky's excited face as he skipped into the porch for the Christmas Eve service. Emma avoided the gates, disregarding their padlocked security and headed for the front door, following Ray. Farrell stopped and whined and Emma whipped round to face him, raising her finger to her lips. He looked at the gate and whined again and Emma doubled back. "Heel, Faz!" she hissed. "Or I'll take you back to the car." She wound her fingers through a handful of the dense hair at his scruff and gave a gentle tug. Farrell whined again, emitting the same noise he made when Rohan's Mercedes turned into the driveway of Wingate Hall.

"What's wrong?" Emma halted, trusting the dog's judgement. Farrell nosed at the gate and stepped back, panting and wagging his tail. Emma's fingers closed on the metal and it moved, emitting a low groan as it swung inwards.

Emma flicked her finger and Farrell shot through the gap and sat next to the door, his mouth open in an enthusiastic grin. She laid the fake plaque behind the gate, hiding it in the dense shadows of the porch. Holding her breath, Emma followed the dog and hissed in surprise to find the wooden doors open a crack. A faint light spewed in an arc around the gap. "Stay!" she told the spaniel, leaning into his ear to make her command more audible. The dog's face settled into an indignant expression, his eyes worried. His tail brushed the floor and he panted, his tongue lolling over the side of glossy lips. "I mean it," she warned.

Emma slipped through the door, cursing her trainers as she heard grit under her feet. She crept through the wide porch towards the nave and peered into the church, listening for movement or voices. Hearing nothing, Emma proceeded forward, creeping on all fours and keeping the toes of her trainers off the flagstones to avoid the inevitable squeak of rubber.

The dull light issued from the altar and Emma

pressed on, unnerved by the neat rows of dark wooden pews offering numerous places for assailants to hide. She checked behind her, discerning a sense of evil in the shadowy corners of the nave. The sound of low voices carried in the cavernous stone and Emma crept closer to listen, feeling the cold through the knees of her jeans. At the foot of the altar stood a man she didn't recognise, surrounded by people. "I just wanted the plaque," he said, an affected English accent making him sound like royalty. "It belongs to my family and I've said I'll settle the debt." Emma heard the sound of bubble wrap moving and crackling and used the sound to cover her as she crept closer to the action. "I don't want to be involved with all this silliness," the man said, thin lips smiling as he viewed the artifact. "Yes, this is it. My grandmother spoke of it; bronze I believe and made by a gentleman in Leicester."

"Is not about some *durak* piece of crap!" Mikhail's voice rasped into the stillness, echoing over Emma's head. "I want my *syn*!"

The grey haired Adam Jameson observed Mikhail through narrowed eyes. A bristly moustache laced with streaks of fading red, covered for the spitefulness of his thin lips as he opened his mouth with a scornful expression on his face. "I know nothing about any sins, despite this being a church. I made a deal, with *her*!" He jabbed a sharp index finger towards a figure in the circle and it moved. Shrouded in a dark cloak, it replied in a gentle female voice.

"So you did, Dr Jameson. But I subcontracted to someone more local, killing two birds with one stone." She lowered the hood which covered her face and Emma stuffed her fist into her mouth to suppress the gulp of fear at the sight of the Contessa, seeing only one side of her face. Graceful and elegant, the woman dominated the circle with her poise and Emma watched as Christopher's gaze rested on the woman, captivated by her presence. An Oriental looking male stood behind the Irishman, a handgun levelled in the small of his back. Christopher's body language was relaxed, appearing unconcerned by the nearness of death.

"This is nothing to do with me," Adam Jameson repeated. "I'll make the transfer of the cash and then I'd like to leave. My sister's waiting for me and she knows where I am. If I don't return, she'll alert the authorities."

"Nobody leaves," Mikhail growled, his Russian accent slurring his words. "I care nothing for authorities; I want my *syn*!"

Emma heaved a sigh of quiet relief that Clarissa was apparently elsewhere. She viewed the Contessa from the side and watched as the pretty mouth curved downwards in a sneer. "You're not in a position to make demands!" she said, her voice calm. The vowel sounds of her New Zealand accent seemed to drag in a soporific drawl as her other companion lifted a gun to Mikhail's temple.

The Russian spluttered in fury. "I brought eight men viz me!" he spat. "Six are outside zis place. I have only to shout."

"Shout then," the Contessa said with a ghoulish smile. "My two outside have already overpowered your six."

Emma looked around her in confusion. She saw nobody on her way into the church, not even Ray. Her eyes raked the dimly lit pews searching for gun toting Triads but saw nothing. Emma faced the circle of adults, seeking Rohan. Her view comprised the heads and shoulders of the gathered crowd and she allowed only her face to peek around the pillar, her sight impeded by the front row pews.

Christopher stood with a bored expression on his face. He showed no respect for the gun in his back, picking at something on his fingernail. Mikhail repeated his demands to see his son, sounding like a droning, broken record in the echoing space, while the Contessa sneered at him from beneath long eyelashes.

"I've transferred the money," Adam Jameson said, cutting across Mikhail's whining. He looked at Christopher and hefted the plaque under his arm. Bubble wrap trailed from the artifact like a wedding train. "Check if you wish."

Christopher shrugged and pressed keys on his phone. His fingers moved quickly and after a moment, he nodded. "Cheers then," Christopher said and returned to his heavy boredom.

Adam moved and one of the Russians next to Mikhail pulled a gun from his pocket and aimed it at the surgeon's head. Like a child cranking up to a tantrum, Jameson's face crumpled. "It's not fair!" he exclaimed. "I'm nothing to do with this!"

"For now, you are everything to do viz zis!" Mikhail spat.

"Where's the Actuary?" the Contessa asked Christopher and the Irishman shrugged.

"He couldn't make it so he sent me."

"He sent his tech to make a delivery?" she mused. "Interesting."

Mikhail stared at Christopher and his brow furrowed. "*Da!*" he said crossly. "Ver is he?"

"On another job," Christopher said. "This one was

only small. I handle the wee ones." His Irish lilt added a comic dimension to the scene.

"No, you don't!" Mikhail spat.

"He does sometimes." The Contessa's voice held a hint of flirtatious humour and Christopher grinned at their shared memory of a hotel in Auckland.

"He does *not*!" Mikhail maintained, his wizened face crinkling in a nasty sneer.

"How'd you know?" Christopher raised his voice. "All you've ever done is fund the expenses and take a huge cut. You took forty percent even while you were selling us out and making life harder than it needed to be. How'd you know what we do? Do you think the Actuary would ever trust *you* with details?"

Mikhail bridled and Emma watched his back straighten. He took a threatening step towards Christopher and Emma heard the Russian hiss, his tone surprised and dismayed. "What? Why do dis? To me!"

Emma crept forward, desperate to see the reason for Mikhail's shock and hoping it was the appearance of Rohan. Dropping to her hands and knees again, she crawled between two wide pillars. Nobody looked in her direction and she moved as close as she dared. The last pillar felt cool under her palm, the smooth stone offering a last bastion of cover before the wide space in front of the ornate altar.

The Contessa held a knife in her hand, her arm extended to throw it through Mikhail's face at close range. She couldn't miss. The metal blade glinted in the spotlight over the altar, threatening and deadly in its promise of instant oblivion. Mikhail looked more indignant than frightened, shaking his head from side to side in disbelief.

"Why do I have to stay?" Jameson whimpered, his face pale in the dim overhead light.

"Because you're part of dis job!" Mikhail spat. He jerked his head towards the Contessa. "She vants you dead."

Adam Jameson's jaw dropped. "What? No! She's helping me retrieve a family heirloom."

Emma gritted her teeth at the lie. The archivist in her fought to burst from her hiding place and expose the truth. *Family heirloom*, she fumed inwardly.

Christopher looked suddenly interested. "We don't do hits. We neutralise risk that's all."

"This man *is* a risk," the Contessa replied, her voice silky smooth. "A risk to everyone he promises to fix."

Christopher stared at Adam Jameson and then back to the Contessa. Confusion crossed his face as he pointed at the surgeon. "He already did surgery?" The Irishman didn't hide his surprise. He shook his head and looked away. "Sorry, love."

Emma craned her neck, trying to see the Contessa's face, curiosity driving her further than good sense dictated. The dark hood shrouded the woman from view and Emma wrinkled her nose in morbid disappointment as she sat back on her heels.

"Yes, he performed a very expensive surgery," the Contessa's smooth voice continued. "But unfortunately he was drunk and it didn't go well, did it Dr Jameson?"

The surgeon took a step forward. "I said I'd make it better," he pleaded, his voice wavering. "It wasn't my fault..." He trailed off as if understanding the futility of his plea. Emma winced, suddenly not wanting to see the rest of the Contessa's face and suspecting it was more than an unsightly blemish or a patch of misplaced botox.

"I told you what would happen," the Contessa continued. "You were warned."

Adam Jameson stamped his expensively shod foot like a child, his suit jacket swaying over his meaty frame. "You made me nervous," he complained. "I didn't want to do it but you left me no choice. Your threats towards my family ruined any chance you had of seeing my best work! I had an unblemished reputation before this!"

"*Had!* So, this is my fault and I should just let you go?" The Contessa's voice held a warning which the surgeon ignored.

"Yes!" he agreed. "Completely!"

Emma cringed, hearing Clarissa Jameson-Arden's arrogance and superiority in the man's answer. The Contessa oozed menace and Emma filled her mouth with the sleeve of her sweater, instinct warning her what came next. With a flick of her wrist, the Contessa changed her aim from Mikhail to Jameson, sending the blade straight through the pompous Englishman's neck. His eyes widening in stunned surprise, Adam Jameson fell like a stone snatched by gravity. In the same moment the Contessa released her knife, her foot soldier removed the gun from Christopher and trained it on Mikhail.

"Rohan vas supposed to do dat!" the foolish Russian complained. "Dat vas de job."

"Only you didn't tell him, did you? Why was that, Mikhail? Was it so you could call the wonderful English police and get him locked away for murder?" The Contessa turned and Emma saw her ruined face. She clamped her teeth on the prickly wool to prevent her reacting to the pool of blood spreading outwards from

Adam Jameson's dying body, or the melted scar tissue on the Contessa's visage. Emma heard Jameson's final, gurgling breaths and felt bile rise into her throat.

The Contessa took a step towards Mikhail and the remaining Russians both trained guns on her. She faced each of them in turn, her smile like the two sides of a coin, beautiful and horrific at the same time. "You think there's anything left to spoil?" she asked and Emma felt a flash of pity as the two Russian's looked away, focussing their attention on their boss. "Mr Romanov will be dead before you pull the trigger and so will you." The Contessa took another step towards Mikhail and his bodyguards panicked, not sure what to do next. They babbled in Russian at their boss and he stilled them with a raised hand. "This is all your fault," she breathed, "it all began with you."

CHAPTER FORTY ONE

The ancient church seemed to hold its breath as Mikhail shook his head. "*Net!*" he protested. "Rohan left you in za fire, not me. I vasn't zer!"

"But I was there because of you," the Contessa replied. "I've always had a soft spot for the Actuary but I'd have left him there burning too." Her ruined gaze narrowed, zeroing on the frightened old man. "You, you're the origin of my misery." Her body tipped as she leaned towards Mikhail. "You placed a man in my inner circle. Brilliant, Mikhail. For years he's sabotaged my jobs until Uncle Che investigated him and we fed him false information. This is about you and my uncle and nothing to do with me. Hack, the Actuary and countless others have been pawns in your sad game. He talked, Mikhail; your spy said a lot before they killed him. He told Uncle about your petty revenge over a bad business deal before I was even born." The Contessa leaned closer still, the dark cloth covering her sumptuous breasts almost touching his chest. "How did it feel when he reported how he shot me before I burned? Did your revenge taste good?"

Mikhail shook his head, still in denial. His eyes pleaded towards men who couldn't help him. "*Net*, I had no men zer." His blue eyes flashed with an emotion akin terror and Emma blanched. Someone in the woman's band of soldiers had served two masters. Mikhail pointed a wavering finger at Christopher, who was in the process of edging slowly away from the

Chinese man next to him. "Hack cheated you! It's his fault."

Christopher bit his lip as the Contessa turned the beautiful side of her face towards him. Emma saw his lazy wink and gulped, waiting for a gun to end his reign of seduction. She witnessed the scarred side of the woman's face and the remains of her lip turned upwards in response to his flirtatious Irish smirk. "Oh, I don't think he cheated me out of anything," she simpered, her injuries overridden by the sexual woman still within. The Triad glanced sideways at Christopher and Emma bit her sleeve, surprised to feel a lone tear trickle down her cheek as stress overwhelmed her.

The Contessa turned back to Mikhail and his bodyguards sent nervous glances to each other in silent communication. She produced another knife from her copious sleeves and ran it along the Russian's aged cheek. "No," she purred, "everything began with you. You just couldn't help yourself, could you, greedy old man?"

The Russian nearest the Contessa raised his gun and aimed it at the back of her head. Horror filled Emma and she stood without regard for herself, screeching, "No! Don't hurt her!" Her words echoed around the stone walls, reverberating for moments as the Chinese woman moved and the shot was never fired.

Christopher reacted first, jabbing the nearest Russian in the face with his elbow, disarming him in one fluid movement and savouring his graceful slide to the floor, his nose smashed. The Triads watched in surprise as Ray leapt from the nearest pew and battered the other Russian with a brass candlestick, laying him out next to his unconscious friend. A deep gash along Ray's cheek dripped blood onto his shirt and he moved with great effort.

The Contessa turned her ruined face towards Emma and studied her with great concentration, lowering the blade. Mikhail moved backwards out of range and kept going, scurrying past Emma like a crab. She stood, frozen to the spot as Ray glanced once at her, shaking his head. Rohan appeared in the centre aisle, his hands in his pockets and his nose bleeding, followed by the Contessa's other two men. "You've made a mess, Contessa," he said, his tone casual.

To Emma's surprise, the woman flicked up her hood to cover the spoiled features and eyed Rohan with a look of superiority, staring down her nose at him with undisguised haughtiness. Jealousy blossomed in Emma's heart at the revival of her former belief; the Contessa desired Rohan. The gathered men had viewed the horror of her face but at the tall Russian's arrival, she covered her scars with an immediacy born of passion.

Emma opened her mouth to speak, but found it covered by a hand which reeked of cigarettes. A sharp point pierced the soft skin below her jaw and Mikhail's voice whispered in her ear. "Big mistake, Emma Andreyev. You say too much!"

Fear paralysed Emma and she saw the misty face of her unborn child drift across her inner vision as the blade pressed harder. "Sorry," she whispered, the word unintelligible behind the gnarled hand and couched in her own ragged breathing.

"*Zatknis'*," Mikhail snapped. "Shut it!"

"No, no, don't do that," Christopher called across the distance between the altar and the stone pillar. "This doesn't involve her. This is between us." The worry in his voice exacerbated Emma's dread and she felt her legs tremble beneath her. Mikhail held her up with his hand over her mouth, the blade digging further into her neck as Emma slumped against his wizened body.

Emma she sensed her husband's proximity, desperate to see his face one last time before his spiteful uncle slit her throat. She wanted to beg him to look after Nicky, knowing inwardly she didn't have to ask. Christopher moved towards her, his face wracked with anxiety, wearing a shroud of fear which didn't suit his casual Irish blarney.

Rohan spoke to his uncle in Russian, his voice low and even as he wiped blood from beneath his regal nose and advanced towards Emma. Mikhail ignored him, pressing the blade deeper into Emma's neck and dragging her backwards. It stung, biting into her soft flesh without regard and she felt warmth trickle into the neck of her sweater. "See how it feels?" Mikhail hissed. "You take from me, I take from you." He cackled like a mad man. "This wasn't the game, Actuary, but it's worked in my favour for once."

Emma's eyes darted towards the altar, seeing Ray's ashen face in her fading vision. His expression filled with heartbreak at the panic in her eyes and Emma yearned to apologise for her disobedience and unkind words. She needed to tell him his job was safe; Rohan would honour their verbal contract.

"I'll get Sergei," Rohan offered. He stepped into Emma's eye line and she breathed a sob of relief. Rohan would fix it; Rohan fixed everything. Her husband pulled his phone from his trouser pocket and held it up screen outwards. "Let her go, Uncle and I'll phone him."

"*Net!*" Mikhail spat. "You had your chance,

ublyudok!"

Rohan's eyes narrowed and he lowered his phone. "Why do you call me that?" he asked, his face hardening. Emma groaned, understanding the Russian word for *bastard* and recognising the warning vein pulsing in her husband's neck.

"Because you are!" Mikhail said, laughter cackling in his throat. His palm over Emma's mouth impeded her breathing, forcing her nostrils to flare against his index finger, her brain fighting for oxygen. Her gaze took in the Contessa, her body stood with statuesque grace, a beautiful woman not reduced by circumstance. The four Oriental men flanked her like a stone guard of honour, motionless.

Mikhail's mirth made him lose focus and Emma saw Christopher tense, ready to charge, his fists balled next to his sides. Her heart ached, knowing he was too far away. Rohan's eyes flashed, seeing the old man's distraction. He waved the phone in front of his face again, the carrot before the stick. As Emma's breathing became laboured, she felt Mikhail's grip loosen.

With a stellar effort she clamped her teeth hard on the soft flesh of his gnarly index finger. Emma gripped, feeling the skin flatten beneath her front teeth as Mikhail let out a gargantuan wail. The blade against her neck shifted, drawing a painful wound down her skin, six inches from start to finish and as his hand slipped, she let go and screamed. The frightened sound split the air, deafening her and the old Russian in its intensity.

Rohan moved but not fast enough, listing on his prosthetic leg as he lurched forward. Christopher was too far away and the Triads watched the scene unfold with dispassionate interest as though they collectively studied a TV documentary on how *not* to approach psychopaths.

Emma heard him arrive as she kicked backwards, contacting shin with her heel and seizing another hunk of nicotine stained flesh between her teeth. The frantic scrabbling of claws on the stone floor gave her hope as Farrell launched himself from metres away, sinking his teeth into the soft flesh of Mikhail's thigh. The dog held on, snarling and dragging the man away from Emma, his brown eyes alight with loyalty and the thrill of the game. His front feet gripped Mikhail's leg, claws sinking into the old man's flesh and holding him prone for a volley of savage bites. Rohan reached Emma as the dog pulled the man to the stone floor and he yanked his wife out of harm's way by her arm.

"No!" Rohan shouted, but too late. The Contessa's skilful blade zipped through the air like a silver trick of the light and pushed itself through Mikhail's right eye. His hands flapped uselessly as he fell backwards, dead before he hit the stone floor with a dull thud. The dog let go, looking momentarily perplexed until Christopher's shrill whistle gave him focus and he bounded over to his friend.

"Emma, Em, look at me!" Rohan's soft fingers stroked Emma's face as she gulped against his shirt. She heard the dog's happy panting and felt Christopher pull her hair back to check the wound on her neck. Rohan widened his eyes and shook his head.

"Not the doctor," Emma gasped. "Don't get that doctor." Emma's irrational heart told her she'd rather die than have the Ukrainian abortionist's hands on her.

"I won't, Em," Rohan promised, cradling her into him and bearing her weight as she sank earthwards. "We'll clean up and get out of here," he whispered. "It's not safe."

Emma bit back a hysterical laugh. *Not safe* meant something very different from the mess surrounding her. It meant asbestos and busy roads, not men with stab wounds to the face and their blood pooling on a mediaeval church floor. Farrell jumped up and licked Emma's fingers as she clung to Rohan, offering comfort and doggy solidarity. She sank her fingers into his ruff and held on, feeling his excited trembling.

"Clean up Em's blood and leave the rest," Rohan commanded.

"What?" Christopher sounded aghast. "We can't do that!"

"I mean it! Get rid of our prints and Em's blood and let's get out of here."

Emma smelled a flowery fragrance and pulled her face from Rohan's chest, seeking its powerful origins. The Contessa's half smile, half grimace greeted her. "Thank you," the Chinese woman said with grace, her speech slurred on the melted side of her face. She reached out a scarred hand and touched Emma's wrist. "I thought I didn't care about dying anymore, but I do."

Emma nodded, a million words crowding into her brain. She let go of the dog and used her sleeve to wipe her tear stained face, alarmed by the blood on the front of her sweater. "Is it over?" she asked, her voice louder than she intended. She ran a hand over her swelling stomach and the Contessa's eyes followed the movement. "I need it to be over," Emma said, an edge of pleading in her voice.

The Contessa barked an order to the four men standing close and they nodded as a collective and turned to look at Christopher. With a glance at Rohan, the Irishman shrugged and directed the Triads and Ray to wipe any surfaces they'd touched. "We're done," the woman said, bowing regally to Rohan. "A life saved in exchange for a life."

Emma saw something like sadness in her husband's eyes and her heart constricted in misery. Mikhail's death was the cost of hers, in exchange for warning the Contessa before the gun ended her pain; a circle of destruction completed.

Ray ran outside to the white van, jangling its keys in his hand as he jogged through the side door. Farrell sat on Emma's foot, bashing her thigh with his forehead as he repeatedly looked up at her, his upside down face comically comforting with his smiling lips. He panted and Emma saw a line of Mikhail's blood on his flank. She clapped a hand to her mouth and Rohan clasped her round the waist and hauled her upright. "Don't puke, Em!" His voice held an edge of panic mixed with humour. "Hack will hate you forever and we don't have time to clear up. Come on, *devotchka*, don't leave them DNA."

Emma put a hand up to her painful neck, feeling the slick blood move under her fingertips. "Hurts," she gasped and Rohan nodded.

"It's not deep, Em. Trust me; I can take care of it."

Emma nodded and tried not to focus on the bodies littering the sacred church. Her vicar father would have been devastated. Mikhail lay where he fell, his body sprawled with the limbs at awkward angles. Emma pointed at the space where the knife should have been and Rohan followed her gaze. "Gone!" she said.

He nodded. "She took it with her," he replied. "Evidence."

The Triads moved as a unit, obeying Christopher's expert direction, but the Contessa's graceful presence was absent having collected her lethal knives before she glided from the crime scene. "Get her out of here!" Christopher called as Rohan examined his wife's wound in the dim light. Emma watched conflict cross her husband's expression and shook her head.

"I'm fine," she said. "I've got my car keys." She fumbled in her pocket and dropped them, hearing the metallic clatter on the stone floor. "You stay and do your job."

"I'll go with her." Ray appeared next to Emma. "You're better at this." He waved his arm towards one of the Chinese Triads wiping the end of the front pew with precise movements. The white cloth in his hand seemed incongruous in the surroundings.

Rohan looked to Emma for confirmation and she nodded in acceptance as Ray took her upper arm in his capable hands. "Leave the plaque," she said, registering the confusion on her husband's face. "Leave it for the police," she added. "I never want to see it again."

Ray nodded. "Paul will sort it out. She's right. Leave it." He supported Emma to the side entrance, checking the street for anyone passing by. "Act drunk," he told her. "Lean against me and look casual."

"I can't!" Emma groaned, putting a hand up to the stinging wound which smarted in the freezing night air. Her fingers touched sticky blood, no longer running but clotting the void in her soft tissue.

"Do it!" Ray snapped. "Unless you want to be identified when they find this mess tomorrow."

Emma leaned into Ray's masculine body, allowing him to press his head against hers and screen their faces from onlookers. She felt Farrell against her knee and reached down to encourage him for his stellar obedience under duress. "Can you get in by yourself?"

Ray hissed, clicking the central locking remotely. Emma nodded and climbed into the passenger seat, her energy dissipating from shock and injury. The dog scrambled into the foot well and sat on Emma's feet, resting his head on her knee. Ray stripped off his jacket and passed it to Emma before fastening his seat belt. "Put that on and cover your neck," he warned. "In case we're stopped and fasten your seat belt. Let's not give them an excuse."

Emma's fingers fumbled with the jacket, hauling it on over her sweater in the small space. The dog scrabbled over her feet as Ray reversed out of the parking space, not waiting for Emma to finish. They travelled along the main street at a dignified pace and the click of Emma's seat belt killed the flashing light and irritating bleep from the dashboard. An oncoming car flashed its lights at them, sending Emma into a panic. "What's that about?" she asked, her voice high pitched and fretful.

"Cops!" Ray said. "It's a warning there's one parked up or worse, a traffic stop."

"What can we do?" Emma said, jerking her head around. "We need to warn Rohan!"

"How?" Ray snapped. "Just keep your head down and stop panicking." At the junction with Coventry Road he turned right and drove steadily towards the end of town. "They must be on Northampton Road so I'll double back and go across country."

"What about Rohan?" Emma whined and the dog rested his head in her lap, keen to soothe her anxiety. Farrell gave a sigh which summed up Emma's sense of futility.

"They're used to this, miss. They'll get cleaned up and out of there; faster without us getting in the way."

"What did you fetch from the van?" Emma asked, hearing Farrell's collar clink under her foot. The dog jerked to attention, his tail thudding against the carpet as his face disappeared to check it out.

"Gloves and stuff for cleaning up," Ray replied, concentrating on the road ahead. He slowed the vehicle and looked around him. "I'll head out to Lubenham," he confirmed. "Then take the back roads through Marston Trussell and Clipston and come out on the main road south of Great Oxenden." Having made his decision, Ray settled and drove with care.

"What will Rohan and Christopher do when they leave the church?" Emma asked, her mind inevitably straying back to her husband's plight. "Will they run into the police?"

Ray shook his head. "I doubt it. My guess is they'll lock up the church the same way they unlocked it and then head out somewhere nearby to disable the camera feed. Any security person checking in the last hour would see the feed looping and assume it's all ok. But the boys can't leave it that way. Hack must disable it and then screw it up so there's no view from before they arrived. He'll stay around to log in and do that."

"How do you know this stuff?" Emma asked, distracting herself from the pain under her jaw. The smarting was replaced by a dull ache which spread across the right-hand side of her face and into her temple. "Did you learn it in the army?"

"No." Ray shook his head and concentrated on the road ahead as he made the turn onto back roads in sleepy Lubenham village. "Hack explained when I helped him load the van this afternoon."

"I'm sorry I said you were fired," Emma whispered, the engine noise almost obliterating her apology.

Ray smirked. "You can't fire me, miss; I know too much."

Emma watched the dark countryside whiz by. "Where did you go when you left me in the car?" She sat up straight. "The plaster cast! I left it by the side entrance."

"They'll get it, don't worry. Your husband's good at this; Hack said so."

"I'm not sure I want him to be," Emma muttered. She remembered Adam Jameson's blank eyes and pooling blood and shivered.

Ray saw and pressed his hand over hers, wincing at the wet nose which pushed its way into the embrace. "Hold on, miss. We'll be back at the house soon."

Emma laid her head back against the head rest and Ray shook her hand. "Don't go to sleep, miss. Keep talking." He glanced sideways and removed his hand to navigate a tight bend. "I told you to stay in the car and then cut round the front of the church." His lips pursed as he stressed the words, '*stay in the car.*' "The front doors were unlocked but closed and the wood creaked as I opened it. I saw them gathered around the altar."

Orange flashing lights strobed into the night from a distance and Emma's heart clenched. "What now?" she panicked, opening her eyes and slurring her speech.

"Tractor," Ray reassured her. "It's nearly spring so the farmers will be out with the newborns. There's nothing to worry about."

The tractor turned into a gateway, bearing wrapped bails of silage for a herd of cows huddled near a hedge. Ray navigated its back end and continued up the road. "Emma, listen to me." He slapped her thigh and she groaned. "I heard a scuffle and investigated, finding

Captain Andreyev and the Triads dealing with the Russians. I waded in and between us, we dispatched them."

"You killed them." Emma's voice sounded flat and the effort of speaking seemed to sap her remaining energy.

Ray shook his head. "Knocked them out. They'll wake up and disappear, hopefully before the police arrive. Those Triads fight like machines." He smiled, admiration in his square face as the headlights from an oncoming vehicle lit the car's interior. "I didn't know the Captain spoke Mandarin," Ray commented and Emma rolled her eyes.

"Something else I never knew," she muttered, sealing her right hand over the wound. Warm blood trickled over her fingers and she panicked. "It's bleeding again," she sobbed. "And I don't feel well."

"Not far now," Ray confirmed. "Just listen to my voice and focus on that." He indicated and turned again. "I couldn't risk using the front doors because of the noise, so I crept in the side. I met the dog in the porch and told him to stay there. They were arguing, so I managed to slip around the rear pews and make my way forward. I saw you doing the same and felt the overwhelming urge to tan your bloody, disobedient backside!" Ray looked sideways at Emma to see if she registered the rebuke. Her eyes were closed and her head lolled on her chest, held up by the seat belt. He swore and shook her. "Miss! Miss! Don't go to sleep until I've looked at that wound."

"Rohan," Emma slurred. "Rohan."

Ray slapped her thigh again and moved his hand quickly as Farrell growled and bared his teeth, his irises glinting blue in the reflected light from the headlamps.

"Steady on, boy," Ray breathed. "I'm trying to help her." He made the turn onto the main road struggling not to panic, indicating and driving normally, despite the pounding in his chest. "Emma!" he shouted and she stirred and turned to face him, her eyes drooping. "Rohan stayed outside the church with the Triads and I didn't see him come in. What you did was brave, miss, really brave. Stay awake, please. Meeting you and getting this job is the best thing that's happened to me in years. Please, miss. Stay awake!"

Ray indicated right and bounced into the turning circle before the high iron gates of Wingate Hall. Met with the keypad he realised he didn't know the number. "Miss! What's the code?" He tried to wake Emma without touching her, the dog's growl threatening every time his fingers crossed the centre aisle.

The gates crept open before him, the motor giving a high pitched hiss in the silent night air and Ray grappled to close his driver's window against further danger.

"Where'd you go?" Rohan's irritation was apparent as he emerged from the shadows, his brow furrowed. "We've been back ages." His blonde head poked through Ray's window and he observed Emma's slumped form. "Get her up to the house, now!"

Ray powered through the gates and drove up to the main house, hearing gravel spit from the wheel treads behind him. The Mercedes nosed from between the trees in his rear view mirror and reversed onto the drive, following Emma's car up the hill.

Emma woke as Ray cut the engine, pushing her door open and falling sideways. Farrell shot straight out, taking Emma's legs with him. The gravel came up to meet her but the seat belt kept her pinned, embracing her like a sling. She saw Rohan's strong forearms in her blurred vision and sighed with relief. "I think I'm dead," she slurred and heard the low rumble of his laugh. Light streamed out from the house and for a moment, the horror of the night threw her back in time to the burning Scottish mansion and the loss of Christopher.

Emma panicked, scratching Rohan's fingers as he tried to release her. "Christopher's dead too!" she wailed.

"Don't be daft, woman!" The Irishman's laugh cut into her fog as he leaned across her to unfasten the seatbelt. "Yer window's open," he said, directing the jerk of his head at Ray, who turned the key and restarted the engine. Emma heard the whirr of the window closing. "This rain should wash away any traces we left outside the church."

"This is too freaky," Emma breathed, fighting to regain her sanity as huge drops of rain pelted the top of her head. As the belt released her, she slid into Rohan's welcome arms and he cradled her against him like a child and lifted her into the air.

"Want me to take her?" Christopher asked as Rohan limped towards the front steps and breached them with great difficulty. Emma heard the rumble through Rohan's chest wall as he swore at the Irishman in Russian, the old rivalry alive and well. She pushed her face into his shirt and closed her eyes to avoid the sight of the damp blood stains, not wanting them to be his; but equally afraid they might be hers.

Rohan heaved himself onto a kitchen chair and kept Emma on his knee, tutting as Ray and Christopher argued their way into the room behind him. "Why'd yer do a bloody tour of the country?" Christopher asked, his Irish accent making worry into humour.

"Because of the cops!" Ray defended his actions, putting shaking hands on his hips. "Another car flashed me in the high street and I didn't want to get pulled over!"

Emma felt Rohan's sigh through the side of her head but Christopher's exhalation was more vigorous. "You eejit!" he snapped. "He was probably tryin' ter tell yer to put your headlights on!"

Ray shook his head. "I did have them on!"

Rohan's voice sounded calm as Christopher crashed around in a biscuit tin containing first aid supplies. "You had side lights on; you didn't click the lever fully."

Ray used a dirty expletive too awful to repeat and turned away from the men to give himself time to collect his face. Rohan rubbed Emma's shoulder and sat her up. He offered her a bright smile in his pale face and she felt a wave of nausea overtake her stomach as she reached an upright position. "I feel sick!" she announced, grabbing at the plastic pudding bowl Christopher slid across the table.

"You will," Rohan replied with calm assurance. "You lost blood but not enough for a transfusion." He tipped her face towards him, ignoring the presence of the pudding bowl. "We'll get you sorted and then you can sleep. Tomorrow I'll take you to the hospital and get you checked." His hand strayed across the signs of pregnancy, caressing her swollen abdomen and knitting his brow. "I need to make sure my *doch'* is well."

"She's kicking," Emma whispered and Rohan smiled with relief. She felt so exhausted it was an effort even to hold the pudding basin up to her face, but after a couple of hearty retches she conceded nothing would happen.

"Did you eat today?" Ray asked, ignoring Christopher's nasty glare as he spewed bandages and tape onto the table.

Emma shook her head and he nodded. "Then that's part of the problem." Ray shot a nervous look at Rohan. "Do you want me to deal with her wound?"

"Why?" Christopher roared. "How come a bloody grounds man is suddenly the expert in everything? He can't even drive home without drama! Just call the usual guy."

"Shut up!" Rohan's calm voice broke with irritation. "He was a medic in the army and a good one. And I'm not calling the Ukrainian to my wife." His hands clamped around Emma's upper arms as she began to struggle. "I promised." Rohan glanced across at Ray. "Just do it, man. Where do you want her?"

Ray jerked his head towards the table and Emma squeaked as the men lifted her onto its wooden surface. Rohan slipped his blood stained jacket off and rolled it up, laying it under Emma's head as a pillow. Breathing heavily, Ray used antiseptic wipes to isolate the cut from the blood. Emma closed her eyes at the cold, stinging sensation and Ray saw. "Sorry," he whispered. "Sorry for not keeping you at the house and for the round country ride too."

"Bit late for that!" Christopher snapped in the background and Emma tensed, sensing an explosion.

Ray sighed as the tendons in Emma's neck flexed and he stood up, sounding exasperated. "You're making things worse!" he bit, focussing his anger on the Irishman. "Yeah, I made some mistakes tonight but I'm trying to put it right and you're not helping."

"Take the van back." Rohan's low voice cut across the brewing argument, commanding and definitive. "Sort out the gear and get some sleep."

"But..." Christopher began, waving his arm at Emma's body, prone on the kitchen table.

"Hack!" Rohan warned. Relenting, he offered, "I'll text you when she's fixed up. Ok?"

With a grunt, Christopher left the kitchen and Emma heard his steps thudding along the corridor to the main doors. Farrell's claws clicked on the tiles and then floorboards as he decided to accompany the Irishman outside. With the tempestuous Hack gone, Ray relaxed into his role as medic, his hands shaking less as he cleaned around the cut on Emma's neck. Rohan stood near Emma's face, holding her hand and passing wipes to Ray as he requested them. "It's a mess," Ray breathed, glancing nervously at Emma as he made the tactless remark. She closed her eyes and fought the nausea again.

"Do you need an IV line in?" Rohan asked. "We've got the gear."

Ray gave a heavy sigh. "Captain, I haven't done this stuff for more than a decade. I came out of the army when I was forty."

"But you can put a line in?" Rohan demanded, his tone urgent.

"I don't know!" Ray's voice cracked with the strain and Rohan nodded.

"I understand," he replied.

Emma heard movement and recognised Rohan's heels on the floor of the corridor outside as he moved away. She opened her eyes and stared towards the open doorway, panicking. "Where's he gone?" she asked, feeling weak.

Ray shook his head, his face white. "I don't know, miss. He'll come back." His hand shook as he wiped along the ridges of the cut and Emma hissed with the pain.

"Sorry I passed out," she whispered. "It hurt."

"And you're dehydrated," Ray said, his face close to hers. "Stop trying to look at me and keep your head turned that way." He pushed her temple, so she faced away from him and resumed his cleaning. "That's better."

"You didn't say you were a medic," Emma said, watching the kitchen cupboards swim around the room like a weird psychedelic trip.

"I didn't think it was important."

"You must have told Rohan," Emma said, her voice weak.

"Nope," Ray replied. "Stop talking, miss. Save your energy."

Emma closed her eyes and heard Rohan return. He walked through a mist in her brain carrying a bag of clear fluid and a plastic box of complicated pipes and items she couldn't identify. "I don't want that," she tried to say, hearing her voice slur and laughing at how drunk she sounded.

"I don't know if I can do this," Ray said, sounding anxious.

"That's ok; I can," came Rohan's reply.

Emma felt something cold in the crook of her left elbow, then a sharp scratch which made her jerk. An odd sensation worked its way up her arm, spreading out like an icy touch. *Then nothing.*

CHAPTER FORTY TWO

"What's happened to Mummy?" Nicky's shrill voice carried through the bedroom and Emma groaned as she moved her head. Her right hand sought the crook of her left elbow, feeling for the thing which disturbed her repeatedly during the night. The skin ached when she pressed it but the needle wasn't there anymore. Emma glanced upwards to where the bag of rehydration fluid spent the night hanging above her head, attached to the top of the four poster bed with a length of string. *Nothing.*

"I'm fine, Nicky," Emma said, her voice sounding cracked from disuse. "I had a silly accident but I'm all better now."

The little boy ran to the side of the bed, looking down on her with a worried expression. He pointed to the white medical pack on her neck. "Is that an operation?" he asked.

Emma pushed herself to a sitting position. "Kind of, baby." She put her hands up to touch the sore spot and winced. Rohan shook his head to warn her to leave it. "How was school?" Emma asked, dropping into her maternal role with relief. "Was Mo back?"

Nicky shook his head with sadness in his wide, blue eyes. "No. His dad found them so Mel had to leave and take New Mo somewhere else. I asked Mrs Clark, but she just said, '*He's safe, Nicky, don't you worry.*' But I cried until playtime anyway 'cause I was worried. What if the bad mens find him? What then?"

Emma smiled at her son's impression of his gentle hearted teacher and cradled his head against her chest. She stroked the soft blonde hair and kissed the top of his head, sensing his agony and knowing words were futile. Emma closed her eyes and breathed in the scent of her son, jumping as the unborn sibling in her womb began its frantic movements. "Baby's talking to you," she whispered, smoothing Nicky's hair back from his forehead.

"To me?" he asked, looking up at her and jabbing her collar bone with his chin.

Emma nodded and took his small hand, placing it over her stomach. "Can you feel?" she whispered.

Nicky shook his head and a deep furrow appeared in his forehead. He opened his mouth to complain and then beamed. "Yeah," he said, his eyes widening in childish delight. "What's she sayin' to me?"

"I don't know," Emma laughed. "That's between you both. But remember it might not be a girl."

"It is," Nicky replied, sounding cocky as the small movement fluttered against his palm. "It's Stephanie."

Emma raised her eyebrows, feeling the pinch of the wound at her neck as she peered down at her son. "What if it's a boy?"

"Then I'll call him Mo," Nicky answered insolently. "And you won't like it."

Emma sighed, tiredness paralysing her body. "Definitely not, thanks. I think we've had more than enough boys called Mo in our lives for a while."

"Boys called Mo are nice though," Nicky argued. "They make amazing friends."

"They sure do." Emma smiled at her son. "There's cake in the tin in the pantry. Why don't you get some?"

"Yummy!" Nicky said, pulling away from his

mother and unwittingly causing pain in his carelessness. He skipped to the bedroom door. "Oh, Mummy, I like that new man, Ray Barker. He mended my skateboard."

"Cool, that's awesome, baby." Emma lay back against the pillows as her son departed, bounding along the hallway towards the stairs. She sighed as the inevitable sounds of his palms squeaking against the bannister reached her ears. "Don't slide down the bannister!" she called, but her voice carried no further than her husband's smiling face.

Emma lifted the sheets and peered at her body. She heaved a relieved breath and lay back against the pillow again. "I thought for a horrible moment I was still covered in blood," she said. "Thanks for changing my clothes and cleaning me up."

"It's fine." Rohan sat on his side of the bed and swung his left leg up, his right one following with the aid of his hand. "I enjoyed it," he said with a small laugh.

"Pervert!" Emma replied.

Rohan reached to clasp Emma's hand in his. "Your neck's fine but it will be scarred, *devotchka*. Ray did a good job once you passed out."

"Did he do big ugly stitches?" Emma asked, wrinkling her nose and raising her hand to touch the white tape.

"Na, we glued it and he butterflied the top. Neater than stitching."

Emma snuffed. "But what if something was wrong inside and you just glued over it?" she complained.

"Trust Ray," Rohan soothed. "He spent years patching people up. He checked inside and made sure it was clean. The blade went through a few fatty layers and could have been nasty, but the Contessa ended that possibility."

Emma put her hands up to her face and breathed deeply. "It makes me feel ill." she muttered through her fingers.

Rohan squeezed her thigh through the sheets. "It's over now. We can live our lives in peace."

"I keep seeing it happen over and over. I see the knife flying through the air and..." Emma's body tensed and the wound on her neck tightened, producing a dull ache. She banished the image of the dying men as she had in the Scottish mansion. Placing a hand on her gullet, Emma saw the knife slicing through Adam Jameson's throat and gasped. "Mikhail could've cut something major," she breathed. "I might have died."

"He almost *did* cut something important." Rohan pulled Emma's hand away from her throat. "But he didn't. Mikhail was good at making money but always rubbish with his hands."

"This isn't funny!" Emma bit her lip and faced her husband. Rohan looked chastened, but she recognised his desire to change the subject. "What if Paul Barker wants to come back and talk to me about the man who died at the gate?" Emma panicked. "How can I cover this?" She flapped her hand towards her neck. "It feels like a mess so it probably is."

"*Net*. It's fine. If you make a big fuss you'll draw attention to it. Wear one of those jumpers that go right up your neck."

Emma shuddered and gave a huge sigh. "Who discovered the bodies? I hope it wasn't a poor little old lady with a heart condition."

"Freda," Rohan replied.

Emma turned to her husband with a look of amazement. "What? How?"

"She does the flowers for the Sunday service. I rang her and warned her there'd be unusual items in the church and she did the rest. She's playing the sobbing old lady card right now and enjoying the attentions of Detective Barker."

"What day is it?" Emma asked in a small voice. "Why isn't Nicky in school still? Isn't it early for him to be home?" She craned her neck to see the clock, trying not to disturb the wound. "It's lunchtime."

"It's Saturday." Rohan shifted closer and put his arm around his wife. "He was telling you what happened yesterday. We did the drop on Friday night, remember?"

"Then how did Nicky get home?" Emma pushed herself up the bed and flicked the covers off her feet, feeling as though the world had passed her by and she needed to catch up. Her tee shirt ended at her thighs and her bare legs stretched under the sheets. Her body felt wooden as she tried to stand.

"I drove to town and fetched him this morning," Rohan soothed, pulling her back into the bed. "Everything's taken care of, Em. Trust me."

"What about Sam? He gave us the plaque. If he makes a statement to the police and…"

"Sam will say nothing," Rohan assured her. "Ray and I had a chat with him earlier this morning while you slept. I told him partial truths which fitted with his experience of Adam Jameson. Last weekend, Clarissa Jameson-Arden visited Sam and they had an unpleasant conversation. She told him Adam wanted the plaque and Sam must find it. Adam had a mean reputation within the family for his violence and unpredictability so Sam was scared."

"Sounds like a Jameson trait from generations ago," Emma interjected and Rohan shrugged, unaware of the angry faces peering from decades of class photos.

"Sam stole the plaque but when Clarissa turned up to get it, he lied and said he couldn't find it, feeling overwhelmed by his loyalty to you." Rohan stroked Emma's dark fringe back from her forehead. "He said he'd promised to help you when he found out you were pregnant and alone."

Emma nodded. "He did. It was very sweet."

"You're not alone, Em and you never were."

"I felt it," she whispered.

"I know, but you weren't." Rohan kept the steady stroking motion on her hair and Emma sighed, fighting exhaustion.

"So who offered him money?" she asked, yawning.

"Clarissa. Adam pressurised her to persuade Sam and she tried the promise of a baby to make him comply. She saw him weakening and visited a few times to raise the amount of cash she was offering but Adam Jameson lost patience and engaged us via the Contessa. Sam got a visit yesterday from Clarissa and he sent her away and told her he'd call the police if she didn't leave him alone. Then he was shaken up by a nasty phone call around tea time from an angry Adam, telling him to watch his back and say nothing to anyone about the plaque. It was probably the last phone call he made. Nice guy, hey? Nobody seems sorry Jameson's dead; except perhaps his sister."

"And Mikhail killed the man at the gate," Emma said. "It doesn't make sense, but it kinda fits."

"*Net*, he didn't." Rohan shook his head. "I don't know why the Triads came right to the front door but wonder now if it was to warn me about Mikhail's games. It's possible they wanted a truce anyway but then the foot soldier died and the plaque was found. I'm not sure. That one remains a mystery and Barker's told Ray he's no nearer to solving it."

"The Contessa clearly thought Mikhail did it," Emma said, rubbing her eyes with her left hand.

"He definitely didn't," Rohan replied. "Hack saw the whole thing and it wasn't Mikhail or anyone connected with him."

"If he saw it happen, why didn't he 'clear up' as you both like to call it?"

Rohan shrugged. "You'd have to ask him that."

"I don't like things unsolved," Emma complained. "It doesn't feel right."

"It's fine," Rohan chuckled. "You're a perfectionist. Hey, Ray's settled into the other apartment over the stables; is that ok?"

"I'm not bothered." Emma yawned. "I think it's a mess though."

"*Da*, he wants to renovate it himself and I said that's fine. I hope it was the right thing to say?"

Emma peered at her husband sideways, enjoying his deference to her for a change. She pouted. "I guess it's ok," she said. "He'll have to do it in period style though. And it will probably draw the council inspector and heritage people to Christopher's apartment, which is definitely not in keeping with their idea of how things should be done."

Rohan pulled a face and Emma detected a hint of sadness. "He needs to move it anyway. If I'm no longer the Actuary, I don't need a tech so it's pointless him staying." His voice sounded wistful and Emma chewed her lower lip and thought of life without Christopher.

"There's a folly which the Ayers built deep into the property near the woods on the Great Oxendon side. It's turn of the century but mock gothic and nobody seems interested in that. Apparently it's where Freda's sister was conceived." Emma saw her husband turn away with a smirk and kept her smile to herself. He didn't want Christopher to leave either. "Can this thing get wet?" she asked. "I need a shower."

CHAPTER FORTY THREE

Emma's breath caught in her throat as the blonde man emerged from the Mercedes. Rohan slammed his driver's door and took the baby while Sergei's wife climbed out. The breeze felt cool on Emma's legs as she formed the welcoming committee, an Arctic wind whipping around her and teasing her clothes away from her body like a selfish lover.

Nicky rode his skateboard along the wide coving between the front lawn and the gravel driveway, balancing like an acrobat. He ceased for a moment to look at the blonde baby which looked unerringly familiar but also different.

"Mum!" His shout sounded panicked as he ran to Emma, staring over his shoulder at the visitors, his eyes wide with wonder. "Mum, it's..."

"No!" Emma clasped his shoulders, not wanting the thought to take root in the fragile heart. "It's not Uncle Anton, baby. It's his brother, Sergei." She swallowed, trying to gain control as a stranger approached the steps, a stranger wearing a loved one's face and body. Emma took short breaths to ease her pounding heart and plastered the smile on her face.

They could have been twins, Anton and Sergei. Anton's smile met Emma's and she choked with emotion, covering the telltale action with a fake cough. Anton's loss hit her afresh with the arrival of his doppelgänger, raking over the shallowly healed wounds. Sergei held out his hand in greeting, treating Emma to a smattering of heavily accented English.

"Please to meet," he offered.

Nicky laughed, a raucous blurt of merriment. "You sound just like Uncle Anton," he giggled. "He used to do that funny accent too."

Emma glared at her son, paralysed on the front doormat. Sergei smoothed his blonde hair back from his face like a model and bowed to Nicky. "*Da*, he did too. He does me and now I do him."

Rohan followed the slender beauty, who glided up the stairs and offered her hand to Emma. She leaned in and gave an air kiss to both Emma's cheeks. "Bella Romanov," she said with a smile. "*Zdravstvuyte*."

"Hello," Emma replied with cordial grace. Her eyes fell on her husband and she felt his waves of misery, but didn't understand them. Finding his brother after losing Anton should be a happy occasion but Rohan seemed distant as though going through the motions. Emma gave her husband a nervous smile and he returned it, his perfect teeth adding to his striking good looks. The smile didn't reach his eyes and faded before he closed the front door behind him.

"This is Artyom," Rohan said, dandling the baby in his arms. The blonde child's face cracked in a grin which displayed four tiny pearls twinkling from extremely pink gums; a picture of innocence.

"What is he?" Nicky asked, pointing at the child.

Bella flapped her arms and looked at Sergei for help, scratching around in their poor joint English. "Er...*mladenets*," she replied and furrowed her brow.

Emma hid her smile and darted a look at Rohan. His face looked blank, giving nothing away. Nicky looked to Emma for clarification, rolling the Russian word for *baby* around on his tongue. "Do they think I'm stupid?" he asked his mother in disgust and Emma narrowed her eyes.

"Don't be rude, Nicky. He's your cousin."

"Cool!" The child's eyes lit up and his elation salvaged the moment. He reached out a dirt covered hand to the baby and Artyom gripped his finger and squealed with pleasure. "Can he do skateboarding?" Nicky asked, turning the question on Emma when nobody else answered.

"Not yet," she replied. "I don't think he can walk but you can teach him when he can. Maybe if they stick around you can teach him lots of things. *Good things only,*" she added in warning.

Nicky's face crumpled at the thought of being denied the child's company even in the future, but the baby grinned with delight. "He looks like me doesn't he, Mum?" Nicky asked and Emma nodded.

"In lots of ways, Nicky." She looked at the shape of the chubby cheeks and earnest expression on Artyom's tiny face. "And not in others."

A glance at her husband revealed a stony expression and she saw his jaw working through the stubbly skin of his cheeks. The moment became awkward.

"Let's go through to the sitting room," Emma said, indicating the corridor with a flapping hand. It induced a flurry of shoe removal and seemed ages before everyone was seated in the sunny room. "I'll make hot drinks," Emma suggested, looking around. "What would everyone like?"

In the kitchen she heaved a sigh of relief. Christopher sat at the table eating toast and Ray washed his hands in the sink. Emma shook her head at the Irishman. "You've got your own kitchen!" she snapped and he shrugged.

"So I have," he replied with a grin. "But it's got no

food in it. Yours does."

"Sorry, miss." Ray looked guilty, drying his hands on a towel. "The lawns are finished and I'll start on the flower beds tomorrow."

"I didn't mean you," Emma said. "I meant him." She pointed at Christopher with a jab of her index finger. "He takes liberties."

"Lawn mower's going fantastic," Ray said, beaming. "It just needed oil." His rugged good looks contrasted with Christopher's more photogenic profile. Emma compared them to Rohan and realised she'd surrounded herself with beautiful men.

"That's awesome, Ray," she agreed. "The place is starting to look loved."

"How's it goin' with the rellies?" Christopher asked, jerking his head towards the open doorway and dripping jam in a line across the table.

"Awkward," Emma replied with a sigh. "Something doesn't feel right and I'm not sure what."

Both men pulled faces and shrugged, leaving her none the wiser. Emma clattered around with coffee and tea pots, laying them on a tray with a glass of water for Nicky. She returned to find the sitting room empty but for Rohan, who stood in the bay window looking out at the front lawn and the main road beyond the trees. "Oh." Emma laid the tray on the coffee table and looked around her. "Where did everyone go?"

Rohan jerked his head towards the driveway. "Nicky's showing them how to skateboard." Her husband's hands were jammed into his front pockets and his back felt rock hard under Emma's touch, every muscle tense. She felt it again that sense of misery coming off him in waves of static.

"What's wrong, Ro?" Her heart fluttered in alarm.

"Nothing, *dorogaya*." He released his left hand from its pocket and put his arm around her shoulders, pulling her into his chest. "I love you, Em," he said and she heard the cry of his heart, unable to decipher the coded message it threw into the ether.

"You're right; Sergei's Anton's twin. I find it difficult to look at him," Emma admitted.

Rohan nodded and looked away, a tight smile on his face. "Yeah."

"We'll be ok, you know," Emma said with reassurance. Her gaze followed the slender blonde man as he skipped alongside Nicky's precarious balancing act. Unable to skate on the gravel, the boy traversed the concrete boundary steps which separated driveway from lawn. The council heritage advisor said they were laid in the 1800s and showed open horror at Nicky's disregard of their protected status. Emma closed her eyes and connected with the child which would join him as an accomplice in badly planned, childish escapades. She ran a questing palm over the growing bump which protruded from her trousers, feeling the fluttery movements of her daughter.

Rohan saw, laying his big hand over Emma's and swallowing in a painful action. His blue eyes filled with anguish. "Em?" he said, turning towards her. She smiled with encouragement but his nerve failed and he shook his head. "I love you, Em," he gushed with a sigh. "You're all I have, you and my babies."

Emma cocked her head and knitted her brow at the strangeness of the statement. Anton's double laughed and caroused on her driveway with Nicky, taking a turn on the skateboard and balancing his lithe, athletic body on the thin board. Every fibre of him demonstrated Alanya Harrington's ballerina grace and heritage. She watched her husband's jaw work and felt again that same sense of foreboding.

"When will the food be ready?" he asked.

Emma replied, "Soon." Watching him from the corner of her eye, she pushed away the nagging sense that Rohan wanted the afternoon over.

CHAPTER FORTY FOUR

"Wait here and Mrs Harrington will be along shortly," the man said, his medical uniform belying his role as prison guard. He smiled, completing the paradox. "She's heavily medicated so her mind will occasionally wander and she may say things which make little sense, but her health is good and she's excited to see you." The man left the room and the door clicked behind him, sounding more like a jail.

Emma swallowed, fear making her jumpy. The room resembled a waiting room with comfy chairs and a coffee table, the walls adorned with trendy wallpaper and bright, happiness inducing paint effects. The absence of handy ornaments for mental patients to fling, gave the room a stark minimalism. "Does a guard stay with her?" Emma whispered and Rohan frowned before nodding.

She fidgeted, smoothing her hands over her unborn baby until Rohan gripped her fluttering fingers in his and held them tightly. "It's ok," he whispered.

"Why is she medicated?" Emma asked and Rohan's eyes widened.

"She's not violent, Em!" he hissed. "The antidepressants make her spacey, that's all." His look of horror made Emma feel guilty and induced another set of nervous finger spasms.

"Sorry," she said, putting enough contrition into her voice to appease Rohan's sense of injustice.

"*Net*, I'm sorry." His brow furrowed. "You're

bound to be scared; it's understandable."

Emma jumped as a different door opened with an electronic hiss and Alanya appeared in the gap. Her slender build verged on emaciation and Emma shot a look of question at Rohan. He stood and held his arms out to his mother. "*Zdravstvuyte*, Mama," he greeted her, enfolding her in strong arms. Emma swallowed and watched the white coated guard seat himself in a chair near the door. His eyes were watchful but the smile he gave her was gentle.

Alanya kissed Rohan on the cheek and sank into the chair opposite, her face devoid of makeup. Emma remained silent, attempting to blend into the furniture until the torturous visit reached its natural conclusion. She expected Alanya to resent her presence, the interloper in a private moment between mother and son. Rohan sat back on the sofa next to his wife, allowing their thighs to touch and drawing attention to her presence. Emma cringed as the vibrant blue eyes of her stepmother rested their gaze on her face. "You came," Alanya said. "*Spasibo*."

"It's ok," Emma whispered, acknowledging the other woman's thanks.

"I'm glad you're vell," Alanya said, indicating Emma's blossoming pregnancy with an arthritic finger which barely unfolded. "Rohan said it vill be summer baby."

Emma nodded, the familiar Russian cadence of Alanya's speech washing over her like freezing water.

"Rohan vas vinter baby," Alanya sighed, locked into her memories, her eyes flickering like fading candles. "Anton vas autumn so not too cold yet. Nadia vas summer baby. She vas beautiful." Alanya's brow knitted and pain lit her eyes, the colour of the irises dimming in response. The old lady shook her head to clear her mind, but her ghosts haunted her without relief. "Nadia vas stubborn child," Alanya said softly, her gaze flicking back to Emma's face. "You always remind me of her."

Emma gulped, realising Alanya spoke of her dead daughter and her body froze in horror. She opened and closed her mouth but nothing came out.

Alanya waved a hand closed by painful, bulbous joints. "The doctors say she wouldn't survive vis her health problems. She vas..." Alanya searched the ceiling for the word, coming back empty. "*Kaleka*."

"Crippled?" Rohan translated, his tone disbelieving.

"*Da!*" Alanya smiled in recognition. "Never walk or speak like boys. But ve love her."

"She have *vdokhnoveniye*." Alanya looked hopefully at Rohan again.

"She had spirit," he said, his voice growing quieter.

"Born in difficulty," Alanya said, "but full of life." She smiled, at once a beautiful woman.

Emma gulped, her age old assumption that Alanya killed her daughter falling to the ground like a dirty accusation. Her stepmother looked at Emma's bulging abdomen and touched her own stomach. "I couldn't protect Nadia," she whispered. "She catch..." Alanya closed her eyes in thought. "Measle? *Da*?" She looked at Rohan but he didn't answer or move. "*Da*," she concluded for herself. "I vas punished and new baby die. He vas gone before I vake. I don't see him." She gave a tiny smile. "Maybe he look like Anton, or Rohan." She nodded to herself. "Like Anton Stepanovich."

Alanya leaned forward. "I don't feel him, my baby boy. I know others and sense in my heart." She touched the gnarled fingers to her breast. "Nadia and Anton are der but not baby boy. Where is he?" she asked, staring straight at Emma.

Emma shook her head. "I don't know," she lied.

Alanya nodded. "Safe, maybe?" she pointed at the ceiling to indicate heaven and Emma moved her head in jerky agreement. A sickness began in the pit of her stomach at Alanya's uncanny perception.

"*Izvinite*," Alanya said abruptly, focussing on Emma. "I make...vitamins for children. You don't get disease, *net*? I make better, *da*. I not protect Nadia and boy from death so I do better wiz you." She jabbed a crooked finger at Emma.

Emma's face paled and bile surged in her stomach at Alanya's misconception that her poisons were vitamins, intended to keep her family safe. A sense of wretchedness pervaded her senses and she grabbed for Rohan's hand, missing and seizing his thigh. A glance showed how pale his face was, an unnatural tremor reaching Emma through his leg. Alanya's blue eyed stare fixed on Emma's face, the manic flares coming and going on a strange loop in her head. "I just vant little girl to call me Mama," she sighed, pointing her finger at Emma. "To make up for Nadia."

"I'm sorry," Emma choked, her throat furring up so she couldn't speak.

Alanya cocked her delicate head and suddenly she was there, fully alert and present, blue eyes flashing with life and vigour. Emma inhaled and gripped Rohan's thigh harder, her eyes wide and frightened. "I always loved you, child," Alanya said, her voice soft and caressing. Emma waited for the backlash, the spiteful whip of her venomous tongue but it didn't come. Her breaths came in frightened gasps as she looked sideways at her husband, digging her nails into his flesh. It was as though Rohan's body remained but his essence stepped out, leaving a shell for Emma to cling to. When he turned to meet her eyes, his complexion was ashen and Emma knew. He remembered. She watched the snapshots of their childhood run through his brain in technicolour misery and saw him hide from it, battening down the hatches and seeking fact and logic to save him.

"Is true," Alanya whispered, exhaustion creeping into her voice and bowing her slight frame forwards. "I loved you as my own but you don't say *Mama* to me." She tapped her breast and smiled, her eyes sad but conscious, lucid and vital. She looked beautiful, the Russian damsel in distress Emma's father loved. Emma craved the touch of gentle, maternal caresses, letting Alanya's words of love heal her. '*I loved you.*'

Emma's lips parted and she felt her soul relent, releasing bitterness and pain in a whoosh of emotion. "You loved me?" she breathed, desperate to believe.

Alanya nodded. "*Da*, Emma." The Russian woman balled both hands together, her fingers writhing in a dance to the death as her eyes dimmed and her sanity ebbed.

"Don't go," Emma gasped as Alanya receded before her. "Don't go, Mama."

CHAPTER FORTY FIVE

Emma made it to the final set of gates accompanied by the prison guard, who nodded Rohan through the gap first and jangled his keys wanting her to follow. "Miss?" he said, his eyes narrowing. "This way, please."

Emma peered down at her boots, their immobility seeming to startle her. Her brow furrowed and she looked at Rohan, opening her mouth to speak and panicking when nothing came out. The hands which covered her mouth shook and Rohan took a step towards her just in time. "*Net*, Emma, don't do this, *dorogaya*. I shouldn't have brought you. Emma, Emma?"

The wretched woman slid down the smooth wall, landing on her bottom with her knees raised. Rohan managed to keep hold of her arms but overbalanced on his prosthetic leg and tumbled next to her in the corridor, wrapping his arms around Emma's trembling body and trying to soothe her.

"You can't stay here, sir," the guard said politely, activating an emergency switch on the wall and closing the gate.

"I know, I know," Rohan said, kissing his shaking wife's temple. "I'm sorry."

The first sound Emma made was a sob, quickly followed by another. She felt detached from her body as though someone else sat on the clinical floor of a prison for the criminally insane and wept for Alanya. Rohan's arms offered more security than the tiled floor or the thickly plastered walls and Emma sank into their safety as the sobs and groans came tumbling from her pink lips.

"We need to move, sir." The guard's voice was authoritative, a supervisor summoned by the emergency switch. Rohan nodded and let go of Emma. He rolled to his side with difficulty and braced his prosthetic limb so he could kneel on the other knee and haul himself up. His trouser leg moved, exposing the metal shin of his false leg and the supervisor's face changed. "Sorry, sir. Would you like a hand up?" His late offer caused Rohan's jaw to clench as he reverted from the 'dangerous guy with the unstable wife' to 'the disabled guy.' He ignored the empty gesture and used his hands to push himself to a standing position.

"Emma," he said with softness in his voice. "*Devotchka*, come. Let's go home."

His wife's face tipped upwards, a salt river pouring down either side and she heaved a fractured breath. "She just wanted me to call her Mama," she sobbed. "I only needed to say one word."

Rohan's face softened and he shook his head. "No, Emma, no. None of it's your fault. Think of our baby, Emma. Let's go home."

Upright, Emma's feet fumbled every step. Her body ached as though pushed from a moving vehicle and they cut a pitiful crowd, the limping Russian supporting his broken wife. One guard went in front, opening gates and nodding them through while the other brought up the rear and watched them leave.

In the car, Emma dabbed her eyes with tissue from the glove box and Rohan kept his hand lightly on her thigh, staring blankly through the windscreen. He exhaled a slow breath and pushed his head against the seat. "Mikhail's selfish wife broke her," Emma whispered. "What she did broke her."

Rohan nodded. "I know, Em." He swallowed, his own emotion near the surface and his resolve cracking. "How do I make it right? It's too late for her and Sergei now. And I couldn't ask her; the question was all planned out in my head but I couldn't say it."

"Ask her what, Ro?" Emma pushed away her own emotions and dealt with the turmoil before her. "What did you want to ask, baby?" she sniffed.

Rohan stared at the steering wheel, his head bowed and his face a mask of agony. "Who my father is," he said. His chin wobbled as the striking Russian fought tears of his own, remaining strong for his wife and abandoning Alanya to the cruelty of fate.

CHAPTER FORTY SIX

"Shall we begin?" the priest asked, straightening his stole and pushing his shoulders back as Rohan nodded. Emma glanced sideways at her husband in his black suit, the crisp white shirt sealed at the neck by a black tie. She reached out and clasped his clenched fist in her slender fingers and he released his hand and allowed her to comfort him.

The priest tapped his microphone and began. "The death of our dear sister, Alanya Nadia Harrington was a shock to her family, but the silent passing into the hands of our Lord during her sleep, a blessing they are grateful for." His eyes roved the empty church and Emma followed the direction of his brown irises as Rohan kept his head bowed, his eyes closed against the reality of his mother's death. Sergei and Bella sat on the other side of Rohan, their faces ashen and their lips moving as they tried to follow the priest's colloquial English. The journey into the small nave carrying the coffin was sombre. Sergei and Rohan each took a handle of the slender casket and the funeral directors provided the other four pairs of hands. Alanya entered the beautiful church flanked by strangers, the irony not lost on Emma.

Emma chose the hymns and liaised with the priest as Rohan grew more distant with each passing day, dreading the finality of the funeral. St Di's seemed wholly inappropriate as a funeral venue with the stain of Mikhail's blood still a pale but present feature. The tiny Anglican Church on the border between Market Harborough and Little Bowden was the only one to welcome the body of a murderess, even one not yet convicted. Allaine looked after Bella's baby and offered to meet Nicky from school, sparing the children the childish boredom of a silent confinement on behalf of a grandmother they never knew.

"Let's stand for our first hymn, '*When I Survey the Wondrous Cross*'."

Wood creaked as the tiny congregation stood, Sergei and Bella leaping to attention as Rohan hauled himself to his feet. Bella whispered something to her husband and he nodded and smiled at Emma, the language barrier proving an unforeseen problem. As the organ chimed into the silence, Emma heard only her voice singing the powerful words of redemption and love. Rohan remained tight lipped and head bowed next to her and Sergei and Bella stared at the words in a hymn book which Bella held upside down. Emma's singing faltered until she realised the futility of leaning across and correcting them.

"I'm sorry, it's a private funeral; you can't come in!" The funeral director's voice echoed in the silence at the end of the hymn and everyone turned to look for the source of the commotion.

"That's why we're here," said a familiar voice and Emma sighed with relief. Sergei and Bella craned their necks behind them, but Rohan gnawed on his lower lip and didn't take his gaze from the stone tiles between his feet.

Freda rode her trusty scooter down the centre of the nave. Behind her trickled a slow moving queue of elderly men and women, neatly dressed for the occasion with trilby hats and an assortment of black veils and apparel. They filed in, filling the front of the church with their creaking bodies and wavering voices. Freda rode down the side aisle and parked next to the family's pew, disgorging her tweed clad self into the seat next to Emma. "Thank you," Emma said, sniffing and missing the opportunity to swipe at the escaped tear which plunged down her cheek. She yanked the collar of her dress higher to cover her healing wound.

Rohan glanced sideways at Freda and offered a tiny smile, his eyes glazed over with a frightening numbness. The priest waited with his hands clasped as the shuffling army of pensioners seated themselves on the hard benches. Emma leaned towards Freda and kissed her on the cheek. "Why are they here?" she whispered. She peeked back at Rohan, finding him still lost in his silent reverie. "I thought they were scared of her."

Freda leaned towards Emma and whispered, her denied deafness making it louder than intended. "Funerals are to respect the living, dear, as well as the deceased. They loved your husband being at the apartments. In just a few days he called three ambulances, gave CPR in the lift and carried more shopping than you can imagine. He reversed cars in the underground garage and picked numerous residents off the floor." She glanced over her shoulder at a woman wearing a blonde wig who waved back eagerly. Emma smiled at the woman and nodded as Freda continued. "Cissy woke up in the lift with your gorgeous husband's lips over hers," she snorted. "She thought she'd died and gone to heaven, although she was a little confused to find her teeth in her handbag."

Emma squashed the inappropriate mirth which bubbled inside her. Rohan licked his lips next to her and Emma reached for his hand, alarmed when he used it to pull her towards him, his face filled with terror. "I can't do it," he hissed. Reaching into his inside pocket he pulled out the tattered eulogy he'd agonised over. His fingers shook as he pushed it behind the pages of a worn bible in the back of the pew in front. He shook his head. "I can't do it."

As the clamour around the church stopped, the priest spoke, thanking the new arrivals for their attendance. "And now I welcome Alanya's son to speak," he said, smiling and nodding in Rohan's direction. There was an awful silence and Rohan worked his jaw and swallowed several times. The priest's panicked eyes roved from Rohan to Sergei and back again and he raised his eyebrows at Emma.

With great dignity, Emma stood, her rounded bump showing through the dark fabric of her fitted dress. She smiled at Freda and stepped along the pew, negotiating the abandoned scooter and walking towards the priest. The man hid his confusion well and indicated the lectern and microphone.

Emma gathered herself and viewed the gathered crowd. "I'm speaking on behalf of my husband, Rohan," she began, swallowing in the wrong place through nerves and forcing a pause. "Alanya was my stepmother from the age of six and it wasn't a happy relationship. I took her at face value and that was my mistake. I only learned about Alanya's sad history recently when I stopped to listen and kept my judgements to myself for once. She was a woman of many tragedies and I came to realise she was a product of circumstances outside her control. Losing two children through no fault of her own drove Alanya in a direction which fed a debilitating mental illness. All she ever wanted from me was to be loved and hear me call her Mama. By the time I humbled myself enough to say it, it ended up being the last word I spoke to her." Emma glanced at Rohan and found his blue eyes fixed on her face with a look of painful intensity.

"She loved her boys; nobody could ever doubt that. And they loved her, particularly Rohan. I hope when I come to the end of my life, I'll have experienced the same loyalty, affection and steadfast love which Alanya could claim. She was in that respect a fortunate woman and I hope she knew it." Emma looked at the priest and he released her from her duty with a smile.

Rohan's eyes followed Emma's progress across the front of the church and back to her seat. As she slid into place he reached for her hand and dragged it across his stomach, clinging to it with both of his. His palms were clammy and an unnatural shiver wracked his body, making Emma concerned for his wellbeing. "Nearly over," she whispered as they stood for the last hymn, squeezing his fingers. Rohan nodded.

Alanya's casket departed to a tune Emma hadn't picked, carried by the funeral directors and the Russian brothers. As the hearse bore Rohan's mother away to the crematorium, Freda's army dispersed with hugs and kisses, accepting Emma's thanks with embarrassed shakes of grey and white noble heads. They filed into waiting minibuses and raced back on scooters decorated with orange warning flags, leaving two lonely couples standing on the street.

"I need coffee," Emma sighed and Bella agreed with enthusiasm.

"Cigarette," Sergei stated, putting two fingers to his lips and making a dragging motion. Bella wrinkled her nose and slapped his arm.

"*Net!*" she said in reprimand.

"Rohan?" Emma asked, staring at her husband and he jumped, lost in his private world. "It's a bit of a walk into town but shall we go for coffee?" His brow knitted and Emma regretted the selfishness of the question. "We don't have to," she said. "It's ok."

Rohan shrugged and then nodded. "What about the pub," he said. "I need vodka." He reached for Emma and put his arm around her shoulders, pulling her into him. "*Ya lyublyu tebya, Emma Andreyev*," he whispered and kissed her temple.

"I love you too," she replied, smiling for him as though nothing else mattered.

CHAPTER FORTY SEVEN

"Hello and good morning to you all out there, lovely Harborians. It's a fine Spring Friday and everything in our town is finally quiet. I'm Brewer Bowden and you're listening to your favourite local radio station. Today we have historian, Freda Ayers talking about her harrowing experience at St Di's last Saturday. Hello, Freda."

"Hello, Brewer."

Emma buttered toast and sat at the kitchen table, smirking to herself as her friend played her final, damaging hand. The radio presenter's jovial lilt bounced through the kitchen, highlighting the holiday mood.

"So, Freda, you were the unlucky young lady who found the bodies in St Di's last weekend. What can you tell our listeners about that?"

"Ooh, it was shocking!" Freda intoned. "Blood and bodies everywhere..."

"Er, thanks, Freda, we've been asked by Detective Barker not to go into specific details as the investigation's still pending. Talk us through your movements on the fateful morning."

Emma heard Freda take an exaggerated sigh of annoyance and smirked as the presenter stripped the wind from the old lady's copious sails. "Well, I bought the flowers from the Saturday market as usual. Orchids were cheap, so I grabbed a handful of those and scooted on down to the church. I struggle with my key because the church warden doesn't do his job properly and that front door's heavy on its hinges. If we've asked him once, we've asked him a million times..."

"Yes, thanks Freda, so you're inside the church and as you described, the scene's pretty horrific. We won't go into that again but what were your first thoughts?"

"Annoyance," Freda said. "Yes, definitely annoyed."

"Annoyed?"

Emma laughed out loud at the sound of a man who'd bitten off far more than he could chew.

"Yes, young man, annoyed! That irritating Jameson boy died right in front of the steps to the altar. I needed to get up there. My friend, Edna always fills the vases with fresh water for me on a Friday lunchtime after her shift at the coffee shop. I can't carry them, you see, not at ninety years of age. Adam Jameson lay right in front of where she stands them, silly boy. Did you know he'd bought the old folks' home over at Farndon Fields and put them all on notice? He doubled the rents on their tiny rooms and the Ministry refused funding to those poor souls. The Council's scrambling to find them somewhere else to go. That's wicked at their time of life!"

"No, I..."

"You should do a story about that! I expect one of the old folks beat him to death with his walking frame; we get driven to it, you know. Nobody listens to the old people anymore. When I was a girl..."

"That's right, you were born and raised here, weren't you?"

Emma stopped licking the butter from her toast and held her breath, sensing Freda's victory across the airwaves.

"Yes, dear. You're a Bowden aren't you? I went to school with your grandfather. He was always telling tales and getting himself into trouble. Our teacher, Mr Jameson beat his sorry bum black and blue for the stories he made up; it's probably where you get your journalistic tendencies from."

"Er...thanks, I think. So, you helped out at the school getting ready for the big celebration coming up, I hear? Tell the listeners about that."

"There's no need to talk to me like I'm senile, young man," Freda grumbled.

"I'm fifty two." The presenter started to lose his nerve. "I'm not really a young man."

"Compared to ninety, you're a babe in arms!" Freda bit. "Ah yes, the scandal at the school. My colleague found the plaque and advised the headmaster. We were waiting to see what he wished to do about it."

"Ah, yes. Little Arden School has issued a statement saying the event will go ahead as planned but more as a celebration of the work of the school in the community rather than a commemoration of any particular date."

Freda cackled, the sound carrying across the airwaves like the trumpet blast for Halloween. Emma suspected she did it on purpose to watch the technical staff scramble for switches and volume controls.

"So how did the plaque end up at St Di's in the possession of one of the deceased?" The presenter sounded a heady mix of perplexed and depressed.

"No idea," Freda said. "Can we talk about me now?"

"Er, well, we're going to the news item in a minute or two."

"No, you're not. It says ten minutes on that little

digital thingamy. I can see it counting backwards. I came all the way here on my scooter. It's not easy being ninety, you know."

"I'm sure. Perhaps our listeners might like a few more minutes of history then. I understand you became one of the famous Ayers of Market Harborough after the war when you married John Ayers." The announcer sounded dangerously smug. "That's quite a rags to riches romance, isn't it?"

"No." Emma heard Freda's smile through her voice, carrying from the radio station offices in town and broadcasting her interview to the community's eager listeners. "My sister, Charlotte and I were the children of Geoffrey Ayers. I was born a noblewoman and I'll die one."

Emma touched the healing cut on her neck and smiled as the presenter covered the huge silence with a song from the 1950s. Freda's secret spun through the airwaves and would land in Clarissa Jameson-Arden's ears before the day was out. Emma shook her head and wondered if the spiteful family would cool their heels for a while and allow the town to settle after the series of revelations and the death of the toxic Adam Jameson. The plaque generated a whirlpool of excitement, especially when Sam and Emma claimed it went missing from the school's attic. Emma stayed away from work for the last few weeks of term, giving Mr Dalton and his board of governors time to decide whether they still wanted an archivist or not. It allowed her neck to heal and gave her space to reflect on her changed circumstances over the last months.

Paul Barker visited Emma at home and commented how pale she looked. Wearing a high necked jumper, Emma blamed it on her pregnancy, signed her verbatim statement and smiled sweetly. "It's a bit of a mystery," the detective sighed, smiling as his father handed him a mug of tea. "Quietest town in the county for years and now three murders I can't solve." He shook his head and wrinkled his nose. "I'm sure Clarissa Jameson-Arden's in this up to her neck but I can't find any evidence of it. And the dead Russian came here on a false passport so nobody knows who he was, not even the Russian embassy."

Ray glanced at Emma and shrugged before patting his son on the back. "Ah well, son," he said. "Ya can't win em all."

The front door slammed and Emma heard the sound of running feet. She tensed as Christopher Dolan burst into the quiet kitchen. "You'll never guess what?" he blurted. His face changed at the sight of the detective and he bit his lip and backed away. "Sorry, I'll tell youse later," he said. Paul Barker knitted his brow and looked to his father for explanation.

"He's a wally," Ray snorted, drawing attention away from Emma, who rolled her eyes and watched the kitchen door close behind him.

"Yeah," she breathed and chewed on her lower lip, dreading whatever latest mayhem the Irishman had dragged to her front door this time.

Dear Reader,

If it were not for you, there would be no point me writing. It's the thought of another's enjoyment and their ability to lay aside their cares in the glorious pastime of reading; which keeps me striving.

I want you to lose yourself, to enter the worlds of others and be released from your own troubles, just for a time.

I hope this novel kept you turning the pages and if it has, I would be grateful if you could leave a review on Goodreads.com and the site where you purchased it from. In the shifting sands of writing and publishing, reviews are the only way of building a reputation and reaching other readers.

Thank you for spending time with the Andreyevs. There will be another book available in 2016.

ABOUT THE AUTHOR

K T Bowes has worked in education for more than a decade, both in New Zealand and the United Kingdom and has been writing since she could first hold a pencil. She is married with four beautiful children who are all now making their own way in the world. She lives in the North Island of New Zealand between the Hakarimata Ranges and the Waikato River with a mad cat and often a few crazy horses. She loves to ride but unfortunately keeps falling off and breaking bones so has gone back to road running instead. She can't be seen pacing the streets of Ngaruawahia because she runs in the dark, convinced people will laugh. Often accompanied by one of her characters complaining about something, the author appears to have mental problems as she frequently answers back, which is another good reason for running under cover of darkness.

Connect with K T Bowes at:
Website: ktbowes.com
Twitter @hanadurose
Facebook www.facebook.com/Author.KTBOWES

She would love to hear from you.

OTHER BOOKS BY THE AUTHOR:
The Hana Du Rose Mysteries:
Prequel, Logan Du Rose - eBook free to subscribers
About Hana
Hana Du Rose
Du Rose Legacy
The New Du Rose Matriarch
One Heartbeat
The Du Rose Prophecy
Du Rose Sons

The Teen Series - Troubled:
Free From the Tracks
Sophia's Dilemma
A Trail of Lies -eBook free to subscribers

UK Based Mystery/Romances
Artifact
Demons on Her Shoulder

From Russia, With Love
The Actuary
The Actuary's Wife

Go to ktbowes.com and become a subscriber

16171200R00245

Printed in Great Britain
by Amazon